TOM KNOX is the pseudonym for th... Thomas. He lives in London.

Praise for *The Lost Goddess*

"Make[s] you wonder what might really have been going on in dictators' secret laboratories." —*The Wall Street Journal*

"How terrific to find a new thriller in which the dramatic action emerges from an exemplary mix of first-rate research, interesting politics, and credible characters!" —*The Dallas Morning News*

"Combines elements of the best of several genres, shakes them up, then lays them out in surprisingly original patterns . . . Knox doles out enough tantalizing scientific, social, and spiritual lore to sate even the hungriest anthropological thriller reader." —*Publishers Weekly*

Praise for *The Marks of Cain*

"Tom Knox knows the DNA of an astonishing thriller." —Jeff Abbott, bestselling author of *Adrenaline* and *The Last Minute*

"An intriguing, well-told story." —*Booklist*

Praise for *The Genesis Secret*

"[*The Genesis Secret*] makes one want to tear through the pages to find out what happens next." —*The Dallas Morning News*

The Lost Goddess

Tom Knox

A PLUME BOOK

PLUME
Published by the Penguin Group
Penguin Group (USA) Inc., 375 Hudson Street,
New York, New York 10014, U.S.A.
Penguin Group (Canada), 90 Eglinton Avenue East, Suite 700,
Toronto, Ontario, Canada M4P 2Y3
(a division of Pearson Penguin Canada Inc.)
Penguin Books Ltd., 80 Strand, London WC2R 0RL, England
Penguin Ireland, 25 St. Stephen's Green, Dublin 2, Ireland
(a division of Penguin Books Ltd.)
Penguin Group (Australia), 707 Collins Street, Melbourne, Victoria 3008, Australia
(a division of Pearson Australia Group Pty. Ltd.)
Penguin Books India Pvt. Ltd., 11 Community Centre, Panchsheel Park,
New Delhi – 110 017, India
Penguin Group (NZ), 67 Apollo Drive, Rosedale, Auckland 0632,
New Zealand (a division of Pearson New Zealand Ltd.)
Penguin Books, Rosebank Office Park, 181 Jan Smuts Avenue,
Parktown North 2193, South Africa
Penguin China, B7 Jiaming Center, 27 East Third Ring Road North,
Chaoyang District, Beijing 100020, China

Penguin Books Ltd., Registered Offices: 80 Strand, London WC2R 0RL, England

Published by Plume, a member of Penguin Group (USA) Inc. Previously published in a Viking edition.

First Plume Printing, January 2013
1 3 5 7 9 10 8 6 4 2

Originally published in Great Britain as *Bible of the Dead* by Harper, an imprint of HarperCollins Publishers

℗ REGISTERED TRADEMARK—MARCA REGISTRADA

The Library of Congress has catalogued the Viking edition as follows:

Knox, Tom.
The lost goddess : a novel / Tom Knox.
p. cm.
ISBN 978-0-670-02318-9 (hc.)
ISBN 978-0-452-29898-9 (pbk.)
1. Excavations (Archaeology)—Fiction. I. Title.
PR6070.H6555L67 2012
823'.914—dc23
2011032996

Printed in the United States of America
Original hardcover design by Alissa Amell

This book is dedicated to the Tibetan villagers of Balagezong,
Yunnan, southwest China.

Author's Note

The Lost Goddess is a work of fiction. However, it draws on many genuine archaeological, historical, and cultural sources. In particular:

The Plain of Jars is an ancient site in remote central Laos, southeast Asia. It comprises hundreds of large stone vessels, maybe two thousand years old, randomly scattered across the meadows and fields of a limestone plateau. No one knows who made the jars, or why, or how. Burned remains of humans have been found nearby.

In the late nineteenth century, prehistorians working in Lozère, in southern France, discovered a series of skeletons in the cave systems of the region. These human remains exhibited curious and troubling wounds.

In 1923 Joseph Stalin asked a team of French scientists to examine a peculiar kind of crossbreeding, with an eye to creating a more perfect soldier. The laboratory constructed for these experiments still functions today, in Abkhazia, by the Black Sea.

Acknowledgments

Thanks are due to the many authors I have read, over the years, in the various subjects pertaining to the themes of this novel. In particular I owe a huge debt to Karen Armstrong, Nic Dunlop, Dith Pran, Haing Ngor, David Lewis Williams, Jean Guillaine and Jean Zammit, Steven A. Leblanc, Roland Neveu, Dave Grossman, Jean Clottes, Robert Wright, Jon Swain, Philip Short, Steven Pinker—and dozens of others.

My great friends and colleagues Peter Dench and Dan White, brilliant photographers both, have always been ready to tell me—over a warm beer in London, or a cold beer in Bangkok—just how wrong I am about almost everything. Without them, this book wouldn't exist in any sensible form. I am similarly indebted to my editors Jane Johnson, Joy Chamberlain, and Josh Kendall, and also to Coralie Saint-Genis.

Above all, I am grateful to the many people who helped with my more difficult research in China, Cambodia, and Laos.

I'll not forget the Hmong family who helped me as much as I helped them, when we were all stuck in the Laotian jungle one long muddy night. And thanks to Paksan for not being embarrassed when I nearly blubbed at the beauty of the snow mountains near Zhong-dian. And I owe a debt of gratitude to the Lozère tourist authorities in France and the guide who showed me around miraculous Gargas cave on that sunny day in late September.

A darkness will settle on the people of Cambodia. There will be houses but no people in them, roads but no travellers; the land will be ruled by barbarians with no religion; blood will run so deep as to touch the belly of the elephant. Only the deaf and the mute will survive.

—Ancient Cambodian prophecy

The Lost Goddess

1

The cave was cold. And dark. Bitter dark. Even though the last autumn sun of the Cévennes was shining outside, as soon as Julia made that descent, down the metal ladder, into the Cavern of the Swelling, the chilling blackness grasped at her—and sucked her in. Swallowing.

Why was she always unnerved by the initial descent? Surely she should have become accustomed to it by now? All summer she had been doing this: doing her job, digging and scraping in the dank limestone cave systems beneath the Cham des Bondons. Yet the first moment of the working day never got any easier.

Reaching a hand up, she switched on the torch of her headband and crouched through the gloom to her tool roll, left there on the damp cave floor, from yesterday.

She knelt and unwrapped the plastic and laid it all out, exposing the trowels and eyeglass, the brushes and plumb lines. The tool roll was a gift from her devoted yet sighing parents. The tiny family she had left behind in Michigan.

The wind whistled outside, fluting across the cave opening like a child blowing air over a bottleneck. The sound was plangent and sad. Julia picked up her tool roll and crawled farther, painfully barking her shin against rock despite the protection of her soft neoprene knee-pads. A few minutes later she halted under a limestone ceiling barely a meter high. Here was her patch. It looked forlorn.

She was used to working down here in the Cave of the Swelling, with her colleagues Kanya and Alex and Annika. But in recent days the little platoon had dwindled: Kanya had left for California, finishing the digging season a week early. Alex was elsewhere, working in a cave along the plateau, with the rest of the team. And Annika, her good friend Annika, she was nursing a cold, in her little cottage in the deserted village of Vayssière, high on the Cham.

But at least, thought Julia, adjusting the beam of her LED headlamp, at least she *was* still doing proper archaeology. And she had only one more week to make the most of this disappointing season. One more week to find something, to justify her sabbatical, to justify all the time and money spent here, in the most remote and isolated part of southern France: the *departement* of Lozère.

They had a week left; the final slice of the digging season.

And then what?

The vision of a winter in London, and many winters after that, teaching yawning eighteen-year-olds, was a drag. Julia cursed her meandering mind and concentrated on her work. Just do it. Even if she knew she wasn't going to find anything more than a broken bone pin, she also knew she was lucky to be here at all. And the sheer metronomic rhythm of her archaeology was, as always, rather soothing: brush and trowel and sieve, trowel and tweezer and sieve.

The tinkle of her metal tools echoed down the empty cavern.

Julia tried not to think of her loneliness. What if some mad shepherd came down here and raped her? In *speleology,* no one can hear you scream. She smiled inwardly, at her own fears. She'd gut the guy with her six-inch survey peg. Just let him try it.

The hour passed. She bent to her task; sorting through the drier dust, at the end of the cave. Troweling and sifting. Troweling and sifting.

She brushed and troweled. And paused. Feeling her own heart. Beating.

An eye stared back at her.

Julia nearly dropped her brush.

A distinctive white circlet of bone was visible through the black soil, like a crescent moon on a very dark night.

An eye socket. In a human skull?

Julia squinted, closely, at the orbital bones and the fine nasal cavity. She felt the pulse of her professional excitement accelerate. *An actual human skull.*

How old was the cranium? Maybe it was some medieval goatherd, who fell down the hole after a night of rough wine. Maybe it was the corpse of some eighteenth-century Protestant, fleeing the war of the Camisards, but more likely it was Neolithic. *The real thing.*

The debris of the cave floor was largely Stone Age. They knew that. The other day she had found her tiny fragment of antelope bone pin—dated from 5000 B.C. This skull *had* to be of the same epoch.

Julia's hand trembled, for a moment, with excitement. This was the best find of a desultory season in the cave systems beneath the Cham des Bondons. Hell, this was the best find of her entire and desultory *career.*

She brushed, and scraped, then used the most delicate trowel, her precious four-inch silvery leaf-trowel, to wholly disinter the cranium. As she pushed the grit away, she realized—there was something odd about this skull.

It had a hole, high in the forehead.

Slipping on her working gloves, Julia lifted the cranium into the white and weakening light of her headlamp. Her batteries were on the fade, but she didn't care. This was too good.

The ancient teeth gleamed in the shivering light, white and yellow. And smiling.

The hole in the bone was, in itself, no revelation. Julia had seen enough damaged bones to know that splinters and fractures were only to be expected in ancient remains: *Homo sapiens* emerging from the Ice Age had to fight savagely for food and survival, with cave bears and wolverines, with leopards and hyenas. Accidents were also common: from cliff falls and rock falls, and hunting wounds.

But this hole in the head had been made precisely. Carved. Sculpted. Not intended to be lethal, yet drilled into the bone.

She put the cranium on the cave floor and made some notes. Her grimy gloves soiled the white pages as she scribbled. She had discovered, surely, a skull deliberately pierced, or "trepanned," in a form of early surgery: this was a Stone Age lobotomy, someone diligently excising a disk-shaped hole in the high forehead of the cranium.

Trepanning was well attested in the literature. It was the earliest form of surgery ever discovered; there were several examples of it in museums dating from the probable age of this skull: 5000 B.C.

But no one had any proper sense why Stone Age men did it. So this discovery was still quite something.

A noise disturbed her excited thoughts. Julia set down her notebook and stared into the murk, beyond the faint cone of light cast by her headlamp; the shadows of the cave danced around her. She spoke into the gloom.

"Hello?"

Silence.

"Hello? Ghislaine? Annika?" Silence. *"Alex?"*

The silence was almost absolute. Only the vague whistle of the distant wind, up there on the Cham, answered her question.

No one was down here. No one but Julia Kerrigan, thirty-four years old, single, childless, with her degree from Montreal and her antistatic tweezers—her and this unnamed human skull. And maybe a rat.

Julia returned to her inviting task. She had two hours left before the day was done. And she was truly looking forward to supper now: when the archaeologists got together, as always, in the little Brasserie Stevenson in Pont de Montvert, to discuss the day's finds—tonight of all nights would be fun. She would nonchalantly say to the oleaginous team leader: *Oh, Ghislaine, I found a skull. Trepanned. I think it is Neolithic.*

Her boss would beam and glow and congratulate her, and her friends would smile and laugh and toast her success with Côtes du Rhône, and then she would call Mom and Dad in the little house in Marysville and she would make them understand why she had left them to go to Europe. Why she still wasn't coming home. *Because her willful ambition had been justified, at last. . . .*

But wait. As she turned her head from her notebook to her bone brushes, she noticed a *second* whiteness, another gleam in the corner.

Another skull?

Julia brushed, very delicately, for a moment, and confirmed. It was a second skull. And this, here: in the farthest corner. What was this? A *third*?

What was all this?

Now she was working—and working hard. She knew that as soon as she told everyone, they would come and take over her cave, but this marvelous cache, this trove of bones, this was *her* find, she had spent all summer waiting for something like this—she had spent fifteen *years* waiting for something like this—so she was damned if she was going to surrender it without giving it every wallop of energy, this one last day.

Away down the passage, rain was falling, spattering on the metal ladder—no doubt blackening the sober old monoliths of the Cham des Bondons—but she didn't care: now she could see that the cave floor was barely concealing, quite astonishingly, *entire human skeletons*.

All of them wounded.

She stared. Appalled. The light in her headlamp was almost gone, but it was still strong enough to illuminate what she had found.

Three skulls had holes in them. Bored holes. Trepanations. The four other skeletons, a man, woman, and two children, did not have holes in the head, but they exhibited another, deeply disturbing feature.

Julia rubbed some grit from her eyes, as if she could wipe away the unlikeliness of what she was seeing. But it was incontestable. The creamy-gray ribs and neck bones of these skeletons rammed with flint arrowheads. At all angles. The flesh that these arrows had once pierced had rotted away, thousands of years ago, but the stone arrowheads remained, lying between ribs, jammed between vertebrae.

These four Stone Age people had been brutally murdered, or even executed. Shot with arrows from all sides. Overkilled. Ritually. Julia couldn't help feeling this had something to do with the other skulls, the trepanning, the holes in the head. But what?

Her thoughts were halted. Abruptly.

That noise again.

This time it was utterly unmistakable. Someone, something, *someone,* was descending the metal ladder. The rusty steel rattle seemed overloud in the darkness, darkness intensified by the fading glimmer of Julia's dying headlamp.

She lifted a hand to the lamp and tapped. No good. The light was all gone. The batteries were dead; she could see almost nothing. But she could still hear. And the noise of someone approaching, in the somber darkness, made her back away, reflexively.

"Hello? Who is it? Who's there?"

The darkness did not reply. A black shape was just visible in the

gray sketch of light admitted by the cave entrance. The dark shape
stopped. Big. Imposing. Julia strained to see a face but all she could
discern was an ominous silhouette. Now the dark shape was hurrying
down the passageway, straight toward her. Coming close, and closer.

Julia screamed.

2

Vang Vieng was the strangest place Jake had ever been. Two years working as a photographer in Southeast Asia—from the full-moon parties of Ko Phangan, where thousands of drugged-up young Western backpackers danced all night on coralline beaches next to raggle-taggle Sea Gypsies, to the restaurants of Hanoi where Chinese businessmen ate the beating hearts of cobras ripped from living snakes while making deals for nuclear power stations—had inured him, he thought, to the contrasts and oddness of tropical eastern Asia.

But Vang Vieng, on a tributary of the Mekong River halfway up the long, obscure, serpentine little country of Laos (and as he had to keep reminding himself, Laos was pronounced to rhyme with *how*, not *house*), had shown him that the eccentric contrariness of Indochina was almost inexhaustible. Here was an ugly concrete town in a ravishing ancient valley—where hedonism, communism, capitalism, and Buddhism collided, *simultaneously*.

He'd been here in Vang Vieng three days, taking photos for a coffee-table book on Southeast Asian beauty spots. It had been quite a long assignment, and it was nearly over. They'd finished the tour of Thailand, spent two weeks in Vietnam, and already had Halong Bay in the can.

The final Laotian leg of the journey comprised Luang Prabang, up the river, and Vang Vieng, down here. They'd flown to Vang Vieng from Luang; tomorrow morning, they would go by cab to Vientiane, the Laotian capital—and jet back to base in Phnom Penh in Cambodia, where Jake had his flat.

That meant they had just one day left. Then the joy of invoicing.

It hadn't been the greatest assignment in the world, but then, there weren't many great assignments left for photographers, not these days. Jake had been a photographer for a decade now, and as far as he could tell the work wasn't coming in any quicker; in fact, it was dwindling. All those people with camera phones, all that easy-to-use, foolproof technology, autofocus, Photoshop, they made it all so simple: anyone could take a decent snap. Literally anyone. With a modicum of luck, a moron with a Nokia could do a decent Robert Capa.

Jake didn't resent, morally or philosophically, this democratization of his "art form." Photography had always been the most demotic of arts, if it was an art at all. Let everyone join in. Let everyone have a go. Good luck to them.

The pain of the process was merely personal: it just meant that his business was disappearing. And the only answer to this dilemma was either to become a war photographer, to become so brave or foolhardy he could and would take shots no civilian would ever dare—and he was increasingly tempted that way—or he could accept boring, commercial, uncreative but comfy assignments, such as coffee-table books on Southeast Asian beauty spots, where at least the air tickets were paid for, the hotels were decent, the toilets nonsquat, and he got to see the world, which, after all, had been one of the reasons he had become a snapper in the first place.

He drank the last of his Red Bull, flipped the empty can into a bag of garbage on the roadside, and got back to work.

Photography.

Wandering down the languid, sun-setting, wood-and-concrete main street of Vang Vieng, Jake paused, looked to his right, and quickly assessed—and took a quiverful of shots of the riverine landscape, framed by a teak-built house and a ramshackle beer shop.

It was a predictable view of the spectacular karst mountain scenery, across the languid, shining Nam Song River. Long and slender motorboats were skimming down the torpid waters, churning up white cockerel tails of surf: the water was beautifully caught in the slant and westering sun, setting over the Pha Daeng mountains.

The view was predictable, but still gorgeous. And this is what people wanted to see in these books. Lush tropical views of stunning scenery! With friendly peasants in funny hats! So do it.

Snap. A stock shot. Snap. A stock shot. Snap. That was a good one. He checked the screen. No, it wasn't. Jake sighed. This was the last day of work, and when would he next make a buck or a *kip* or a *baht* or a *dong*?

Maybe he *should* have become a lawyer. Maybe he *should* have become a banker, like half his friends back in London. But his family tragedies and his own willfulness had combined to send him abroad: as soon as he had reached eighteen he'd wanted to get the hell out of Britain, get the hell out of his own head.

He'd wanted to travel and he'd wanted drugs and he'd wanted seriously dangerous adventure—to rid himself of the ineradicable memories. And to a point his running away had worked, until he'd hit the wall of near-bankruptcy and he'd realized he needed a job, and so he'd remembered his childhood yen for art, and he'd squeezed into photography: begging for work in studios, laboriously teaching himself the craft, crawling back to a real kind of life.

And finally he'd taken the plunge, and stepped into photojournalism—just at the time when photojournalism was, maybe, dying on its feet.

But what can you do? You can do your job. *Photography.*

A young suntanned, barefoot, ankle-braceleted Australian girl was ambling down the main road of Vang Vieng in the tiniest bikini. Jake took a surreptitious shot. There wasn't much light left. He knelt and clicked his camera once again.

The girl had stopped to throw up in the street, quite near a saffron-robed Buddhist monk on a bicycle. Jake took another shot. He wasn't remotely surprised by the girl's outrageous behavior. No doubt she was just another of the kids who inner-tubed down the river all day, every day. Because that was the unique selling point of Vang Vieng.

Every cool and river-misty morning minibuses took dozens of backpacking kids upstream, the kids in their swimsuits all sober and nervous and quietly excited. Then the buses decanted the kids into riverside huts where they were given big, fat tire inner tubes to sit in, and the tubes were cast off into the river flow, and then these Western teens and twenty-somethings spent the hot Laotian day floating in their tubes down the river, occasionally stopping at beachside beer shacks to get drunk on shots or doped on reefer or flipped on psychotropic fungi.

By the time the inner-tubers berthed at Vang Vieng in the late afternoon they were blitzed and grinning and sunburned and adolescently deranged.

Jake slightly pitied these kids: he pitied them for the way they all thought they were having a unique, dangerously Third World experience—when it was an experience neatly packaged and sold to every sheeplike teen and twenty-something who came here. Laos was remote, but not that remote: thousands had this "unique experience" every week of every month.

But Jake also *envied* the youthfully uncaring backpackers: if he had been just five years younger and five times less mixed up he'd have jumped in a tire himself and drunk all the beer his spleen could take as he tubed down the Nam Song. Fuck it, he'd have sailed all the way to Ho Chi Minh City on a tidal bore of Kingfisher lager and crystal meth.

But he wasn't a kid anymore. He wasn't eighteen or twenty-one. He was thirty and he'd done enough messing around; and anyway, latterly, when he took drugs, especially something mind-warping like Thai sticks or magic mushrooms, it reminded him of his sister and the car accident and the memories that lay under his bed like childhood monsters. So he didn't do drugs anymore.

The light was nearly all gone.

The languidly pretty local girls were riding mopeds in flip-flops, and the mopeds had their headlamps on; the half-naked backpackers were buying dope cookies from shrewdly bemused hill-tribe women. Jake pocketed his camera and made his way to the Kangaroo Sunset Bar.

Ty was there. Tyrone McKenna, the American journalist doing the words for their travel book. Jake definitely envied Tyrone. The red-haired, hard-bitten, sardonic forty-five-year-old New Yorker didn't have his job threatened by a billion people with camera phones. Ty was a proper *journalist*—a correspondent—and no one had perfected software that could write a decent foreign news report. Yet.

"All right, Jake?" Ty smiled. "Got all your shots?"

"Got them. Startling new visual angle on Vang Vieng."

"Let me guess," said Ty. "Sunset over the karst?"

Jake admitted the cliché. Ty grinned, and laughed, and lifted his glass of good Lao beer. Jake quickly drank his own beer, and felt the tingle of pleasurable relaxation. The beer here *was* good. That was one of the surprising things about Laos: Jake had heard back at the Foreign Correspondents' Club in Phnom Penh that Laos was primitive and poor even compared to Cambodia, and indeed it was, but it was also effortlessly beautiful, and the beer was excellent.

Tyrone was leaning forward.

"Tell ya something, I have got a *scintilla* of gossip."

"Yes?"

"Chemda is here."

A bar boy came over. Tyrone turned and breezily ordered some more Lao beers—tucking a few dollars into the kid's hand as he did. The kid bobbed, tried to say thank you for his lavish tip, blushed, and then smiled.

The English photographer assessed the Laotian waiter. Probably three years ago this waiter had been a barefoot tribal lad, living in a hut in the hills, not even able to speak Lao. Now he was serving beer to laconic American journalists and dreadlocked French girls and beery London college boys with "Girls Are Gay" written in lipstick on their sunburned backs, and the boy was earning more money in a week than his father earned in a year even as his culture was destroyed.

It was sad. And maybe Jake was making it worse, taking photos that would only attract more people to spoil what was previously unspoiled. And maybe, he thought, he should stop punishing himself for the way the universe worked.

His mind clicked back into gear; he recognized the name. Chemda. *Chemda Tek.* A beautiful Cambodian girl from Phnom Penh. She spoke English. American-educated. A lawyer or something with an NGO. Maybe the UN? The tribunals by the airport in Phnom Penh. He'd met her at the Foreign Correspondents' Club.

"Chemda Tek. What's she doing here?"

"Well, it's Tek Chemda, technically. Khmers reverse their names like the Chinese. Family name first, pretty name second. But she's Americanized, so yep, Chemda Tek."

Jake said nothing.

Ty said, "So you remember her. Cute, right?"

Jake shrugged.

"Well, I hadn't noticed."

"Yeah . . . rrrright."

"No. Really. The fact she looks like one of the dancing *apsaras* of Angkor Thom had completely escaped me. Mate."

They chinked glasses and chuckled.

Tyrone said, "She's at the hospital."

The single word *hospital* unsettled Jake, somewhere deep. He moved the conversation forward.

"She's OK?"

"Yeah, yeah, she's fine. But it's an odd situation."

"Why?"

"She's with some Cambodian professors."

"Here in Laos?" Jake was mystified. "I thought she was working on the Khmer Rouge stuff. Reconciliation. In PP."

"She was, sure." Tyrone repressed a burp with a drunken hand and gazed out at the street. A hammer-and-sickle flag hung limply from a concrete lamppost in the gloom: in the jungly darkness the Communist red looked darkest gray.

Jake pressed the point: he wanted to know more. Tyrone explained. He'd met Chemda on the street near the hospital. She was in Laos to visit the Plain of Jars with a pair of old Cambodian professors, themselves victims of, or associated with, the Khmer Rouge, the onetime and long-hated genocidal Maoist government of Cambodia.

"Why the Plain of Jars?" asked Jake.

Tyrone finished his beer and explained.

"Apparently, during the Khmer Rouge era, these historians were made to go there—seems the Communists made them go to the Plain of Jars to look at something."

"Sorry?"

"You know what the Plain of Jars is, right?"

Jake faltered a reply: "Big . . . old . . . stone . . . jars. Sitting in . . ."
He paused. "A plain?"

They laughed.

Tyrone continued: "Plain of Jars: two-thousand-year-old jars. Big
fuckers. Near Phonsavan. Saw them years back. Boring but curious.
No one knows who built them or why."

"But what've they got to do with . . ."

"The KR? The Khmer Rouge?" Ty smiled affably. "Ain't got a
clue. But the Rouge and the Pathet Lao were obsessed with the Jars,
it seems, and they researched them in the seventies, coercing these
historians, maybe—and Chemda is trying to find out why—"

"And?"

"The whole thing back in the seventies obviously freaked out the
professors. Something happened there, or they found *something* there."

"But why the hospital? Why's she *here*?"

A tuk-tuk clattered past, two-stroke engine coughing fumes into
the soft tropical night. Barefoot German girls were laughing in the
back as they counted out wads of *kip*. *"Kharb jai, danke schön, kharb jai."*

Tyrone smiled at Jake. "The prof, it seems, stepped on a bombie.
One of those little butter-yellow cluster bastards. You know that
whole area is mined and lethal—all that fine American ordnance—"

"That bit I know. You guys did a proper job on Laos."

Tyrone nodded; Jake persisted: "Didn't the Yanks drop more
bombs on Laos, in the Vietnam War, than on the whole of Germany—
in the entire Second World War?"

"Hey. Please. We dropped more bombs here than on Germany
and Japan *combined*." Ty sighed, personally. "Anyhow. Where was I.
Yeah. This crazy professor took a wrong turning and got half his
fucking leg blown off. And Chemda had to bring him to the nearest
hospital, which—given what a crappy little squatter of a country Laos

is—was all the way here to Vang. A long day's drive with this poor bastard bleeding out in the back of the pickup—"

"And now?"

"She's heading back. Finish the job, get the answer. She's a determined girl, that one. Like her dynasty." Tyrone turned and motioned to the bar boy. "*Sabaydee.* Two lao beers? *Kharb jai.*"

"Heading back to the Plain of Jars?"

"Tomorrow. Yeah. 'S what she told me. She heard on the vine we had finished our assignment, so she wondered if I'd like to cover the story. For the *Phnom Penh Post, New York Times,* ya know. I told her I didn't care how intriguing it all is, I'm doing this coffee-table gig for fun, I need a break from the wartime stuff—and anyhow, I'd rather have drunken sex with a senior ayatollah than spend four days on Laotian roads, going to see a bunch of enormous stone cookie jars."

Tyrone paused and gazed at Jake's pensive expression. He groaned.

"Oh God. Color me fucking stupid. *You* wanna do it, don't you? *You* want the story. *You* want to cover it. Make a name for yourself at last!"

3

"So what happened here, in the Plain of Jars?"

Chemda stared at Jake across the cabin of the pickup. Her eyes were deep dark brown, like whiskey aged in sherry casks; she had a slight nervousness about her, mixed with fierce determination. Intelligence and anxiety. She was maybe twenty-eight years old. He had met her only once or twice before: on the fringes of passionate conversations, dark and heavy discussions about Cambodian corruption and peasant evictions and journalistic power plays, on the roof terrace of the Foreign Correspondents' Club in Phnom Penh, the terrace that gazed over the noisy boulevards and the wide, lazy Tonle Sap river.

"You are a journalist? You do understand Cambodian politics?"

Jake felt the pinch of sarcasm in her words.

"Well, yes, I do. But . . ."

"The Cambodian government is under intense pressure to . . ." She sought the words. "*Atone.* To put the Khmer Rouge leadership on trial, to seek the truth of what happened in the 1970s. When so many died. As you know?"

"Of course. Though . . . the genocide, I'm never sure how *many* died. I mean, I hear different opinions."

"A quarter of the population." Chemda's firm but quiet voice, lilting, almost tender, made her revelation all the more sobering. "The Khmer Rouge killed, through starvation or extermination, a quarter of my people. *Two million dead.*"

A chastening silence ensued. Jake stared out of the pickup window. They were way up in the misty hills now, in central Laos; they had been driving for *fifteen hours* on the worst roads he had ever encountered: he understood why Tyrone had refused to make the journey; he understood why they had been obliged to leave before dawn if they wanted to do it in one day.

The route on the map showed the distance was just a few hundred kilometers, and theoretically this was the main road in Laos, but when the road wasn't rudely potholed it was badly waterlogged or simply blocked; dogs and goats and chickens and cattle wandered on and off the asphalt, children played an inch from thundering trucks. Several times they had been obliged to halt by broken-down trucks, or by muddy washouts where they had to lay big flat stones under the helplessly whirring wheels.

And now they were heading for the mountains, the Annamese Cordillera, and it was damp, even chilly: not the tropics Jake was used to, not Luang or Vang Vieng, let alone Phnom Penh. Fog wreathed the vines and banana trees, wedding veils of fog, kilometers of dismal gauze.

Night was dimly falling, along with the saddening mists. The car rattled through another pothole. The wounded Cambodian man had been left at Vang Vieng Hospital, where Jake had tracked down Chemda.

When they had met, late last night, she had appeared pleased by his eagerness to tell the story, to come along. She said she wanted the world to hear what the Khmer Rouge had done: that was her job, as the press-officer-cum-lawyer for the UN Extraordinary Tribunal in Cambodia. And so far she had only got a couple of articles published, on minor Asian websites. Maybe Jake could do better; he had contacts. She was keen.

But now she seemed displeased by Jake's relative ignorance of Cambodian politics. And Jake didn't know what to do about this. He didn't know how to act, because he sensed an unnerving disparity between them: he was older, yet she was the one doing the important work. Chemda was the one with the knowledge; the proper purpose; the real job. And her seriousness was visible, tangible, in the sharp young profile of her dark face, framed by the car window beyond.

Their silent Laotian driver swerved to avoid a water buffalo that was belligerently munching ferns by the side of the alleged road. Jake gripped at the frame of the rocking pickup. A soldier slept on top of a stationary car as they drove past.

Jake stared across the gear well. He wanted to befriend this slightly daunting woman, with her earnest loveliness, her irrelevant beauty. He was here to do a task; he desired to be a proper photojournalist, do a serious job like her. But for that he needed her friendship—and her candor. If only she would open up.

He asked about her background. Her replies were polite but terse. She was born in the chaos that came after the Khmer Rouge genocide, and her family had fled to California following the Vietnamese subjection of Cambodia in the 1980s. She was educated at UCLA, but she had returned to Cambodia, like many of her close relatives, to rebuild the country, to restart, reboot, rejoin. To reset an entire nation.

Jake wanted to ask if all her family had escaped—survived the Khmer Rouge killings.

But he dared not touch on this most difficult of subjects. He knew from sad experience that if you asked this of Cambodians you got, quite casually, the most harrowing of replies. "Oh no, my mother and father died, they killed my sister. Everyone died." Even worse was the answer: "I don't know what happened to them. I am alone."

So Jake had stopped asking this question of most Cambodians after his first year in Phnom Penh: just looking around the city was information enough. There were hardly any old people. All the people who would have been old had been murdered.

Whether that included Chemda's wider family, he didn't know. It seemed she wasn't going to tell him. He certainly wasn't going to ask. Not yet. He got the sense of something—something bad. But every Cambodian had something bad and tragic in the past, something best not discussed.

The driver turned on the headlights: a small wild animal's eyes reflected in the glare, then shot off the road. It was almost freezing now, a freezing twilight in the high hills. Jake buzzed the window shut to keep out the cold and the damp. Then he spoke:

"This is it, isn't it? The Plain of Jars."

They had topped out. The exhausted car rounded a final turn and stopped climbing—now they were very slightly descending onto a plateau. They had reached the plain, after sixteen grueling hours of solid, hard, bone-wrenching car travel.

It was an unnerving landscape. The villages scattered across the moonlit plateau seemed to be bereft of electricity. That much was obvious from the lack of lights. But it also seemed that many of these wooden tribal hamlets lacked heat and running water, because people were bathing themselves in gutters, or from parish pumps. And the villagers had also lit countless small fires outside their wooden shacks, presumably for heat and cooking. Didn't they even have chimneys?

Whatever the answer, it made for a frightening vision: a medieval depiction of hell. The flat, darkling plateau was speckled with those thousands of tiny fires, flaring in the cold and mist. And everywhere, old women were crouched by the pumps, their ribbed and seminaked bodies garishly illuminated by the lurid scarlet flames.

"Fifty kilometers," said Chemda, "to Phonsavan. That's where we are based."

As they neared the destination, Jake seized the moment; he needed more facts.

"Who is pressuring the Cambodian government? To do this, to reckon with the past?"

"The Cambodian people. The UN. Many Western governments."

"Not all Western governments?"

"The Americans supported the Khmer Rouge in the late seventies, so they are more ambivalent."

"OK."

Her slight smile was pitying.

"Yes, a fine irony. The Americans thought the Khmer Rouge could be a buttress against Vietnamese communism. But now many Americans, of course, do want the past to be examined, ah, especially the Khmer diaspora."

"People like you?"

"People like me. Cambodians like me are coming back. And we want the truth."

The car slowed.

Ahead of them, Jake could see real streetlights. It was a town. With shops, or at least garages open to the road: selling colorful packets of instant noodles, and mobile phone talk time, and lao-lao rice whiskey. Faces stared at Jake as they passed, faces blank yet inquiring, impassively curious, faintly Mongolian. Men wrapped in anoraks pointed and shook their heads; two of them scowled. There weren't many Westerners up here on the chilly plain. This was not Vang Vieng, it was like another and very different world.

They sped on into the gray-black countryside once more.

"The Chinese are also involved in what happened here. During the KR regime."

Jake was glad to get to the center of the issue.

"So what did happen here?"

"We're not *entirely* sure. But in 1976 Pol Pot gave an order. That's the famous Khmer Rouge leader—"

Jake bridled. "I have heard of Pol Pot, Chemda. He was a famous weather presenter, on morning TV?"

For the first time since he had met her this morning, she laughed, sincerely; her serious face was transformed, delicate white teeth revealed, eyes wide and smiling.

"OK. Sorry. OK. My professor at UCLA once said I was 'a tad didactic.' Am I being . . ." her brown eyes met his ". . . a tad didactic?"

"Well. Yes. A bit."

A silence. The driver buzzed down a window and spat. The in-rushing cold was piercing and stark. Jake shuddered, wishing he had brought a proper coat. All he had was a raincoat packed in his rucksack. No one had told him he would need to keep warm.

Conversation might keep him warm.

"So, Chemda."

She was staring at the darkness: the bombed and lethal plain. She turned.

"Sorry. I was thinking. But let me finish the story. We know that in '76 the Khmer Rouge, and the Pathet Lao, and the Maoist Chinese, they all sent a team here, to the, ah, Plain of Jars. A team of historians, academics, experts who knew something about the remains, the Neolithic ruins. Then they made people search the whole area, despite all the lethal UXO."

"Unexploded ordnance."

"Yes. Hundreds died. The KR didn't give a damn . . . nor the Chinese. They were looking for something. We don't know exactly what. In the scale of things"—her eyes sought Jake's and found them—"in the scale of things it is a pretty minor atrocity. Just a few hundred killed, a thousand injured. What's that compared with two million dead?" She shook her head. "But it's a puzzle, and it was cold-blooded murder. And Pol Pot and Ieng Sary and Ta Mok the butcher, all the Khmer Rouge leadership, they were, ah, obsessed with this project, likewise the Chinese. They had no money but they spent lots on this, in the summer of '76. Searching the plain. Searching for what?"

"And these historians?"

"Most of the academics were later purged by Pol Pot. Murdered at Cheung Ek. The killing fields, of course. But two survived. I tracked them down. We asked them to come with us, to show us where they searched. All this is part of the UN's work . . . to, ah, dig up the truth. But these guys—they were very unwilling."

"So what did you do?"

"They were ordered to help us, by the Cambodian government. They had no choice. But they don't have to *say* anything, we can't force the truth from their mouths. Can we? Now one is in the hospital, and there is one left. Doctor Samnang. Not happy. Sometimes I wonder . . ." She sighed. "I wonder if I am doing the right thing, in forcing these old men to rake over the past. But it is my job." The steeliness had returned to her soft Khmer vowels; her English was only slightly accented. She turned to face him, square on, and she stared him out.

"And then. There is a personal angle."

"OK."

"My grandmother died here."

Jake said nothing. Chemda's face was ghosting in the twilight.

"I think she died up here. In the Plain of Jars. She was one of the academics the Khmer Rouge brought with them."

"How do you know this?"

"I have a Khmer friend in Los Angeles. Her father was also sent here. And he claims he saw my grandmother, on the plain, that she was one of the team. My grandmother was quite well known; my family is quite well known. So, my grandmother was an anthropologist and, ah, we know she disappeared around that time, and we know there were rumors she came here. No one will tell me the truth because maybe no one knows *the truth*."

Chemda's words were like a litany, softly and reverently repetitive, a whispered prayer in the gloaming of a church.

"That is one of the reasons I am doing this, Jake. By uncovering the truth about my family I can uncover the truth about Cambodia. It doesn't make me popular—many people want to forget. *But I don't care.*"

They drove in silence for fifteen minutes. The cabin was cold. Then Chemda's cell phone chirruped, an incongruously jaunty song. Cantopop. She picked up the call, but the signal was bad.

"Tou? Tou? Can you hear me?" Rattling the phone, she cursed the reception, and explained. "Our guide, Tou. Trying to reach me. Cell phones are almost useless up here. Outside the towns."

Jake was not surprised. A place without electricity was hardly likely to be superbly linked with telecommunications. Nonetheless the thought added to the growing sense of isolation.

An hour passed in even more subdued silence. And then:

"Phonsavan!"

The driver had spoken for the first time since the morning. They were entering what was, for Laos, a largish city. Straggling and busy and concrete, it was an ugly place, especially in the harsh glare of rudimentary streetlights. Jake saw an Internet café, people in scarves locked on bright screens in a dingy room; a few closed tourist shops had *Plain des Jarres* scrawled in crude paint on their windows.

The pickup swerved a sudden right, onto a very rough and rubbled track.

"Here we go. The only hotel in the area. *Home*." Chemda smiled, with a hint of sarcasm. "My guide, Tou, is here. And the historian. The one who can, ah, still walk. . . . It is good we are arriving at night; this is less conspicuous. The Pathet Lao do not want us here. Of course. They want us gone."

"You are intruders. Raking up the past."

"Yes. And also . . . there is tension. The Hmong."

"The hill tribesmen?"

"They live in the uplands right across Southeast Asia, but here is the real Hmong heartland. And the jungles and mountains south of here. There are still Hmong rebels down there. Some say. Still fighting the Vietnam War."

"I heard a few stories."

Now Jake could see lights of a distant building. Chemda continued:

"The Hmong helped the Americans in the Vietnam War, when Laos was a secret battle zone. The North Vietnamese were using Laos as, ah, a route, to ferry arms to South Vietnam."

"The Ho Chi Minh Trail."

"Yes! You know your history." Her eyes brightened, momentarily. "Yes. It came right through here, the Plain of Jars. So the Americans secretly infiltrated Laos, and secretly bombed the trail, and they recruited Hmong to help them, in the air war, because the Hmong hated the Communists, the Pathet Lao, the people still in power now. The Lao regime." Her voice softened to a wondering tone. "The Americans actually had a whole secret city in the hills south of here, with airstrips, warehouses, barracks. And maverick pilots, specialist bombers, fighting a completely clandestine war. The Hmong helped, some actually became fliers. . . . So there is still a lot of, ah, *very* bad feeling, and the Lao don't want outsiders here, stirring things up."

The car jerked to a stop outside a blank concrete building. The parking lot was almost empty: just a couple of dirty white minivans. Chemda got out and Jake joined her, yawning and stretching; the cold upland air was refreshing now, and he inhaled deeply the sweet night scent of pollution and burning hardwood.

"Let's unload. Then you can meet the team. What's left of it."

Their baggage was meager. It took a few seconds to shift the rucksacks and luggage from the pickup to the parking lot and into the echoing and utilitarian lobby.

No one was around. Three clocks, on the wall above the reception, gave the time for Paris, Vientiane, and New York. They were all stopped.

"This way."

The walk to the room took a minute, along a wood-railed path to a door, where Chemda knocked. Silence replied. She knocked again; there was no reply; Jake leaned against the doorjamb, impatient with weariness. As he did he realized he was standing in something *sticky*.

The revelation was a slap of horror.

"Jesus, Chemda, is that *blood*?"

Chemda flinched and gazed down; then she stepped smartly aside, so the dim light of the walkway bulb could shine on the pooling fluid.

It was vivid and it was scarlet.

Immediately Jake pushed with a shoulder; the door wasn't locked, but it was heavy: something was inside, blocking the way. He pushed again, and once more; Chemda assisted, resting a hand on a door panel. The door shunted open and they stepped into the bleak, harshly lit hotel room.

It was empty.

Where was the blood coming from? Jake followed the trail: the thickening flood of redness emanated from behind the door, the heavy door he had just swung open. Jake pulled on it, so they could see behind.

Chemda gasped.

Hanging from the back of the door, by ropes attached to a hook, was a dead man. A small, old Cambodian man, in cotton trousers, bare-chested. But he was hanging upside down, his ankles were roped to the hook, his body dangling; his hands trailed on the ground and his head bobbed inches from the blood-smeared concrete floor.

The man's throat had been cut, slashed violently open. Blood had obviously poured from his jugular onto the floor: as with the bleeding of halal butchery, he had been hung upside down so the blood would drain out. A smeared knife lay discarded nearby.

The old man's hanging hair was just touching the pool of blood beneath: with a delicate, even tender finesse. The blood glistened.

4

"Jesus, Ghislaine?"

The large dark shadow was illuminated: she could see Ghislaine's white face. He had flicked on his flashlight when he heard her scream.

"Ghislaine!" Her heart was still thumping, protesting. "What the *fuck* are you doing, creeping around down here in the dark?"

He came closer. His dark leather clothes squeaked, slightly, in the moist air of the cavern.

"Miss Kerrigan, *calm down*. There was no light, I was concerned: I thought Annika was working down here. With you." His face was gray, and indistinct behind his torch. "Where *is* Annika?"

Julia felt her trembling subside—very slowly. It was *just Ghislaine*. Just Ghislaine Quoinelles, *just her boss*. Yet her terror had been very real: the dark shape, looming down the cave passage, so big. Like an animal. Maybe she had spent too long reading the local legends, the werewolf on the Margeride, *la Bête de Gévaudan*. The beasts and the skulls and the overwhelming darkness.

The mutilated skulls.

She spoke, urgently: "Annika is at home. She's got a cold. She's fine."

"But the light? What happened to your light?"

Julia knelt and picked up her helmet—which she had dropped in her panic. "I guess I just forgot—and the battery ran dead. See?" She tapped the headlamp glass. "The battery's flat. Totally dead. But, Professor. I had a *reason* to be distracted."

"Yes?"

"I believe I have found something. At last."

A glint of sly brightness lurked in his expression, like an old philanderer gazing at another ingenue actress.

"Show me."

They crouched together, down and along the stone corridor. Julia held the torch aloft as Ghislaine moved closer still and leaned to scrutinize her discoveries. He lifted the skull with his large white hands.

"*Oui, oui.* I see. Yesss. . . . Yes, I see. Of course. . . ."

Ghislaine was kneeling so close to her, she could sense his body heat in the chilliness. The smell of his leather clothes was distinct, and pungent. What was it with the leather clothes? Ghislaine Quoinelles dressed thirty or maybe forty years too young. Today's leather jacket and leather jeans combination was especially risible. His haircut was the normal drugstore-black pompadour. Ridiculous.

Hunching herself against the cold as they knelt in the dirt of the dimly lit cavern, Julia wondered if she was being hard on Ghislaine, letting her anger at his foolishly creepy approach infect her thoughts. But why had he been creeping around like that? Maybe he *was* just looking out for her? He was a pretty strange man.

She knew a little of his background. She knew that Ghislaine had been something important a long time ago, a student revolutionary, a *soixante-huitard:* an upper-class leader of the leftish student rebels in the socially turbulent Paris of 1968. Indeed, she'd been shown black-and-white pictures of him—shown them by Annika—grainy shots of a handsome Ghislaine in Paris leading the kids, photos of him in sit-ins, interviews with him in *Le Monde*, profiles of him alongside Danny the Red and other famous young radicals.

So he had once been a tall and cerebral young Communist—in a country that worshipped daring and sexy intellectuals. Once he had been in possession of an exquisite future. Now he was, somewhat mysteriously, an aging professor in a remote part of the country doing an obscure job on the periphery of French archaeology: and perhaps the absurdly young clothes were Ghislaine's way of holding on to the better part of his life, when he had been haloed by fame, when his hair wasn't stupid.

A hint of pity for Ghislaine stung at Julia, in the cold of the cave. She wanted not to dislike him. She didn't like disliking people. Such a waste of time. And someone must have loved him, once.

Besides, she needed his approval of her find. That's how it worked in France: she needed his say-so to make this her project, to secure her rights to her own discovery, to quarantine the cave until she could return next season and investigate further; then she could write a paper and make her name. Or at least, begin to make her name. And this was maybe her best chance. Ever.

"What do you think, Ghislaine?"

"Wait. Please. *La patience est amère, mais son fruit est doux.*"

Another agonizing pause. He was scrutinizing one of the wounded neck bones, and the arrow flint cruelly embedded between the vertebrae. At last he turned. The thick hair was very black on his large, white, gesturing hands.

"The skull, it is obviously male. Yes, yes. But the skeletons . . ." Ghislaine hesitated, and took out his eyeglass to once more scrutinize the neck bone. Then he stood. Abruptly.

"I am finished, Miss Kerrigan." With a beckoning signal, he retreated into the higher, wider part of the cave. "Yes, it is quite an interesting discovery. Quite interesting, but . . ."

"But what?" Julia quelled her rising sense of panic. Surely Ghislaine could see the extraordinariness of her find?

With his expensive German pen, he pointed down and along, at the wholly disinterred skull. "*You see?* These trephinations are moderately common in this region, and this era. The Gorge of the Tarn, and the grottos in the Causse Méjean, they have yielded similar fruit. We see this quite a lot."

"But the wounded children, the flints? Professor?"

"*Eh.* They are *typique.*"

"Typical? Typical?? I've never seen anything like this and—"

"Please. *Calm down.* We can talk on the Cham. The cave is . . . unpleasant."

His reply was polite, yet somehow sharp. Ghislaine turned and walked toward the ladder. She watched his bulk as he ascended the steel rungs, to the winds and skies of the plateau. Supplicant and pleading, she followed. What exactly was Ghislaine doing? What was he saying? Was she going to get the chance to exploit her find? As they reached the surface, Ghislaine put a hand in his leather pocket. For his cell phone.

The twilight air was cold and dank, almost colder than the cave. Julia gazed about. The dark forests of the Cévennes stretched away beneath them, rolling down to the very distant coast. A crackle of lightning flashed in the east; black Luftwaffes of clouds were rolling in, scudding over the gravely sober stones of the Cham des Bondons.

Ghislaine was on his phone, chattering away in quick, cultivated, impenetrably Parisian French. Julia walked a few yards away, tuning out. Waiting nervously for the final verdict. What was happening? Ghislaine *must* see the relevance, the importance, of her discovery. For all his superciliousness, his oleaginous bullying, he was a smart man, he spoke so many languages; he spoke very good English— which Julia appreciated, as she was embarrassed by her own poor, probably Québécois-inflected French.

Tense, she waited, as patiently as she could, as Ghislaine strode this way and that in the drizzle.

The professor had finished his phone call. She waited for him to speak: to pronounce. To turn and smile his sickly smile, and say *Bien sur. You are right, this is the most interesting find of the season.*

But instead, he shrugged, and tutted, and turned—and started marching straight to his car, parked on the road by an abandoned farmhouse. Just visible in the gloom.

The rain was falling harder, persistent and annoying. Half frantic, Julia pursued her boss. She had to *know.* Her heartbeat matched her excitement. She stammered:

"Ghislaine, sir, I mean, Professor—*please.* I need to know. Can I do the next season? Can I? Please? I am sure there is something here. The bones, the skulls. That is OK, isn't it? I have ideas. I know you think this is typical but really, really I do have an idea and—"

He swiveled. There was a look on his face she had never seen before. Contempt. Not the laughable pomposity or the risible vanity of before. *Contempt.* He snapped.

"The crania will be taken tomorrow, and the skeletons. There are museums that can accommodate them, perfectly. They will find their home in Prunier, of course."

"But—"

"You have heard of Prunier? Ah, no. Obviously not." Another contemptuous snort. "Miss Kerrigan, I will not need you anymore, not next season. Not ever. Your job is complete."

This was stunning. This was a stunning disappointment.

"What?"

"You are relieved, is that how you phrase it? Retired. Finished. I need you no longer."

"But, Ghislaine, *please,* this is the best find I have ever made, I know I make mistakes and—"

"*Ça suffit!*" He pouted, angrily. "Go home, go home now. Back to the States. They have history there, do they not? Some of your post offices are thirty years old."

The rain was heavy, the thunder rumbling. Julia felt the blackness closing in on all her dreams. Her wild dreams of this afternoon. The Find of the Season. The Justification for Everything.

"But this was my find! This is unfair! Ghislaine, you know it is unfair."

"Pfft. Your discovery is mediocre, and indeed it is *shit*." Ghislaine's black hair was damped by the rain, his leather trousers were smeared with mud; he made an absurd yet slightly menacing figure.

And now Julia found herself backing away. She was alone here, in the emptiness, not a farmer for miles, all the villages abandoned: alone with Quoinelles. And she had the horrible sense of *physical threat*. His angry finger was jabbing the air.

"What do you know? You learn in your American colleges and yet you have not heard of these things? You know nothing. The skulls and skeletons are just typical. Typical shit. Shit. Just shit. I expect you to return your *carte d'identité* tomorrow."

His aggression was palpable, yet also strange. She got the queer impression he was threatening her for some kind of nihilistic *fun,* for his own bleak amusement. Trying to frighten her, trying to make her flee the scene first.

Standing her ground, with a tilt of her chin—thinking *fuck you,* if you're going to sack me, *fuck you*—Julia stared straight back.

The silent hiss of the rain surrounded them.

With a weary shrug of repugnance, he turned and walked to the car once again. She watched as he disappeared along the path; he didn't seem at all absurd anymore.

And now?

Her own car was the other way. She had to trudge through the drizzle, carrying the weight of her disappointment, her crushing let-down. She wouldn't be able to call her father, or her mother, and vindicate her decision to go to Europe; she wouldn't be able to tell her friends, her colleagues, the world about her discovery. She felt like a teenager spurned in love; she felt like an idiot.

She had been dumped.

Julia walked. Her bleak route took her past a steel cowshed, a run of barbed wire, and the very loneliest of the moonlit megaliths. And there, despite the pelting wet, she paused and looked around, feeling her anger and anxiety evolve, very slightly: as she surveyed the stones of the Lozère, the Cham des Bondons.

Truly, she still loved this locale—for all its saturnine moods. It was somehow bewitching. This ruined landscape, of legends and mega-liths. This place where the werewolves of the Margeride met the elegiac Cham des Bondons.

The rain fell, and still she lingered. Remembering what had brought her here.

The only reason she was in Lozère at all was an offhand remark by a friend, in her college department in London, a year ago, who had mentioned a dig in the south of France. Not far from the great Ice Age caves! And there was room for an archaeologist from Eng-land! For a season! The offer had immediately gripped Julia with that old and giddy excitement. Proper archaeology. *Dirt archaeology.*

Enthused and animated, Julia had scraped together her savings and begged for a sabbatical from her mildly sneering London boss, and then she had left for the Continent with high hopes and had spent a sum-mer digging in France—in *France*—and yet she had found nothing, because there was nothing to find anymore. Nothing. And right up until today it had seemed her sabbatical was going to dwindle away into disappointment, like everything else, like her career, like too many relationships.

Until today. The skulls. *Her Find.*

Julia gazed at the standing stones.

The megalithic complex of the Cham des Bondons was one of the biggest in Europe—only Carnac was bigger, only Stonehenge and Callanish were more imposing—yet it was virtually unknown.

Why was that? She could think of one obvious answer: the remoteness was crucial. The *departement* of Lozère had been depopulating for centuries. The highest limestone steppe of all, the Causse Méjean, just west of the Cham, was said to be the single most deserted part of France: a great plateau of rock with just a few shepherds remaining. Everyone else had gone. Every*thing* else had gone.

It was, therefore, no wonder almost no one knew about the cold and windy Cham des Bondons: there was no one here to see the stones, and no easy way to pierce the guarding wilderness.

And yet maybe there was some other explanation, too—maybe the *atmosphere* of the Chem des Bondons had something to do with the stones' lack of fame. The dark, mournful, off-putting ambience. They were like sad soldiers standing around the grave of a beloved king. Like the *moai*, the great and tragic monoliths of Easter Island, erected by a dying and maybe violent society.

A flash of insight illumined her thoughts.

Could it be?

Fat raindrops were falling, yet Julia did not feel the cold. This sudden idea was much too intriguing: it was a long shot, fantastical even, yet sometimes in archaeology you had to make the intuitive connection, the leap of faith, to arrive at the new paradigm.

Walking briskly to her car, she fumbled for her keys even as she fumbled for the truth. The dating of the Cham des Bondons was late *Neolithic*. The dating of the skeletons was *Neolithic*. They came from the same long era of human history. Could there be some link between the Bondons and the strangeness of those bones?

Yes. No. Why not? Who could say?

Hell with Ghislaine. This was her Find. It was her puzzle to solve: and now she had an intuitive lead. There *must* be a link between the stones and the bones. And the link was that echoing sense, that chime of insight. The fact that she got from the skeletons underneath her feet, down there in the cave, the very same emotional sense she derived from the stones:

Guilt.

5

The Lao policemen had guns in shoulder holsters. The smell of male sweat in the hot and stuffy room was distinct and intense. The questioning became more aggressive.

Why were Jake and Chemda here? Who was the dead man? Why had Tou disappeared? Why had Tou telephoned them last night? Why would anyone kill a harmless old historian? Why were they looking at the Plain of Jars? Who had given permission? What did they expect to find? What could be interesting about a bunch of old jars? What? When? Where? How? *Why were they here?*

Chemda stared at the ground, saying nothing, saying as little as possible. Jake did the same. But the thinnest cop, with the sweatiest shirt, seemed enraged by their muteness. He glared and he shouted. His face was so thin, everything about him was thin, the nylon of his clothes, the plastic of his shoes, the vowels in his curses. He was thin and angry and fifty and sweating hatred for everything Jake represented: money, the West, youth, privilege, the English language—all the Western kids puking on the steps of the temples of Vang Vieng, all the Westerners polluting beautiful ancient Laos.

Jake almost wanted to say sorry.

He said, "Sorry?"

The man shook his head angrily and spat out a question; but he spoke barely any English. He stood and he shouted at Jake, incomprehensibly. What was he shouting? It was all said in Lao. Jake tried not to cower in his chair. He got the sense this particular policeman was a millimeter away from whipping out his gun and slapping it across Jake's face, breaking his nose like balsa, squirting blood onto the desk. Was that already a bloodstain? On the wall?

Jake stayed mute. Staring ahead. Meek and polite—and mute as possible. That's what Chemda had advised. *Say nothing.* But this *was* nasty. Jake had heard vague stories of Western journalists being seriously abused in Laos, for going where they were not wanted: journalists flung in jail, and tortured, by a prickly Communist regime, a cornered country, now surrounded by capitalists. He'd seen men on the terrace of the FCC in Phnom Penh with limps and bruises and ragged, disbelieving expressions: I just got back from Luang, where the beer is good and the girls are cute, but *man, oh man.* . . .

The cops turned for a moment. And walked away.

Chemda whispered: "Remember what I said at the hotel."

He couldn't forget. The hours since the discovery of the corpse were now a stark and unforgettable tableau, luridly lit in his mind.

When they had discovered the body, Chemda had stifled her immediate shock and suppressed any hint of tears, and with extraordinary calmness she had turned to Jake and intoned, *"The police will use this against us, try and get rid of us, or worse. When they interview us—say nothing."* Then she'd gone straight to the hotel manager, leaving Jake with the corpse, swinging gently as the door creaked on its hinges.

Soon after, Chemda had returned with the manager, a fat man with red eyes who gaped at the body in horror, and who tiptoed past the blood like a bizarrely corpulent ballet dancer.

The rest was a series of grisly procedures. The ambulance. The sirens. Lights in the parking lot. Dirty white police cars behind. Frantic phone calls and texts. Tou had been searched for—and not found. Eventually Jake had collapsed onto a bed in a spare room for a few meager minutes of sleep.

And then the police had come back, just after dawn, to snatch Chemda and Jake and take them to the station—for the interrogation, maybe more. And so they were brought here, to the Ponsavan police station, an anonymous yet menacing concrete block in this anonymous yet menacing concrete city, a building adorned with three Communist flags hanging limply in the dawn light over the concrete porch.

The young Lao officer who had first collected them was polite enough. Just enough. He spoke some English. He'd led them through corridors of dusty policework to this stuffy room, where his desk loomed large, and handcuffs and batons hung from a hook. Jake had wondered what tools they had in the basement. And then, at last, the questioning had begun: long and incessant, remorseless. Hours of grinding questions. Repeated relentlessly, like the cops expected them to suddenly change their answers if they asked the same question for the tenth time.

Hours later, they were *still here*. Was this ever going to end?

Jake stared, now, at the hammer-and-sickle flags hung around the room, as the thin cop questioned Chemda. So many flags? They implied a very defensive insecurity. This was a *nervous* place. The flags said: We are Communists, *definitely*. Ignore the rampant capitalism everywhere. Look instead at all the *flags*. Jake wondered again how many people were taken to the basement. Such a big concrete building would definitely have a large and chilly basement.

The questioning of Chemda continued. Jake reached into his pocket and took out his light meter. It was the only bit of gear he had. All his cameras were back at the hotel: he felt like a soldier forcibly deprived of his rifle. He fiddled, uselessly, with the meter.

And now the cop came back to Jake with his questions, interpreted by the English-speaking policeman. They were the same questions, all over again.

Why were Jake and Chemda here? Who was the dead man? Why had Tou disappeared? Why had Tou telephoned them last night? Why would anyone kill a harmless old historian?

Jake replied quietly, and meekly, and honestly. And repetitiously. For another hour.

At some unspoken signal, they were both asked to stand, and separate. The authorities were dividing them. They were apparently going to be questioned individually. Chemda gave Jake a long glance as she was led away, then she reached and subtly grasped Jake's hand. The touch was like a mild electric shock. Then she let go.

Jake stared at her. She was turning now and regarding the smiling, faux-polite, English-speaking cop: her regal Khmer expression was proud, uptilted, daring the police to do their worst. There was a shamelessness to her loveliness in that tiny moment. A kind of unabashed and aristocratic pride. Imperious and defiant.

He admired her stance, her confidence. And yet he worried for her. He wondered what the Communist cops would do to this beautiful and well-born girl who openly defied them.

The door closed; he was alone with the thin cop. All the other policemen had gone, along with Chemda.

The assault came at once. Like the anorexic cop had been just waiting for his moment, when he was at last unobserved, he leaped from his chair, grabbed Jake by the hair, and yanked his head back, painfully, pulling at the roots. Now he spoke over Jake's face. Spoke down. Salivating. Angry. Hoarse. Speaking Lao.

There was something foul in the cop's breath, some overripe Asian food, a pungent meat, or last night's Chinese liquor; Jake blocked out the man's spittled words. He closed his eyes and said nothing, letting the policeman rage and snarl. How else should he respond? What else could he do? He counted the seconds as the cop slapped his face. Once, then again, then a third time. Hard.

Jake kept his eyes shut. He heard the cop say a name. He opened his eyes. The cop gestured angrily, and then eagerly stepped to his desk, like a boxer going to his corner, impatient for the next round. A drawer was flung open. The cop was rifling, briskly searching. Looking for what? A knife? A scalpel? The fear tingled in Jake's fingers.

The door swung open. Chemda stepped through, followed by the policeman who spoke English. She lifted her cell phone and explained: "I did it—I got hold of people in Phnom Penh! They confirmed it all . . . our presence in the Plain of Jars. We're OK, Jake, *we're OK*."

It was true. The mood had altered. Somehow. She had done it: she had saved them. She had saved Jake from a real beating. The English-speaking policeman nodded at the room, nodded at everyone, as if he were saying *This is over, for now*.

Jake stood and said nothing about what had happened. The thin cop was staring furiously, but quietly, through the grubby window.

Doors were opened. Hands were very cursorily shaken. The English-speaking officer escorted them from his office. As they walked, he told them they were free to go, but only free *to leave the police station*. He wanted them to remain within Ponsavan city, until his initial investigations were concluded.

When they reached the street, the English-speaking policeman rewarded them with another unreadable grin. "So. I think your bus tour is over. This is a murder case. I believe you do well to remember this. Laos is not Cambodia. *Sabaydee*."

After six hours of questioning, they walked down the police station steps into the dusty whirl of Ponsavan.

Muddy pickup trucks were ferrying sandaled farmworkers down

the main street. Girls with inclined eyes, wearing brightly colored jerkins adorned with silver coins on chains, were smiling at shops full of Chinese snacks and tiny bananas. "I need coffee," said Jake. "Jesus Christ. How much do I need coffee."

Chemda nodded. "There is a café down here, in the market." They crossed the whirling main street; the shattered concrete of the roads and pavements led to a carless square full of people. And tables. And chattering traders. And flies.

Many of the tables and counters were shaded from the sunshine by battered roofs of zinc. The tables were laid out with local food and game: dead wildcats, owls, strangled stoats, and small jungle dogs, their teeth wild and snarling even in death; there were bottles of yellow-and-black hornets pickled in vinegar, stinking river fish on counters of blood-tinged ice, and piles of slaughtered field rats. Jake was used to the extraordinary fecundity and exoticism of Southeast Asian eating habits, but he had never seen *piles of rats* before.

Chemda sat down at the rickety market café table and glanced at Jake as he gazed across the market aisle at the heaped-up piles of brown rats.

"Field rats," she said. Her voice was thick with exhaustion. "They are famous here. I mean, as far as rats go, these are top-notch. You can't get a better rat in Laos."

"I'm sure," said Jake, smiling at her brave if tired attempt at humor. But the blood in the muzzles of the slaughtered rats reminded him of the blood on the floor, the blood of the dead Cambodian still in the tread of his boots. Ghastly. How close had he been to a real beating?

"What just happened, Chemda? Did Tou kill him? I don't get it."

She stared down at the grain of her elegantly narrow indigo jeans, now dusty and smudged. She shook her head and hid her eyes with a poetic gesture, like the cultured shyness of an Angkor princess.

At last she dropped her hand and spoke.

"Can we sit in the sun?"

They shifted down the pewlike benches of the café into the light; the sun, Jake noticed, was actually strong, sharpened by upland cold—but strong. Healing. Warming. They both turned their tired faces to the heat and said nothing for a second, absorbing.

Then she said, "It can't be Tou. It just can't. He was, ah, part of the team."

"But he's run away."

Chemda shrugged. She had taken off her gray and tailored leather jacket, and he noticed the slenderness of her topaz-brown shoulders.

"He's scared. He is Hmong."

"OK . . ."

"And he has contacts with other Hmong, of course, which is why we employed him. The Hmong have been helping us. Because this is Hmong country: they know the plain better than anyone. They farm the rice paddies, they slash and burn the forests. They also know which areas are, ah, too risky, too saturated with unexploded ordnance. Of course that is—that was—pretty important for our work."

"He rang you last night—trying to get through. But why . . ." Jake was trying to puzzle it out. Something was incongruent. A shard of memory like a piece of grit in a shoe.

Chemda interrupted his thoughts: "They *really* don't want us here, Jake. As I said. And a murder case gives them a great excuse to make things extremely uncomfortable. It took the UN ages to get permission for this investigation in the first place. Now they have the whip hand. You noticed they *didn't* take our passports? It's because they want us to quit, to go. To give up and fly home. That was his hint about Laos—you heard it? '*This is not Cambodia.*' Ahh." Her sigh was brief. And unsentimental. And somehow undefeated.

Jake sat back. Their coffee had arrived, two chipped little cups of thick blackness, plus a tin of condensed sweetened milk already pierced and bubbling. Jake dribbled the viscous milk into his coffee; Chemda wanted hers black.

They drank quietly.

A man across the market was holding a chunk of honeycomb. It looked like a thick slice of intensely rotted wood. The man was digging into each cell of the hive slice with a finger, and retrieving a wriggling blob of whiteness. A larva. The man popped the white living larva into his mouth, munching and smiling, chasing it with slugs of Dr Pepper from a can. Then he winkled out another and ate it.

Something slotted into Jake's mind. He looked at Chemda and said, "You think *they* did it. Don't you? The cops."

Her eyes met his halfway.

"Yes." She frowned. "I do. Because of the way he died."

"Why? It was a brutal death. But how does that prove it was the cops?"

"You never read the stories of what the Khmer Rouge did in Tuol Sleng?"

"The torture garden, S-21," he said. "Yes, I know the history of Tuol Sleng: *horrific*. But maybe I missed . . . some details?"

She gazed across the café seats. The market was closing up; dried rats lollipopped on wooden sticks were being piled in cardboard boxes. Then she spoke:

"I have read two accounts of some experiments there. Accounts verified by the guy who ran the camp."

"Comrade Duch."

"Yes. Comrade Duch. Apparently, in Tuol Sleng they used to tie prisoners to iron beds, and they would attach pumps to them, and then drain every . . . drop of blood from their bodies. They wanted the blood for Khmer Rouge soldiers, but they turned it into, ah, a form of torture, a sadistic game."

Jake was sweating; the sun was now directly overhead, the hard plateau sun. A sadistic game? He thought of the cop searching in the drawer as Chemda elaborated.

"They drained all the blood from these chained prisoners just to see what would happen. Over many hours they took out all the blood until not a drop was left; the prisoners would writhe and gasp, someone described them as sounding like rasping crickets at the end, gasping, stridulating, croaking like insects as they died."

Chemda looked briefly away, gazing at two barefoot boys sucking on the bloodstained ice from the fish counters; then she turned her dark, serious eyes on him.

Jake spoke: "Grotesque. Truly grotesque. But why repeat that experiment on *Samnang*?"

"It's a *message*. Someone is giving me—us—ah, a message. To scare us or warn us, or remind us of the horrors of Pol Pot. I don't know. But Tou wouldn't know any of this, and anyway, if he wanted to kill Samnang he wouldn't do it so bizarrely. But it surely cannot be coincidence: no one dies like that, as horribly as that, for no good reason. They are trying to scare me away. Ah. Because they know what I do—investigate the Khmer Rouge and their barbarities. They want me to give up. But I'm *not giving up*."

Her expression was dark.

Jake felt a need to move. "OK. Let's go for a walk, Chemda. Somewhere with fewer *rats*."

They stood and stepped from the market, paced through a busy side road into the main street. It was more crowded and hectic than ever. And it was obviously full of Hmong people now: many of the women were dressed in the most splendid finery.

For several moments Jake and Chemda observed, together and silent and alone. They stared at the passing people: the cavalcade of girls, twirling delicate silken umbrellas, escorted by proud young men in ill-fitting suits. She answered his question before he asked it.

"No, they don't always dress like this. It's the Hmong New Year. The most important three days, when people meet their future husbands."

"So . . ."

"They are fiercely traditional. Animist . . . but wait—is that— over there?"

She was pointing, and trying not to point. Jake scanned the scene: the parasols and the pickups, the Chinese noodle trucks and the silver jangling coins on summery dresses.

A small figure was discreetly waving at them, down the road, half hidden between two large jeeps.

"It's Tou," she whispered.

Jake marveled. *This was Tou?* He was barely more than a boy. And this was the crucial figure? Their all-important guide? This was the chief suspect in the homicide of Samnang? It was indeed a ludicrous concept: this boy looked more street urchin than murdering villain.

Tou's smile was broken; his shirt was grubby and worn; his face was young and brave and eager and frightened.

Glancing both ways, Tou slipped into the shadows, then seconds later he reappeared, directly behind them, speaking quick, anxious, and fairly articulate English.

"Come, please, quick, Chemda—come!!"

His nervous glance flickered over Jake.

"It's OK," said Chemda. "It's OK. He's a friend, he's with me. What is it? Are you all right? I know the police are—"

"Chemda, I have seen what they look for."

"What?"

Tou gave his anxious reply. "The Stripe Hmong! One of them come to me yesterday, old Hmong man. And he tell me—he tell me stories of the Khmer Rouge come here, in the seventies. And others. That's what I tell Doctor Samnang last night. That's what I try tell you on the phone. Then Samnang he get sad, crying, and I run away—"

"What? What stories?"

"Chemda. I show you. We must to be quick, but . . ." He lifted a finger, invoking their silence, and their discretion. *"I show you."*

"What do you mean? Show me *what*?"

"I show you what the Khmer Rouge find. Many, many years ago. *On the Plain of Jars."*

6

"Chemda, why are you taking this risk? Why not just give up? And go home?"

She didn't answer. Jake wondered whether to try again. They were speeding south, jeeping into the heart of the plain, with Tou and the old Hmong man, Yeng. They were taking a terrible risk, disobeying the cops, quitting Ponsavan, going to see what Tou had discovered.

Yeng had swiftly agreed to help them, as he had already helped Tou: he apparently hated the Pathet Lao, the Khmer Rouge, all the Communists; he was a wiry, determined old guy, maybe an ex-fighter, Jake suspected—certainly he was toughly contemptuous of everyone and everything. Yet likable.

Jake had been told Yeng was *Hmong Bai,* Striped Hmong, one of the most rebellious and warlike of Hmong tribes. Jake could see *his* motivation.

But why would Chemda suddenly be so audacious, so foolhardy? The cops in Ponsavan were truly menacing; rustic and clumsy, but menacing. If he and Chemda got caught doing this, with the prime suspect for the murder—Tou—they would, of course, be immediately deported, if not arrested and beaten and imprisoned. As Chemda herself had implied.

Yet Chemda's dark and serene Khmer face was impassive; only the tiniest tic of nerves showed in the corners of her eyes. Nothing else.

Frustrated, Jake looked out the window, wary and nervy.

The old jeep was rumbling along lanes that were little better than cattle tracks. Wooden houses of Hmong villagers lined the way, large wooden rice barns standing beside the laurel trees and the elephant grass. Some of the barns had strange metal struts supporting their thatched or iron roofs, fat pillars of steel curving to a point.

With a jolt—a physical jolt as the ancient American jeep vaulted a crack in the sunbaked muddy track—Jake realized the pillars in the rice barns were *bomb cases*. The Hmong were using bomb cases to construct their barns: there was obviously so much unexploded ordnance around here, so many old bombs and shells and grenades providing so much metal, the swidden-farming Hmong were scavenging the stuff for buildings.

And now, as Jake looked closer he could see American hardware everywhere: rusty shell cases used as flower pots; meters of corrugated tank tracks utilized for fences; huge bombs sliced in half and employed as water troughs for oxen.

"Why don't you tell me. Why are *you* taking this risk?"

It was Chemda, at last. She had spoken. Her brown eyes secured his gaze; her expression was demure, clever, and opaque.

"'Cause I want the story," he said. "I want to get a decent story for once in my life."

"You want it that badly?"

"That badly."

"And that's it? Just that?"

Jake paused. Obviously Chemda sensed there was more: and she was right. But he couldn't tell her the truth. Could he?

Two little Hmong boys were chasing a rooster—the car slowed just enough not to kill them, then speeded up again. They were blithely unaware that death had come so close. Nearly snatched them away. Abducted them.

He thought of his sister. The guilt was a burn on his brain, an ugly scar, never properly healed. He thought of his mother, and his sister, and their deaths: and the absence of femininity in his life.

Living his life was like living in a jail, like being in the army. Everything was crudely masculine. It was all beers and jokes and danger and ambition and cynical laughter with Tyrone. So maybe he needed something different, something feminine, something gracious? The idea was absurdly premature, but something in him already craved the elegant, mesmeric, intelligent femininity of this strong, resourceful Khmer girl; to fill the hole in his life, the bomb crater of the past, the sense of emptiness.

Alternatively, maybe he just didn't know *what* he wanted.

They were headed deeper into the rough. The pitted and shallow hills where the lethal golden "bombies" slept, unexploded, beneath the pine trees: like fallen Christmas baubles of death.

"All my life," Jake said at last, "I've wanted danger and risk. The adventure. And yes, the story."

"But why? What, ah, motivates that?"

Her gaze was shrewd, even knowing. Jake now felt an enormous urge to confess: just get it out, cough it, purge the pain. Puke up the poison like when he was a teenager, drinking too much, drinking the pain away, with the room spinning: best to go and throw up.

"My sister died when she was five. Run over."

"God. I'm sorry."

"Don't say that. Everyone says that, it's bollocks."

"OK. OK. And?"

"My mum was more broken than any of us. She was Irish, Irish

Catholic. Devout. Before it happened. You know. Then Rebecca was killed and she just fell apart. Mum lost her faith. Stopped going to church. Then she stopped going anywhere. She . . ." He found it hard to say; he said it. "She changed. When I was about nine years old, she abandoned us, me and my brother, and my dad. Overnight. She never even said goodbye. She just walked out one night."

"Jake. Ah. God. That's awful."

"She died of cancer ten years later. We were only informed when the police came to tell us. They took us to the hospital. We never knew she was living alone, in a different city."

Chemda's face was framed by the placid green hills beyond.

"In the end I just quit the UK. Just wanted to go anywhere else. Take risks. I didn't care. Did lots of drugs, nearly killed myself."

"So it was nihilistic. Your reaction?"

"Yep. Drink, coke, drunken rock climbing, you name it, I did it all. And then, eventually, photography. That was my solution. I wanted to do a job that entailed risk, you know? Because . . . when I was in danger I didn't feel so sad, I just felt scared. And I had a job, an excuse, a purpose. It wasn't just drugs. So I went to Africa, southern Russia, looking for action, seeking the work."

"But you didn't get *the* story?"

"Not anything amazing. There are a lot of guys—and girls—out there doing what I do. Lunatic photographers. Most of them are better than me. At least I can write a bit, so I can work on my own if I need to—but these guys are better photographers than me and—" He looked at her, he looked beyond her, at a flat blue lake surrounded by bushes with blue flowers and teak houses pillared by bombs. "And some of these guys are even more fucked than me. They will do anything. They don't care. Really. They are broken. Damaged. Flawed. Junkies of one sort or another. Sometimes just basic junkies, heroin addicts. At least I managed to stop the drugs. I did a deal with Fate.

I said, *Just let me keep the booze, something to kill the guilt and grief—I'll quit everything else.* So that's how I have survived my family. Now I stay cheerful. Sort of. When I'm not being threatened by cops."

There. It was done. He'd said it. He had confessed. He felt a kind of lightness, his spirit unburdened; like he was on a better and smaller world, where the gravity was less punishing.

"And you?" he said. "Chemda? Why are *you* taking this risk?"

She was quiet again. Pensive. He didn't know whether to insist, so he stared ahead at the track, at the widening landscape.

All around them stretched the plain. In the bright, harsh sun, the scenery had an astringent beauty: flat, whispering lakes, groves of silent bamboo, docile parades of brown cattle pursued by bored-looking boys with willow sticks and, in the distance, modest green hills.

Even from ten kilometers away, Jake could see the hills were marked by the smallpox of bomb craters, regular indentations of shaded circles. This region really had been *bombed to fuck*, as Tyrone put it, and now it was like a landscape that had survived death, a land in traction, floating on its memories of pain—but alive. Even the landscape was a survivor.

Chemda inhaled and said, "As you know, my grandmother was killed by the Khmer Rouge, probably somewhere around here, in the Plain of Jars. Somehow she was killed. Maybe UXO." Chemda hesitated, and then added: "But I don't know, just don't know. And that, Jake, is the real cancer in Cambodia's past. Not knowing. Ah. I just know she is not here, no one is here, they all disappeared, got swallowed up. Dissolved. Maybe she wasn't even blown up . . . maybe she just did her job and then they got back to Phnom Penh and *Angkar,* the Organization, the KR, they took her to Cheung Ek and smashed the back of her head with an iron bar. Because that's how they killed, Jake, they didn't even waste bullets—they just crushed heads with car axles and cudgels . . . two million heads. Babies or children they smashed to death against trees. Smashing babies against *trees*."

Her voice was dry, faltering; for the first time it was breaking: her demure composure was gone. She shut her brown eyes and opened them and shook her head and she was quiet, and then she said: "How can you do that? How could anyone do that? They weren't even doing it to the enemy. They were killing their own people. Smashing their own babies. So I want to know what happened to my grandmother and, ah, ah, all the rest of my family. Because: if I can find that out, maybe I can understand what happened to my country." She stopped short, then spoke again: "The third jar site is over there. The red-and-white blocks are MAG warnings, Mines Advisory Group; warnings not to walk beyond the blocks. They mean the fields beyond are uncleared. One misstep and—bang."

Jake stared. The pretty green meadow, just visible through the trees, was scattered with large stone jars. That was the only word for them—enormous *jars*—carved from old and coarse gray stone.

"Tou," said Chemda, leaning forward and tapping the lad on the shoulder. "Where is this jar site the Khmer Rouge discovered? How far?"

"Not so far," Tou said. "Jar Site Nine, is called. But very, very difficult road. Two hour. Maybe three? Only site left, not touch."

The road was, inconceivably, deteriorating: it was now little more than a linear stripe of mud, just coincidentally the width of a car. The jeep banged and jumped and rocked. Yeng hawked and laughed and talked in Hmong.

"I've seen the evidence. The pyramids of skulls," said Jake. "At Cheung Ek." He hesitated. Should he pry further? "Horrible. But . . . but all this must have happened before you were born?"

"Yes," said Chemda calmly. "I only heard of it. My father never got over the genocide. He lost so many relatives. As, perhaps, you *understand*?"

"I understand."

Jake knew what it was like for your family to disappear. To dissolve.

Chemda continued: "So my father died in California, years later. That was not suicide, strictly speaking. A broken heart, maybe. Many others in my family were killed by the Khmer Rouge. My surviving cousins and uncles won't even talk about it. My mother is the same. It shattered us as a family. Ah. The only true survivor was my grandfather."

She gazed his way, her eyes candid and searching, seeking maybe for some reassurance that he could be trusted with these truths.

He said, "Go on."

"He is a powerful man, my grandfather. Sovirom Sen."

"Sovirom Sen?" Jake had heard of him. A businessman. In Phnom Penh. Fiercely anti-Communist. Rich. Powerful. Connected. *"He's* your grandfather?"

"He is my grandfather. He is the man the police spoke to in Ponsavan."

"You said it was the UN."

Chemda shook her head. "They tried the UN first, of course, but it was my grandfather who really pulled their stupid strings. Got us released. I didn't want to say it out loud, at the police station, not so bluntly as that."

It all made sense. Jake sat back. It made a lot of sense. *That's* why Chemda felt able to take these risks. She had a powerful man in her family. That counted for a lot in Southeast Asia, a patriarchal culture. That was almost everything. Face and money and masculine power. Sovirom Sen. First name Sen, family name Sovirom, a regal name, a rich Cambodian name. Most Cambodian family names were short, perfunctory, monosyllabic; the rolling polysyllables of *Sovirom* meant money and class.

"He's involved in import and export, right?"

Chemda shrugged. "Business with China. His family is . . . or we *were* . . . upper class. It sounds absurd but that is the case. We were friends of Prince Sihanouk. Nearly all the bourgeoisie and the upper classes were slaughtered by the Khmer Rouge, as soon as they got the chance. But Grandfather *didn't* die. He survived. I have always admired him for that, loved him."

"So it was his idea you came here. To find out what happened to his wife?"

"No," said Chemda. "It was my idea. But he was proud of me."

Jake fell silent. The track was now so rough, so barely there, so narrow and unused, trees and bushes were reaching in through the windows, clawing. They all shut the windows; conversation was stifled by the crackle of the undergrowth, the squelch of the tires, the jerk of the car slapping from rut to rut, then up onto the rattling craquelure of sunbaked mud. He was still trying to solve the somber puzzle of Samnang's murder: he didn't believe Tou did it, not for a moment. The boy was incapable, he had no motive; but then, what? Who? Why?

"Here."

They had emerged from the woodland onto another flat meadow. And there were the large stone jars, in direct view.

The jeep parked. Yeng climbed out, smiling proudly: pointing. Jake looked at the fields and the shining rice paddies stretching to hills; a water buffalo, tethered to a wild magnolia, stared back at them, pugnaciously bored.

"Is it safe?"

Tou nodded, leading the way. "No bomb here. Yeng say no bomb." The young Hmong man was almost running. "The Khmer Rouge take most of the remain in other place, but here you can still see some. In here. And here. And here. Soon this will be gone. They want to destroy this. But they wait because Yeng say people come here, last year. Still looking. American."

Jake stepped closer. "Sorry?"

"He say . . ." Tou turned to the Hmong man, whose dark face was lined with a smile. Tou repeated the question, and again Yeng gave his answer; then Tou interpreted: "Yeng say he was driver for them. Many days. He know the area, the bomb. So they hire him. Last year. American. Fishhook. Fishwork? Don't know."

"They came here to examine the jars."

"Yes!" Tou said. "Last year. See. Here. Look. Yeng say this is what they find. And this is what I tell Mr. Samnang. He sad then, scared."

He was pointing inside one of the nearest jars. The large, two-yard-high, very crudely carved vessels were made of some prickly stone, rough to the touch; Jake leaned over and stared into the fetid darkness of the jar indicated by Tou. His eyes adjusted.

Several human skulls stared back at him, sitting forlornly on the stone floor. Next to them lay a small pyre of burned bones, ribs or femurs, pelvic bones, maybe, with the appearance of old, charred wood.

The skulls had holes in them. Like the skulls at Cheung Ek, smashed by the cudgels of the Khmer Rouge. But the holes here were at the front, smaller. And of course the skulls were much, much older. Jake was no scientist, but he could tell these skulls were ancient—by the moldering. Yet they were also preserved somehow. By lids, maybe? Some of the jars had until recently possessed lids—he had read that. The lids may only have been wrenched away in the last few decades: by the Khmer Rouge, or by this mysterious American. Exposing the archaic remains within.

It was intriguing. But even so, these were just old bones and skulls. Why would the rediscovery of these bones provoke such emotion in Samnang, *and how did it cause his murder?*

Chemda was obviously working the same mystery. She was peering into the jars, talking quickly with Tou in English and French. Maybe Khmer. Jake couldn't quite follow.

"Many people have speculated," she said, coming over to Jake a little breathless. "Speculated that the jars were urns, funeral urns, for a civilization we do not understand, but this is nothing amazing. I don't see why the Communists got so excited by this. Or Samnang. It merely proves an existing theory. Tou—Tou—" She swiveled on the young man. He was smiling shyly. Anxiously. In the silent countryside with the solitary water buffalo still gazing their way.

"Tou, ask Yeng what the Khmer Rouge found, why they were so drawn to this site—more than others?"

Tou shrugged. "I already know: I ask him that. He hear the American talking, he know some English."

"So?"

"Thousand year ago. Many people here, Khmer people, Black Khmer. They have . . . much war, many killing, many war. And then . . . then they . . . suicide themselves, kill themself. And they put each other in the jar. Like tombs, hide themselves. Kill each other and burn the bone."

Jake intervened. "How did they establish this? The Khmer Rouge? The American?"

Tou pouted his ignorance, then turned and asked in Khmer a question of the Hmong man—who was now glancing anxiously at the horizon. The old man shrugged and muttered. Tou interpreted.

"We not know. But he know the people in the jar were Khmer. And the hole in the head . . . the skulls. They were . . . in the story, I think. There is the Khmer curse. . . . The Black Khmer?"

Yeng interrupted, unprompted, gesturing and very agitated. There was a frown of genuine fear on his face. Jake turned.

Noises.

The silent countryside was silent no more. The trees bent, the sun glared, the noises grew. The water buffalo was straining at his tether. Loud car noises were coming toward them. Jake strained to see: then he saw. Rolling over a hill, maybe five kilometers away. Big white four-by-fours. Like the ones that had arrived at the hotel before dawn: dirty but new.

The police. Surely the police.

Tou said: "Now we run."

7

The cold winds moaned and howled right outside Annika's cottage. The sound was distressing, like anguished mothers were wandering along the derelict lanes of Vayssières, crying at the ancient doors, searching for their murdered children. Here in the very middle of the Cham des Bondons.

This was Julia's first visit to the Cham since she had been dismissed by Ghislaine last week. She was glad to be with Annika again, with her friend. Yet she was also, as always, unsettled by the surroundings. She couldn't understand why Annika lived *quite* so close to the stones. The Cham was wonderfully atmospheric, but why choose to live in the only habitable cottage in an otherwise abandoned village?

It was just a little *too* eerie.

Annika was crossing the low-ceilinged living room, bearing a tray with a pot of tea.

"A habit I collected in China. Green tea. *Cha!*"

Julia's friend was originally from Antwerp: she was a demure, wise, and graciously elegant sixty-two-year-old Belgian. So her mother tongue was Flemish, but her English was nearly as good as her French. Annika was also an archaeologist, although semiretired. As two single women in the macho world of archaeology, they had bonded almost as soon as Julia had arrived in Lozère.

Annika was graciously pouring the tea. Julia sat back and stared around the little cottage. She found her Belgian friend's taste in decor consistently intriguing: the drawing, the paintings, the elegant sketches, the wistful etchings of winter scenes, of skaters and frozen lakes. Maybe from Belgium, or Holland.

Annika stood and returned to the kitchen to fetch some cake.

Taking advantage of the moment, Julia looked farther along the wall. Hanging next to those wintry, Breughelish scenes were several prints of French cave paintings. Julia recognized the lions from Chauvet and the "sorcerer" of the Trois Frères. And there, on the far wall of the sitting room, a picture of the Hands of Gargas, from the Gargas cave in the mid-Pyrenees: stencils of hands made on cave walls by men, women, and children in the early Stone Age.

Sitting here in this weather-beaten cottage, aged thirty-three, Julia could still vividly recall the day she first saw the Hands of Gargas. In a way those hands were the reason she was here.

She was only fifteen when it had happened. As a special treat, as part of a long, unique holiday in France, her mother and father had taken her to see the great ancient caves of the Dordogne and the Lot, Lascaux and Cougnac, Rouffignac and Pech Merle, with their famous and glowing cave paintings.

There, confronted by these stunningly ancient tableaux—some painted twenty thousand, even thirty thousand years ago—Julia had almost cried, ravished by their primeval yet timeless loveliness.

But that was only the beginning. After the Dordogne they had driven south, to the Pyrenees, to go and look at Gargas. And the Hands. And where Cougnac and Pech Merle had delighted, the Hands of Gargas had troubled her, and *truly* moved her.

They were just plain, simple, humble stencils of human hands: but they were so silently poignant, so piercingly mute. And so vividly new. It was as if a Stone Age family had walked into the cave just an hour before Julia and placed their hands against the rock face and blown the pigment through a straw around the fingers, creating the stencil. Somebody had indeed lifted up a little child in one section of the cave—or so it was supposed by the experts—so the tiny infant hand could be stenciled alongside the adults'.

Why?

And why were so many of the hands disfigured? Julia had wondered about this then, even as she wondered about it now. Why the disfigurement? Fingers were severed or bent in most of the Hands of Gargas. No one knew the reason. Since the discovery of the cave in the nineteenth century, many theories had been provided for these "mutilated" hands—a hunting code, a disease, frostbite, a ritual and tribalistic disfigurement—yet none of them really fitted.

The mystery was everlasting. Painfully unanswered.

It was, therefore, the Hands that had decided Julia's fate. Standing in Gargas feeling giddy and awkward and flustered and adolescently attracted to the young French student who was their guide, Julia had resolved—there and then—to make these precious subterranean cloisters her world. At that moment she had resolved to study prehistory; and then to become an archaeologist.

To solve the puzzles.

At first her parents had been pleased by her impetuous decision: their precious daughter had a charming vocation! But when the mid-teen ideal evolved into late-teen reality, those familial attitudes had changed. First she'd shocked Mom and Dad with her decision to leave not just Michigan but the country: she wanted to study at McGill in Montreal. This was partly, as she had patiently explained to them, because McGill had a great archaeology department. Also, living in

Quebec, she could learn to speak French, by immersion, by actually living with French-speakers: something she really desired.

But there had been other reasons for her decision that she had *not* explained. Barely hidden inside her was a simple yearning to go somewhere different, somewhere real, somewhere with history and culture and a European flavor—just somewhere with flavor—to get away from the stifling, boring flatness of the Midwest, the boring snowy no-man's-land on the border, the bored kids doing boring meth in the boring mall next to Meijer's. And there was one further memory of Michigan she couldn't bring herself to address: yet it, too, chased her away.

And so she had done it: she'd moved to Montreal and a freezing apartment in a handsome city where fat Americans spoke French and ate fries with curd.

The memories faded, just for a moment. Julia stared up at the Hands of Gargas. Apologetic, tragic, mutilated. Full of remorse. And then again her mind flicked back, through the mental photos: to that day she left Montreal—for London.

If their daughter's quitting Michigan had been troubling for her parents, her decision to quit North America entirely, to do her PhD in London, had been bitter. Then the remorse had *really* kicked in, the guilt of an only child entirely deserting her family and pursuing a career—instead of giving them grandchildren.

To compound Julia's growing sense of error, her subsequent career had begun to disappoint, it had all trailed off into a mediocre teaching job at a mediocre London college. Soon after that, the weekly transatlantic phone calls from her beloved mother and father had become an unspoken ordeal, a silent yet insidious reproach: No, I am not coming home; Yes, I am still "just teaching"; No, I haven't got a fiancé; No, there is no prospect of grandchildren. Goodbye, Dad, goodbye, Mom. Goodbye.

Julia sighed and shook her head.

Annika set a plate of sweet cakes on the table; she was speaking.

"You must understand Ghislaine, he is a disappointed man. A very disappointed man, but determined, too."

Julia knew that Annika and Ghislaine went way back. They were the same age. They had been friends, apparently, for decades. Annika had worked under the ludicrous Ghislaine since the 1970s, across France, now in Lozère.

She leaned forward.

"Annika, do you mind if I ask a personal question?"

The older woman shrugged in a neutral way and pulled her gray cashmere cardigan a little tighter around her shoulders. "Not at all. You have told me all of your life! Why not ask me about mine?"

"Were you and Ghislaine . . . were you . . ."

"Lovers. Yes."

"In Paris?"

"In 1969. We shared political ideals. We were at the Sorbonne together. We learned Maoism together! We even went to China together in the early seventies. Hence, Julia, the tea." Annika puckered her slightly overlipsticked lips to take a hot sip, then she set down the handleless porcelain cup.

"So?"

"Do not blame him, Julia, for the way he acts and is. He has . . . beliefs, even now. Beliefs that brought him here. And me. There was a time we shared ideals as well as kisses, and we were both interested in the caves, in prehistory. Archaeology." The two women simultaneously looked at the wall pictures, the cascading lions of Chauvet.

"Of course, we are no longer together now. We do not share kisses." The smile was brief and unmirthful. "But we are still friends, after a fashion. À la mode. I will not betray him. He is a sad man, conflicted. And he has his family name."

Julia was bewildered.

"Why won't he take my find seriously?"

"What makes you think he doesn't take it seriously?"

"The way he just dismissed me! Sacked me!"

Annika squinted at Julia, then she looked out the window, where the wind was searching among the stones, lamenting its widowhood. "He wouldn't do that lightly."

"Why?"

"Think, Julia. Think." Her older eyes assessed the younger woman for a moment. Then she continued: "You do know he is attracted to you, yes?"

"Sorry?"

Her friend sighed, quite patiently. "He may seem older to you, but he is a lover of beauty." Her smile was sad. "Youthful beauty. . . . I know him, Julia, I saw the way he reacted, when he first met you. And you were blithely unaware of this?" A shake of the head. "You are one of those women, if I might say so, Julia, that does not realize her own attractiveness to men. This is true, isn't it? Mmm? Yet your blue eyes, the blond hair, the blond hair you always keep tied back—"

"No. Annika, really, it's idiotic. *No.*" Julia was blushing fiercely. And yet a thought was also tugging at her: the way Ghislaine had approached down the cave, like an attacker, like a man intent on . . . No, she chided herself, this was absurd. *Not all men are like that.*

She sat forward, seeking answers.

"Annika, even if it's true, what's the relevance? What's any of *that* got to do with my dismissal, for God's sake?"

"What I'm trying to say is he . . . liked you." She lifted a hand. "Please. It is true. But he is also professional. He sincerely *admires* you as an archaeologist, that's why he hired you. And for all these reasons, he would not dismiss you summarily. No."

The picture clouded. "But then, why do it?"

"Perhaps he takes your find *very* seriously. Too seriously. And remember, he is conflicted."

Julia could only feel lost.

"There are many mysteries in Ghislaine's past. But it is not for me to reveal, not for me to shine the lamp on the cavern wall. But do not think less of yourself. That is all."

Her cake uneaten, Julia brooded.

Annika was always a little evasive; self-consciously mysterious in her thoughts. But all this stuff, this was a seriously new level of annoying coyness. Even though she liked and admired Annika, Julia couldn't help thinking, *Get over yourself.*

She tried again. And this time she would be more specific.

"What did he mean by Prunier'?"

"You can Google this yourself."

"I did. And I found out. Prunier is a tiny village, twenty kilometers away. North Lozère."

"Yes, I know."

"So I *went there,* Annika. *And there's nothing there.* I expected a collection of some sort. A small museum of archaeology, more skulls and skeletons, that kind of thing. But all I discovered was a boulangerie and a church. And some old lady who scowled at me. There is *nothing in Prunier.*"

Her Belgian friend smiled distantly.

"So you did not find. Do not worry. It probably will not help you anyway."

Julia silenced her desire to swear, by drinking tea.

Annika added: "Consider it possible: some things are meant to be hidden."

"And the relevance of that is?"

"The truth is hidden in the caves! But it has always been hidden there, hasn't it? And we still do not know quite what it is." The Flemish lady allowed herself another long, melancholic glance at a picture on the wall: at the beautiful twinned horses of Pech Merle, peculiar, elegant horses cantering away from each other since the Ice Age. "I always think, even today: why did they paint so many animals and so few humans? Isn't that strange, mmn, Julia? And when they do paint humans, they are so sad or forlorn, no? The poor boys of Addaura, the terrible Hands of Gargas, the little stick man at Lascaux, with the slaughtered bison and his intestines, his chitterlings, like so many andouillettes, pouring out of the stomach! There is some more green tea."

Julia flinched at the image: the spilled intestines of the wounded bison, at Lascaux, one of the more horrifying tableaux of Ice Age art. Troubling, like the Hands of Gargas. But why? What did any of this mean? The frustration was piercing, not least because Julia felt she *deserved* proper answers. After all, Annika had invited *her* over—after Julia had mentioned her find, the skulls, the argument. Yet now the older lady was being difficult, and shrugging, and mysterious, and stupidly European.

"Annika. I came over to talk. *Can't you just tell me?* We're *friends.* Why is Ghislaine being so obstructive? If you can't tell me anything then I don't—"

The telephone rang. Annika rose and crossed her little living room. Phone in hand, she stood under a wall poster of the Cougnac paintings. Julia tuned out from the overheard dialogue, not wishing to intrude. It looked like Annika was having a slightly painful conversation: whispering, white-faced, nodding tersely.

"*Oui . . . oui . . . bien sûr. Merci.*"

The receiver carefully replaced, the older woman came back to the coffee table, wrapping her cardigan even tighter—as if the wind were blowing down from the werewolf-haunted steppes of the Margeride and directly through the room. Picking up her cup, Annika drank some tea and cursed:

"*Merde*. The tea is cold." Then she looked at Julia. "That was the police. Ghislaine has been murdered."

8

Gaining. The police were gaining. "Faster," said Chemda. *Her hand gripped Jake's momentarily, maybe unconsciously.* "Faster. Quicker. Please." *Then she spoke in French, and then Khmer. Urging on the driver.*

Jake doubted Yeng knew any of these languages. He spoke Hmong. But the meaning was plain.

Faster. Quicker. Please.

But no matter how fast they went, the noises behind them proved how swiftly they were losing. The roar of the big police Toyotas was drowning the growl of their own wheezing vehicle.

"Faster!" said Jake helplessly. He saw images of the blood-drained Cambodian man in his mind: did the cops really do that? Why not? Who else? Perhaps it was that thin, unsmiling Ponsavan officer. Jake could easily envisage him briskly slashing a neck, like severing the arteries of a suspended hog, watching the blood drain and belch. Nodding. Job done.

The jeep accelerated into a desperate turn.

They had no choice but to escape. Even if they surrendered to the Phonsavan police and Chemda used her grandfather's leverage, again, to save them—and there was no guarantee that this technique would work a second time; indeed, Jake was sure it wouldn't—that still meant surrendering Tou, who would certainly be beaten and imprisoned and convicted and possibly executed. And what would those clumsy and brutal police do to old man Yeng? The openly rebellious Hmong?

But their vehicle was old, asthmatic, and rusty; the police SUVs, however dirty, were fast and new.

Yeng spun the wheel, racing them along the soft earthen banks of rice paddies, ducking the car under the slapping branches of oak, bamboo, and glossy evergreens; the jeep slid and groaned in the mud, then sped on—grinding, desperate, and churning—but the cars were overtaking them. It was happening. They were being overtaken.

Jake swore; Tou shouted; Yeng accelerated. Jake thought of the thin police officer, his repressed anger and hatred: maybe he would happily hoist them by their ankles, open a throat—

An explosion blossomed in gold.

A huge and sudden explosion flayed the windshield with mud and water and leaves; the jeep toppled left and farther left, nearly flipping over; but then the driver-side tires found some purchase and surged forward and crashed back onto level ground, and somehow they sped onward.

Unharmed?

Smoke. There was smoke behind them. And wild flames of black and orange and billowing gray. Jake guessed at once: it must have been a bombie: an unexploded shell. The cars behind had surely hit some UXO. Jake stared, quite stunned, watching men falling out of one flaming vehicle, men on fire, screaming. Muffled screams.

Tou was whooping.

Jake gazed in horror.

"We have to stop." He grasped Tou's shoulder. "We must stop, they could be hurt—"

"No!" Tou said. "Crazy! They kill us. They kill Samnang, they kill you and Chemda, we go—"

Chemda looked Jake's way. "We have to. He's right—"

"But—but, Jesus—"

"No. No no no! We escape!" said Tou. "We escape now! See, they are stopping!"

It was *true*. All the police cars had been halted by the lead vehicle's disaster. The cops were stuck in the smoke and the mud. They had all been saved by the American ordnance hiding under the softly petal-shedding magnolia trees.

"Escape. We escape."

We escape.

Jake stared. Quite dumbed. Their old jeep rattled over the paddy-field bumps, screeching uphill and away. They were indeed going to escape—and maybe this was no accident, maybe this wasn't just outrageous fortune. Jake had forgotten that Yeng knew what he was doing. Yeng knew the bush, the forest, the paddies. He was Striped Hmong. *Hmong Bai*. He knew all along where he was going, perhaps knew the route, and where to lead their pursuers: into the bombs.

Whatever the answer—luck or skill—the smoke and fire were a long way behind them now. The policemen, mobbing the wreck of their burned-out car, were visible but tiny. The jeep was already climbing into the mountains, quitting the Plain of Jars. And so their fate was boxed and mailed. They were on the run. If Jake really wanted adventure and danger and risk: *this was it*.

The plain stretched into the blueness of the distance as they ascended. The scenery was queerly serene, untroubled, as if this place had seen so much worse. And the serenity was paradoxically beautiful, too. Jake clutched his camera in his perspiring hands, and took a shot. The way the mosaic of rice paddies shone out so blue in the reflected sun: it was like the tessellated pieces of a stained-glass window.

Where had that image come from? His childhood. The stained-glass window, the blue robes of the Virgin. It was a visual echo of himself, as a little boy, with his mother in a Catholic church, holding her hand, staring up: there's Saint Veronica, Jacob, and there's Saint Francis, and that's the blue of Saint Lucy, Saint Lucy blue.

Jake took another photo to mediate the sadness away. The spire of smoke became a wistful line, and then it was gone. All was blue, the blue of the sky and the blue of the reflecting paddies and the blue of the horizon, anxiously smudged with faint cloud.

No one spoke for many minutes as they made a lonely ascent through tiny hamlets and empty woodland. The return to the tranquillity of deep rural Laos was a small welcome death. They passed villages where girls threw tennis balls at young men, all of the men in suits, the girls in splendid dresses. The jeep sped on, urgent and noisy in the quiet of the woods.

"A mating ritual," said Chemda. "They sing to each other and throw tennis balls at New Year. That way they can find husbands . . . and wives. . . . This damn phone."

Chemda was again frustratedly checking her cell phone. But she shook her head. Agitated. Frightened. Determined. No signal. She leaned over and asked: "Tou! Where are we going? How can we get out of Laos? We need to find a way out!"

The lad turned.

"Yes, yes, big danger. But Yeng say he have friends. We go. But we drive long time, long time. Road dirty."

Jake guessed immediately who these friends must be: Hmong fighters, tribal renegades, hiding out in the rugged hills. They were surely beyond government jurisdiction: this was surely rebel territory.

He had been in just enough lawless regions to recognize the sensation: that liminal frisson as you passed into a no-man's-land, the interzone, where the laws of the city no longer applied.

That's where they were now. There were no police here. No civilian laws. Just endless thick forest and orchids and fungi and wild camellias astir in the sunny breeze; and in the distance, thin strings of waterfall tasseling in the wind as they dropped from the misty peaks of the high cordillera.

The journey was lengthy and anxious. Every so often they passed clearings in the forest where Hmong children, carrying wicker baskets full of freshly chopped hardwood, stopped dead and pointed, evidently stunned, astounded by what they saw in the jeep.

One boy gazed Jake's way, his mouth hanging wide open, goggling and laughing. The child's mother came behind, pushing a long-handled wooden wheelbarrow. She also paused and stared at Jake; her expression was so shocked it was beyond alarm, it was pure incomprehension: like she was seeing an extraterrestrial.

Tou laughed unhappily. "They never see a white man before. You like a god. Or demon."

A cloud of gray dust showed a vehicle approaching, coming the other way. It was an army truck. Troops in khaki were hanging on the back. The fear was congealing. No one spoke in the jeep. What troops were these? But the soldiers just gazed vacantly at them, half curious, half bored. Tired, maybe. The apathetic gaze of conscripts across the world.

Nothing further happened. The army truck disappeared. The onward trail ran its ragged way through the hills, sidling around mountains, climbing higher, giddily high. The first hints of mist and cloud appeared, bashful centaurs and unicorns that fled as they approached.

The light was dwindling; night had conquered. How long had

they been driving? Chemda was half-asleep, her head bobbing against the window of the jeep. Jake yearned to stop, to get out, to take a pee, to stop. But could they risk it? Maybe the police were just a few kilometers back. Maybe they were closing.

But they had to stop—so they stopped. For a second. In the middle of the dark jungle. Now it was truly night, and it was cold up here, in the hills. Jake walked a few yards into the dank and clammy darkness of the chattering forest, full of night sounds. Frogs croaking. A concerto of insects. Nocturnal howlings in the distance. He thought of the wildcats and strange jungle dogs he'd seen in Ponsavan market.

He relieved himself. Trying not to make the mental association: all the blood, the blood in the muzzles of the dead jungle dogs, the blood on the floor of the hotel room, the man with a gaping throat, hung by his ankles to bleed out like a kosher lamb. Probably Samnang was killed by the police. But why? And why so cruelly? Was it really to frighten them? Surely murder was frightening enough.

Jake shuddered. Sometimes, despite his convinced and angry atheism, he could sense death approaching, like a black god, a god he didn't believe in, yet who still hated him. *Your mother and your sister are mine. You're next.*

The moon was lonely overhead. Fireflies twinkled blue and green like shy and tiny ice stars in the undergrowth.

He walked back to the car. Chemda talked, nervously, as they drove on. She was speaking of ancient history: speculating about the remains they had found in the jars. Jake marveled that he had forgotten about them. In the midst of it all he had mislaid that image: the skulls kept in the jars. The sad old bones. Reproachful. *You left us behind.*

No. He got a grip on himself.

No.

Chemda was talking about the prophecies of the ancient Khmer.

"If the people in the jars, the people who made the jars, if they were Khmer . . . maybe they really *were* Black Khmer."

"And they are?"

"The ancient Khmer: a cursed people. There are stories in the Khmer tradition of the earliest Khmer being a kind of terrible breed—no, that's the wrong word—of making a terrible mistake. Losing God. Losing faith. Becoming violent. What is the prophecy? Tou mentioned it."

The jeep's headlights were struggling against the dark and the mist of the mountain forest. Chemda remembered the words:

"A darkness will settle on the people of Cambodia. There will be houses but no people in them, roads but no travelers; the land will be ruled by barbarians with no religion; blood will run so deep as to touch the belly of the elephant. Only the deaf and the mute will survive."

Tou and Yeng were silent. Jake nodded. He didn't believe in prophecies, he didn't believe in legends, he didn't believe—he certainly didn't believe in any kind of god, because what kind of brutal god would allow all the terrors of the world? The Khmer Rouge? The death of children? *His sister?* But the skulls in the jar: they were certainly real; he had seen them, and the holes carved in their foreheads.

Why?

Chemda's words echoed his thoughts.

"It is highly suggestive. What happened on the Plain of Jars two thousand years ago? To the Black Khmer? Maybe they did something terrible—to their gods—to each other. That is the prophecy. That, then, is why they would be cursed. Ah. It could explain the legends."

"It's like a kind of Noah legend, of a flood. God wiping out the people as revenge."

"Yes," said Chemda. "And also no. And, ah, I still don't know why this so upset Doctor Samnang."

Jake turned from her and looked out the viewless window. Out there it was cold and dark and chilling, like a sickening. The jungle was shivering.

Where were they going to sleep? Were they *ever* going to sleep? Devil-black darkness had descended on them, broken by the feeble beams of the headlights. They were churning mud now, the truck swaying. The fireflies twinkled. Above them shone the moon, bemused and still. The jungle yawned and sucked. The mud sucked them farther in. And at last Jake fell asleep.

He dreamed of a man throwing a tennis ball. A tall, dark man. A little girl picked it up. Her face was blemished with a vivid, port-wine birthmark.

He awoke with a startled pain. Tou was shaking him roughly.

How long had he been out? It was dawn. They were on the lip of a canyon. A long, mist-churned valley stretched ahead and led down to a flat expanse with a kind of airstrip and a dilapidation of buildings: low cabins, concrete and steel—but tumbledown and old. And there were ruined roads, strangled with weeds, or so it looked from this distance.

Tou said, "The secret city."

So they'd reached the American airfield, the old base hidden in the mountains. The Secret City of the Raven War, where the disavowed American bombers flew their missions to drop their secret golden bomblets on the people of the plain.

He yawned and felt a hit of nausea. Disorientation or altitude? He couldn't tell. Rubbing the sleepy grit from his eyes, he got out of the car. Tou handed him a bottle of cold water.

Jake drank, thirstily, lustily. They had escaped—for the moment—but what now? And where was Yeng? And Chemda?

There. Down the road, in the clearing mist, between a clutch of dwellings, he could see Hmong men gathered: young men with guns and rifles and belts of ammo slung brigandishly over their backs. Hmong rebels. In the middle of them all was the slight yet animated figure of Chemda, talking and gesturing.

That girl. She had grit and steel and guts and backbone, and Jake felt, again, the stirrings of moral admiration not unmixed with blatant desire. She was tough. A tough, determined Khmer princess. Five foot two of royal energy. Her ancestors, Jake suspected, would have been proud.

Tou shook his head like something bad had happened.

"What?"

"Chemda ring her grandfather again. He say you go Luang. Then he save you." Tou pointed at the distant airfield. "The Stripe Hmong have plane, we can get you Luang, same-same, no problem."

"OK, that's good, isn't it?"

Tou shook his head. "Chemda nearly cry. She not cry, but nearly. Sad."

"Why?"

"People here know her face and they hear grandfather name. They tell her." Tou looked shyly at his own muddy, broken sneakers. Jake reminded himself to thank this boy, to thank him for saving their lives; but Tou was not for thanking, he was explaining everything. "Hmong lady, she tell Chemda, she know her grandmother, royal Khmer lady, everyone know what happen to her. To grandmother. When the Khmer Rouge come to the Plain of Jar, in 19 . . . 19 . . ."

"In 1976."

"Yes. Then they do something to Chemda grandmother. They cut open her head. For . . ." Tou searched for the word. "For an experimen? Medical experimen. In her head. Cut her head open like she was a goat, in market."

Jake stared at Chemda down the road. What did it mean? Cutting open? *Experiments?*

A parakeet flashed overhead, cinnabar and yellow, screeching in fear of some unseen pursuer.

9

The plane was waiting for them, parked on the muddy airstrip. From two hundred meters away Jake could count the seats. Four. Just a little four-seater: tiny and old and functional. Jake wondered precisely what function the plane had, normally: Crop spraying? Drug dealing? Arms smuggling?

He didn't have time to ask. Already the propeller was turning, and the Hmong rebels escorting them to the tarmac wore extremely frayed and anxious smiles, keen to see them gone.

Jake stared at Tou and Yeng, who were talking quietly. He felt a tingle of suspicion. Someone had betrayed them back at Phonsavan: the police had known where to find them. Could it be that *Yeng* had betrayed them? Tipped off a policeman? Twenty dollars was a lottery win in Laos. Maybe *they* had bought his loyalty.

But that didn't make sense at all. Why go through all the pain of the last twenty-four hours, rescuing Tou and Chemda and Jake from the police, if Yeng's immediate or even ultimate intention was to turn them over? So, no, it wasn't Yeng.

They were approaching the airfield proper, passing a barricade of rusted, empty Budweiser kegs. Jake marveled at all the emptiness.

What had once been the busiest airport in Indochina was now a museum of tropical weeds and concrete decay, surrounded by shacks adorned with ancient Coke signs rusted into a purple-red: vintage and resonant.

The whole place vibrated with memories, with jungly and luxuriant nostalgia: the air was moist with ghosts of young Yankee pilots and dead Hmong heroes, and the whiff of marijuana and china white heroin, and big slangy guys in jeeps and talk of Charlie and LZs and Willy Peter, and cartridge players blasting The Doors—

He glanced back at Chemda. Her brown eyes were full of gratitude and weariness. Not the alertness she had shown, staring in the jars at Site 9.

Jar. Site. Nine. This partial answer to the puzzle slid into place in Jake's mind with a satisfying exactitude. Site 9! The Laos government *knew perfectly well* what had been discovered at Site 9. *And they were still protecting it.* A Communist government protecting what fellow Communists had discovered in the 1970s. A final site that had been kept untouched, maybe for this American. Fishhook.

This made perfect sense. Jake and Chemda had already been conspicuous on the streets of Ponsavan—he was virtually the only white guy in the city. Tourists were scarce. Then someone—it could have been anyone—had spotted them heading south, toward the Plain of Jars. This person told the police. Paranoid and dangerous, the thin and smiling Ponsavan cops did their job, protecting Site 9. They came after them.

But why did it mean so much to the authorities, and to Samnang, then and now? A bunch of old skulls and burned ribs in a jar?

Jake scanned the horizon, as if the answer would be hanging from the mango trees. There was no answer. Just a monkey hooting in the jungle; vaguely human, yet distinctly inhuman. A macaque? A gibbon?

A langur? The jungle thronged with life. And there were Laotian soldiers in there, too, chasing down the last Hmong rebels. Not conscripts: real soldiers. Trained soldiers. Killers. Aiming their guns this way.

Now.

"OK, OK," Tou said, turning and calling to Jake. "Hurry. Please?"

They paced quickly across the concrete. Jake's anxieties were winding ever tighter. They needed to be gone. But who had organized this? How were they going to repay the Hmong?

"Chemda," he said, eyeing the plane, "how do we sort this out? I only have about a hundred bucks—"

"My grandfather," she answered. She lifted her phone. "I have talked with him. Grandfather Sen is helping us. . . . He has persuaded the Hmong—"

"Come," Tou interrupted. "Come quick, please quick."

As they ran the last yards, Jake remembered. And turned. "Yeng?"

The old man had halted. He shook his head. He was standing on the broken asphalt: he was not going to accompany them to the plane; instead he grasped Jake's hand, and then Chemda's, and then he cracked a weary smile and said, *"Sabaydee."*

His conscience tolling, Jake grabbed a fistful of dollars, virtually all of the dollars he had on him, and thrust them into Yeng's hand. Yeng refused. Jake tried again.

Yeng accepted just ten dollars and said, *"Kharb jai."* Then he motioned with his free hand at the green mountains all around them, and he did a machine-gun action with two fingers pointing and shooting. "Pathet Lao! Bang bang!"

The phrase didn't require interpretation. Jake raced the final ten yards to the plane. Chemda was already inside the minuscule cabin. The "pilot" was another skinny, grinning Hmong lad, barely eighteen, in ripped jeans stained with motor oil; he smelled faintly of last

night's lao-lao whiskey. Jake reached for the ladder, but now he realized Tou was also dawdling. Backing away.

"Tou? You're not coming either?"

"I stay here for . . . Luang no good. Police. My Hmong friend are
here. Better for you go Luang."

Reflexively, Jake once again reached into his pocket for cash. Tou
frowned at the idea and the gesture. No! He didn't want anything.
Instead he stepped back and did a mock salute and he laughed.

"Number one plane! Royal Hmong Air Force."

Jake laughed, very anxiously—and said goodbye, trying to repress
the fear that this was all a setup. Tou and Yeng weren't coming
because they knew that the plane was going to crash? No, that was
ridiculous. The pilot didn't look like a potential suicide. But the mystery was so mazelike he felt trapped by his ignorance.

"Quick please!"

He climbed the ladder.

There were no seat belts in the tiny plane. There were barely any
seats. The carpet of the cabin had worn away so much that the steel
of the chassis was visible: bare rivets and bolts.

A rusty door slid shut and the pilot clicked a switch and slammed
a pedal; the old wheels rumbled down the cracking concrete, and
Jake wondered if this plane had enough life to reach the end of the
runway, let alone the royal capital of Laos, and then they were up and
away and banking left and up and up and . . . *just about* over the crest
of the surrounding hills.

The lushly forested peaks were lavishly mustached with white
mist: the plane banked left and ascended again, and the green and
rugged summits of the cordillera stretched beneath to a hazy horizon
of more hills and blueness.

"Fuck," said Jake, resting his head against the tiny perspex

window behind him. Chemda's worried and weary smile was about
ten inches away. The plane was that small. It was just the two of
them, sitting opposite each other, and a hungover pilot, in a plane the
size of a dinghy.

"Hmong Air Force One?" said Chemda. And then she suddenly
laughed. And Jake laughed too, because he needed to relieve the tension, and because he just liked her laughter: there was something
lyrically and infectiously sarcastic in it, pretty yet grounded—and
clever. Aware of the absurdity of everything.

"What a night." Jake shook his head, the laughter dying on his
lips. "What a fucking horrible couple of days."

"Samnang." She sighed, and swallowed away some emotion. "I
still can't work it out. *Aiii. Khoeng koch . . .*"

She was speaking in Khmer; it was incomprehensible.

But Jake did comprehend. He felt like he had, this instant, flown
through the clouds to the dazzling blue of the truth.

"Suicide!"

"What?"

"Samnang wasn't killed. *It was suicide.*"

She gazed at him, perplexed.

"Explain?"

"It must be suicide. No? Otherwise, it's too much coincidence.
Think about it. Your other guy just runs into a minefield, knowing
the danger? Do you believe that is likely? Why would he do *that*?
Now this other guy dies—slashes himself, hangs himself—"

"But why, why kill himself?"

The plane banked. Jake raced on: "Maybe someone is, or was,
intimidating these men, telling them not to help you—putting on
intense pressure, maybe getting to their families?" Jake was speculating, wildly, unscientifically. But he was sure he was right. "And that's
why he killed himself, that way. There is a *message* in the killing,

Chemda! He did it to *himself,* like a suicide note no one could erase or steal, knowing someone would see the terrible parallel."

Chemda frowned. Jake continued: "Think about it. Tou comes to him and says, 'We've found the jars, rediscovered the jars,' and then—you see?"

"OK. . . ." Chemda nodded. "And then, ah, Samnang realizes something terrible is about to be revealed—something he was involved in, all those years ago. He sees no way out. But he wants to leave a note, that no one can erase—" She hesitated, pensively, then said: "But still, suicide. How can we be sure?"

"The knife," said Jake, almost triumphant. "The knife was just lying on the floor. Would a cold-blooded killer do that? Leave the weapon lying by the body? We know Tou didn't do it. He has absolutely no motive. If it was the cops, they would have taken the knife and used it to frame Tou—"

A brief silence between them ensued, while the pilot talked quietly and cheerily in Lao via the cockpit radio. Jake stiffened with renewed tension; he *might* have solved the puzzle of Samnang's death, but their situation remained precarious. Exceptionally precarious. Who was the pilot speaking with? *And what was he saying?* Jake realized he hasn't asked a question of Chemda, a question that had been ripening in his thoughts for a while.

"Why aren't we flying straight to Phnom Penh? It's just an hour or two."

Chemda's oval face was smudged with dirt and tiredness.

"They will know if we try to fly straight across the frontier. International air traffic control. That could cause very big problems. But if we go to Luang, there are other ways out of the country. . . . Much more discreet exits. Roads, ah, through the jungle."

"And there are lots of tourists in Luang."

"Yes," she said. "It will be safer for you there. You won't be quite so visible." She twisted in the painfully small cabin, looking down at the ruched green pelt of the countryside: the forests already were thinning, the hills mellowing and softening.

"That is the Mekong. We are nearly there."

"Where shall we stay? I know some hotels."

She shook her head. "My family has very good friends in Luang. A French couple. A little hotel by the river, hidden away. Good place to hide for one night. . . . Sleep, we need to sleep. No? Then we work out a way to get out of Laos."

Already they were descending. Jake saw roads and a truck, the metal roofs of rice barns and farmhouses, sugarcane fields. Moments later they bumped to a halt on a brown dirt airstrip. It was another random airport in the bush, even more ramshackle than the Secret City. Just a hut at the side of a broad boulevard of mud and a man in the hut who nodded, knowingly, at the pilot, when they walked from the plane to the perimeter gate.

"Luang Prabang," said the pilot, pointing beyond the wall at a sunlit road. *"Sabaydee."* The pilot slapped Jake on the back, and then did an elegant *wai*—the hands-pressed-together, all-purpose, praying-and-bowing gesture of Indochina—to Chemda. She did the same in return.

The pilot, Jake noted, still smelled of lao-lao whiskey. Maybe he had been drinking on the plane. *But they had made it.* Jake and Chemda grabbed their bags, their pathetic remnants of luggage, and walked out onto the road. The traffic was light, bordering on nonexistent: a few farm trucks, then nothing, then a Honda motorcycle carrying an entire family—father, mother, two infant children, piglet. Then nothing. But a few minutes later a yellow metal tuk-tuk coughed into view, rounding the lush bamboo stands, decorated with stencils of Australian and British flags.

They hailed the tuk-tuk and climbed aboard. They were heading into Luang. Jake felt his spirits rise and his nerves subside for a moment as the warm air breezed his face. He had loved Luang Prabang when he had first seen it, just a week ago—though it felt like a year. Luang Prabang: the ancient capital of the kingdom. Half French colonial resort, half glittering Buddhist citadel, royal and sacred *Louangphrabang*.

And here he was again, where smiling girls bicycled quietly by the boulangerie; where old Laotian men played petanque by the water tamarinds; where the orange-robed monks walked from temple to temple every morning past a hundred Buddhist shrines, teakwood bars, and rambling Chinese shops.

Street vendors were hawking pyramids of tangerines arrayed on wicker baskets. Barefoot men slept on rushes in the shade of papaya trees. The mighty Mekong River slid past unnoticed, like a great and famous actor, forgotten in his dotage.

"Here," said Chemda.

The hotel was indeed discreet, beyond the royal palace and the tall scruffy stupa: so discreet the road gave up before it reached the building.

They climbed out of the tuk-tuk and paced the last hundred meters of dirt. The hotel door was closed. *Le Gauguin,* said a sign. Chemda pushed open a large door and they slipped into the coolness of a wooden lobby scented with teak and cedar and incense—expensive, private, tranquil. Jake yearned immediately for a shower. Sleep. Then escape.

"Chemda! Chérie! Bonjour!"

A late-middle-aged French woman strode into Reception. She was introduced: Madame Agnès Marconnet. She hugged Chemda and smiled warily at Jake. The two women spoke quickly in French, too fast for Jake to begin to understand; before he could say please or *merci* they were escorted by a girl in a silk *cheongsam* to two guest rooms, and Jake struggled through a couple of *merci beaucoups* and *kharb jais* and Chemda said she would see him later, and then he fell straight into his bed without even showering and slept immediately, hungrily, like a starveling famished of sleep for a century. He slept so hard he didn't dream, at first, but then something in the darkness of his subconscious disturbed him and he woke with a vague but ungraspable sense of panic.

For a few moments he lay there, perplexed, collating his wits. He didn't know what time it was. Dawn, maybe. The thin filter of blue light, through the slats of the shutters, pierced the darkness of the room.

Then he stared. Hard.

Something was hanging from the door. Three meters away.

He wished he were dreaming, but he was awake. Wide awake.

This was something truly and purely terrible, something beyond hellish.

Jake's mind swarmed with the horror.

Please. No.

10

The French policemen arrived at Annika's cottage an hour later. The sleek Peugeot oiled into the drive with an authoritative scrunch; red-and-blue police lights flashed exotically across the dark and drizzly wastes of the Cham.

The Belgian woman was needed to identify the body; Julia immediately offered to accompany her friend for this grisly task—though Annika's composure was so superb, Julia wondered if any help was truly required.

The same red-and-blue lights shone briefly on Annika's impassive face as she climbed into the back of the police car, and sat, almost rigid, staring ahead. Julia followed; the car started; they drove the moorland miles up onto the Causse, heading for Mende.

Ghislaine Quoinelles had lived in a large, isolated villa near Marvejols—but his body had already been moved.

Annika shared a few words in French with the fifty-something officer, his hair brindled gray. Officer Rouvier had arrived with a suitably dignified demeanor, and a junior officer behind the steering wheel, for the somber task of escorting them to the morgue at the hospital in Mende. After a few minutes, Julia added her own halting comment to the conversation.

Her interruption silenced the car. The officer turned in the front passenger seat and briefly smiled at Julia. And then he said in perfect and very educated English, his words punctuated by the melancholy percussion of the windshield wipers, "You are from Québec?"

Julia groaned inwardly. She answered in English: "I talk like a lumberjack from Chicoutimi, don't I?"

"Please. Your French is . . ." The smile persisted. "Charming. But I speak very good English. So it is not remotely necessary. But thank you."

Julia sat back and was quiet, trying not to feel insulted, trying not to feel anything selfish: she was in the middle of *Annika's* shock and horror. But that was the problem of being an only child: the selfish reaction was conditioned and immediate, and Julia was always on the watch for it, in herself.

She gazed at the metronomic smearing of the rain on the windshield, and the brief glimpses of other cars shooting past them on the narrow country roads. It was only fifty kilometers to Mende but the drive would take an hour in this weather, on these circuitous roads.

A memory returned, importunate, like a meek child knocking timidly at the door: a memory of her infant self and her father and mother, driving in the rain, the snow and rain of eastern Michigan, watching lonely snowflakes settling on the car window, trusting her father's driving, absorbed by the way the flakes were beaten and crushed by the wipers, dissolved.

Julia recalled the way she felt safe and privileged, yet sad: the only child, alone in the too-big backseat of her parents' SUV; it was a family vehicle, all the seats were meant to be filled, but she had no brother to argue with, no sister to play with. So she sat upright in the middle of the empty space. Importantly. Talking to the adults. Precocious and garrulous and selfish, like so many only children.

And also lonely.

The Peugeot was quiet now; this was truly a morbid business. Yet Julia felt the urge to converse. She found silence—when she was on her own—quite soothing and enriching; but silence between people she could not bear. It made her feel lonely again.

A question recurred. Why was Annika going to identify the body? She and Ghislaine were not married, they were just friends—and ex-lovers. Surely he had someone else, someone related? Hadn't there been a mention of children, or siblings? Nephews, maybe?

Julia knew it might be an insensitive inquiry, but she couldn't help it: she was intrigued as well as horrified by the whole scenario.

"Annika?"

The Belgian woman didn't even turn to face her questioner. But she answered coldly, *"Oui?"*

"Ghislaine has no other family?"

"No." Annika's reply was curt, and barely softened by her continuance: "There is a sister but she lives in Tahiti. Retired. No one else."

"But I thought . . . I thought he had kids from a—"

"No children!" Annika's composure had fractured, momentarily; and now she turned: "Nothing like that. He was alone."

Then the studied calmness returned, like the older woman had neatly zipped her unwanted emotions into a bag and dropped this bag disdainfully into a bin. Julia noted that Rouvier had turned to observe this female exchange. His frown was not unhappy, it was the frown of curiosity. Professional and clever.

Julia guessed he was very senior in the Lozère police force, because she likewise surmised that there weren't many murders, out here in France's loneliest *departement*. So any such crime would attract the most senior policemen.

The lights of suburban Mende glowed fizzy-drink orange on the rain-blurred horizon. Rouvier spoke quickly and quietly with Annika. Julia tried to listen in, even as she tried to pretend she was not, out of politeness; she definitely caught the phrase *prepare yourself*.

For what? How had he died? Who had murdered him?

The shock of the situation kicked in, once again, or maybe for the first time properly. Julia felt a shiver of fear run through her. *Murdered.*

Now they were in Mende, the car was actually speeding up, emancipated by these empty urban highways, which were virtually deserted at this time of night—and in this type of weather. They slashed through rainy Mende, jumping amber lights, their police siren howling in a satisfying way.

She watched the sights of her adopted and temporary hometown flee past the windows. The cathedral, the museum, the *Hotel Lion d'Or*. Why did every French town have a *Hotel Lion d'Or*?

And then the hospital. Julia had never visited the hospital before, but it was just like any hospital. It could have been a hospital in Chicago.

"Par là . . . je connais bien la route."

Doors opened, nurses passed, old people lay on gurneys, staring grimly at nothing: people cuckolded by their own bodies, betrayed.

The four of them took an enormous steel elevator to the basement. Again Julia felt the absurd urge to fill conversational silence. What could she say: *Hey, isn't this a big elevator?*

She said nothing. Shut her eyes. Tried not to think of what they were about to see. Would she even see anything, would they allow her in as well? Ghoulishly, Julia wanted to observe the body. She had never seen a murdered person. She desired the unique experience even as she despaired at her own heartlessness. Poor Annika. Poor Ghislaine.

The French being spoken was urgent, but whispered, like they were in church, as they walked the long corridor to the mortuary.

Julia asked herself why people always whispered in the presence of the dead. The dead, she thought, are also deaf.

A wide door swung open automatically. As they crossed the threshold, a man in light-blue rubber gloves came over, briefly smiled at Rouvier, scanned the other faces, and met Annika's eyes with his own. She nodded.

He motioned: this way.

It was all happening very quickly. Julia had expected more of a palaver, a prologue, some polite and ritual ablutions. But this was brisk French efficiency, verging on harsh unsentimentality. The four of them filed through a wide, overbright room, full of gurneys and the vague forms of bodies under plastic sheets—the sleeping dead, all patiently waiting.

Now they paused, but only for a fraction of a second, and then the doctor pulled the top of the plastic sheet down to the neck.

It was Ghislaine's face. He seemed almost calm. The eyes were shut, with just a smudge of blood on the nose. The skin was ghastly pale, but the relaxation of death gave the professor, oddly, a more youthful appearance. No longer straining and posing; the absurd hair was tousled, like a young man's hair, charmingly unkempt. It looked better that way.

What a horrible, horrible pity. A huge, engulfing wave of sadness and pity nearly knocked Julia down. She steadied herself, gripped her feelings. Poor Ghislaine. Why had he died? How? Who?

"*Oui. C'est lui.*" Annika had spoken; she had *identified le corps*. The doctor went to pull the sheet back, but Annika reached out a dignified arm and gripped his wrist.

"*Non, laissez-moi voir—*"

She wanted to see the rest of the body. The doctor threw an anxious glance at Officer Rouvier, who hesitated—and then nodded, discreetly.

The doctor pulled back the sheet. They stared.

And they recoiled. Even the two men, who must have seen the body before.

Ghislaine had been almost *ripped apart*. That was the only description: he had been cut up with such savagery it was practically a dismemberment. The blood was splattered on the underside of the plastic sheet; so much blood was smeared on his wounded corpse that he looked like he was tattooed red and purple, all over.

Whoever had knifed him to death had done it with wild anger, lust even. Slashing his arms and legs, plunging a knife into the groin—several times, cutting and slashing. A bestial attack. Revoltingly pornographic.

Lost in her own thoughts, Julia only now realized that Annika was sobbing.

Softly, but wrenchingly, the Belgian woman was crying, trying to hide her flowing tears behind her hands. Rouvier gestured to his junior officer and requested, in French, that Annika be driven back to her cottage. The junior obeyed, taking Annika gently by the arm. The doctor did his duty and wheeled away the transformed and brutalized corpse of Professeur Ghislaine Quoinelles.

Rouvier and Julia were alone in the mortuary. He sighed.

"These places. Always I think—one day I shall come in here, and I will never come out again. But, let us be thankful, not today."

They took the elevator to the ground floor. Rouvier seemed keen to talk, lingering by the front door of the hospital, where a few patients in dressing gowns were smoking the midnight hours away under a steel-and-glass awning.

"There is a machine over there with the most terrible coffee. I believe I need one. And for you?"

"Black. Thanks."

Rouvier jangled some coins and went to the machine.

Julia breathed in the rainy night. In the chaos and confusion she had left her car at Annika's. She had quite forgotten. But she couldn't be bothered to arrange a wearying or expensive lift to the Cham now—especially as she'd just have to drive all the way back, the same night.

She would sleep here in Mende, in her nearby apartment, and maybe get a lift from Alex in the morning. After all, he would want to go and see Annika. Offer comfort.

Moreover, she was happy to be right here, at the hospital, surrounded by people. She didn't want to go home alone to her empty rooms, not right now, not immediately. She was actually scared. Who did that appalling killing? The randomness and barbarity was frightening. Julia noticed her hand was shaking as she reached to accept the white plastic cup of coffee from Rouvier.

She sipped.

"You're right. It's disgusting coffee."

"It is a miracle, *non*? To make coffee this bad is practically a biblical event."

"And stupidly hot, too."

He nodded and smiled. She noticed he had very neatly manicured hands. She liked Rouvier. He reminded her of her father at his nicest: gentle, clever, protective.

It seemed a shame not to take this opportunity to ask him a few questions. Julia's scientific brain was keen to take control again, to exert a grip on her febrile emotions. That way she could fend off the sadness, and fear, and memories. The raped body of Ghislaine chimed unhappily in her mind. *That day her father drove her back from Sarnia. Sobbing.*

She purged her thoughts and asked, "Do you have any theories? Any suspects?"

Rouvier shook his head, blowing cold air on the coffee.

"No. But there are some clues. The arrangement of the knife blows is interesting. He has many, many cuts on the hands and fingers."

"I saw."

"The distribution of the cuts shows he had his arms, hmm, what is the word . . . elevated. *Elevated.* To protect himself."

This was a little mysterious.

"Protect himself. How?"

"Maybe the killer was trying to stab him high in the head. That is our suspicion. The front of the head. The forehead or the eyes. Naturally, there is a reflex: to lift your hands. In that situation."

It was a horrible image.

"How do you know it was one killer?"

"We don't. But I think, just a guess, I think I am right. One big man, frustrated, and then frenzied. Yes, that is a very good English word. *Frenzied.*"

"Who found the body?"

"A neighbor. I understand she is very upset."

"Not surprised. Jesus. *Jesus.*" Julia was gulping her coffee now; it was cooler, and she needed it. The bitter taste was apposite. "So. Do you have any theories about motivations? Did Ghislaine have enemies?"

"Motivations?" said Rouvier, half smiling, half avoiding her gaze. "No. Yes. No. A man with no close family? No girlfriend. No rivals in his small field. Yet a man with a famous name."

"Famous?"

"OK, perhaps not famous. But well known." Rouvier crushed the plastic cup in his hand and chucked it in a trash can from a distance; he smiled at the accuracy of his aim. Then he sobered and turned. "I knew Ghislaine Quoinelles. He was, perhaps, a little *haunted* by his surname."

"How?"

"His grandfather was a famous scientist." Another moue of a shrug. Rouvier was looking ready to leave. "I do not know much more. But I often wondered why he came south, to little Lozère. In France a famous surname can be a wonderful advantage. We are meant to be a meritocracy, the great republic! But *énarques* descend from *énarques*. The sons of small Hungarians in the Élysée get to run La Défense at the age of twenty-three. Quoinelles was rich and clever and descended from famous men, politicians, scientists—yet he came here to tiny Mende, where literally *nobody* lives! For a Parisian, Lozère is like Siberia. Maybe he tried to escape the shadow of his surname."

Julia absorbed the sudden information. It attained a sort of logic. A hint of a pattern. Perhaps.

"Oedipal. Yes. But what has that got to do with the murder?"

Rouvier smiled in a valedictory way. "*Hélas.* Nothing. Probably nothing. But we have no clues and no witnesses and no suspects, so I will try anything. Perhaps you can help us?" He warmed to his own theme. "Ask Madame Annika, maybe, she may know more, you are her friend. She is a difficult woman to pry open, like an oyster. Find the pearl. And now I am talking rubbish, is it not so?" He laughed, quite cheerily, and reached in the pocket of his smartly dark uniform. Then he produced a card with a debonair flourish. "Call me, *telephone* me. Anytime. But now it is late, I go, I must drive a long way home. You live in Mende? You need me to drive you? Let me drive you—" His hand reached for her arm.

She flinched. She couldn't help it.

"No!"

Her voice was way too sharp—punchy and aggressive.

Rouvier gazed back, perplexed and confused, and Julia winced at what she had said. *But she couldn't help it.* The words had ignited the memory. A car, a dark winter night, crossing the border to Ontario, to drink underage. "Hey, babe, let me drive you . . ." Her resolve never to let that happen again.

"No. Sorry. Please. I . . ."

His frown was sincerely tinged with hurt.

"I was merely offering to assist. Miss Kerrigan?"

"I know. I know. It's just that . . . You know. My apartment is quite near."

"*D'accord.*" He gazed her way again, puzzled still. But then his frown subsided and he glanced up at the weeping sky. "And now it is raining. *Il pleure dans mon coeur / Comme il pleut sur la ville.*"

Julia nodded, keen to move on, to forget. "'It rains in my heart like it rains on the city'? I know that line. Rimbaud, right?"

"Ah, no. It is in Verlaine, in the works of Verlaine."

His smile was renewed, but it was sad, and it was distracted; it was obvious he really wanted to leave. Julia focused on the present. She still had questions: she had so many questions, but there was one she needed to ask now; she felt it was important, but didn't know why.

"Monsieur Rouvier—"

He was actually walking away; but he turned.

"*Oui?*"

"You said Ghislaine's grandfather was a famous scientist. What was he famous for?"

The officer stood beneath a streetlight; rain tinseled in the glow as he pondered the question. Then he smiled faintly, his face illuminated by an answer.

"I might be wrong, but I think it was breeding. Yes, something *audacious*. Like that? Yes—I believe it was crossbreeding."

"Crossbreeding—between what? What species? What animals?"

His smile faded to nothing. "Men."

"Sorry?"

"*Men and animals.* He tried to crossbreed men *with animals,* or so I believe." The smile returned. "*Au revoir,* Miss Kerrigan. *Au revoir.*"

11

Rising from the bed, Jake slowly approached the door. Hanging from the hook was a terrible thing.

What was it? A tiny dead monkey? A dried fruit bat? *What the fuck was this?* A brown leathery mammalian corpse just hanging here? Surely it couldn't be worse, surely it couldn't be what he most of all feared?

His revulsion mixed with his furious curiosity. He walked closer. And then his stomach surged with the bile of confirmed disgust.

This was no monkey. This was unmistakably *not* animal.

It was a human embryo.

A human fetus, somehow dried or mummified, was hanging by its own umbilical cord from the coat hook on the door.

The fetus stared at him. Its blank open eyes were milky white.

He heard a scream.

He stared.

The scream didn't register; it was like a distant car alarm, not really meant for him. He was so transfixed by the sight of those eyes, dead eyes rolled back, like his sister. *No, don't think this way.* But he couldn't help it. Slowly he pulled on his jeans and a shirt, and all the time he kept staring at the baby, the dead fetus, the possessed, hor-rifyingly white eyes, like his sister's, lying in the road; until he real-ized it was Chemda. Screaming.

Chemda!

He kicked open his door and the scream was still loud in his ears—her room was next to his. Shunting through her door, he found her, sitting on her bed, panting and gasping, her face wrought with fear. She was pointing at something, wordless and terrorized.

He didn't have to guess. Hanging by its umbilical cord, from the rafters of the timbered room, was another fetus.

"Chemda. *Come on*—"

She was naked, wrapped in sheets. She didn't move.

"Chemda. Please. *Now!*"

He walked over to her, took her damp hand; her gaze yearned beyond him, through him, at some fearful horizon. Then a lucidity reappeared; she nodded, dumbly, and he turned away as she hurriedly put on a dress. Before they could open the door a maid was in the room; the maid also screamed. And her scream was unbearable, exis-tential: like she sensed her own approaching death. The maid's rubber-gloved hand was weakly pointing at the limply hanging fetus; her mop had fallen to the floor. Then she screamed again. A wild klaxon. Shrieking and shuddering.

Jake didn't know what to do: rescue Chemda, or calm the near-hysterical maid. He grabbed Chemda's hand once more, and they fled into the garden.

He was agitated for an hour; it took Chemda two hours to calm down. Madame Marconnet brought tea and a blanket and the maid hovered nearby, distraught, her small, dusty hands trembling and shaking as she smoothed down her dirty apron, over and over. Sitting next to Jake, Chemda stared fearfully at the river and the boats and the algae nets and the singing fishermen, and for a hundred minutes she said nothing. And then, finally, she spoke.

"Talismans." The voice from the back of her throat. "They are talismans."

"What?"

"In Khmer—*koh krohen* . . . or *kun krak*."

Once more she fell silent.

They were alone again in the secluded riverside garden of the Gauguin. Madame Marconnet had withdrawn, the maids had finally gone back to work—to clean the rooms, to take away those horrible *things*.

The garden, he now noticed, was beautiful. In front of them the milk-chocolate waters of the Mekong communed with the dark-chocolate waters of the Nam Khan. But all Jake could think about was those cold and dead and horrible milky eyes. Above them the leaves of the tamarinds tinkled and whispered, yet Chemda was still shivering with fright.

He needed to know.

"Talismans. What kind of talismans? How?"

She looked his way; she was visibly struggling to master her emotions. "It will all sound insane. But you must know the Khmers are very superstitious. Ah. For instance, you see the little spirit houses everywhere in Cambodia, to trap evil ghosts, the *neak ta*? Right? And gangsters with sacred tattoos, to ward off bullets: Phnom Penh is full of them."

Jake nodded. He had seen these tiny, sinister shrines. And yes, the tattooed gangsters were everywhere, draped with blessed amulets.

"I've seen all that. But why here, us, why those *things*?"

"The belief in spirits goes deep in my culture, Jake." She shuddered again. "Very deep. Even the Khmer Rouge, for all their atheism, were the same: animist and superstitious. And it's not just Khmers who believe in the power of Khmer voodoo."

"Sorry?"

"Khmer voodoo, Khmer black magic, is feared right across Southeast Asia. The Lao hate it, the Thais fear it, the Malays, the Burmese, the Chinese all pay homage. The Thai prime minister is thought, by Thais, to use Khmer talismans, *kratha*."

Down by the pier, fishermen were hauling in nets, a meager catch of little silvery fish. Pungent and flapping.

"So what exactly are these talismans in our room? You called them something. Just now."

"*Koh krohen*. They could be *koh krohen*. Ah. Dead babies. Embalmed."

He shook his head, revolted and disgusted, watching the watermen on the river speeding past in their long-tailed boats, churning the chocolate-milk water.

"They are miscarried fetuses. *Mummified?*"

"Yes. But sometimes they can be worse than that. I suspect the *kratha* in our rooms are even *more* evil."

"Worse? How could they be any *worse*?"

"The babies in our rooms . . . ah, I don't know for sure, but my guess is they aren't *just* miscarried fetuses." She gazed away at the river, torpid and decaying; "I think the ones in our rooms were the worst of all. Even worse than the ghost children. You saw the maid's reaction. Pure horror."

"So? What are they?"

"What we saw, hanging from the door, was probably *kun krak*. Smoke babies. They are babies that have been . . ." She blinked, twice, and then again. "Ripped out of a woman's living womb, then doused in some kind of sacred oil, then smoked over a fire. Some call them *kuk krun*. Well-done babies."

She paused. Jake gazed between the papayas and the jackfruit, trying not to dwell on this truly appalling information. Murdered babies of a murdered woman; fetuses anointed and smoked.

"Sweet fucking Jesus." His voice was choked.

Chemda's eyes were moist and shy. "The fact that someone put them in . . . my room, our rooms, means someone wants us out. It is a direct and devilish threat, Jake. Designed to unnerve. And I am unnerved. The smoke babies. It scares me. Ah."

He regained himself. Angrily.

"But Chemda. You're a Californian, right? You went to UCLA. You know it's all bollocks. This is just, just voodoo. Juju dolls, dead chickens, zombies. It means nothing—"

"I can't help it. I *believe* it, Jake. Somewhere inside I do fear it, horribly; it's part of my root culture. Maybe more than that; maybe it's genetic. I wish I didn't, but I can't help it. Ah. Can't help it."

This was the closest she had come to breaking. So far, Chemda had been relatively unfazed by the bloody death of Doctor Samnang; she had been determined, and decisive, when they were fleeing the police at Site 9; she had arranged their escape from the Secret City with a valiant coolness bordering on sangfroid; but a brief if chilling encounter with black magic—*that* had thrown her.

But if Jake was honest with himself, it had also thrown him. Like someone were taunting him with his worst fears and guilt. The little dead child, eyes rolled and white.

Trying to void his mind of this revenant image, he looked around—Agnès Marconnet was standing, once more, at the edge of the riverside lawn, anxiously gazing their way. The hotel owner had been in a state of anguished nerves ever since the ghastly discovery, apologizing and speculating. Who had put these hideous things in the room. *Mais pourquoi. . . . C'est pas croyable. . . . Mes propres employés? Je suis vraiment désolé. . . .*

But as he stared, Jake also became aware, through the screen of trees at the edge of the garden, of a police car, parked on the road that concluded at the Gauguin. A police car? When did that arrive? A few minutes ago? What was the policeman doing inside? Talking on his radio? To whom?

"OK. Fuck this. Superstition or not, Chemda, we need to go, *now*. Look!"

He tilted his head, significantly. Chemda squinted at the police car.

"How long has he been there?"

"Who knows. Maybe someone called them, about the . . . talismans. C'mon, we need to *go*."

"But *where*? The roads, they are so long, and so bad. It will take two or three days. We cannot fly out."

"Just grab the bags."

Their luggage was still stacked at the rear of the hotel, in a pile, on a cart. A melancholy brace of tiny rucksacks, dirty and ragged. They had been left there as if their stay was expected to be brief. Jake turned at a noise. The policeman was stepping out of the car. The door of his Toyota closed. A two-way radio crackled.

The cop was walking to the hotel door. He was knocking at the door; he was talking to someone there.

They stood in the garden, screened by the trees—but paralyzed. There was no way out of the hotel now. Indeed, a second police car was sliding down the narrow road, lights flashing, pointlessly, in the tropical sunlight.

Agnès emerged. Her voice was tremulous. She stammered, for a minute, in French, gazing at Chemda.

Chemda explained.

"She says someone called the police, about the . . . *kratha*. She doesn't know who. A maid, maybe. She says her husband is holding the police at the door, but they will force their way in if necessary—"

"So we're screwed."

"No." Chemda looked at Agnès—and Agnès nodded. "There's one other way, a path, down here, by the river, it leads around the wat, we can evade the police . . ."

Despair filled Jake's thoughts. The idea was feeble. The path would still lead them back into Luang Prabang; but Jake also realized they had no choice.

"OK. *The rucksacks.*"

They snatched their bags, Chemda whispered a goodbye to Agnès, and then the two of them fled through the tamarinds, slipping into the cooler shadows, running down the lawn. As the garden approached the river, the lawn sloped, more severely, until it became a very serious incline. They were half scrambling, half crawling, almost rappelling to freedom.

Freedom? Jake winced at the idea. This wasn't an escape to freedom, this was fucking futile. The riverside path would get them away from the hotel, around the police, but it would lead them straight back to town, emerging onto a main street, dirty and conspicuous, where they would immediately be spotted and arrested.

The riverside path led on, past the pier where the fishermen darned their nets in the sunshine. Jake stared.

The river. The pier. The river.

He gazed at the long-tailed boats. The sun of an idea dazzled on the Mekong's dark ripples.

"Chemda. Stop!"

She was three meters in front of him, hurrying along. She turned.

He snapped, "How about the river? Doesn't it go to Thailand? Eventually?"

Her face darkened—and then it brightened, a fraction.

"It does . . . Ah, yes, yes, it does!"

"So we get a boat. Right away. Hire one. *Anything!*"

The two of them hurried onto the wooden jetty. A few more boat-men were gathered at the very end, in the shade of a palm-roofed shelter, playing dice, some bare-chested, some barefoot, some laughing. Chemda walked straight up and talked urgently with one of the men, in Khmer, or Lao, in some language—yet another language Jake did not understand. His sense of isolation intensified. He was so foreign here; indeed, he was beyond foreign, he was like a different species. Chemda seemed excited, as well as frightened: she turned and interpreted.

"This man, Pang"—she indicated the wiriest of the boatmen—"he knows Agnès. And he knows a place, a day upriver. He can take us past Pak Beng. It's wilderness up there. After that we can just walk into Thailand. Then, at last, we are out of Laos. *Then we fly to PP from Chiang Rai.*"

Jake glanced at Pang. He was an old Laotian man dressed in faded denim shorts and a Manchester United shirt. He was the pilot of this small, narrow riverboat, a *pirogue*. He smiled. He seemed trustworthy. Jake wondered at his own fatuous speculations. What choice did they have, anyhow? The police might be searching the gardens this minute. Then they would hunt along the riverbank.

Bags were flung, and thumped. Chemda hurried down the wooden ladder and into the wobbling boat. Pang was silent. Everyone was quite silent. No one spoke about the smoke babies, the well-done babies, the ghost children, hanging from the rafters. White-eyed. Jake couldn't stop thinking about them.

Who had hung them there? Who was doing all this, trying to frighten them away?

The mighty river beckoned, implacable and unanswering. Swiftly he climbed into the boat, following Chemda aboard. Pang was already at the engine. Then Pang yanked the outboard into life and they pushed out from the shore, against the slowly surging waters, constantly fleeing their own tail plume of muddy water.

The staggered white stupas and golden wats of Luang, framed by the banana-tree green of Mount Phousi, receded at last. Jake watched the city of incense disappear behind them. He was very glad to leave, yet he knew he wasn't really escaping. How could you escape your own memories? New memories or old, they stayed with you, forever.

The Mekong was apathetically vast. Broad and slow and wide. For the first few miles they had the unsettling company of tourist boats drifting lazily downstream, full of Western and Chinese tourists in ungainly shorts waving at them like kids; Jake cursed them and wished them away. Sometimes speedboats accelerated past, rocking them with backwash, trailing gauzy isadoras of blue diesel exhaust and making Jake think they were going to be surrounded and arrested.

But within an hour they were virtually alone. And the loneliness was possibly worse than the traffic. They were scarily alone, deep in the jungled upper reaches of the Lao Mekong.

Bamboo reeds bent in the breeze, silent red petals fell on milky-brown water. River birds flew overhead. Wild lychees, black herons, silence.

Occasionally they passed a little tribal village, lost in the jungle, where naked, dirty children ran down to the shoreline brandishing small, crude carved wooden dolls, desperately shouting, almost hysterical.

"Souvenirs," said Chemda. "Sometimes tourist boats get this far, and they buy crafts from the villages. Otherwise these people live on nothing. Fruit from the forest. Monkey meat. Ah. Desperate conditions."

In another village an old tribeswoman was sitting on a log, her withered breasts quite bare: the woman looked and smiled, and Jake felt the electricity of shock. *Her mouth was full of blood.* She was smiling and her mouth was full of blood. Then he realized: she was chewing betel nuts. The woman smiled her lurid scarlet smile.

The boat slid from one empty shore to another, avoiding mud slopes and rapids, ducking under bamboo overhangs. Water snakes slid beneath the boat, sinister sine waves of yellow. At one point they turned a grandiose bend in the river and Jake saw a huge cave: in its dark recesses glittered a hundred or a thousand little smirking Buddhas, gold and silver statues sitting on rocks and sand. There were boats tethered here. Pilgrims?

"Sacred caves," said Chemda.

The sun was wearyingly hot, an enemy, ogling them. Jake felt increasingly ill at ease, once again. Were they being followed? Every so often he looked back, but the torpid waters stretched to a horizon framed by banana trees and bending palms and nothing else.

Pang the boatman was silent as the river. He was old, yet tough and wiry: one of those East Asians who looked like he could never die. Smoked by age and sun. Kippered. He smiled sometimes, but said nothing.

Chemda had, it seemed, fully recovered her wits. She wanted to talk. She was trying to explain Khmer culture to Jake, its superstitions and legends.

"Some people believe there is a particular darkness in the Khmer."

"Meaning?"

"It's difficult to explain it concisely. But here is an example: *kum*."

"OK."

"*Kum* is the desire to take revenge, a typically Khmer desire to do down your enemy. Ah. To crush him, over many years."

"Like a vendetta."

"Yes, but also no. Vendetta is just eye for an eye, isn't it, you kill mine and I kill yours; *kum* is even more deadly—but no, *deadly* isn't right." She stared at the riverbank, where an egret sat on a branch. "*Kum* is more . . . satanic. Kum means the desire to take, ah, disproportionate revenge."

"How?"

"*Brutally*. If someone hurts you, he becomes an enemy, a *soek,* and you must take revenge, *sangsoek*. But the principle of *kum* means you must hurt him ten times over in return. If someone rapes your sister, you must kill his sister and his brother *and* kill his father *and* his mother. Kill everyone."

Jake sensed the proximity of personal grief. He was quiet. Then she continued, her noble profile framed by the troubling green jungle and the painful blue sky:

"The legend is that the Khmers adopted Buddhism, the most peaceful of religions, because it put a restraint on *kum*. And that"—she leaned out of the boat and trailed delicate fingers in the water—"that is why communism was so particularly vicious in Cambodia."

"Explain?"

"The Khmer Rouge took away the constraints of Buddhism. They burned down the temples, tortured and slaughtered the monks. They tried to murder God. And the result . . ." She shrugged, and winced. "Was the killing fields. The nihilistic brutality of the killing fields. Because if you take away the Khmers' religion, we are just left with *kum*—plus tyranny."

Chemda withdrew her hand from the river abruptly, as if she feared it might be bitten. "And then again, sometimes I think that maybe we are still a cursed people." She gazed into the mirroring waters. "Ah. Lacking something, lacking humanity. Maybe we are *still* the Black Khmer. Steeped in blood."

The boat was slowing. Jake turned: they were approaching a larger village, with a pier and stores and one or two fishing skiffs, a place where village children played in clothes, rather than shrieking and naked.

"Pak Beng. We can stop for water, briefly, it is surely safe here. No one comes here. Then we have another few hours and we can get to Thailand. I hope."

They tethered the boat. Jake stepped ashore and grabbed a warm cola from a man running a stall in the village. He had one eye and one arm and one leg, and a full set of grinning white teeth.

Jake returned to the boat. He didn't feel refreshed, he felt utterly exhausted and still very hunted. The sun was so ferociously, predatingly hot; even the cooling river breeze did not help as they motored slowly upstream. The silence of the river and the memory of the smoke baby, hanging from the door, weighed on him, like oppressive humidity before a storm. He wanted to talk. He didn't know what to say. Chemda spoke.

"Why do you feel guilt, about your family?"

It was one of her direct, even piercing questions.

He shied away from answering. "What do you mean by that?"

"When we were on the plain. You said . . ." She softened her voice, as if she knew her words might hurt him. "You said that you felt guilt, about surviving your family, or your mother and sister. Why?"

Again, something in Chemda seemed to invite the truth from him, and again he yearned to tell her everything; maybe because she had darkness in her past, too.

"When my sister was run over, I was . . . holding her hand. I was looking after her, but I was only seven, and she was five. Stupidly young. But I was still in charge, you know? And still I let go and, and, and she ran into the road." He half-swallowed the rest of the story, eyes fixed on the walls of jungle imprisoning the river. "It was after that my mother fell apart, and then she walked out. Broken heart. I don't know. But in my mind it was all my fault. If I hadn't let go of Becky none of it would have happened. None of it. Kids blame themselves, don't they? That's what I did, and sometimes still do. When I'm not working. Or drinking. Or watching football. You know."

The motor puttered as they curved another, tighter riverbend.

Pang was staring rigidly ahead to where smooth rocks protruded from the brown-and-silver water.

"I have a photo. Of Rebecca. It's the only thing I keep, the only bit of her left."

Chemda said nothing. Instead she put her hand briefly on his, offering that tender electric shock. Then she sat back.

He reached for his rucksack, unzipped it, and took out his wallet. *There.* The photo. One of the first photos he had ever taken. Of his sister just before she died. He handed the little Polaroid to Chemda like he was trusting her with his most precious possession. A pathetic photo. By a seven-year-old. But it was precious: a photo taken by himself of his five-year-old sister, smiling her impish smile, wearing a hat three sizes too big. Laughing.

Chemda's eyes moistened.

"She was . . . very pretty. I'm so sorry."

Jake shrugged and took back the photo and put it away. Carefully zipping it up safe.

"Sometimes I wonder if I'm being a bit morbid. Keeping it all this time. But it's my only purchase on the past. You understand?"

"Of course," said Chemda. *"Of course. . . ."*

He watched her as she gazed at the rippled water. Her expression was maudlin and quiet.

"Tell me about yourself, Chemda."

"Yes?"

"Well, twenty-eight. Unmarried. Boyfriend?"

She faintly smiled his way. "I am a virgin. . . ." A pause. She added, with a more sincere smile: "In Cambodia."

He laughed, somewhat uncertainly.

She said, "It sounds absurd to talk about all this, now."

"Hey. What else can we talk about?"

"OK. OK. How to put it? I was not quite so chaste in LA. There were lots of boys. The wrong kind of boys." Her eyes met his. "The insecurity was appealing. I was always drawn to boys who wandered away, adventurers, boys who couldn't be tied down. Probably because I didn't want to be tied down. Ah. You have to remember, Khmer culture is quite conservative, girls are expected to marry young. My parents have *seriously* started to worry about me. Especially now I am over twenty-five. . . . Ah well."

The river birds were swooping again, silver and blue, maybe some kind of kingfisher. They talked some more, but then the silence fell, and with it the fear returned—and then the oppressive heat drove them to separate corners of the boat.

Jake gargled horribly warm water from the dirty water bottle, then dipped a T-shirt in the river and draped its wetness over his broiling face.

The motor chirred. Wearied by his own anxiety, and the sadistic heat, Jake lay back against the uncomfortable planks of the pirogue, and almost immediately felt the mermaids of sleep dragging him under. Soft female arms pulling him down. And down. Into the darkness of sleep, with the murmuring bones.

When he woke, his watch showed three hours had gone by. Now Chemda was asleep. The sun was filtered by the riverside palm fronds. Twilight. Pang was gazing at him.

Pang said, "We are soon there. You and Chemda very tired, I think."

This was startling. It had not occurred to Jake that Pang spoke English. All this time he had presumed the man's silence was due to his not understanding their conversation. Jake hadn't even offered the boatman a proper word of hello.

"Please, Pang. I didn't realize you spoke English . . . you know. I'm so sorry."

"Not problem. I understand, much danger. Do not worry." The old man nodded, distractedly. He was steering them carefully around floating logs and sudden rocks.

The river had become notably narrower, the current faster, the shorelines steeper, almost cliffs. Impenetrable jungle adorned the cliff-tops on either side. A younger Mekong.

"I take tourist up here, many years, for Madame Agnès. In the hotel. I know her family long time." The boatman hesitated. "One time I know *her* family, too, they friend with Agnès."

"Who did you know?"

"Her grandmother. Madame Sovirom. She live in Luang after the war."

Jake paused, and pondered. Surely not. The grandmother was killed by the Khmer Rouge. But surely it had to be. The Hmong knew her, or knew of her; why not someone in Luang?

Pang revved the engine, steering for the opposite shore. Chemda was still fast asleep, her delicate head resting on a folded sarong, her bare dark legs smeared with mud.

The boatman's Manchester United shirt was stained with salt and river and oil; the grime of honest hard work. He said, "I not like tell Chemda. Sad story. Maybe she not know?"

"What story?"

"I tell you. But secret. Everyone pretend they know nothing. Madame Agnès, everyone. The famous lady from Phnom Penh, royal lady. She lived at the Gauguin after the war, for a few year. She sit every day by the river, in the garden, and every man with a boat know who she was. She just sit looking at the river, every day for three year, maybe four. Some men call her bad name, Khmer name—*vierunii*—"

"It means?"

"Lao-lao. Whiskey. But also it mean . . . stupid woman, made bad by drink. Like she drunk." He cocked his head and slacked his mouth, doing a caricature of someone palsied, or retarded. "She like this. Spitting."

"She just sat there? Was she ill?"

Pang shrugged, his frown deep and troubled.

"Not ill. Own fault. She say, 'Give me.'"

"What?"

"They cut her up, but they say she want this." Pang sighed. "I do not know, maybe I say nothing."

"But I want to know."

A pause. They were just a few meters from the shore. Jake spotted a modest mud bank, and a rough track leading up the steep river cliff into the bush. He realized this must be Thailand, this shoreline: beyond the cliff was Thailand and roads and proper airports and 7-Elevens and safety—*they were close to safety*—but before he alighted he wanted more information, as much as possible.

"Pang, are you saying that Chemda's grandmother volunteered to be experimented on?"

"Vol . . . an . . . ?"

"Volunteer. It means, it means . . . Are you saying she asked them to do it to her? To cut her head open?"

"Yes. Yes! *Doi!* That is it. She *ask* them to do this, to cut her open, to make her brave like lion, like brave animal, but it go wrong and then she like . . . dead woman. Sitting there. For many year. Staring at the river. Sad story, so sad." Pang nudged the boat onto the mud, darkly frowning, almost despairing. "I always ask. Always. Why? Why anyone want that? Why anyone ask to be cut open? To be cut into many pieces?"

12

Only when Officer Rouvier had driven away, swinging out of the hospital parking lot, did Julia begin her walk back to her apartment. It was a walk through the biting cold of the rain, but she didn't mind.

She was glad for the cold and she was glad for the drizzle. It matched her sober and melancholy mood. And her slow footsteps were a soft and suitable backbeat to her thoughts, her deep deep thoughts. Of irritation at her own overreaction to Rouvier, and of fear and sadness at the murder of Ghislaine—that grotesquely brutal savaging. Raped by knives, or claws, or teeth.

Raped by animals.

Wearied by her own pensiveness, Julia stopped on one street corner; she was standing under the softly illuminated awning of an old bank. Crédit Agricole.

She couldn't resist anymore. The past had been hammering at the present for so long: it was a jangling phone that wouldn't stop ringing. A shrieking car alarm, waking up the neighborhood. She had to confront this painful memory, or it would drive her mad.

She had been nineteen. When it had happened. In Sarnia.

It was a teenage rite of passage in Marysville. To cross the border into Canada, where you could drink underage—by American standards. And her friends' usual stop was Sarnia, a small, ugly Canadian border town of warehouses and derelict railroads and bleakness and freight trains and the Charity Casino. And liquor stores selling cut-price bourbon and Labatt Blue Light.

She and her friends must have done that trip a dozen times, yet that one night it went wrong. Maybe they drank too much, smoked too much skunk. Maybe someone had done some pills, E, she didn't know. She couldn't remember. But suddenly the evening was out of control and someone with a VW kombi offered to drive her home, but they didn't go home; minutes later, an hour later, she was in the back of the kombi with a guy she liked, Callum, and he was kissing her, and she was half undressed, and kissing him, and laughing, and drinking more and more, and barely aware there were other guys in the van. Watching. Predatory. Watching.

By the time she began to realize, it was too late. She was naked and the other boys were laughing, because they thought she was enjoying it—was she enjoying it?—then she had done it: she had sex with one, maybe two of them, and the others were watching and laughing, and she shuddered to remember the way they touched her, grabbed her, like animals, slavering; and as she sobered the terror began, and she screamed and screamed and someone took pity and slapped down the others and bundled her from the van. The friend had called her father, who had arrived in Sarnia at two a.m. to find his daughter half dressed and weeping and refusing to talk, standing in the lobby of the Charity Casino like a whore. Like she was a whore. Wondering if she was actually a whore. Worse than a whore.

She'd loved her father that night. His delicacy and tact, the way he didn't ask too many questions; the way he just hugged her and protected her and rescued her. And then he played his favorite jazz on the car radio, to fill the father-daughter silence, as they drove home through the comforting dreary suburbs, silent in the frost.

Three months later she had the abortion. She'd kept that to herself as well. Another shameful secret. Half a year later she got into McGill and she left it all for good.

The cold Lozère rain eased a little. Julia stepped from under the awning of the Crédit Agricole and recommenced her walk home.

Why was this memory seeking her attention now? Her childhood, however bland and ordinary and boring, had been largely happy. She loved her parents; her parents loved her. She'd enjoyed a decent education. There was just that one incident that clouded it all, just one. And she had gotten over it, in principle. So she thought.

Maybe it was the animality of the attack on Ghislaine that reminded her. She thought of the boys in the van; they had been her friends, then they became a pack, just like that. A wolf pack. How easily man was reduced to animal.

Or maybe it was the blood on Ghislaine's body. Like the imagined blood of her abortion. The crimson of her guilt.

The echoes were many.

Her apartment was near now. Puddles on the gray pavement reflected the Mende streetlights; they also reflected her pensive, downcast face. Julia let her mind wander away, away from the past. To the conversation with Rouvier.

Yes.

The sudden revelation was like the reflection of a moon unexpectedly emerging from behind the clouds: large and startling.

Yes.

In Verlaine, that's what Rouvier had said. *In Verlaine.*

And that's what Ghislaine had said, in his own way. *You'll find it in Prunier.* The same way Rouvier had said *in Verlaine.*

You'll find it in *Prunier*!

Could this be the answer? To the puzzle? Was this why she was stymied?

She had presumed when Ghislaine had said "in Prunier" he meant "in Prunier, the village in north Lozère"; and last week she had visited the place and found nothing.

But maybe when Ghislaine had spoken that day on the Cham he meant his phrase in the same way an academic might say "in Shakespeare" or "in Darwin." Ghislaine's meaning must have been: You'll find it *in the works of* Prunier, *the scholar.*

Quickly, she collected her chastened wits. Prunier or Prunières was a not entirely uncommon surname. It belonged to no scholar she knew, but this was evidently an obscure corner of French science. Maybe a local man? Or someone very dead, from very long ago.

Two minutes' walk to her apartment, and two hours in front of her laptop screen, laboriously translating the most obscure and recherché French websites, finally gave her the answer: Pierre-Barthélémy *Prunières*.

She was *right*.

It turned out he was an antiquarian who flourished in the mid-nineteenth century. Pierre-Barthélémy Prunières did much research in Lozère; and he came from Marvejols. Long forgotten, he was once, the website said, known for his research in osteo-archaeology: skulls and skeletons he unearthed in the caves and dolmens of his native region, like the *Baumes-Chaudes* in the Tarn. And near Saint-Pierre-des-Tripiers—in "*la grotte de l'homme mort.*"

La grotte de l'homme mort?

The cave of the dead man.

She wrote down the phrase on a pad, circled it, stared at it. The name was poetic, but it meant nothing in itself. She circled the name again, then returned to her computer. And ten more minutes on the laptop brought her a much more sincere frisson, a real buzz, a frightening revelation.

The word pulsed on the screen: *trépanation*.

Trepanned.

Her thoughts whirred. It seemed this man Prunières had unearthed precisely the same kind of remains as Julia. A hundred and fifty years before.

Trepanned skulls. Horribly wounded; deliberately drilled.

Julia pushed back her chair and walked to her rain-scribbled window. The gray slate roofs of Mende were framed by the dark hills beyond: the Causse Méjean, and the Cham des Bondons. And the wild and empty Margeride.

The word resonated in her mind.

Trépanation.

13

"Hell of a story," said Tyrone. "Hell of a story."

"I guess."

"I'm serious." Tyrone lifted his beer bottle. "Dude, you're on your way. Nail this one, and you could make your name."

They were drinking on the top floor of the FCC, the Foreign Correspondents' Club, in Phnom Penh. The top floor extended to a terrace that stared out over the Tonle Sap river, sluggishly reflecting a fat and queasy moon. Beneath them the clattering lamplit riverside boulevard was full of motos and cyclos and taxis; and jingling snail sellers and wandering tourists and unemployed tuk-tuk drivers arguing over rancid glasses of palm wine.

Jake had been back in the chaos of the city just three hours. It was only twenty-four hours since they had crossed the border into Thailand. From there they had walked for two hours into a village, then got a cyclo to a taxi, caught a taxi to Chiang Rai. Then jumped on a plane to Phnom Penh.

He stared around: the FCC was its normal, comfortable, languid, semicolonial self, with its yellow shutters and overhead fans and wicker chairs. Journalists were talking with UN workers, photographers were boozing with bohemian locals.

But it had changed; or Jake had changed. By rights he knew he should be exhausted, but he wasn't. Why? Maybe he was pumped with adrenaline, and maybe he was still energized by the fear, and the unforgettable horror. The dead baby swinging from the rafters, with the little milky eyes. It was impossible to forget *that*.

He was being tapped. Tyrone was rapping him on the knee with the butt of his bottle.

"Dreamboy. You OK?"

He snapped out of his reverie.

"I think so. It's just—you know. It was pretty unnerving. And the mystery goes on. It's freaking me out."

"Uh-huh."

"You've been through all this, Ty. Bosnia. Darfur. Chechnya. You've been in danger. It resonates for a while, right?"

"It does. Dude, you have to let yourself down. Or you could drink it away. Or do some number four."

"I'm done with drugs, I want *answers*."

"Shame. It worked for me, till it fucked me up. China white heroin, like Himalayan snow. Ahh." Tyrone slugged the last of his Angkor: *"Où sont les neiges d'antan?"*

Jake had heard this spiel before, Ty romancing the powders; he diverted their dialogue onto more useful territory. He urgently wanted *explanations*.

"So, please, what do you think of it all. The jars, everything?"

"Obviously the Lao government was very keen to get this research—Chemda's project—aborted."

"Agreed."

"The Commie Lao, the Pathet Lao, they are *still* in power up there. And if they did anything dodgy in Laos back in the seventies, they'll wanna keep it under wraps, even now."

"Again, agreed."

Tyrone sat back, his empty beer bottle in hand.

"So that's your answer. The government put the frighteners on the two professors. Scared them, menaced their families. Yet these poor historians were also getting pressure from the Cambodian government, and the UN, and KR victims, to do the right thing." Tyrone accepted another Angkor lager from the waiter, and continued. "No wonder they folded: pressure from all sides. Sounds like your ass-over-tit guy got so shit-scared he killed himself, no other way out, especially when he found out the jars had been rediscovered. But, like you say, he did it in a way that sent you a message, the draining-blood stuff, a Tuol Sleng torture. He was telling you that it was the Communists that were pressuring him. A final despairing signal."

"Yes, my thoughts completely, that has to be it. But . . . Chemda isn't quite so sure it's suicide."

"Well, I think you're right. But what happened up there back in '76, anyway? Madness. And the dead fucking baby hanging on the coat rack? What's that about?! What kind of fucking hotel *is* this? Maybe they do that to all the guests, as a welcome gesture. Like a chocolate on the pillow—"

Tyrone was laughing at his own black humor. Jake was not laughing; he was wholly unnerved.

"But Ty, why didn't they just deport us, why did they let us go into Ponsavan—"

Black mosquitoes buzzed between them. Tyrone flicked the air with an irritated hand and speculated: "Say they *were* planning to kick you out, but you went straight to the jars. Possible. And of course the Lao cops were well aware who Chemda was, by then. A Sovirom. Not a family to mess with easily. If it had just been you—they would probably have taken you down to the basement and got all Torque-mada on your ass."

Jake sat back. It was true. He had been saved, paradoxically, by Chemda. She had led him into danger and then saved him. And the thought of Chemda stirred his anxieties further. He had told her, on the plane, Pang's backstory of her grandmother: she had reacted quite calmly, or just wearily. But with flickers of sadness and puzzlement.

And he knew that she was right now confronting her family, down the road, in their large villa, beyond the vast, ugly concrete pagodas of the Cambodiana Hotel: telling them everything. Did they already know? What would they say? Jake checked his watch again. He thought of calling her. But maybe he should wait for her to call him.

Tyrone had guessed his thoughts.

"Ahhh . . . Missing her already? Bless." The American smiled. "Jake and Chemda, sitting in a tree."

Jake attempted a dismissive and nonchalant laugh, and failed. He couldn't fake it. He knew there was truth in Tyrone's implication: he was deeply drawn to Chemda, already. And their lives were now entangled by what they had been through.

Tyrone leaned forward, cynical yet smiling, like a conspiring cardinal.

"You want some advice?"

"No."

"Just *be careful*. Be careful with this girl. That is one *powerful* fucking family. You get involved with Chemda, and you're involved with the entire clan, Teks and Soviroms. Especially her grandfather."

"Sovirom Sen. You've met him?"

Tyrone affirmed. "Just once or twice, embassy parties. Y'know. He is tough, very smart, and has that old-school charm. Same as the Khmer Rouge leaders."

"Come again? The Khmer Rouge . . . *charming*?"

"It's true."

"Not a word I'd associate with mass murderers—"

Tyrone lifted a hand.

"Remember. *I have interviewed some of these men.* KR leaders. It's actually a pretty unsettling experience. Because, like it or not, they do have this wit, this intellectual wit, and very good manners." He tilted his beer bottle and drank, and elaborated. "Guess it's the background, the old-world culture. Pol Pot was a dullard, a mediocrity, a functionary like Himmler with, I dunno, a weird gift for management—and killing. But lots of them went to the *best* schools here and the *best* universities in Paris. So they can quote Baudelaire and Rimbaud and Byron, they tell intellectual jokes and they know about Schubert. It's *most* fucking unnerving, 'cause you're sitting there, thinking, Jesus, this bastard helped run maybe the most evil government in history, his government used to crucify people *and burn them at the same time.* Yet he is making me smile, he is interesting."

"And Grandfather Sen is like this?"

"A touch. Upper middle class, Chinese Cambodian. His wife was true royalty, I think. . . ." Tyrone paused. "And then there's his daughter, Madame Tek. Oh wow. Let's not forget your potential mother-in-law." Tyrone was chortling. "She may be three inches high, she could probably run under a weasel, but *man.* These little Khmer women, they *wai* and scrape and make your noodles, but you cross them, just once?" He did a scissoring gesture. "Snip."

Jake winced. Tyrone snatched up a menu.

"Hey, I'm hungry. Aren't you? Must be. You've probably been eating bees for a few days, no? In Laos? You gotta love that *variety.*" Tyrone turned to the attendant waiter. "Burger, please. Rare. Properly rare. *Aw kohn!*"

"I'll have the . . . the *pad thai*. Whatever. Thanks. *Aw kohn*." Jake handed the menu to the waiter, who executed a *wai*, then returned to the kitchen.

Tyrone was quiet for a moment, then he turned to Jake.

"There's one other thing that worries me. Your story."

"Yes?"

"One bit you skipped over."

"What?"

Tyrone spoke quietly. The moon was sickly yellow in the sky behind him.

"Jake. You say those police cars coming after you—one of them hit a bomb or a mine."

"Yes."

"And possibly some cops were thrown, maybe injured—even killed?"

"I'm not sure. I saw one of them stumble out. Jesus. Jesus Christ . . . *of course*—"

The ugly reality dawned on Jake, like he'd woken to a nasty breakfast. *The police car that exploded.* Now he dwelled on it, conceptually, for a moment—it was obvious. Trouble. Serious trouble. They wouldn't just let this go. Would they?

Tyrone summed it up: "Maybe a cop died, maybe he didn't, but that's serious. Add it to the doctor's death—murder or suicide—and you have a very serious incident. Perhaps the Lao government will forget about the problem, rather than publicize it." He squinted at Jake. "That is possible. But maybe they *won't* just forget it. They could go through the Cambodian authorities, ask them to arrest you. Or someone might just quietly tell someone . . . who hires someone. Maybe you should watch your back on Monivong Boulevard."

The scorpion of fear scuttled down Jake's collar, under his shirt, and

down his spine. He shivered at the sensation. Red-haired, war-chewed
old Tyrone McKenna was surely right. *Watch your back on Monivong.*

Jake stood. He felt ill at ease again, very ill at ease.

"I need a leak."

Turning on a heel, he crossed the bar to the toilets. He unzipped
and sighed, and gazed anxiously out the bathroom window at the
river. On both riverbanks, people were out walking. Poor families
were frying eggs in braziers on patches of scruffy grass. Bonfires
burned. The squid sellers hawked their racks of dried translucent
squid. Dried and swaying, like the *kun krak*.

Jake felt the scorpion move under his shirt. The fear. This city: it
always got to him. He found Phnom Penh addictive in its anarchy
and energy and exoticism, but it was also a truly harrowing city.
Menacing by day and haunted at all times. A city spooked by an
unknown future—and a tragic and appalling past.

Down there on those crowded boulevards, on Monivong and
Sisowath and National Highway 5, the Khmer Rouge had marched
two million townspeople, out of the city, in two sunburned days in
April 1975: they had cleared the whole capital as soon as they had
won the civil war. People were tipped from hospital beds and forced
to walk. The elderly who stumbled were left to dehydrate in the gutter. Children were lost in the chaos and never found again. The
capital city was emptied, society was deconstructed, all was dissolved.
Two days.

They even blew up the central bank, destroying all the money in
the country, sending banknotes and government bonds flying into
the shattered streets. The banknotes hung for weeks from the wilting
jacaranda trees, like old confetti. Money was officially useless. And
then the Khmer Rouge sent the nation into slavery, and they worked
and starved a quarter of the population to death, and bludgeoned half
a million more. Killing their own parents, their own sons, their own

brothers, their own families. Devouring themselves in an orgy of self-harm. The nation that hated itself. *The nation that killed itself.*

His phone was ringing. It was Chemda.

Her voice was an urgent whisper.

"I got a call from Agnès, in Luang."

"And?"

"One of the hotel workers, a bellboy. He confessed. He put the things in our rooms."

"But why—"

"He was told to do it. The smoke babies were ordered, by the *kra*, the Neang Kmav of Skuon."

"The who? Who is that?"

The line hissed and deadened for a moment. "Sorry, Jake. I—" The voice was gone, then it returned. "My mother is crying. The whole family is in chaos. Have to go—maybe I can call you back—"

The call ended. Jake waited for a moment, and another moment, and nothing happened. Slipping the phone into his pocket, he returned to his bar stool. His plate of *pad thai* was sitting on the table. Tyrone was already assaulting his burger. Jake picked up his knife and fork, but he didn't feel remotely hungry anymore. His stomach was full of fluttering nerves. He had already dined, too much, on fear and angst.

He told Tyrone what Chemda had told him. Tyrone stopped eating.

"The Neang Kmav of Skuon?"

"What? What is the Kmav? What is Skuon?"

Tyrone looked atypically rattled. "Skuon is a small town near here. They eat spiders there. Tarantulas."

"What?"

"And the Neang Kmav is the Black Lady, a notorious fortune-teller who lives there." Tyrone was shaking his head. "It sounds like a stupid cartoon, but that . . . that is *bad news*."

"But—"

"She's an extremely powerful sorceress, one of those Khmer witch doctors that gets hired by Thai generals, Malay sultans, Chinese billionaires. Jake, this is the spider witch of Skuon we're talking about. *The spider witch of Skuon.*" He gazed at Jake's frightened face. *"Hey.* Chillax. At least if she turns you into a frog it will make a good headline."

14

The air was still and cold above the Cham des Bondons. The stars looked down, protectively, on the standing stones. And on Annika's little cottage, in the abandoned village. Vayssière.

Hunched over her laptop in the low-ceilinged sitting room, Annika was drinking wine and typing furiously. And drinking wine.

Her fingers paused. She squinted. The ambient light was rich and low and yellow in the room, cast by her antique table lamp with the lemon silk shade. The light from her screen was harsher, and brighter—and it stung her eyes.

Or was this stinging actually tears? Annika rarely if ever cried. She was proud of her scientific logic; she was proud of her coolness. But the emotion of confessing, after so long, was profound. Agony and relief at the same time. Because it was so hard to be honest. That's why she was drinking, that's why she was drunk: she needed the courage to do this. To wrench the lies away.

The years of complicity and deceit, with Ghislaine, meant the deceit had become part of her, grown deeply into her being. She was like one of those sad old trees on the Cham: a tree that had grown too close to barbed wire, so that the tree had eventually grown *around* the wire, and absorbed it, slowly and painfully, until the cruel iron wire was part of the tree itself. But she had to rip out the lies, because they were killing her, slowly.

Another slug of wine. Côtes du Rhone.

Her fingers tapped again, for a minute or more. She was an expert typist, even after a bottle of red. Yet now she had reached the crux. This needed a pause. A significant pause. And a deep breath.

Annika stared through the small open window of her living room, across the barren Cham. The silhouetted and distant stones looked like Victorian scholars, dressed in black and posed in thought. The chill autumn wind was gusting through the window, making her shiver.

Werewolves. Werewolves on the Margeride. Sometimes she wondered what exactly was out there. She knew it was something terrible. She didn't know it all, but she knew enough, and that's what she had to confess, before it was too late. Just tell the plain truth. Because the truth was terrifying enough, and more terrifying than any werewolf.

But first—another slurp of wine. Some more courage. Another pause.

She stood and stepped and leaned to the window, swaying slightly, gazing into the darkness. Waiting. Waiting for what? Death. Or worse.

The wind answered her questions, the cold, cold wind and nothing else. Shivering in the chill, she shut the window tight, and her heart filled her throat with terror at *the face she saw.*

But then she almost laughed, in shock. It was herself, reflected: she was gasping at her *own reflection* in the dark glazing. The living room interior, unlit and reflected.

Momentarily, she regarded her own aging face. How would she describe it? How did one describe a face? How accurate could one be with just a glimpse?

A few days ago, someone had come forward with a description of the possible killer, or, at least, of someone acting suspiciously near Ghislaine's house, on the night the archaeologist was butchered. A neighbor had been walking his dog along the semirural road near Marvejols and had glimpsed a strange figure over a hedge. Why would anyone be skulking in a field on a very dark and wet evening?

But the description of the killer was so bizarre: short, slender, very probably a young woman; long dark hair, a chalky-white face. Could a woman do all that? It seemed a little incredible. Something else was assuredly out there. Something stronger, stranger, more brutal than the police conceived. And more people were dying. Annika had to confess, to admit what she knew—before the murders got worse, before they were completed.

Annika walked back to her desk, wineglass in hand, gazing around the room as she paced: at her pictures from the Ice Age caves: of the mute and wounded Hands of Gargas, the great black frieze of Niaux.

This tableau of a life seemed slightly *insulting* now. Once, these pictures, these mementos, they had meant everything—truly everything— but now all this, her life's work, the ceaseless work and the tireless lies and the childless journey she had shared with Ghislaine, it was a historical, ideological, and actual dead end: it had *literally* ended in death.

Ghislaine had been cut open like the bison of Lascaux, his intestines falling to the floor. And more people would follow if Annika did not confess. There was no reason to maintain the deception one moment longer.

She set down her glass with an unsteady and unhappy hand, and she pulled out her chair, and she sat at her lonely desk, and reopened her e-mail. But even as she tapped the first words she hesitated. There was a large, agitated shadow on the wall. Cast by a moth. The moth must have flown in before she shut the window, and now the insect was trapped in the lampshade, its little wings beating desperately.

The dying struggle of the moth made the lamplight flicker on the walls, animating the pictures: the Hands of Gargas opened and closed, showing the severed fingers; the dying boys of Addaura struggled in the dust, watched by the men with sinister beaks.

Annika tried to type, to continue. But the moth was so desperate, trapped and hysterical.

Enough. Her thoughts were unraveling, the tears were not far away. She needed to rescue the moth, remove this last distraction, and then return to her computer and write it all down.

Approaching the lamp stand, she reached her hands inside the shade. A subtle shiver drove through her as she touched the madly flapping wings of the moth; she still nurtured childhood fears of moths trapped in her hair, flying into the mouths of sleepers, choking them on dusty wings.

An absurd phobia. Clutching her hands carefully, Annika caught the struggling thing between her fingers, caging it, not killing it. Slowly she moved to the nearest window, a small, leaded medieval window; it was unlatched. She just had to nudge the handle with her elbow and she could release the moth into the night. Just like this.

A white face passed in the darkness outside.

The shock was arctic. Liquidly chilling. What was that? What had she seen? Surely she had seen a face: it was meters away, a chalky-white face, staring, barely visible in the gloom, like a ghost. And now it was gone.

But had she? Had it even been there? Yes, perhaps no. Perhaps yes. She was quite drunk. Maybe she had imagined it. Her thoughts were fierce and turbulent and melting. She calmed herself as best she could. It was probably her deeper anxiety making her foolish—she had surely imagined it, and now it was gone. So she could return to her computer.

A noise rattled across the garden.

Annika spoke, timidly.

"Hello?"

It was so black out there, almost moonless. A deserted village with no streetlights. A dark so dark it could play tricks. But there—there!—that noise again. Was it just the wind, rattling an ancient door—or something lurking among the crumbling walls, maybe in the neighboring, wholly ruined cottage.

Annika leaned farther out of the tiny window.

"*Bonsoir?* Hello?" Were these words in her head? It was all doubt. "Is there someone there?" She felt absurd as she did this. A drunken old woman imagining things, talking to the silence; it was the last indignity.

Silence. Then more silence. Annika pulled back a fraction.

The face loomed again. The white face was rushing toward the window at incredible speed.

Annika choked with shock.

A dark hand was reaching in. Gripping her.

Who was this?

What was this? An angry face, showing animal anger, growling, murderous. Bestial. Shameless. And now the *body* of this *white-faced creature* was *pouring* through the open window, pushing her back, hands enormously strong, muffling her mouth, all over her. Annika was grabbed by the throat and her arms and her legs: she was grappled by something unexpectedly and luridly powerful. Like a monster. *A childhood monster.*

A jab of sharp pain pierced her neck, just under her chin. She had been injected. At once she felt the cold of paralysis slam into every limb, yet her brain was quite functional, she could sense and think and fear, and feel her heart straining at the terror.

Annika tried to scream—but the paralysis was too strong. Yet she could feel pain, too, searing pain. She was being dragged by the killer, this brutish mutant, this beast from Gévaudan. She was being dragged out of her sitting room by her own hair, yanked at the roots in her scalp.

Her hip bone banged against a table; now she was in the kitchen, her elbows knocking against the fridge, the oven, the door. The kitchen door. Lights dazzled her eyes and then more lights, and then she felt coldness and darkness. They were outside. She was being dragged over the front doorstep and along. *By her hair.*

The attacker was effortlessly potent. Annika was tugged and pulled all the way down her path, past her trash cans, past her little flower bed, out onto the track that led to the Cham des Bondons. Sharp, cold skies sang the night; Capricorn spun above her.

Where were they going? The stones? It had to be. She, it, this white-faced thing, this monster was dragging Annika *to the stones.* Again the Belgian woman tried to scream; again she heard nothing. Had she gone deaf?

No. She wasn't deaf. She could hear the coarse and rasping breaths of the killer, the animal-like panting. She could hear the sounds of her own body slishing over the dewy turf as she was hauled along by the hair.

The stones awaited.

The nearest stone to her cottage was one of the tallest, *the Soldier,* three brutal meters of impervious granite, a pillar of black in the black of the night: she saw it coming toward her. The stone was standing like an executioner, medieval, in a horrible black hood, waiting to do a silent duty. The killer lifted Annika into position. He, she, it—this thing jerked back Annika's head. The monster was going to smash her head against the rock. Just slam her skull into the stone, crushing the cranium. The front of the cranium. Yes, of course.

In her last moments Annika thought of her e-mail, in her laptop, waiting. Pulsing in the light. Unfinished. Everything she had done in her life had come to nothing; even this one last attempt at honesty.

The first hot tears ran down Annika's face as she stared up at the sky, as the killer pulled her head back as far as it would go. Ready. Ready to slam her forehead against the rock. To smash open her skull and pulp her living brain.

Annika wept for the end of her life. The stars above the stones were like a million fireflies, in a dark and freezing jungle.

15

The road out of Phnom Penh, once the road of ghosts, was now a cavalcade of
makeshift Asian capitalism run amok: cyclos and fuming buses and whining
motos and angry Mercedes passing impromptu gas stations where tinkers sold
bottles of pilfered gasoline from suspended glass vessels. The liquid in the big
upside-down bottles was blood-red and urine-yellow. Jake thought of men
turned on their heads, leaking blood.

"Yes," said Ty. "Let's try the National, the new one in Abu
Dhabi."

Tyrone was sitting next to Jake in the back of the taxi, but Ty was
apparently talking to someone in Jakarta. Or maybe Sydney. Or
Hong Kong. He was schmoozing and huckstering, pitching and
charming.

Jake envied Tyrone his contacts and his ruthless ambition, almost
as much as he envied Tyrone his war stories, that elegant war weariness. *Oh yeah, Bosnia, been there, done that, saw a brain in the road.* Jake
did sometimes wonder if Tyrone actually played up to the image of
the cynical, war-weary correspondent; perhaps Ty had molded his
persona to fit the cliché.

Whatever the answer, Tyrone McKenna had been doing it long enough that he really had become the stereotype, *par excellence*. The hard-bitten hack with hair-raising tales from global war zones.

Jake was glad Ty was with him; Jake was not so hard-bitten. Jake was properly scared.

"And let's try Tamara. Yeah. That new ed at the *Observer* mag, slept with Marcus Dorrell—you hear that?"

Corralling his nerves, Jake locked his camera lens on the view through the window and took photos.

He didn't want to think about their impending meeting with the spider witch of Skuon. It was cartoonishly unsettling, like a cheesy anime film come to life. Leaning out of the taxi, he took a photo of a garish, blinging red Buddhist temple surrounded by big, black, cockroach-glossy Toyota SUVs. Gangsters' cars.

They were on the outskirts of Phnom Penh now, heading past the airport. Aimless concrete buildings straggled along the hot and disintegrating road; a mobile phone outlet, adorned with lurid pink balloons, stood next to a butcher's shop with three orange pigs' heads on a counter—and then Jake glimpsed the first dusty sparkle of paddy fields.

He was glad they were leaving the city: it meant less chance of their being successfully pursued. Any one of the cars around them in the city could be the police sent to arrest him, or just someone sent to *do him in*. But outside Phnom Penh, Jake could see exactly who was following, if anyone.

No one was following.

Calmed, a little, his thoughts reached for Chemda, working in the UN's Extraordinary Tribunal, the Khmer Rouge Courthouse—not far from here, in the big building near the airport, where a handful of old men confessed to killing a hundred thousand little children. Every day, five days a week, eight hours a day.

Chemda had immersed herself in her UN court work by day and paperwork on the death of Doctor Samnang; she and Jake had talked long into the night. Yet Jake didn't quite know what to say to her during these phone calls, so they had talked about other stuff, their lives, their daydreams, school days, the origins of Buddhism, the origins of penang curry, anything. And the conversation alone seemed to be enough, meandering and mutual reassurance: we are in this together, please be careful. *Watch your back on Monivong.*

"So, Ty."

The American clapped his phone shut. "Yup?"

"Let's go over it again—the plan."

"I thought we did all this?"

Jake set down his camera on his lap, stared at it for a second.

"We did, but . . . indulge me? This is pretty unsettling stuff."

"Fair point. OK. *We are what we are.* I'm a journalist, you're a photographer."

"Working for?"

"The *Bangkok Post,* that's quite a big paper. Important enough to make the witch sit up, not so important she will actually, like, check. We're doing a story on her, how famous and powerful she is, the Neang Kmav, the best sorceress in Cambodia. These people are vain, and they like to whip up business—"

"You sure she'll buy this?"

"As long as we pay cash, and lay on the flattery, she'll buy it."

"Then we slip in a question?"

Ty nodded. "We certainly try. Play it by ear. We ask her about famous clients, rich notable Khmers. Because whoever ordered the *kun krak* has got lots of money. These aren't bits of dead toad you sell to the villagers to cure their sniffles; smoke children are very, very expensive to procure, upper-class juju, aspirational. She must be proud of having such a prosperous customer. We'll try and get a few names."

The next question almost didn't need to be asked, but Jake did: "And the risk, the downside, the worst that can happen?"

"She guesses who we are. She freaks. She casts a spell on you and turns you into a gecko. *She tells her clients and they come after you.* But Jake, what does it matter? You already have the Laos government on yer ass. You're fucked, you're double fucked, you're a first-time virgin on a porno shoot and King Dong is in the studio."

"Jesus."

"Trying to make you laugh. So you won't be scared."

"Too late, I'm scared." He forced a very weak smile. "Nice image, though. Thanks. Why did you never win a Pulitzer?"

"Dunno," said the American. "Strange, isn't it? But maybe this story will do it: *New Yorker*, front cover, ten thousand words, 'Kiss of the Spider Witch.'" He stared at Jake with those been-to-Chechnya eyes and he sighed. "That was a joke. I'm *joking*. This is your story. I just want to help. And I can help. We simply have to keep our nerve."

"And how do we do that?"

Tyrone's shrug was not so reassuring. "She will try to scare us, try to spook us out, that's how these people operate. Don't fall for it."

The car rumbled over potholes, the road worsening even as the landscape was improving. They were more than halfway to Skuon, skirting the river lands, the water meadows and swamp zones of the Cham, the secretive, Muslim, animal-sacrificing, river-fishing tribes of innermost Cambodia: descendants of the ancient kingdom of Champa, inhabitants of these desolate riverside settlements for centuries.

Jake knew the Cham had been almost wiped out. Yet more victims of the Khmer Rouge.

Water buffalo twitched their pink ears and stared at the passing car, truculent, inert; Cham fishermen patrolled the brown-yellow waters, gathering bamboo cages half immersed in the mud. Wooden stilt houses loomed beyond the stooping palms. Dark houses where old faces stared from the empty sockets of windows: old Cham women in strange white veils and robes.

The car jolted and swerved, abruptly, to avoid a barefoot child. She had just run out onto the road, between the cactus hedges.

"Fuck," said Jake. "That was close."

Tyrone said, "Lucky girl. The one thing you never get used to is the damn roads—the danger."

Jake watched the girl disappear in the rearview mirror. She was playing with a ball, entirely unaware of how close she had come to dying.

He shuddered. His little sister hadn't been so lucky. She was knocked to the ground, her eyes rolling white. Milky white, and staring; staring at her brother, who didn't hold on. Who let her go to her death.

"You OK?" said Tyrone.

Jake shrugged. "Thinking about Becky." He had told some of his story to Tyrone long ago: his guilt trips and his grief trips. He hadn't told Tyrone as much as he'd told Chemda.

The American sighed. "Families! Jesus." He cleared his throat, aggressively, and spat out the window. "What the fuck are families for? What do they give you but grief and guilt? What do they give anyone?"

"How about love?"

"Oh yeah. Love. Nice. And toasted sandwiches. Fuck that shit. You *have to move on,* Jake. *The only exit is survival.* Remember that's what Duch said, at the Khmer Rouge trial? Last week? He may have been a mass-murdering cunt but he got that right. He could have been talking about the average nuclear fucking family. The only exit from your childhood is *survival*."

The palm trees thinned. The river lands dried. The car took a left and a right and rattled down one of the more appalling roads in Southeast Asia, and then, at last, the haze of dust ahead showed they were approaching another dusty Cambodian town.

Skuon.

They pulled into the main square, essentially a sunburned round-about with old buses waiting by beer shacks, and noodle stands, two hairdressing shops, and dirty palm trees. Jake and Tyrone climbed out of the car and stretched for a second, and then they were mobbed.

Cambodian ladies were running toward them. Young ladies, old ladies, fat ladies, lots of ladies were zeroing in, with tin trays balanced on their heads. And on top of the trays were pyramids of fried black tarantulas, decorated with rose petals.

"They dip them in Knorr ready-mix soup," said Tyrone, waving away one lady. "No, *aw kohn,* no spider, *aw kohn,* not today—"

He turned and motioned to the driver: *wait.* Jake stared at the trays piled high with fat, ugly, greasy black spiders. The women were pointing at the spiders, smiling, begging them to buy.

"No. No thanks—" He edged away. "What is it with the taran-tulas?"

"Tell you in a minute. C'mon, let's go. Before we are forced to eat one in a bun." Tyrone was already walking away from the car, and the women, and the trays of fat spiders, down a lazy dust-hazed street. The American elaborated as they walked.

"They claim it's a tradition, the spider-eating. But I reckon it just goes back to the Khmer Rouge. In the late seventies everyone in Cambodia was starving—absolutely everyone. But they weren't even allowed to eat their own rice or they'd get shot by Khmer Rouge soldiers. So I reckon someone dug up a tarantula one day and thought—hell with it, let's roast this massive eight-legged mother-fucker and eat it, and then they developed a taste, now they are a delicacy: people drive for miles to buy 'em." He lifted a hand. "OK. You wait here? I'm gonna ask some questions. Find the house."

Here was a collection of plastic tables outside a concrete beer bar. Jake sat down, watching his friend disappear. Tyrone spoke Khmer, after a fashion, and that meant he could do this kind of thing quicker if alone; Jake's muted presence might unnerve people. But that also meant Jake would just have to wait. And watch. And perspire. And wait.

The sun was violently hot. Jake shifted his little chair into the shade of a red parasol. He ordered an Angkor beer. The beer arrived, it was stupidly warm. He left it undrunk, and gazed around. Two kids at an adjacent table were sipping 7 Up through straws, and staring at Jake with blank, cold expressions.

Jake looked the other way. Across the street in a small, scruffy square lot, a circle of men were sitting on their haunches, shouting and gambling, and drinking.

A cockfight.

He surreptitiously reached for his camera and took a few clandestine shots. The men were excited, calling out numbers, yelling. A flurry of dust in the middle showed where the cockerels were fighting. Jake used his telescopic lens, his sweaty hands urgently locking the gear into place.

There. He could see the roosters now, scrabbling in the dirt. One of them had pecked out the other's eye; the defeated rooster was stooped, half blinded, bleeding and dying. A hand swept down and collected the victorious bird while the men laughed and chinked glasses and swapped wads of grubby riel banknotes. The blinded chicken was taken to the side and its neck was wrung, contemptuously. It flapped in the dust for a few moments.

"I found her house."

It was Tyrone.

"That was quick—"

"Small town. Everyone knows her, she only lives around the corner. I've already spoken to her . . . secretary. If that's the right word." Tyrone exhaled. "OK, let's get on with it. I really don't like this town. Lot of people died here under the Rouge. A bad *ambience*."

"And? The witch?"

"Her assistant said she can give us half an hour. So we need to work fast."

The walk was as brief as promised. Two hundred meters of sandy road, past wilting stores selling Pringles, bottled water, and tarantulas, brought them to a large vulgar white house with fake Corinthian pillars. Like something particularly nasty in Miami.

Stupidly, crassly, Jake felt a slight tremor of journalistic disappointment. Somewhere inside he had hoped for something romantic and witchy, something vividly characterful to photograph, an old incense-sooted shack, cauldrons boiling with serpents, chicken blood on the walls. Not a coke dealer's villa.

The big new wooden door was painted an insistent blue. It opened. A young woman with dark, dark eyes stared at them and conversed with Tyrone as they crossed the threshold.

The house was air-conditioned. Mercilessly air-conditioned: it was actually cold, like the owner was trying to prove something. Jake felt the blast of chilly air on his bare arms.

The girl escorted them down a hallway with kitsch paintings of Buddha and Jesus and Princess Diana, and showed them into a large room.

The spider witch of Skuon was a middle-aged woman wearing too much makeup and jewelry. She had a Chinese aspect to her eyes. She was seated on a leather sofa with her legs tucked under her, like a girl, oddly neat, even gamine. Her turquoise jumper was decorated with hearts made of sequins; around her neck, dangling from a gold rope necklace, was a glass amulet: a monastic talisman of luck. Jake reckoned she was maybe older than her face implied. An older woman who could afford a face-lift.

The lady offered a cold hand to be shaken, a queenly gesture. The bangles on her wrist jingled; her fingernails were long and lavishly varnished. The lady wafted the same bangled hand toward a large plate of huge black spiders, sitting on a glass coffee table in front of her.

Jake declined the spiders, and accepted instead a cup of water from a large jug. The bangled spider witch gazed at him. Then she smiled, and yawned, as if too busy and important to be intrigued; her left hand hovered over the plate, and plucked a large tarantula.

She munched on a spider leg, delicately. Then she ate the fat, oozing black thorax of the spider, staring at Jake as she did so. She ate with her mouth open. He could see the pulp of black spider flesh inside her mouth; he was staring at an old woman's mouth with red lipstick on yellow teeth. And masticated black tarantula within.

A shudder of revulsion convulsed him. He was actually swaying. Maybe it was dehydration; he gulped down some more water, then busied himself with his camera, but he could feel the *tarantula* of fear slowly stalking down his spine. This was stupid. She was deliberately trying to spook him, as Tyrone had forewarned. The witch was trying to unnerve him; she was maybe succeeding.

The interview began almost at once. Ty asked questions in Khmer and the witch answered languidly, with a hint of vanity at certain points. She ate three whole spiders as they conversed. Jake watched her, helplessly fascinated. She was plucking off the big spider legs and popping them in her mouth, or chewing them like toffee strings. Her bangles chinked. She had crumbs of tarantula on her chin. One spider leg got stuck between her teeth—she pulled at it and then ate it, licking her fingers. Then she coughed another leg straight into a napkin.

Jake stared at the napkin as it unfurled itself on the table. The half-chewed black spider leg lay within the nest of uncrumpling paper, glistening, faintly pink and creamy with spider blood.

The urge to gag was overwhelming; but this, too, was maybe part of her act, her shtick. Her modus operandi.

Photography. Jake needed to take photos. That way he could distance himself from this grisly scene. But as he fumbled with his camera, he realized, with dismay, that his lens was smeared with his own sweat. The images he was getting were distorted. The witch was just a leering mouth full of blackness. A yawning insectivore in jewelry. Jake cursed. *Always keep your camera clean.* The first rule of photography; like a soldier learning to oil his rifle.

Seeking wet wipes from his bag, and dry tissues, Jake shivered in the cold of the overly air-conditioned room as he urgently cleaned the lens. He was barely aware, as he worked, of the silence in the room, then he noticed it.

"What?"

The witch had said something that had apparently given Tyrone pause. Jake noticed that the witch was staring his way now.

"What?" he asked. "What's happened, Ty? What did she say? Is it about me?"

Ty shrugged, with an awkwardness. Silent.

"Tell me."

"It's just her doing her thing. Trying to freak you."

"Ty!"

"She says you have sadness in your life. . . ."

"And?"

The witch spoke quickly in Khmer. Tyrone translated further:

"She sees a ghost child. Uhm . . . The ghost of a ghost, a little girl? A girl who was snatched away."

This was absurd—and grotesquely degraded. Jake waved away the idiocy. It was so chilly in this stupid room; why did they have the air-con turned so high?

But the woman was persistent, pointing at Jake. Tyrone continued to translate:

"She also sees a floating head, long hair, white face, a head with . . . I don't know, don't know the word. Something to do with your mother's spirit, her ghost?"

"My mother? What does she know about my mother?"

"Don't know, pal. I think it's a Khmer ghost image, the *arb,* the floating woman's head—trailing blood—"

Now the anger surged: Jake felt his own shameful and angry stupidity. He had walked into this. The woman had researched them. She was, of course, a charlatan.

"Fuck all this, Ty. Fuck her."

"Calm down."

"No. *Fuck* it. 'S obvious. She's got some inside gossip on me. Trying to spook me—"

"Heck. I did warn you. These people make a lot of money for a *reason.*"

"OK, let's spook her back, the spider-eating bitch. Let's just *ask her* about the smoke children. Watch her choke on her bloody arachnids *then.*"

"But Jake—that's a big risk—"

"Tell her we know about them!"

Tyrone paused, and pondered. Then he swiveled on the woman, and threw questions at her, urgent questions. The interview had become an interrogation. The witch waved an angry hand, bangles jangling. Her teeth were stained black from the roasted tarantulas.

She didn't care. She was irked and aroused, but she wasn't saying any names. Jake heard no name in her stream of Khmer consonants.

Abruptly, the lady clapped her hands, twice, as if summoning guards. And then her voice deepened, to a weird and guttural muttering. Barely human. Growling.

"What the hell is she doing now?"

Tyrone backed away.

"I don't know, I don't know—maybe she's casting some spell, some hex. Come on—let's go!"

"We're done?"

"I think we need to *go*? Don't you *think*?"

The witch was swaying from side to side; her growling had evolved into a hissing; and she was pointing a varnished fingernail. But Jake was not done. He swerved on the woman.

"Who ordered the babies, you bitch? Who?"

She hissed once more through her black, spider-stained teeth. A snake at bay.

"Tell us? Who the fuck was it? Who ordered the *kun krak*? The smoke children? Who paid you to do that?"

Tyrone grabbed Jake's angry arm; Jake angrily shook him off.

"Ty. You do it! *Ask her.* Tell her if she doesn't help us we will write a story, tell everyone she is ripping babies out of women—"

"But—"

"And *threaten* her."

Ty stiffened, as if finally snapping to attention; then he turned and he barked the question at the witch. He made the threat.

Her expression froze. Her eyes iced with hatred. Jake wondered if she was going to faint, or shout, or curse them again. But then she said, very slowly and distinctly:

"Madame Tek."

The infernal, serpentine hissing recommenced. Jake grabbed his cameras and Tyrone snatched his notebook: they were fleeing, escaping the chilly house, racing for the door—and ignoring the protests of the assistant, lurking in the hallway.

The door slammed shut behind them; the heat was intense and immediate after the overly conditioned air of the witch's villa.

"Sweet Jesus!" Jake said. "Is that who I think it is? Who ordered the smoke babies?"

Tyrone shook his head. "Yes. Yes, it is." He hurried on. "Jake. It was *Chemda's own mother.*"

16

Jake called Chemda as soon as they got back from Skuon. It was dark. He sat at his empty desk in his sparse apartment overlooking the Tonle Sap, and murmured the truth.

"Chemda, I'm sorry."

"She said it was *my mother*?"

"Yes. I'm sorry."

Chemda was silent; as silent as the Tonle Sap itself. Jake stared through the window at the reflection of a jaundiced moon in the sleepy waters.

"But it doesn't make any sense. My own mother paid for the *kun krak*? I . . . so . . . she was trying to frighten us? How does it relate to Doctor Samnang? Ah. I don't understand."

Jake was bereft of an answer. He muttered some consoling words, meaningless sympathies. But Chemda was in no mood for sympathy; her next reaction was much more articulate, and brisk:

"Please come and see me tomorrow, at my house. I need support. I am going to confront her."

"What?"

"This is too weird. So. Jake—I can't live with this, knowing this, ah, I need to understand what is going on—"

"But what can I do?"

"Be my friend. Please, I need a friend. Just a friend. This is going to be hard."

The words were alluring even as the idea was discomfiting.

Chemda sighed and explained further. She told him her grandfather was away, as ever, on business, she had no one else to turn to, and she wanted Jake's support, his physical presence.

She said it twice: his *physical presence*. A man. By her side.

"Please. Will you come?"

The last words were murmured: sultry, dark, whispered.

He got the sense she was almost hypnotizing him, leading him somewhere. He thought of her sleeping on the boat out of Luang. Her naked legs. He thought of the *apsaras* he had once seen at Angkor Wat, the bare-breasted dancing girls of King Jayavarman. Dancing their endless nubile dances, wreathed in smiling inscrutability, twirling and alluring, teasing and divine. And always, in the end, unreachable.

Yet he was reaching.

"OK, Chem. I'll be there."

"Thank you, Jake. Ah. This means a lot. Thank you."

With a sense of great apprehension, and also the insistent stirrings of desire, he shut down the phone and turned from the view of the dark and aged river. He tried to distract himself with research on his shining laptop.

He scoured the net, seeking information about the Plain of Jars, the burned bones. He researched the strange holes, the wounds in the crania. Jake looked at trepanations, he winced at medical images of opened braincases, he gaped at dissected human heads floating disembodied on the screen; he disturbed himself with stories of neurosurgery gone wrong: early lobotomy patients turned into drooling zombies, like Chemda's grandmother.

This wasn't helping. He turned off the computer and retreated to alcohol, hoping to lull his agitated soul to sleep with some Aussie wine. But his night was long and disturbed.

For some reason, he woke at three a.m. and he was sweating, heavily. Was he ill? He rubbed the sheet over his perspiring forehead. Drenched. Then he heard low voices outside his building. Why? Stepping to the window, he surveyed the humid nighttime streetscape. No one was there. Just the moon shadows of palms rustling in the breeze, and ranks of parked mopeds. A rowing boat was drifting down the Tonle Sap, with no one on board.

He went back to bed. Fought his way to a fretful sleep.

Early the next morning, he walked out onto a sunlit, empty, Sunday-ish Sisovath Boulevard and caught a tuk-tuk south along the corniche, deeply apprehensive.

The house of the Tek and Sovirom dynasties was auspiciously situated near the Imperial Gardens and the embassies, very much the superior end of town, where the Mekong braided with its sister rivers, the Brassac and the Tonle Sap, in a languorous troilism of the waters.

Whitewashed walls surrounded the Sovirom compound. He pressed the bell, said hello to a tiny camera, and the black electric gates swung smoothly ajar. He crossed a sunlit lawn of vivid green grass, and approached the impressive front door.

Behind it was a barefoot young maid, sweet, uniformed, humbly performing a *wai,* and also glancing anxiously at the ceiling. He soon realized the cause for her agitation. The house was filled with shouting.

Two women. It had to be Chemda and her mother. He could hear Chemda's normally soft voice raised in real anger. Then an older woman snapping back. What were they saying? Even if Jake had understood Khmer he probably wouldn't have understood the angry torrents of words.

The maid blushed, said nothing, looked left and right in confusion. Then she escorted Jake down a wide parquet-floored hallway to a large white sitting room. This house was *big*. The maid departed, and he was alone—alone with the voices screaming upstairs.

He didn't know what to do—intervene? Surely not: this was domestic, this was family, this could get nasty. But could he *not* intervene? What if it got *nastier*? Bewildered and uncertain, Jake sat down on a modernist leather chair and gazed around the enormous room.

It was sunny and bright, and decorated with antiquities. A Garuda stood in a corner, a winged and beaked Hindu demon carved in red sandstone—like a mute and flayed opera singer. Next to the Garuda was the enormous stone head of a Naga, a Hindu snake deity, snarling at a large black Samsung TV. Behind the antiquities was a huge wall of window, then a garden of gray sand, small trees, and soft gray rocks.

The argument upstairs was getting worse. Jake stared at the garuda. Its stone mouth shouted back at him, soundlessly, like it was trying to ventriloquize the screaming upstairs. The demon's stone wings were batlike, enormous. A flying djinn, poised in heraldic cruelty.

The shouting upstairs was undimmed.

Steeling himself, he stood up: he had to take action, step between these women. But as he walked to the door he was met by the door swinging open.

A man entered. A small Asian man, with a yellowish complexion, attired in a beige linen suit. Jake instantly recognized this man from the newspaper and TV as Sen, Sovirom Sen, the businessman, the banker, the friend of prime ministers, confidant of Sihanouk.

The patriarch.

Jake felt intense relief. Now someone else could intervene and solve the argument upstairs.

Grandfather Sen smiled and put a finger to his lips. Then he gestured at the ceiling and spoke.

"I always think *cherchez la femme* is a rather absurd expression, don't you? Women are not exactly hard to find. They are so *audible.*"

Jake didn't know what to say; Sen was shaking his hand warmly. Sincerely.

"Please. I am Chemda's grandfather. And of course you are Jake Thurby. My granddaughter discourses on you, *nightly.*" A delicate hesitation. A smile. "Ah. Shall we step into the garden? Women are like the weather. Their moods are tropical depressions. We must simply wait for the rains to pass."

Outside, and with the glass door shut behind them, the noise of Chemda and her mother was almost completely muffled. Sen led the way along a path to a kind of summerhouse, with wooden benches and silk crimson cushions, that looked out over the sands and posed rocks and the small, pale-green trees.

"Please, Mr. Thurby. Be seated."

Jake sat down on the wooden bench. Sen smiled and regarded the exquisitely raked gray sand. Jake noticed the man was wearing beautiful shoes of fine-grained leather. Probably bespoke: handmade in London or Paris.

A pause.

Sovirom Sen leaned an inch toward Jake, and said, "This garden is . . . one of my greatest passions."

Jake wasn't sure how to reply. He attempted a sensible remark. "It's beautiful. Japanese, right?"

"Of course. It is closely modeled on the famous withered gardens in the Zen temples of Kyoto. You have seen them, I imagine?"

"No, I've never been to Japan."

"But you must, you *must go*! I visit Japan regularly, for my business. I adore the great Zen temples of Kyoto. Ryoanji. The Silver Pavilion. *Nanzenji.* Hence my garden here." He raised a modest hand. "The essence of the Zen garden is abstraction. The more you take away— the more you have. And that is the true genius of Japanese culture, they see the beauty in nullity. Abstraction is perfection. The haiku is but a few parched syllables. Japanese cuisine is rawness and purity. And Japanese Zen Buddhism—that is the greatest of religions. Why? Because there is no god, no afterlife, no superstition, there is *nothing*."

Fittingly, this speech was concluded by silence. But Jake had to break it, he had to say something.

"Mr. Sovirom, I want to thank you for saving us, in Laos. The airplane, the soldiers."

The patriarch smiled, distantly. "It is nothing."

"But I also have questions."

"Yes, yes. Of course. I am aware what has happened. In Ponsavan. In Luang. You must be confused. Please accept my profound apologies for this."

"OK. . . ."

"Happily, I can explain everything. If you will permit."

"Please?"

The grandfather spoke quietly. But with firmness.

"My daughter, Madame Tek, is a shrewd and educated woman— like her daughter in turn. But, Jacob, they profoundly disagree. Madame Tek believes that Chemda's determination to dig up Cambodia's tragic past is, shall we say, not ideal. She thinks the bones of the killing fields should be left to molder. Why open the coffins, why break the tombs? Why dance around with our skulls, like Mexicans after too much tequila?"

"I . . . don't know."

"Well, there is one answer. My willful granddaughter would say, with her American education, that we cannot 'move on' as a country until we have confronted the past. And it is not an argument without merit. Perhaps we should stare at the head of the *naga*, the snake, Kali. I myself have truly difficult memories of the Khmer Rouge regime. Maybe I have not dealt with these memories."

Jake felt a need to be bold.

"You mean your wife? We know something terrible happened to her."

The elegant old man continued.

"Yes, indeed. We don't know *precisely* what happened to her. Or why it happened. We *do* know they did some experiment, on her body and her mind. Perhaps akin to brainwashing."

"Your wife volunteered for this, uh . . . experiment. That's what we heard."

Grandfather Sen looked at the concentric circles of sand.

"This is apparently the case. And it is quite plausible. You see, my wife *believed* in that absurd regime, she was a true *cadre*. She *supported* the Khmer Rouge."

"Why?"

"You must understand, at the time many people believed in the new regime. Because they wanted to believe. The Americans were bombing us. The country was in uproar. The king was on all sides at once. The Vietnamese were abusing us. The fascist, Lon Nol, was in power. Brutal and gangsterly, a son of a bitch, as they say. The Americans' very own son of a bitch."

"Therefore?"

"The Khmer Rouge seemed like a salvation. They were unsullied, pure. Incorruptible. Of course, we heard reports from those places in the country where they had already seized power, reports of killing. Horrible killing. But these reports came from the CIA. When they said, 'The Khmer Rouge will kill your mother and your father and your sister and your daughter,' we did not believe the stories. My wife certainly did not believe them." Sen gazed almost longingly at his garden. "And yet . . . in my heart, *I believed the stories.* I knew some of these Khmer Rouge leaders from Paris, at least by reputation. Ieng Sary, Khieu Samphan, Hou Yuon. Brilliant scholars, every one—and also the most *passionate* of ideologues. From the beginning, I suspected they were capable of . . . extraordinary acts."

"Why didn't you do anything?"

"Take my family out of Cambodia?" Sen smiled a bitter smile. "I am Cambodian Chinese, but my wife, she was pure Khmer, dark Khmer, royal Khmer, daughter of a concubine in the court of King Monivong. She was not going to leave. Besides, as I say, she supported them, even as they burned the monks alive. Even as they manured the rice paddies with the ashes of the bourgeois."

"Then they took her . . . to Laos."

"She was a scientist. The government said they needed her. I watched her go. And then I heard that she had let them perform their strange brain surgeries, their experimental interventions, that she actively volunteered, or so we were told. . . ."

"When did you find all this out?"

Sen was silent, regarding his rocks and tiny trees. The gray sands of the Zen garden shifted in a slender breeze off the river, whispering like something sleeping, but restive.

The old man spoke: "In 1980. After the Vietnamese invasion. I was living like a peasant near Battambang. Starving, like everyone. Starving but surviving. And finally she returned from Laos, from the Plain of Jars, and she was . . . a dribbling doll, a creole zombie." His steady gaze became an anguished frown. "But we struggled on. There was so much pain in those years, this was merely an addition. And miraculously she had survived the mercies of Pol Pot and Ta

Mok—survived their religion of holocaust and hatred, their god of smoke and ash. Yet it soon became apparent that whatever they did to her in Laos, and for whatever reason—it was irreversible." Sen touched a single fingertip to his forehead, and closed his eyes.

"By that time, my daughter and her husband had already escaped to America, where they had baby Chemda. They were safe. The paradox is quite piquant: first America tried to kill us, then it saved us. Ah . . . America with her bipolar moods, so generous and so unhinged."

"And you?"

"I remained here. I was proud. I am proud. I stayed silent. And I decided to send this emptied husk, this creature that was once my wife, back to Luang. I sent her to our good friends the Marconnets, to live out her remaining years beneath the shade of the papayas, in beautiful Luang Prabang, Xien Dong Xieng Thong, the city of the Golden Lord Buddha. You see, she always loved Luang: it was emotionally appropriate. And I told no one she had come back. We did not want her to be ridiculed, to be gawped at in Phnom Penh as the monkey woman, the smoke woman, one of the *araks brai*. My proud wife would not have wanted anyone to see her salivating. In a wheelchair. And we did not want anyone to know her shame: that she had volunteered herself for this terrible surgery, that she had selected herself to be turned into a living corpse."

The wind had dropped. Silence was sovereign. Sen murmured, "But now you have the story. *In toto*. There it is."

Jake felt the old man's pain, it was searing, and still visible; and yet Sen seemed strong, despite it. A true survivor.

He thought of his own guilt and grief: the aching sadness that never entirely quit, the insidious remorse for something he didn't do: hold on to his sister, protect his mother from despair. If Sovirom Sen could survive his far greater tragedies, Jake could surely endure his own. He recalled the phrase from the Khmer Rouge tribunals, the one Ty quoted: *The only exit is survival.*

But had they exited? And how had they survived so far? *How had they survived Laos?*

"But, Mr. Sovirom—"

"Sen. I am Sen."

"Sen. Can you also explain what happened to *us* in Laos? Chemda and me? The professors?"

The patriarch smiled Jake's way, and answered. "We suspect that Khmer Rouge loyalists, still active at the heart of the Phnom Penh government, are keen to derail Chemda's investigation. They tried to obstruct the tribunals, but they failed. Now they are trying to suppress Chemda's work on the Plain of Jars. They must have threatened the academics, who maybe slew themselves; surely they are working with the Pathet Lao, their old comrades, the Communists still in power in Vientiane."

"So everything that happened, in Luang . . ."

"When we heard of the death of Doctor Samnang, Madame Tek and I immediately feared that Chemda's life was in danger if she continued working in Laos—or here in Cambodia. However, Chemda is so stubborn, we knew that if she was pressed too hard to leave she would be even more determined to stay."

It was true enough: Jake had already experienced Chemda's obstinate passion. It was one of the reasons he admired her.

"But *dead babies*? Jesus! Why do *that*?"

A withered tree rustled in the near-silent wind.

"My daughter and my granddaughter, they are educated, but they are also very *superstitious,* like all Khmers, like so many Asians. Why is this? I often wonder. I have struggled against it, the exorcisms, the divinations, the luminously risible tattoos." He shook his head.

"Whatever the case, Madame Tek believes in the power of Khmer magic, as does Chemda. So Madame Tek arranged to frighten her daughter with the most forbidding talismans in Khmer occultism. The *kun krak*. The smoke fetuses." He frowned once more. "Madame Tek knew that Chemda would be unnerved by them, and her plan worked. To a point."

"Go on."

"You fled, and you escaped Laos, but of course you are still in very grave danger, Mr. Thurby. As is my granddaughter."

"What should we do?"

"Consider your options. Chemda is a beautiful young woman. She is *krangam*."

The wind blew a wisp of sand. The rocks shone black in the sun.

"Y-y-yes. I guess."

"The fusion of Chinese and royal Khmer genes is fortuitous. And also my granddaughter is very intelligent, and she is unmarried. She is a prize."

Jake was silenced.

"I also know, Jake, that she has developed a certain *tendresse*." Sen gestured, poetically. "But to enter the *guha* you must leave the country, take her to England, or take her to America. She has an American passport. You *must* leave the country because you are both in danger and I can no longer protect you. The Lao government seeks revenge for its dead police officer. The descendants of the Khmer Rouge even now are working against me and my interests. Against Chemda and you."

Sen continued: "You have my permission. She will marry you. We can do it today or soon. *You* must take her, only you can persuade her to leave. But before that happens, of course, for the sake of propriety, a wedding. At once."

"A wedding?"

Grandfather Sen patted him paternally on the knee and said, "This is the most bizarre of surprises, I know."

"What the hell—a *wedding*?"

Jake could barely grasp the idea. He was being offered Chemda: like a casual meal, or a rather trifling gift.

Sen smiled regretfully.

"I understand the shock. You probably need to think about it. I shall step inside, to see if these two typhoons have exhausted themselves. Wait here and I shall bring my daughter."

The old man quit the garden. Jake stared blankly at the gray rocks, the perfectly positioned tree, the tenderly raked circles of sand, all parched and delicate in the ruthless sun of the remorseless dry season.

He was stunned, and perspiring, almost feverish. This wasn't good; this was horrible. These people were so desperate to get Chemda safely out of the country, and get her swiftly married, they were prepared to foist her on some man they hardly knew. Maybe fear was driving this. Maybe even the great Sovirom Sen was scared; maybe everyone was scared.

Jake was scared.

A further, darker thought occurred to him. Could Chemda be *part* of this? Was this some peculiar conspiracy to entangle him? But why had she asked him to come this morning? Had she lied about her grandfather being away on business?

The confusion was bewildering, even painful. He needed to get out, to think clearly. Get some advice, go home, drink too much coffee, call Tyrone.

He got up and walked to the door and quickly crossed the hallway. The house was quiet. The maid stared at him from behind a door. The mother-daughter argument had apparently been calmed by Sen, or blown itself out. But he had no desire to linger and enjoy the domestic harmony. Not in this pristine prison of a house.

Jake paced very quickly to the front door, and then virtually ran down the long, curving drive to the boulevard. Jumping in a tuk-tuk, he sat back, trying to clarify his thoughts in the sweet, warm, polluted Phnom Penh breeze. His mind was churning.

It was Sunday, so it took just a few minutes to reach his corner. He tapped the driver on the shoulder.

"Here. No problem. I can walk from here."

Handing over two dollars, Jake turned the corner. And saw a boy climbing off a motorbike—and casually walking to the door of Jake's apartment block, carrying a glass bottle. Something about this was odd. Jake felt an instinctive wariness: who was this? What was going on? He slowed his pace, observing. The boy was fiddling with the bottle in his hand. And a lighter. He was setting fire to a cloth stuck in the bottle; he stepped back and threw the flaming bomb through a first-floor window. The glass crashed.

The Molotov cocktail exploded inside Jake's apartment.

Flames woofed, fire streaked from the windows. Jake stood there, gawking, quite stupefied.

It was all so casual, so fucking casual.

The street was still quiet, it was Sunday morning, a young woman was cycling past the end of the road. Couples were strolling along the riverfront. And someone had thrown a Molotov cocktail.

As Jake watched, the boy climbed back onto his Suzuki and sped away from the scene. The flames were already roaring, hoarse and hungry, licking up the walls. And then, incredibly, it happened *again*. A second lad drove up, on a moped, and repeated the process, calmly, half smiling—like it was an amiable household chore. The youth climbed off, Zippoed a wick in a glass bottle—and walked toward Jake's flat. Ready to throw.

The urge to run and stop the boy was almost irresistible. Jake wanted to sprint and kick and stomp and hurt—but some deeper logic held him back. Some inner, concealed, subconscious sense of self-preservation restrained him, despite his fury.

Trembling with helpless anger, Jake watched. The boy hurled. The bottle smashed. The flames gained in strength, eating and roaring.

The fire was big now. Someone, somewhere, screamed. People were running from cafés and pointing, fear on their faces. The fire bombers were long gone.

Jake sank into the shadow of a frangipani tree. He realized, with a lucid terror, that he had just witnessed an attempt on his own life. No one knew he wasn't in there, it was still quite early, it was Sunday, they probably presumed he was asleep, inside.

Someone had just tried to kill him.

17

Chere Julia

I don't know how to begin this letter—this e-mail. It is perhaps the hardest thing I have been summoned to write. But I also feel I have no choice. You are owed an explanation; more than this, I want to give you an explanation, you above all people. My friend.

Firstly, you need some essential facts. We are scientists, we are nourished by facts, n'est ce pas? Though I am a melancholy sort of scientist, these days. And perhaps this is a deformation professionelle, the inevitable destiny of the archaeologist. All the bones, Julia, all the many many bones. And the skulls. The wounded skulls and bones. They sadden me. They sadden me so much, now I know what I know.

But I am hurrying away with my story. Here is your first fact, the first of many I must tell you.

Three years ago, an old academic colleague of Ghislaine's and mine, an academic named Hector Trewin, was killed in his Oxford college. You may have heard of him, or at least of the case. The murder, I believe, attracted a brief but intense flurry of interest, because Hector

*had been tortured before he was killed. Electric shocks had been applied
to his hands, and his scalp, and, I believe, elsewhere. The homicide was
apparently motiveless. No suspects were named or located, Julia. No
one was arrested. The unsavory murder soon disappeared from the
news.*

But, you see, not everyone was quite so mystified.

*From the start, Ghislaine and I were suspicious that the killing
could have been linked to our trip to Cambodia—Democratic
Kampuchea—in 1976.*

I have never told you of this. But it is crucial to my sad story.

*Decades ago, Hector Trewin, Ghislaine Quoinelles, and me, we
were all part of a mission, a kind of mission, a team, an invited party.
Most of us were French, there were also some Americans and Britons,
myself from Belgium, as well, perhaps a German. I forget precisely,
Julia, it was so long ago.*

*But I remember the basic facts. We were all invited by the Chinese
and Cambodian governments to visit Beijing, and Phnom Penh, in
Spring 1976. The party comprised biologists, anthropologists,
archaeologists—thinkers and scientists. And all of us were committed
Marxists, supporters, or at least fellow-travelers, of the Pol Pot regime
and the Maoists in China.*

*What we did there I can barely bring myself to admit. Let me come
to that later. What I can tell you now is that the murder of Trewin is,
or was, I believe, related to this mission. Because, I mean, of the bru-
talities, the murder, they were so distinctive. So echoing.*

*Therefore when Ghislaine and I read of Hector's death, we thought,
as a consequence, that perhaps someone was taking revenge: for our
own terrible actions in the 1970s.*

*Therefore we too began to fear, to indulge our horror of this chilling
idea: that the killer was going to come for us, too. And take their*

revenge. This conviction grew over the following months. Earlier this summer Ghislaine openly speculated that we should flee, leave the country. I rejected his suggestions, and made him stay; perhaps, deep inside, I felt this looming fate was condign? Deserved? Maybe I deserved to be punished. My unadmitted guilt held me back.

But again I am confusing you. Please forgive me. What I am strug-gling to enunciate is that all this, Julia, explains Ghislaine's bizarre behavior in the cave, the day you discovered the skulls. He was genu-inely concerned for my safety. He thought I was going to be attacked, like Trewin. . . . All the time he was looking out for me, for us. For himself too of course. He was very afraid he was going to die the same way, someday soon. We were all afraid we were going to die. One by one by one.

Because all those legends were coming back to haunt us. Man reduced to animal to werewolf to beast.

You may think I am going mad? I am not. Not now. Non. The madness was indeed ours: but it happened long ago. In '76. And this is the truth of the matter, and this is why I need to tell you this. At last. Someone needs to know, and I sense that you, of all people, will understand. My friend. My female friend in the brutal male world of the caves of the skulls.

Please forgive my previous opacity. J'espère I hope that this e-mail will shed the light you need. There is a moth in the lamp. It is trapped.

I wonder if me and Ghislaine we were like the moths. Once and long ago we thought we were pursuing the truth, the great truth, the secret of the Ice Age caves, the secret of the blazing paintings in the dark-ness of the caverns, Julia, but we were so wrong, we were like moths who sought the moon, by instinct, but flew inside a lampshade and . . . and we got trapped by our delusion, dying burn singed to death by the deceiving light trapped by a terrible mistake.

And that is why I cannot bear the lies anymore, Julia. I cannot live with myself, and these corruption Les lilas et les roses. Therefore t k t

Julia dropped the printed sheet on the café table.

"That's where it ends?"

"Yes."

"And she was about to send this e-mail? To me?"

"Of course. Yes."

"But how . . ."

Rouvier set down his absurdly large cup of latte and explained:

"The murderer reached her before she could finish, or even get halfway through, perhaps. However, she was using webmail. The draft message was, therefore, automatically saved. We retrieved it yesterday."

Julia stared at the table, at her coffee, at nothing. Trying not to reveal her deepening disquiet. But it was impossible. This new revelation destabilized everything.

Ghislaine's death had been ghastly enough—but she had not been emotionally close to her boss. She was, moreover, able to *rationalize* that crime: she had pretty much convinced herself his death was a unique, if horrible, atrocity. An ex-lover taking mad revenge, maybe. Or just a robbery gone wrong.

But *Annika*? Julia had *cared* for the woman; they had been real friends. This murder therefore grieved Julia, very badly; it also forced her into fiercer, more horrifying speculations.

The murders.

The brutal murder of Annika following the brutal murder of Ghislaine, that really did mean a chain, a link, a series of crimes—perhaps interwoven with all these mysterious *secrets*. And a series of crimes implied there would be *more* crimes. There would be further killings. She shuddered, inwardly.

Rouvier carefully stirred his coffee.

They were in a suitably discreet corner of the bland and busy coffee shop. Julia had suggested Starbucks, by the Gare du Nord, because Rouvier had said he was *en route* to London by train. She'd also chosen *Starbucks* quite deliberately, because it was so ordinary and non-French and it reminded her of Michigan.

This is what she wanted right now. Michigan, college football, meat loaf, Tim Horton's. And this place was the closest she could get: the sofas, the menus, the vast and oversweet cinnamon buns: they were comforting, so very North American. Insipidly safe. Nursery food for the soul.

Rouvier gazed at her, knowingly, as if he could see her fear.

"Miss Kerrigan, I do not think the killer is after you."

"How can you be sure?"

"Why not read the e-mail again."

She snatched up the sheet of paper.

Chère Julia . . .

Engaging with the puzzle—shunting emotion aside as best she could—Julia deconstructed the information, more slowly this time: trying to grasp the hidden and curtailed meanings; trying not to imagine Annika's obvious fear and distress. The e-mail spoke of a very troubled mind, struggling to confess. Bewildered, frightened, and almost waiting to die, almost yearning to die. And also confessing. But confessing what? What had happened in Cambodia?

She set down the piece of paper on the table, next to her undrunk cappuccino. For a moment she visualized, helplessly, the ensuing scene in the little cottage on the Cham des Bondons. The killing of her friend, her head smashed against a pillar of rock. Smashed to death. She fought back a surge of near-tears, and said, slowly, "I do know the name. Hector Trewin. He is, or he was, quite old, a Marxist anthropologist at Balliol. Respected. Famous in his time, in the 1960s and '70s."

Rouvier nodded. "Yes. I am meeting the English police today to go over such matters. But yes, you are quite right about Trewin. Furthermore, Annika Neuman speaks correctly of their *shared connection*. Our researches *prove* this."

"It does?"

"Here. We have a photo." Rouvier was reaching for his briefcase once more. He extracted a large scan of a color photo and laid it on the table, facing Julia. "We found it among Miss Neuman's files."

It was like a school photo, a group photo: a party of people, with some sitting, some standing behind, all smiling at the camera.

The photo was so obviously taken in the 1970s: it ached with nostalgia for itself. Lots of flared trousers, wide neckties, short, vivid dresses on the women. The faces were mostly young; all of them were keen, hopeful, idealistic, squinting a little in the sun. So many years ago.

Julia touched the photo. There: she could see Annika Neuman. Beautiful, blond, Dutch-Belgian, in a summer dress and sandals. Ghislaine was next to her, his arm around her, slightly awkward, slightly proud. His hair did not look absurd. Leaning closer to the photo, Julia tried to assess where it had been taken: the sun was harsh, tropical. Behind them was a strangely empty city street, distant shadows of palm trees. It was Cambodia, for sure: one of the empty, desolate boulevards of Phnom Penh. How could they be smiling?

"Yes," said Rouvier. "It is Phnom Penh, 1976, a few months after Year Zero, after the genocides had already begun. Rather disturbing, no?"

The policeman laid a finger on the photo. "This is Hector Trewin."

Julia frowned. She vaguely recognized the face: it provoked distant memories of textbooks, maybe an ancient, pompously serious

BBC TV program. Trewin was older than most of the others in the photos; but he was also smiling. His smile was even more ardent.

"So," said Julia. "They all went to Cambodia. As she said. But . . ." Julia glanced back at the e-mail. "What does this bit mean. This word *revenge*?"

"Miss Neuman's intention is, to me at least, *quite* clear." Rouvier placed his fingertips on the photo, gently pinning it down. "Lewin was electrocuted, in various parts of the body, while he was alive. He was finally dispatched with a terrible blow to the back of the head, with a metal bar. Victims of the Khmer Rouge were tormented and then killed in *precisely* this way."

The puzzle cohered; the logic emerged.

"You mean . . . the murderer is . . . a *Cambodian*? A survivor of the Khmer Rouge?"

"Very possibly."

"I get it. The killer is taking revenge on these old academics, old Communists, who went to Phnom Penh in 1976. And supported the regime. It's vengeance! Of course!"

"It seems something of that nature. Yes. I think so."

Julia was somewhat gratified by this solution. It finally made *sense*, after so much disorientating, seemingly arbitrary violence. The murders were just basic human revenge, exacted on old Western Communists, by a victim of the most evil of Communist regimes. She could almost understand it; she could *almost* empathize. If the murderer hadn't brutally killed her friends and colleagues.

She also liked this solution for the most grisly and selfish of reasons: because she was cut out of the picture. She wasn't a target. It had nothing to do with her job, her discoveries, the skulls and the bones.

And yet, a still and persistent voice inside her told her the skulls and the bones *were* connected. Annika specifically mentioned them. There must be a link, then? But a link meant a link to Julia herself.

She was still confused, and she was definitely frightened; she sipped her milky coffee.

Rouvier sat forward. "There is more, naturally. There are many aspects to these murders that still puzzle me."

The coffee was going cold already.

Julia stammered, "A-aspects like what?"

"For a start, there is the sheer skill of the intrusion, the enormous strength, the necessary athleticism—we believe the killer gained entry through a small cottage window at Miss Neuman's house."

Julia remembered the window. It *was* small. How did the killer get through that? A slender young woman could do it, or a boy, maybe; a small Asian man.

"Are you guys sure it is a woman?"

Rouvier smiled approvingly, as if Julia were an elder daughter who had asked a clever question.

"A most important point. Our sole reliable description is of a pale woman with long dark hair. But the kind of expertise we see here must surely come from training, the army, maybe special forces. And a man is much more likely to have this kind of strength and background, this capability. So a man, or a woman. Or what? Who is this?"

Rouvier was frowning through the window at the grand stone façade of the Gare du Nord. It was a bright autumn day in Paris, the streets busy with taxis and tourists.

He turned.

"Miss Kerrigan, this is where you come in, once more. When I considered all this yesterday, I recalled our conversation outside the hospital that night. Your questions."

"*Our* conversation?"

"Cast your mind back. You asked me about the research of Ghislaine's grandfather, the great professor. I told you it was about crossbreeding, between men and animals."

Julia took another quick sip of her enormous cappuccino. It was completely cold now. She put the coffee down, and protested.

"But I was feeling kinda disturbed, that evening. Just asking questions for the sake of it."

Rouvier smiled, very soberly. "Exactly so, Miss Kerrigan, but it is a notion that has some folkloric resonance in Lozère. The werewolves of the Margeride, no? Therefore, two days ago, as I thought of the *animal savagery* of the attacks and so forth, I recalled your question. This is why I asked my assistant to investigate the backgrounds of these academics, these Communists who went to Cambodia."

"Their backgrounds?"

Rouvier once more pointed to the photo. He was indicating another face, a young man, sitting at the front. "This is Marcel Barnier. From Sciences Po."

"And?"

"He was, and maybe still is, an expert in animal science, in hybridization."

"Meaning?"

"Expert in breeding between species."

Julia gripped her coffee spoon. Hard.

"You're saying . . . you're surely not saying . . . ?"

Julia couldn't even begin to articulate it. The idea was insane. But the faces were smiling at her, in the bright Phnom Penh sun, in the dark heart of all that evil, as millions died around them—*smiling*.

Rouvier sat back.

"I'm certainly not claiming that *la Bête de Gévaudan* has returned to prey upon us." He shook his head. "No. That is clearly absurd. But then, what *are* we to think? There is this strange *network of facts*. It cannot be disputed."

The policeman took up the sheets of paper, folded them carefully, and returned them to his briefcase.

"Now I must meet my junior. We catch the train for London. I hope I have not unnerved you?"

She shook her head. He smiled quietly.

"Good. That is good. You are staying in Paris?"

"Alex's brother has a flat here. It's empty. We're here to do some . . . research. Archaeology."

Julia wondered if she should tell Rouvier about their pursuit, the hunt for Prunières. Maybe she should tell him about *her* skulls, the trepanations, the wounds in the vertebrae. The needling and insistent evidence was speaking to the trepanations, and to the injuries to Annika's head, and to Annika's references. But maybe it was still, just about, coincidence; possibly her idea was insane. Possibly it was irrelevant? Possibly?

Whatever the answer, she didn't have the emotional energy to explain her findings and anxieties now. Not the energy, nor the time, nor the courage. She just wanted to get the hell out.

The policeman opened the door of the café to allow Julia through. The morning air was mild, for early November, wistful. He shook her hand. Then he said, "There is one more curiosity."

Julia had already sensed there was more; with a creeping sense of dread, she asked: "Yes?"

"I was prepared to dismiss the crossbreeding as sheer *speculation*. A fanciful idea. But then, yesterday, my junior made another discovery." His smile was bleak. "It seems there *was* a serious attempt in the 1920s to crossbreed man and animals, man and the higher apes specifically. And Professor Quoinelles, the grandfather, he was part of that. The leader, in fact."

A flock of dirty city pigeons clapped into the air behind Rouvier, as if applauding this revelation.

"Why the hell would you do *that*?"

"Military purposes. Supposedly they wanted to create a soldier with the brain of a man and the strength of a wild animal. A real killer. They actually made the attempt! We must remember this was the 1920s, different morals would apply, eugenics was still permissible. But the lengths they went to—they are still incredible, repulsive. They used apes imported from French colonies, and human women. They seized African women, imprisoned them, and tried to impregnate them with animal sperm. *We know this happened.*"

"The French army did this? The French government? My God."

"Ah no, not the *French*. I have misled you, sorry." He hesitated, then explained: "Albert Quoinelles, Ghislaine's *grandpère,* was another well-known leftist. A sympathizer with Bolshevism. Quoinelles did his experiments for Stalin, he was recruited by Moscow. He did his experiments for the *Communists.*"

He bowed her way, then turned and crossed the busy street, heading for the dark, mouthlike arches of the Gare du Nord.

18

An hour had passed since the fire-bombing. His phone was nearly juiced out. He'd called Ty, then the embassy—which was shut. Now he had just enough battery left for a conversation with Chemda. And he didn't have time for niceties. Just the brutal facts. The fire-bombing. Sen's bizarre offer.

She received his story with shocked silence; she stammered her sympathies about his apartment. But he interrupted her with a question.

"Why did you tell me your grandfather was away?"

"He was! He was away. But he came back early. The maid told him you were there. . . . Jake . . . Please . . ."

Her voice faded behind the noise of a tuk-tuk.

Jake was standing in the shuttered doorway of a pharmacy, near the great river. Sidling farther into the hot and tropical shadows, away from the street noise, he pressed the phone closer to his ear, waiting for her explanation.

"Maybe it *was* stupid, asking you to, ah, ah, come to the house. I am sorry. I was nervous, scared. But believe me, please *believe* me, I am perhaps almost as disoriented as you. Can you understand that,

Jake? Hnh? My own mother is trying to frighten me, to curse me, and now my grandfather, the man I most respect in the world, he has—he has tried to marry me off, like chattel."

Another tuk-tuk passed, its two-stroke engine rasping in an ugly and primitive way.

"Jake, I need to know. If you don't trust me . . . then I understand. But then you must leave me alone. I'll manage."

What to do? He pondered her words. But even as he steeled himself he could feel the lush emotions melting his resolve; he was wary of her, yet he also felt a powerful sense of mutuality: they *were* in this together. She knew his darker secrets; she was closer to him than Tyrone now. And besides, he also craved her friendship. Her warmth. That proud and royal smile. He couldn't deny it.

"Meet me."

She whispered her reply: "Where?"

"You tell me, Chem. Somewhere discreet."

Her silence spoke of her thoughts; then she answered. *"A temple. Near the central market. One hour."*

He agreed and closed the call.

Jake stepped out of the shadows. The city stared at him, blankly. A moto hooted, seeking business. Sensing his exposure, he slipped down a side road, then doubled back down an old alley paved with rotting banana leaves. The alley led to the rear of his block. The fires must have been doused, there was no smoke. He could see hoses, and a couple of firemen at the corner, in wet, yellow overalls, smoking cigarettes.

A back door gave onto his stairwell. He walked to the gray metal lockers: he was lucky, the fire hadn't made it to the ground floor. Jake twisted his little key and swiftly grabbed his stuff: his spare passport, some money, a few cards. He kept it all here so he could jump on a plane with a few minutes' warning, imagining himself as the dashing foreign correspondent. He had never imagined this stash would be so useful—*after an attempt on his life.*

Cards and passport zipped in his small rucksack, he hurried to the temple. It took twelve anxious minutes. Chemda was waiting in the courtyard. Her face was beautiful and it was dark and her skirt was very blue. He felt a sudden and unwarranted need to kiss her. Perhaps the surge of the life force, in such proximity to death.

"Jake, we have to hide."

"Where?"

Chemda reached out and touched his hand. Like a nervous bride in church, meekly seeking reassurance from her groom.

"I know a place, my grandfather owns a block of apartments. One of them is empty, it's just come up for sale. Jake, I have a key—*and he doesn't know.*"

He shook off her hand, gazed around.

A young novice monk in his saffron toga was sitting on the steps, vaguely looking their way, lazily swatting flies from his face. His expression was sleepy; it was so hot. The smell of incense, and rotting fruit, spiced the air.

Chemda had chosen this place because it was supposedly discreet, but the ambience was unnerving: blue smoke and hot sun and intense dark shade from the overhanging eaves of the temple. And a languid, skinhead monk, observing them.

Still shaken by the attempt on his life, Jake didn't know if he could trust his own feelings. He swallowed the bitter dryness of anxiety.

Two men wandered through the ornate wooden gate and nodded at the monk, then made a ponderous bow, a *samphae,* at a gilded and gaudy shrine. The men were clean-cut, prosperous, thirtyish. Businessmen? In a temple? Jake watched them leave again, his eyes following them suspiciously, ensuring they were really gone.

Chemda came close, and repeated herself; still meek, but also insistent:

"Jake, there's no one I can trust. Not anymore. Can you understand that?" She bit a lip, shut her eyes. "The only person I still trust in Phnom Penh is *you*. *Only you*. My friends are in America, my mother is . . . I wonder if she knows me. Loves me. My own mother. How could a mother do that? With the *kun krak*? I don't understand, I don't understand *them*. *Not anymore*. Maybe I have been away too long. They are dissolving again, dissolving all over again— like the past coming back. And then my grandfather, how could he just sell me off, like a concubine for Sihanouk, like meat, like the pigs' heads in the market. Jake. And the people at the UN, they are the same, they do not understand, they are not Khmer. I am lost in the middle of it all. So it's you. Just you. Not even my grandfather. Just you."

She was gazing at him, unblinking. "You *are* different. Aren't you, Jake? You come from outside and yet you, you became my friend, you are unsullied. I *trust you*. Jake. But if that is not given back . . . if it's not what you feel, then that's what . . . I understand, of course, ah, but we can't meet again. Never. Because."

She was standing close to him to meet his gaze, standing so close her perfume was discernible. Her face was flushed with urgency; she was looking up at him, feminine and defiant and proud and bewildered all at once.

He was also bewildered. He half understood her, he half shared her feelings. Yet he still didn't quite believe she was telling him everything. Was there something else?

Yet he also *wanted* her: that slenderness. More than he wanted to leave the country, more than he wanted to save himself, he wanted simply to kiss her. Now. He just *did*. Jake thought of her sleeping that day on the pirogue from Luang; the way her delicate head rested on

a folded sarong, with the smear of gray river mud on her bare legs; he
saw the red petals of flame trees falling on the muddy Mekong.

He knew he was being seduced; even if she didn't mean to do it,
she was seducing him. Yet this was not right: his life was at stake, he
had to stay lucid.

"Who tried to kill me?"

Her frown was impassioned.

"It is *obviously* the Khmer Rouge loyalists. It *must be*. The government. Revenge on my family, on all of us. Kumnun. Ah."

"Not the Laotians?"

"Ah, no. Would they be this direct and uncaring of the conse-
quences? No, this is local and powerful people. Very, very powerful."
She looked left and right; a Buddha statue squatted in the corner,
grinning the perpetual smirk of *nibbana*. "This . . . degree of violence, it sometimes happens in Phnom Penh; gangsters, maybe. But
this is also aimed at you, a foreigner, therefore it must surely be political: that means we must have uncovered something in Laos, something very serious. You know this."

She reached out a soft hand once again and took his fingers in
hers, interlacing them, like the waters of the Mekong and the Brassac.
Her voice was soft and clear and sad.

"You must be frightened. Of course. You could easily have been
killed. If you want to fly back to England no one could blame you—
I wouldn't blame you—no, you mustn't stay here for me, my insanity
is mine. I'll deal with it. I will."

Again he shook off her hand, but this time with a certain reluc-
tance. Instead he grasped her by both wrists and spoke to her upturned
face. His masculinity was affronted by her words. Frightened?

"Chem, I'm *not* running away—it's just—I came to Cambodia to
do something. If I let them scare me off I have done nothing, proved
nothing. Where am I going to go, anyhow? Back to England, for

what? Somewhere else? Another war-torn country? What's the difference? This is my job, my home—I want to stay—I'm not *frightened*. But—"

He dropped her wrists, still stymied. What could he say?

Dumb with frustration, Jake walked a few paces, farther into the shade. He was staring through an open door at a side temple. Statues sat on a dais at the end, statues of deities, gods, demons, whatever. It was all so alien, exotic, confusing.

He gazed.

Jake didn't truly understand Buddhism, Hinduism—or how they mixed or differed. He had tried, and tried hard, but some essence always seemed to elude him. Even here, even now, he was befuddled: he'd thought this was a Buddhist temple, Indochinese, but this shrine seemed more purely Indian. The statues were garishly painted, like plaster gnomes, with red lips, yellow teeth, turquoise eyes; a blue woman with many arms and yellow swords danced her frozen dance of death, with her necklace of severed heads. Was that Kali?

Someone had made offerings to the shrine; tiny, poignant offerings had been placed on the steps—a ripe nectarine, two broken cigarettes, some sticky rice on a plastic plate; the ball of rice seethed with black flies.

She came up behind him.

"We can hide in this apartment? No one will know we're there. My grandfather never goes there." He remained silent. She repeated. "Please, Jake. This is it. I'm going to go now. If you don't want to come with me, I understand, but . . . I have no more time. Goodbye. . . ."

Kali waved her many swords, in her blue eternal dance. He made his resolve.

"We got out of Laos—we can get out of this. *Come on.*"

She looked at him briefly, and he thought he saw a flash of shy delight in her eyes—but then her royal determination returned.

They ran to the entrance and stepped over the wooden threshold. It was hot outside, lazily hot: Sunday in Phnom Penh, a few motos jeering, cyclos jangling. Jake felt seriously exposed. He was standing in the sun where anyone might see him; someone could shoot him, snatch him, anything.

A tuk-tuk.

"Here."

They grabbed it. Chemda said some quick words in Khmer. The driver nodded—indeed, he almost saluted. The journey was swift: instructed by Chemda, the driver took back routes and darkened shortcuts; they sped down long, squalid lanes where dogs ran out to snap and bark, they rattled past a row of tenements entirely shattered and burned, still empty, forty years later, *still empty*. Then they briefly turned onto a boulevard with adverts for Delon cigarettes, and big Hyundai showrooms, and Jake shrank into himself, trying to be as inconspicuous as possible. At last they reached the quietness and greenery of the suburbs.

An old wooden house, some gardens, a shady road with frangipani trees. Jake vaguely recognized the district.

"Down here."

It was a modern apartment block. White, clean, quiet, and concealed at the end of a side road.

Chemda paid the driver. She looked at Jake as he stepped from the tuk-tuk, the little rucksack slung over his shoulder.

"That's all you have?"

"It was in the stairwell of my building, my second passport, coupla cards. Everything else is gone. Everything."

"Well, I have money. Ah. We can buy some clothes and things tomorrow. We need to get inside."

The apartment was on the first floor. Sterile but comfortable, antiseptic, air-conditioned, sparely furnished, two bedrooms. A pied-à-terre.

An investment opportunity, waiting for some Cambodian expatriate to show his confidence, at last, in the local property market.

Jake sat on the expensive leather sofa and stared at an almost abstract photo of light and shade on the wall. Another temple.

Chemda sat in the wooden chair opposite him. She kicked off her sandals. Her light cotton, pale blue skirt was notably short. She stared his way. He felt an acute discomfort at their sudden intimacy. And again a tinge, much more than a tinge, of desire. He averted his gaze.

The silence was piercing. The room was oddly hot, despite the AC; like the closeness on the Mekong delta before the wet season.

She rose, and walked across, and stood right next to him.

"If anyone is going to give me away, *it will be me*."

Chemda took his hand. She put it inside her skirt, up inside, between her legs, between her soft, warm thighs.

He stood up and kissed her. Her dark eyes fluttered, yielding, feline, vivacious; her tongue, her lips, her hands were taking him, pulling him into the bedroom. She was a dancing and barefoot *apsara*, and he wanted to be seduced. He wanted to vanquish. He wanted, he just *wanted*.

Dark raw sugar. She reminded him of dark, sweet, fierce unprocessed sugar. There was a harshness to her lovemaking; she sought him with a sly animality. They kissed and stripped, she pulled him closer, closer and harder. He kissed her bare breasts, kissed her again, saw red petals on muddy water, sensed the darkness, the commingling of the rivers, the Mekong and the Tonle Sap. He sensed topaz, lemongrass, her urgent heartbeat, and *prahok*.

They made love twice, and slept for several hours. Then they snuck out to buy food and clothes, ate a twilit dinner, and afterward fell asleep, once again.

When he woke the sun was diagonal at the windows and it was Monday morning and she was fellating him. He gazed down as she sucked, at the veil of her dark hair flung over her head. Jake sighed, tightly gripping the cool cotton bedsheets. He felt himself concentrated into one tiny, intense source of joy and disquiet, down there, as she swallowed him, beautifully, frighteningly, carnivorously; she was voracious Kali, the eater of men, she was a disembodied face, hovering over him, submissive yet delicious, exquisitely devouring— yet this was wrong, something was wrong: there was a shadow on the window, that was it. He jerked upright—

Something was outside. Chemda was naked, and kneeling, gazing down. She couldn't see.

Jake could see. His blood thumped.

A man was standing there, at the window. Staring in.

19

Chemda gathered a sheet around herself, backing up to the bed, calling out:
"Jake, what is it? *What?*"

The figure at the window shrank away as Jake walked across and pressed his face to the glass.

He scanned. His eyes absorbed: a fire escape, metal walkways, stairs, the shadows of jackfruit trees. And *there*—a Khmer man, hiding in a corner, nervous yet staring out, a pleading expression on his face.

There was something deeply strange about him. He had a hat on, a red fleecy baseball cap. In this heat?

Jake wasn't scared now: the man didn't look frightening, just eerie and furtive. Flinging on some clothes and finding the back door of the apartment took half a minute; Jake stepped out onto the shade and heat of the fire escape.

The Khmer man was still there, in grimy overalls, old shoes, that peculiar cap. As Jake approached, the man shrank farther into the shadowed and dusty corner.

"It's OK," said Jake. "It's OK."

This was ludicrous, it was not OK. The man had been staring in at the window when they were having sex, a leering expression on his awkward face: he was a peeping Tom, he was deviant. But as Jake neared the trembling Khmer man, he began to feel pity; he couldn't help it, this disheveled figure was so weedy, so pitiable, like a street urchin unfed for a week.

Chemda had dressed and joined them on the hot shadowed walkway. The jackfruit trees kept the direct glare of the sun off the metal, but the ambient dry-season heat smothered everyone, like a hot blanket, like an arbitrary punishment they all had to suffer.

She spoke in Khmer to the man. He mumbled incoherently, not even words. He pointed to his mouth and shook his head. She murmured, "I've no idea what he is . . . who he is. But maybe harmless."

Again the man pointed to his mouth and shook his head.

But Jake understood.

"You can't talk, can you? *You're mute?*"

The man nodded.

"But," Jake continued, "you can understand English?"

He nodded again, this time vigorously. Then he reached into the pocket of his overalls and pulled out something. Jake flinched, but it was just a small notebook and a stubby pencil. The man was writing in the pad, awkwardly using his knee as support. The little scene exuded sadness.

A glance was swapped between Chemda and Jake. Her dark eyes were wide with mystification.

The man had finished his scribbling. He tore out the note and handed the paper over. Jake took it and read.

I am Ponlok the janitor. I am sorry I scared you.

The English was good. This was bizarre. He showed the note to Chemda and she asked:

"How do you know such good English? Why can't you talk?"

The man's eyes moistened; for a second they seemed to fill with a memory of tears. Jake felt the surge of pity again, the stifling, discomfiting pity.

Another note was rapidly scrawled. Jake snatched it from the man's hand.

I used to be a teacher. English teacher. At the lycee. Then the Khmer Rouge did the experiment on me.

"What experiment?" Jake said. "It left you speechless?"

The janitor, Ponlok, nodded—morosely. And then he slowly reached up to his cap and pulled it off.

A hideous scar lurked beneath. But it wasn't just a scar, it was also a kind of concavity in the upper forehead. As if the skull had slightly caved in, as if a chunk of brain had been removed, then the skull had cratered—though the skin had grown over.

It was horrible, and it was pitiable. The damage was so bad the hair had refused to grow back, the livid pink scar left naked in its strange hollow. No wonder the poor guy wore a cap.

The small Khmer man put the cap back on and cast his eyes to the floor, like a child ashamed of bedwetting.

Jake swore, quietly. He was thinking of the skulls and the bones on the Plain of Jars. The skulls with holes in the same place. Jake remembered the old Cambodian prophecy: *Only the deaf and the mute will survive.*

The first intimations of a narrative glimmered in Jake's mind.

Chemda had taken over the interrogation.

"Why did the Khmer Rouge do this to you?"

I do not know. They took away my memory with some of my brain. And my talking.

"When did they do this?"

In 1976.

"Did you volunteer to have this done to you?"

I do not remember. I hope not. I know some people did.

"Do you know where this happened?"

Yes. Near here. Let me show you.

Chemda said nothing, her expression spoke of confusion.
Another note:

I know who you are. Chemda.

"What?"

*Your grandfather gave me this job. When he built the apartments.
He took pity on me.*

Amid the strangeness, Jake could understand that bit of the story.
He'd never felt such pity. To have your brain opened up, to be turned
into this shrinking, deformed, helpless leftover man? Like an experimental rat, with little pieces of your mind thrown in the trash.
  Grotesque.

That is why I came here this morning. To tell you.

Chemda gazed at the man.

"Tell me what?"

The next note took a long time to write. Jake stood in the heat, trickles of sweat down his back. This man knew who they were, even this wretched specimen of a man had identified them. It was hopeless: everywhere, everyone was watching. The fucking jackfruit trees were watching them. It seemed there was no shade in the entire country. *Everywhere* was exposed to the heat and the danger.

The sweat ran down his back like those tickling claws of the scorpion, the tickle of fear on his spine. He wanted to get back inside the apartment.

At last the note was handed over.

I saw you coming into the apartment yesterday, I watched you. I know who you are, Chemda Tek. Because you are famous and on UN and because you are granddaughter of Sovirom Sen. Everyone knows who you are. But I know more. I knew your grandmother. I saw them bring her to Tuol Sleng and then to S-37. They didn't do anything to her in Laos. They did it here. They brought her back and experimented on her. I can show you. I do remember some things.

Chemda insisted: "I want to see this place. Now."

"Wait—" Jake put a restraining hand on her soft bare shoulder. She was in a midnight-blue undershirt. Her skin was dark and lovely. He could still remember her naked, crouched over him, the man staring through the window.

"Can we trust him?"

Chemda shook her head, frustratedly; Jake whispered in her ear.

"I know he has information, Chem, and I know I feel sorry for him, but look at him! And he might go straight to your grandfather. And he was standing at the window."

Ponlok was waiting, like a lowly servant, a man used to being ordered around, used to abuse and disdain. The Khmer Rouge had turned him into a serf.

Chemda replied, her voice hushed.

"He was just coming to see us! Hnh? He wasn't doing anything. And whatever happened to this poor man"—she gestured at Ponlok—"happened to my grandmother. He may be able to help, to tell us. I want to know more. This is our chance. And besides, he's seen us now, we have to do something. Ah. We need to win him over, make sure he doesn't go to my grandfather."

She was right. And if she wanted to know about her grandmother's fate, he could hardly argue.

"If you *want* I'll go alone with him," said Chemda. "You can stay here."

"Are you kidding?"

A minute later they were climbing down the fire escape, following the small, slightly limping Khmer man in his fleecy cap.

A hundred meters and two alleyways brought them to a slightly busier street. A spirit house stood on the corner, with offerings of dark fish sauce in little egg cups.

Jake waited, and listened. Chemda was explaining to Ponlok: why the janitor should keep this very quiet, that no one should know she and Jake were here, not even her grandfather. Even as he tuned in, Jake felt sure this plan was not going to work; it was too much of a risk, they couldn't trust Ponlok. As soon as this immediate and ghastly task was done, they would have to leave, flee Phnom Penh entirely. Run away into the countryside.

But where the hell could they go?

Jake stared down the leafy suburban road, looking west, away from the sun: thinking of escape routes, places they could hide. He stared, and a brush of horror made him jerk, like an icy hand had been suddenly pressed to the back of his neck.

He realized where they were. The hulking, grimy concrete building at the end of the road was unmistakable. So that's why he had recognized the area.

Tuol Sleng.

They were right by Tuol Sleng, the notorious Khmer Rouge prison.

At the end of the road Jake could see a bus, decanting tourists. People doing the Holocaust Tour. Jake had done it himself, when he'd first arrived in PP. He'd seen the iron beds where people were flayed with electric cables; he'd seen the bleak and fetid concrete cells where women and children were raped with batons, or tied down, screaming as their living organs were removed, in live dissections. Tuol Sleng. The Hill of the Poison Tree. S-21.

Seventeen thousand went through Tuol Sleng alone. And twelve survived.

Just twelve survivors, out of *seventeen thousand.*

Another note from Ponlok. The janitor handed it to Jake.

No. It is not in Tuol Sleng. It is secret place. S-37. Come?

He was guiding them away from the torture garden. Jake felt a brief frisson of relief: they were ducking away from the busyness and tourist police of Tuol Sleng.

But where were they going? Ponlok was heading down an alley, wet with rotting fruit and slimy, bulging garbage bags. The alley curved, then curved back on itself, and narrowed to a long, roofless concrete passageway where they had to *climb* the undulating heaps of trash.

Jake's eyes stung, irritated by the reek and pollution. An empty Royal Ginseng beer bottle seethed with flies; a smear of banana skin stuck to his jeans. Chemda put a hand to her nose to block the stench.

It was a grisly ascent, led by Ponlok, whose farcical cap had slipped, showing his scar. Jake tried not to wince, to show his open repulsion. The old man was muttering as he guided them through the spoil and dreck. This maze of rubbish.

At length the caging walls opened out, and they descended. A dead dog lay prone at the edge of the trash heaps. It was, unaccountably, smoldering. A small fire had been set in the dog's head, like an experiment. Jake looked away, and looked ahead.

The alley culminated in a very dead end: a patch of earth and rubble, and a shattered concrete building. On the face of it, this was just another of Phnom Penh's many, many ruins. But this was no derelict slum, no gutted hovel. This was S-37.

It was surrounded by bamboo stands and high grasses and modest hillocks of glittering and discarded auto parts. Hubcaps and shattered glazing. The building was roofless, and the size of a large one-car garage. A sinister iron bed frame stood in the middle, rusting away.

Two metal cupboards sat next to it, the drawers flung open and empty. Only an ancient, grimy, very broken syringe, lying on the floor, showed that this place might once have had some medical significance.

Chemda spoke: "This is where they did the experiments?"

Yes.

The man was trembling again, glancing at Chemda, looking at her bare legs. Jake wished, suddenly, that she had worn jeans, not the short blue skirt.

Your grandmother was brought here. I know. Then they cut open her head and she was changed. Forever. Like me. Like many members of your family.

Chemda stared at the note.

"Other people? My family? Who else?"

The note fell from her hand to the floor. She was visibly and entirely shocked, her mouth trembling. Jake went to touch her, but she waved him away.

Jake turned to ask the janitor another question.

"How do you know?"

But Ponlok wasn't listening, he was staring at Chemda's legs. He moved closer to Chemda, then stopped. He trembled, quivered, riven with some internal conflict. At last he scribbled a note and handed it to Jake.

You must go. They make me.

"What? Make you what?"

Again Ponlok stooped to his notepad. Jake could see the man's hand, trembling. His scrawny hand shook as he scribbled. The note was handed Jake's way.

They make me like this.

"Like what? Ponlok? What?"

Ponlok stared directly at Jake, his sad old eyes filled with not-quite-human tears. The sadness of a dying hound, a beaten animal. A suffering creature. A mute creature, not quite evolved.

Ponlok's mouth moved. Was he chewing? Spitting? What? With a shudder of helpless disgust, Jake realized Ponlok was trying to speak.

"Shhor . . . Kmmu . . ."

It was impossible. Jake shook his head.

"Sorry. *I don't understand.*"

Ponlok tried again: "Mevv . . . kmm."

Chemda stepped close. She put a hand on Ponlok's thin old shoulder.

"Please. Write it."

The old man gazed at her, the silence held among the three of them, awkwardly, and then he obeyed. He stooped to his notepad one more time. As he wrote, he dribbled. The line of spit from his mouth was shameless and silvery. Laboriously, the janitor wrote his note, with a talonlike hand. Then he moved closer to Chemda and his mouth whirred as he put a hand on her arm. He was stroking her. Pleading. Pleading like he needed feeding. The other hand held the note. Chemda took it and gave it to Jake, shrugging.

The scrawl was so shaky, it took Jake a few seconds to decipher the words. At last he made sense of the spidery writing.

I cant help it. Make me animal.

"What does that mean? Ponlok? What does—"

Too late, Jake realized the danger. Ponlok was already on Chemda, and moving fast. The janitor grabbed her bare legs. She screamed. But the old man had pushed her over, and down, and shoved his hand inside her skirt. Drooling on her neck.

Instantly, Jake grabbed the Khmer man by the arms, pulling him off, tearing at his dirty collar, pulling out fistfuls of hair; but then Jake felt a wild flash of metal across his forehead.

A knife. Ponlok had produced a huge knife from somewhere, he'd swiveled and slashed, slicing Jake hard across the face. The quivering cur of a man was transformed into something powerful.

The pain was momentarily blinding. Jake staggered and gasped. The blood was gushing from his forehead; frantic and angry, he wiped it away, and stared through the crimson pain.

Ponlok was on top of Chemda. Her panties were torn and they were dangling from an ankle. The janitor was unzipping himself, but the other hand was tightly holding the knife, pressing it hard against

Chemda's throat, so hard it was whitening the dark skin of her neck. Chemda's eyes blazed in terror, staring at Jake.

Help me.

Jake stood, frozen with exquisite indecision. One slash of that brutal knife could kill Chemda.

But the Khmer man was going to rape her. In front of him. On the grimy concrete floor of S-37.

20

Alex Carmichael rolled off Julia, flopped back, and lit a cigarette.

"That was nice," he said.

She slapped him.

"*Nice?* You just had sex with me. You aren't allowed to use the word *nice* for at least fifteen minutes."

He laughed, puffed twice on the cigarette, then extinguished it in a used wineglass from last night.

"Coffee, babe?"

"Please."

She watched him swing his arms into a dressing gown and disappear toward the kitchen. What did she feel? She felt more than "nice." Perhaps she was falling for him, properly. So far their relationship had been sexual but recreational, an agreement, friends-with-benefits, one of those things that happens in the intimacy and intensity of an archaeological dig, like actors and actresses on location.

Usually these flings flamed out, quite peaceably, when the season was over. But Alex was turning out to be more than expected: the sex was good, he was properly masculine, clever, unruly, and frivolously cynical in a way that made her laugh when she really needed to laugh; he was forty-two, English, and married, though he was apparently getting divorced. Maybe she could finally accede and relax into love?

Julia sat up. This was cowardly, and it was absurd: this was the wrong time to be thinking about relationships, in the middle of *all this*.

She hastened into the bathroom, turned the steel dials, and showered—but the self-criticism came quickly now, rinsing her, scalding her, like the water gushing from the showerhead. *Was* she a coward?

Almost everything about her life had been too safe. She had let herself settle into a safe job at a mediocre university in London. Home was an average apartment in a quintessentially boring suburb. She led a risk-free life as a permanent singleton, and always made sure the men she dated were unsuitable for real and possibly painful commitment. Like Alex.

Julia stepped from the shower and quickly toweled and assessed herself in the mirror.

Her own nudity often perplexed her. The sense of her own sexuality. Her breasts, her skin, her blond hair. She knew on a theoretical basis that men found her attractive. Sometimes. But she wasn't always sure why, perhaps she didn't want to know why. Did this all come from Sarnia, from what had happened there?—the rejection of her own attractiveness, in case it happened again. Yet with Alex she had found an easiness; and with some other men, too. But they were always men who could be lost, excused, or argued away. Men who wouldn't hurt her too much, if they suddenly *turned on her.* She was intrinsically timid in her choices. Wasn't she?

She paused. The mirror steamed. She wiped it with a corner of the towel and looked at her damp blond hair, her own bare face. Devoid of makeup.

How much of her timidity, her lack of true confidence and self-worth, tied in with her faltering career? Too much, maybe. And yet now—now things *were* different. She had, for the first time, discovered something. The skulls. Prunières. And she had shown tenacity—hadn't she?—in pursuing this. Refusing to be frightened by Ghislaine on the Cham. Refusing to just hide, to go back to London. Coming to Paris to solve the puzzle.

And she still cherished that insight she had, about the skulls and the stones. Guilt. That was *her* insight. Hers. So maybe she wasn't so timid. Maybe she had surprised and revived the steeliness in herself. Maybe she remained the girl who packed her bags and went to Montreal, despite her pleading parents; still the talented eighteen-year-old who got into McGill, the girl enraptured by the cave art.

She toweled away the last dampness. Vigorously. She wasn't going to let go, not now. Moreover, she was involved with these murders, the chain of mysterious events, whether she liked it or not. And she knew the two evolutions in her life converged: the skulls and the murders, there was a link. But what? Even if she was resolved, the complexities were intense.

Dressed and ready, she stepped eagerly into the kitchen. Alex was there, doing his laid-back thing. Consuming his coffee and croissants, reading *Le Monde* very slowly, trying to improve his French and failing.

They had done this many mornings through the summer. The ritual was sometimes comforting; right now, for Julia, it was frustratingly sluggish, a wholly unnecessary delay.

"Please, come on, Alex, this is unbearable, all this waiting, let's go."

He put down the newspaper.

"Right now?"

"Right now."

An hour later they were in a taxi heading north for St. Denis, a rougher part of Paris, not the Paris of Haussmann and the boulevards,

this was the Paris of *les banlieus*—literally, the *"places of banishment"*—
the Paris of Algerian and Moroccan kids with no jobs, the Paris of
couscous and Muslim rappers and nervy policemen in riot gear standing by vans just down the road from teeming mosques.

It was dull and cold and drizzly: late November. Their destination
was the subsidiary archives of the *Musée de l'Homme:* the most far-
flung outpost of the empire of Parisian ethnology.

Alex spoke: "You know I met him. Just a couple of times."

"Who?"

"Hector Trewin." The taxi had stopped at a junction. Alex gazed
out at some Arab kids in Inter Milan shirts, doing nothing.

"I didn't know that."

"Well, it's true. Sort of. I mean, we weren't best mates. But I went
to a few of his lectures at Balliol, the Ashmolean, when I was a student. And we chatted. He was very, very slightly famous."

"And?"

Alex shrugged a laconic shrug. Julia insisted, she wanted to talk.

"Go on, tell me! Trewin, what was he like?"

"A lot of the students revered him, this great Marxist intellectual.
But he creeped me out. Everything was theoretical. The world was
theoretical. Breakfast was bloody theoretical. He simply wouldn't
acknowledge that there was a practical problem with communism; as
far as he was concerned, Marxist theory was fine so it *should* work,
and one day it would. We just had to keep trying. I asked him about
Stalin and Mao and he actually said, 'You can't make an omelette
without breaking eggs.'"

Alex laughed, bitterly.

"I pointed out to him that sixty million dead people was possibly
an oversupply of broken eggs. And the fucking omelette turned out
to be the Gulags, and the Lubyanka, and the Purges. He just looked
over my head and sighed. He was an arsehole, Julia. I'm sorry. An

idealist and a thinker, but an arsehole." The rain was streaking the cab windows. Alex snapped the words. "Arsehole. Like all of them, all of those *soixante-huitards* and those seventies radicals and those CND Marxists, all of those Euro-Communists. I hate them. Wankers. How could you be a Communist after Mao, after the Terror? It's like being a Nazi *after* the Holocaust. How could you be a Communist at the same time as *the Khmer Rouge were killing babies*?"

Julia had rarely seen Alex this sincere and vehement. Normally he was sarcastic and languid to the point of nihilism.

They sat in silence. Then Alex patted her on the knee.

"Anyway, darling—I think we have arrived."

He was right. They'd arrived at the archives of the archives of the Musée de l'Homme. It was a huge gray warehouse, surrounded by nothing much: garages and vacant offices.

Tipping the cabbie, they crossed the rain-stained empty concrete parking lots. Alex said it reminded him of IKEA in far north London. Julia had a childish urge to cross her fingers. This was their last best hope; it was definitely their last hope. They had tried literally everywhere else: the Louvre and the Pasteur, private museums, the Broca archives, and now they were down to a bleak steel warehouse in a dismal 'burb of Paris beyond the Périphérique. One last shot.

The only official presence, the only human presence, was a large grouchy man in a small, depressing office with a sliding-glass window. The archivist of the archives of the archives.

"Eh, bonjour," he said, giving them a curt nod through the open window. *"Et vous êtes?"*

They explained in bad French. He checked their credentials, yawned, and did a magnificently Gallic shrug. *"Pas de problem."* He returned to his sports newspaper, *L'Equipe*.

With an air of tourists approaching the Parthenon, they stepped into the vastness of the secondary archives of the Musée de l'Homme.

It really was like IKEA—but a frighteningly disorganized IKEA. It swiftly became apparent that these archives had not been indexed in any way. It was just *stuff*: vast acres of steel shelves with boxes and artefacts and plastic bags. It was academic debris, the forgotten old dreck in the curatorial attic.

For an hour they wandered disconsolately around the vast building, peeking in boxes of tiny amber beads from Mauritania, staring in perplexity at half a broken bird-god from Madagascar. In this hour they realized they had scrutinized maybe 0.2 percent of the collection.

In despair the couple retreated to the office, to ask the archivist for help.

He shrugged, like they had asked him if he could spit farther than a llama. Like their question was quite surreally redundant.

Pressed once again, the official relented: grudgingly he told them that this cathedral of stuff, this huge warehouse of rubbish, was what remained following the recent translocation of the museum from the Palais Chaillot to its new site at the Quai Branly. Everything the Parisian authorities thought too worthless or irrelevant to be stored in the *official* archives had been thrown in here. The Frenchman specifically used the word for "thrown": *jeté*.

Julia stared down the gigantic aisles of steel shelving in the great cold warehouse. It was pointless. They were defeated. Her determination of the morning had already reached a dead end.

They retreated to the study room. It was a bleak space like a classroom in a fairly poor school: a scattering of tables, a drinks machine. There were two other people there. Two more willing scholars sent to *les banlieues* of anthropology. They had boxes open, or files to study—obviously they had made *their* finds.

Julia approached one of the scholars, a thin young man in black jeans hunched over a dirty and apparently African tribal mask.

She asked him, in her best French, how he had made his find: how he had located the tribal mask among the millions of boxes.

The man answered in cheerful English. He was American.

"It's a total nightmare. That's why no one comes here. They say they will have properly archived everything by the end of the decade. I would give it two decades. I was lucky, I was told by someone else exactly where to find this. What do you think? A death mask of the Cameroonian Fang, eighteenth century, real human hair!"

The death mask was thrust in Julia's face. She smiled, and backed away slightly.

Returning to his work, the man said: "If you haven't got a location, a shelf mark, you're kinda screwed. Sorry. Your only hope is chance. You might luck out."

They weren't going to get lucky. Julia knew it. She gazed at Alex and shrugged and they both walked, defeated, to the door. As she reached the door she realized she was passing another vast pile of boxes. She paused.

"What? Julia? What is it?"

She said nothing. She was staring at the large pile of boxes, dozens of them, stacked roughly, unordered.

Alex said again, "What?"

Julia had been in enough libraries and archives to recognize what this pile implied.

"These are boxes waiting to be shelved. Stuff that's been examined or added, very recently."

"Rrright. . . ." Alex drawled. "And?"

"Think about it! We're presuming the Prunières collection must be here, somewhere in these archives, because we've searched everywhere else. If the collection exists, it must be dumped in this warehouse."

Her lover sighed with a hint of impatience. "Fine. Yes. So?"

"Remember what Ghislaine said about the skulls I found? 'They will be put in the Prunières collection.' If Ghislaine meant that, and we have no reason to doubt him, the skulls would have been *brought* here recently. And added to the collection!"

Alex's frown turned into a bright and flashing smile.

"Got it! Clever girl! So our boxes could be . . ."

"Just in this pile! In fact, they *should* be here. Waiting to be shelved—"

Julia was already wading into the stacks and columns.

The boxes were arranged in piles of ten and fifteen; it took them twenty minutes to sift through a quarter of the columns. Then forty minutes. Then fifty. It seemed they would have no luck, until Alex said, very slowly and rather portentously:

"Julia, look. *There.*" He was pointing. "*Third box down.* By the door."

Looking across, she counted down the column of boxes. Her eyes rested on one with a large and discernible label, handwritten and florid and visible from a distance: *Prunières de Marvejols, 1872.*

There were, in fact, three boxes, all labeled the same way, sitting one on top of the other. Stifling her intense and scholastic excitement, Julia fought through the mess to the boxes, which they then briskly carried from the stack to a table. Alex was smiling at Julia's glee. She didn't care; she ripped open the first carton like it was a take-out Indian meal and she was very hungry.

They peered inside.

The boxes contained several human skulls, obviously Neolithic. All had been trepanned. They were *not* the skulls that she had found. Why not?

Yet these different skulls *were* trepanned.

Besides the skulls, the boxes also yielded several flint arrowheads, in a soft cotton bag, and a file of slender documents, written in exquisitely mannered old handwriting, tiny but entirely legible. The notebooks of a layman Victorian scientist. They were but a few pages long. Ten minutes later she sat back.

Her friend-with-benefits looked up from the wounded skulls he was examining and gave her a sly smile. He said, "C'mon, don't tease. What did he say? Prunières?"

"He found exactly what I found, on the Cham. Skeletons with wounds, lots of them; and skulls with trepanations. Little *rondelles* cut from the cranium. He was hunting in the caves of Lozère, to the west, near the Tarn."

"I see. And?"

"And he made notes for a lecture, summing it up. Here, I'll read it out." She picked up one notebook and stolidly translated: " 'In the Baumes-Chaudes caves, situated in that part of the valley of the Tarn which belongs to the department of Lozère, I picked up numerous bones bearing scars, characteristic of wounds produced by stone weapons. Some fifteen of these bones, such as the right and left hip bones, tibiae, and vertebrae, still contain flint points flung with sufficient force to penetrate deeply the bony tissue. I have also presented to the Congress at Clermont many bones bearing traces of' . . ." She paused. "I'm not sure of this word . . . no, hold on. Ah, it's *cicatrized*. " 'Many bones bearing cicatrized wounds, from the cave of *l'Homme Mort*, and beneath the Aumède dolmen.' . . ." She turned the page and looked at Alex. "There's lots more like this. He found thousands of wounded bones, and dozens of trepanations, across Lozère."

Alex whistled, low, appreciatively.

"Hmm! And the upshot, does he speculate a link?"

She said, "*Yes.* It's vague, and he admits it is kinda theoretical. But he wonders if . . ." She quoted again: " 'If we may posit the existence of a relatively advanced society, in upper Languedoc, many thousands of years before the birth of Christ, prone to severe violence. In this

regard, perhaps the trepanations can be seen as a reaction to the violence. We know from the estimable Doctor Mantegazza, of Peru,
who did such prodigious research in the Sanja-Huara cave, in the
Anta province of that distant land—' "

"He's a bit wordy."

Her smile was excited. "He is. But he gets there! Listen. 'We know
from Mantegazza'—blah blah—'that certain civilizations in pre-
Colombian antiquity practiced the same cranial surgeries, probably
as a way of exorcising evil spirits, allowing demons to escape. It is
surely' "—she leaned closer to the page, squinting at a word—" 'plausible that our ancestors on the wild Causses of the Lozère attempted
similar interventions: they tried to excise the violence in their culture
by freeing the demons in their brains. By drilling holes in their skulls.' "

Alex said, "Intriguing. Very intriguing. He thinks they were all
killing each other, so they tried to save their culture with some primitive brain surgery—to get rid of violent urges. Not *entirely* impossible. It helps to explain Stone Age trepanation."

She lifted a hand.

"This last paragraph is even more curious." She quoted the conclusion: " 'If I am permitted the liberties of a veteran, in our war on
scientific ignorance, I might add one more thought. Could there be
a connection between my modest discoveries and the strange objects
recently reported by Garnier, in his gallant explorations of the
Mekong River in upper Cochin China?' "

Alex sat forward.

"Cochin China. That's the old name for *French Indochina*?"

Her nod was vigorous. " 'The valiant French imperialist, so
recently returned from the terrors of the Khone Falls and the delights
of Louanghprabangh, tells us that he unearthed several large jars, on
a plateau near Ponsabanh, which contained very similar remains as to
those discovered in our very own Lozère: many dozens of skulls,

trepanned, and evidence of disturbing and coeval social violence. The connection is piquant and intriguing, and of course quite fantastical. It is for younger and better scholars to discover if there is any truth in my fantasies.'"

The notebook was closed. Alex was uncharacteristically silent. Then he spoke:

"A link with Indochina. Laos, Cambodia. Wow."

"It's time we told Rouvier about some of this, there are too many links. Too many. *We need to go.*"

Alex agreed; he stood and stretched and said he was impatient for coffee, a proper *grand crème*. A nice bar where they could talk all this over. Quick and efficient, they put lids on the cartons, replaced them on the shelf, then made swiftly for the exit and the rain.

But something nagged Julia as they went toward the big swing doors with the big grimy windows. Something had been nagging her *for a while.* She turned to Alex.

"Meet me at that brasserie, OK? That one we drove past—couple of blocks back."

"Sure. But why?"

"There's something I want to ask that asshole at the office. You go and have your coffee. Three minutes." She stood on tiptoe and kissed him, her arms slung around his neck; she liked the fact that he was taller.

He smiled. "You're getting gay on me, Julia." But he was still smiling as he turned and quit the building. Julia watched him for a moment, happy amid the terrors that she had Alex. But now she had a more difficult duty than kissing Alex Carmichael.

Walking to the office of the dour Frenchman, she tapped on the glass partition. Sighing, tetchily, the curator put down his sports paper and slid back the glass.

Julia asked him about the pile of boxes in the study room.

Obviously, whoever had examined the boxes had *not* used them to archive the discoveries that Julia had made: the new skulls had not been added. So who *had* been in to look at this specific collection? What had been their exact purpose in using the Prunières boxes?

She phrased the question directly: Did the archivist remember anyone who had come searching for the archives of *Prunières de Marvejols*?

The Frenchman nodded, and wearily explained that a scholar had been in for the last three days, frantically hunting down the very same boxes, finally locating them yesterday afternoon. This scholar had been quite annoying in several ways—the archivist yawned theatrically to underline the point—because the scholar had also demanded an obscure back issue of an obscure magazine of French anthropology, so that a specific article could be photocopied.

Julia asked if the archivist remembered the name of the writer of the article.

A petulant sigh.

"Non, mais je me souviens bien du titre. Nous n'arrivons pas à trouver l'article. Il a disparu. Voulez-vous connaître le titre?" No, but I remember the title. We could not find the article. It is missing. Do you want to know the title?

"Oui!"

The archivist sighed and turned and sorted through a pile of documents on his desk; then he handed a piece of paper through the window. The paper had one line written in capitals: it was the title and the author of this missing article.

The author's name might have been underlined in blood, it was so conspicuous and alarming: Ghislaine Quoinelles.

Her anxiety and her speculations were cut short, the archivist spoke: *Is that it? We are finished?*

"Non . . . une autre question."

Julia asked her final question. She wanted a description of the scholar. Picking up his copy of *L'Equipe,* the archivist yawned and answered without looking up: *The woman is about thirty. She is a little strange. She has long dark hair, and a very white face. Perhaps she is Oriental.*

Julia swallowed a surge of true and wild anxiety. She felt like she were about to throw up. The link was proved. They hadn't just got "lucky" with the box. Their find was no coincidence. Someone had been in to use this box just a day before them. But it wasn't some friend or colleague of Ghislaine's.

It was the murderer.

Her fearful thoughts were once more interrupted. The official had slid back the window once more: he was pointing through the glass of the main door.

Look! The same woman is coming again, you can ask her yourself.

Iced along her spine by the terror, Julia turned, and squinted, and saw.

Approaching the building was a strange, menacing figure, a short, lithe young woman, with the palest face, and long dark hair. The face was somehow odd, inexpressive; yet the eyes were demonic. Slanted and brightly dark, and luxuriously intense.

Julia shrank back in reflex. The murderer would reach the door and discover Julia in a few moments. Three seconds. Two. One.

21

Ponlok pressed the knife cruelly to Chemda's pulsing neck. She was screaming and writhing, but if she writhed any harder she would slash her own throat. The blood would geyser. Her legs were being slowly forced open.

Jake had a fraction of a second to decide.

He stepped back as if turning away, then swiveled in an instant and ran two steps and flashed out a boot, as hard as he could manage. At school he'd learned to do the drop kick fast, very fast, *invisibly fast.* Before he got crushed in the rugby maul.

It worked. A sickeningly direct hit. The thudding sound of his steel-capped boot hitting Ponlok's head was queasy and cracking; but his kick did the task. The janitor went sprawling into the grit of the rancid laboratory. The knife spun silver in the sunlight, twirling into shadows.

Ponlok gave a low and ugly moan. The Khmer man was prone, bleeding, half conscious. Jake grabbed Chemda's hands and helped her to her feet and she said:

"*Aw kohn,* quick!"

He didn't need *thank-you*s; he understood *quick;* hand in hand they skeltered down the alley, down the next alley, up the fire escape past the jackfruit trees and into the apartment. Two minutes. Chemda bandaged his head with some torn-up cotton T-shirt; he wiped himself down in the bathroom, then stuffed his few items into a bag. Chemda was in the living room, calling someone on a phone, rattling questions in Khmer. Then she looked Jake's way. "Now!" As one, they sprinted down the steps to the yard and then the boulevard; they were two pitiable fugitives with a couple of bags standing alongside the national drag race of Highway 6—where anyone and everyone could drive by and see them—but then a black-and-white old Citroën taxi squealed to the curb and the driver grinned his six teeth.

Chemda jumped in and said, "Siem Reap."

The man lifted a hand as if to say *whoah—Siem Reap*?

Jake knew this was a long way—two hundred kilometers north, into the jungle, close to Angkor. A day's drive. Yet the taxi driver's skeptical eyes narrowed into shrewd acceptance when he saw Chemda flourish a clutch of dollars from her bag: tens, twenties, hundreds.

"Siem Reap, *baat*!"

The taxi dodged through the traffic, which was thinning anyway as they swiftly exited the brash periphery of the city.

Sweating and trembling, Jake checked behind them. Nothing. Nothing but traffic. They passed Caltex stations, Happy Cellphone shops, grungy garages, then more Caltex stations, more Happy Cellphone outlets, more tire shops; it was like the backdrop to a cheap cartoon repeating itself. Then they passed an old French shop with *dépôt de pharmacie* on the side, then a Sukisoup outlet, a patch of wasteland, and the skeletal bamboo scaffolding of a half-finished apartment block—and then, at last, the water buffalo and the paddies and the sugar palms inclining their heads, like chancellors bowing to a despotic lord.

The royal sun.

They had made it out of the city. They were in rural Cambodia, the land of two seasons and two harvests and two million dead, the land of the killing fields.

"The money is my mom's," said Chemda. "I just took it."

Jake shrugged and didn't reply. He wasn't even sure if he cared, or if he was meant to reply. If he answered her, that meant a dialogue, and a dialogue meant conversation, and a conversation meant they might have to talk about what had just happened: Chemda had nearly been raped by an old man. An old man who had been, what, *altered*? An old man who had endured the same terrors as Chemda's grandmother, and who else?

It was too much. The grief in Chemda's life was mounting like the pyramids of bashed-in skulls at Cheung Ek. And this was just Chemda's family. There were a million more Khmer families in Cambodia, out there, each one with their little pyramid of skulls. No wonder there were so many *neak ta:* so many cages for the unquiet dead.

"Remember what Ponlok said? I was wondering . . . if anyone else was experimented on. So many of my cousins did not survive."

Her eyes were staring ahead, lustrous, in profile. They were roaring through a little village, where women loosely turbaned by the elegant Khmer scarves—the striped or chequerboard cotton *krama,* used as slings or turbans or baby carriers or lunch packs or ponchos— looked up at the car. The women frowned under their *kramas.* Children played in the dust, quite naked.

They were going too fast. Jake didn't care, he *wanted* to go fast. Faster than the police. Faster than light. Faster than life. He was hot and dehydrated. Again. And he couldn't keep saying nothing.

"Look at it this way. Do you remember anyone in your family being aggressive? Demented? Like the janitor?"

"Why?"

"Because, Chemda—" he hesitated, and his gaze failed to meet hers "—because I reckon I have an idea why Ponlok did what he did. 'Cause he wrote those notes. Just before he attacked you."

"What?"

"He said, '*They make me like this.*' He was trying to warn us before he did it."

"How long before?"

"Moments. Just seconds."

"So he knew what he was going to do? Attack me?" She exhaled. "And he tried to warn you and yet—" Her face whitened with understanding. "He is aware of the problem but he just couldn't help himself. An uncontrollable urge."

"Yes, exactly."

Her demeanor was strained, like she was forcing herself to use a matter-of-fact voice, even though her lips were trembling. "But how could this brain surgery they did, or whatever it was, how could that have such an effect?"

"Well. I think I have an idea, maybe. *Just maybe.*"

"OK."

"What I mean is—I did a bit of research on primitive surgery when we got back from Chiang Rai. I read about holes in the head, like the trepanations we saw in—"

"Trepanations?"

"It means holes drilled in the skull."

"OK. Hnh. *And?*"

Jake stared through the grimy cab window. The forests out there were thicker now. Mahogany, rosewood, sugar palm. The banyan of the Buddha. They were driving deep into the soul of the country: Siem Reap, Angkor Wat, the emotional heartland of the Khmer.

He gave his answer.

"I'm obviously not any kind of expert, but it seems, maybe, the frontal lobes of the brain are associated with self-control, commanding

the baser emotions; so maybe if you cut out some of the frontal cortex, you excise the most evolved part of the brain. Therefore, just
possibly, it could make you amoral and criminal. Cruel. Predatory.
Violent."

"A rapist."

Jake was silent. Then he said, "Yes. Why not?"

Chemda spoke quietly: "The skulls on the Plain of Jars. The same.
They were *the same,* Jake."

"I know . . . exactly the same wounds." Jake's eyes focused on the
dust smearing the car window. He was thinking intensely. "There
is—or there must be—a connection. But I can't work it out. Two
thousand years ago, then suddenly again. The violence . . ." He gazed
her way. "Ponlok. Jesus, Chem, are you OK?"

Her hand reached for his across the torn vinyl of the taxi's backseat. She said to him, with softness: "Yes. I'm OK. Ah. I just . . ." She
closed her dark eyes, then opened them once more. "Thank you for
doing that, back there. We saved each other. We are the same. You
lost your sister and I lost my grandmother . . . and God knows who
else." Her kissing lips were a warming whisper on his cheek, momen-
tary and elusive, then she sat back. "We are the same."

Jake yearned to believe this, yet he also wondered, helplessly, if
this were really true. Some of him still resisted the equation. Were
they the same? Were they definitely and entirely on the same side?
Even as he was falling for her, some element inside him still didn't or
couldn't wholly trust her. And yet he didn't know why. He thought
of the black-toothed spider witch. Her muttering and curses, her
kitsch pullover with the sequined turquoise heart. Kali, the Eater
of Men.

Chemda said, "Could *that* be why they did it, the Khmer Rouge?
These, ah, horrible experiments, to actually *make* some kind of
behavioral change? Make people more violent and cruel? Like beasts?"

"Maybe." Jake had already been thinking on these lines. "But why would anyone *volunteer for this*? Like your grandmother?"

Chemda exhaled. "That's the puzzle, isn't it? Why volunteer for that? It simply doesn't make any sense. But we could ask my uncle, he might know."

"Your uncle?"

"My father's brother. Tek Sonisoy. He works in Siem Reap. He's a scientist. Conservation. That's where we're going."

"But—"

She lifted a dark yet somehow pale hand and put a finger vertical to his lips.

"He renounced my family years ago. The wealth and the power and the politics. Resents my grandfather, dislikes my mother, hates all that political stuff. He grew up in California with me, but then he went traveling, disowned my family; ah, he backpacked. And then he ended up in Cambodia. He was a real monk for a while, now he works discreetly at Angkor. We get along. He has helped me before, kind of, when I was researching the Plain of Jars. We've been e-mailing, though I haven't told him everything."

"Why not?"

"Because I didn't want to load this on him; he hates all this. He's spent his life escaping the past. The *recent* past. But now we have no choice. I trust him . . . implicitly. He can shelter us. I'm sure he will."

"But won't your grandfather know where we are?"

"He might guess, eventually. I wonder if my grandfather even *knows* that Sonisoy is in the country. He certainly won't know his precise location in Siem. Why would he?"

Jake sat back. He gazed down at his empty hands. Suddenly and acutely, he felt the lack of his cameras. Lost in the fire. Without them, what could he do, how could he handle it all? How could he mediate and understand the world? Without his cameras, *what* was he? Jake Thurby, photographer? Not anymore. Just a man running, with a girl.

"Chemda, we can't stay in Siem for long. A few hours. We need to find a way to get to Thailand."

"OK, but we can work it out at Sonisoy's place. Ah, please. I need to . . . rest. Just one night?"

Just one night. The phrase was simple. But what it embodied was not: their continued flight, away from the horror and further risk and danger. But Jake also saw no other obvious escape route. And Siem Reap *was* on the way to Thailand. And Thailand would be safe. Wouldn't it?

Rich, developed, comparatively sensible Thailand.

Crossing the frontier would be dicey, but they'd done it before in Laos, and once they were in Thailand he could draw breath—and then at last give vent to his despairing anguish at the trail of violence they had left behind. And yes, he understood why Chemda needed to rest. The ghastly image of the cratered man, the altered man, groping inside her thighs, trying to rape her: that still hurt, like the cut on his head still hurt, under the haphazard bandage Chemda had applied at the apartment.

It was just a flesh wound, but it stung. Jake touched his scalp, then he winced, and sweated, and gazed at the sunlight, serrated by the palm fronds.

Two hours later, as the twilight finally relieved the countryside from the torment of the sun—like a good cop taking over from a bad cop—they arrived in Siem Reap.

Jake had been here, briefly, once before. A sweet little Indochinese town, not unlike Luang Prabang, full of hotels and spas and moonlit walks and *klongs* and night markets, all dedicated to watering and sheltering the millions of tourists who flooded the nearby sites: the clearings of Angkor Wat, where the great temples and palaces of Jayavarman and Suryavarman moldered nobly in the rasping jungle.

But they were not here for sightseeing. They parked by the biggest night market, already busy with stalls selling obese wooden Buddhas and antique incense burners and pirated DVDs of Thai horror movies. Jake glanced at one image as they passed: it was a DVD called *Demonic Beauty,* and the label showed the disembodied head of a woman with her spinal cord and lungs trailing from her severed head like a grisly bridal train of viscera. He turned away.

Sonisoy was waiting for them at a doorway. He looked like Chemda, in male guise. Taller, handsome, older, with the shaved bald head of the monk he once was. He seemed intensely Khmer, but spoke flawless American-accented English.

Hands were shaken. Jake's hands were shaking anyway. Sonisoy escorted them into a house just around the corner from the night market, a house of wood and sweet smells of incense and paper Chinese lanterns, with photos of the Temple of Ta Prohm on the wall.

He served them red Khmer tea as he listened to Chemda tell their story, in one gushing monologue. His face was sober and his head was shaved and his demeanor was monastic. He nodded.

Then he handed out some Khmer sweetmeats: *nom krob khnor,* a translucent blob of gelatin with a yellow mung bean in the middle, like a sweetened little embryo in a placenta. Jake wanted to be sick. He wanted to be at home in England. He could see the blank milky eyes of the smoke babies, the horrible pulsing scar of the janitor; he could see blood and death, the blank eyes of his sister and the disembodied smile of his mother and . . .

He snapped out of it. Turned the wheel of his mind. He had gone off-road, for a moment, he had veered into the bush, where the minefields lurked, the UXO of the past.

The room was quiet. Chemda had finished her story. Sonisoy put down his cup of red tea and, with the nocturnal murmur of Siem Reap just audible beyond the shutters, said:

"Of course, I understand, I believe I have some more information that may piece it all together."

"What?" said Chemda. "How?"

"I think . . ." Sonisoy sighed. "I believe, from what you have told me, that I know who else was a victim of these experiments. Another member of the family. Close, Chemda. Very close."

Chemda said nothing. She stared into the gloom, at the scraped, shaven head of her uncle, now just a silhouette in the candled dark. She had a hand to her mouth; her eyes were shining in the candle-light, moist with incipient tears. She already knew.

"My father? As well?"

"Your father, little Chemtik." His smile was very sad. "My brother. Think about it, about the way he died."

The room was morbid with silence. The plate of mung beans, wrapped in their translucent cocoons of jelly, glistened in the candle-light.

22

The head was floating. Another floating woman's head, with a funereal veil of black gauze, or was it hair? The head was disembodied by the dark, and it was sucking him, sucking his penis, Kali Kra, white-toothed and drooling, fanged and desirous, with her two tongues black and blood-red, licking his erection, painfully, exquisitely, making him cry out.

He didn't want the woman, the witch, the spider witch, the *apsara*, to stop; surely it was Chemda who was blowing him, giving him pleasure, waking him with fellatio once again: and it was beautiful. Jake fought the beautiful feeling in his dreams, he was half awake now, yes, he could see her, it was Chemda's head above his groin in the darkness of the shuttered room above the *krama* shop in old Siem Reap.

"Chemda, Chemda . . ." He wanted real sex. Penetration. He grasped her head, lifted it from his erection, and she looked up, and her eyes flashed and smiled, *and it was his mother, sucking him. His mother, smiling.*

He woke with a myoclonic jerk, rigid with horror. Properly awake this time. It was just a dream, a lucid dream. He shuddered and looked around. The day had barely dawned: ladders of pale and unfading blue showed the slatted shutters of Sonisoy's apartment.

Where was Chemda?

Jake swept a hand across the empty bed.

"Chemda . . ." He could sense the fragments of the dream fleeing him, yet he kept seeing the image of his mother, a head, disembodied, blood dripping from somewhere, the image of Kali, the Mother of Dissolution.

"Hello."

Chemda had walked into the room. She was dressed, and frowning.

"Chemda. Are you OK?"

She shrugged.

"Couldn't really sleep. Ah. Not after hearing that about my father. We talked, me and Sonisoy." Her hands were hovering on her hips, impatient or wary—like a Western sharpshooter approaching a gunfight. "He wants us to see something in Angkor Wat, to tell us something."

"And?"

"We're gonna meet downstairs in ten minutes. Pack everything."

Obedient, he threw a towel over his shoulder and walked to the bathroom. He really needed a shower.

Chemda loitered by the door, watching him, looking at his nakedness as he walked. And lust flashed for a second in that gaze, he saw it: fleshly hunger. Kali, the devourer, with her seven black tongues.

She waved a dark hand at the bathroom.

"Please, Jake, we need to be quick—"

"I thought you said we'd be safe here. For a night."

"I did—I thought we would—until I heard that about my father. Now I wonder: Is my whole family cursed, do they want us all dead? I don't know. But this means everything is worse than we imagined—"

"Let's get to Thailand!"

"But first I want to hear Sonisoy's story. Then we go to Thailand."

"But what *about* Sonisoy?"

"He'd have turned us in by now, if he was with them. I told you. I trust him more than anyone. Apart from you." Her eyes fixed on his. She continued: "Quick, ah, please, be quick. Sonisoy will take us to Angkor. Ten minutes."

It took him two minutes: shower, towel, clothes, socks, boots. Then he loitered in the bedroom, packing his pitiful bag: two pairs of jeans and T-shirts bought from the Siem Reap night market, a little camera, also from the market, then his passport, phone, and cards. Pensively, Jake stared at the cell phone, then took it out of the bag.

He dialed a number. Right now he needed a friendly voice, a Western voice, the voice of a native English-speaker. He felt so lost and isolated.

"Yyyyyo?"

It was Tyrone at his groggiest. Just waking up, probably just assessing his hangover.

"Ty. It's Jake."

Immediately, his friend sharpened. "Jake, for fuck's sake, where are you? The whole of PP is looking for you, you and Chemda."

As concisely as possible, Jake explained the situation—the grandfather, the firebomb, the janitor, the escape to Siem Reap. Tyrone cussed, urgently, a couple of times. Then Jake told his friend about Chemda's father, also lobotomized.

"Fuck," Tyrone said. "How did she take *that*?"

Jake paused. He walked to the window and looked down at the unbusy streets of Siem Reap. He could see a street cleaner with a wicker hat and a municipal jerkin, brushing indolently—and a waiting tuk-tuk close to the front door. "Apparently it happened a few years after her family fled to California. She was young, six or seven.

All she remembers is that her dad was severely depressed, a lot of the time, and drank too much. Silent. Taciturn."

"Sure, but a lot of Khmers were, like, traumatized by the genocides—"

"And that's what she presumed, but last night she told me she dimly recalls a scar, on his head, under his hair. And very deep—nihilistically deep—depressions."

"So he killed himself?"

"No. He walked under a bus, very drunk, Chemda says. An accident. At least, that's what she was told at the time, by her mother. Madame Tek. But, of course, now she wonders if it wasn't a total accident. There was some volition there, some self-destruction."

"Jesus," said Tyrone. "No wonder Grandfather Sen hates the Khmer Rouge so much, they did frontal lobotomies on half his family. Fuck. Fuck. *Fuck.* And now you're going to Angkor on some Indiana Jones malarkey. Nice timing—"

"Sonisoy insists he has important evidence. We're going to see it."

"And then?"

"Then we escape. Thailand."

Tyrone drew breath. "That ain't gonna be easy—"

"Of course, *I know.* How can we do it? Any ideas?"

A pause. Then an answer.

"When you're finished in Angkor, head for Anlong Veng. Most remote border crossing. Chong Sa. I've got friends there, from when I did my Ta Mok story. Maybe they can help you. Just get there, asshole, as stealthily and as quickly as you can! Anyone, repeat *anyone,* could be a danger. Anyone at all."

"Anyone? Surely we are a little safer, this far out of Phnom Penh—"

Tyrone whistled impatiently. "Thurby, *you're not getting me.* You don't understand what's fucking happening here in PP. It's mayhem, man. The police are *hunting* for you, it's all over the FCC, everywhere. Grandfather Sen has an advert in the *Post* this morning, asking for help in locating his granddaughter. And the article is worse: it has quotes from the Phnom Penh police, claiming you kidnapped Chemda Tek. There's even a fucking price on your head. You're actually *wanted. Like in a Western.*"

"You're joking."

"I'm sorry, Jake. It's true. Why don't you just go? Fuck the evidence. Just fucking run."

"But Chemda wants to see—"

"Leave Chemda behind, Jake. Go. You're better off without her. Fucking safer."

The idea was sensible; the idea was ludicrous.

"I can't leave her, Ty. You know that. . . ."

He groaned. "But they're after your ass! With guns. This is not a goddamn rehearsal. The chief of police says it, literally: *any means necessary may be used to rescue Chemda Tek from the kidnapper,* i.e., they can take you dead or alive as far as the authorities are concerned." He hesitated, then added, "And knowing this is Cambodia, what that really means is—"

"I can't leave her."

Tyrone sighed. "I know you can't. I know."

23

Julia pressed herself into a corner, a kind of vestibule between the office and the main doors of the archives. Perhaps the killer would walk straight past, not see her, walk on.

Then she could run for it. If the killer walked straight down the lobby into the study room or the main archives, she would have a few seconds to flee, without even being spotted.

The door swung open.

The Asian woman stood there, looking left and right. Julia was hidden behind some coats and a stack of boxes, crushing herself backward against the wall. She could feel her heart beating in her lungs and her spine, so hard was she pressed to the rough brickwork.

Again, the Asian woman glanced left, and then right. The face of this woman was pale to the point of unearthliness. There was something wrong with it, something strange.

Now she was staring directly into the gloom of the vestibule. Squinting. Surely she had seen Julia. Surely this was it.

But then the woman walked on into the hallway, and she tapped on the glass. She wanted to speak to the curator. The grouchy old Frenchman.

This was another vortex of anxiety. Assuredly, the French curator would say, "Oh, there is someone here looking for you, she is in the building, she was here a minute ago," and then—then the killer would turn and narrow those dark eyes and she would see Julia and the knives would come out, or worse.

The curator appeared to be asleep, or to have disappeared. There was no response to the woman's persistent tapping.

Tap, tock, tap.

"*Bonjour?* Hello? Anyone there?"

No reply. The small, lithe woman had a soft, deep voice. Maybe an American or Canadian accent. Yet the face was not European, and was bewilderingly pale.

The murderer leaned close to the glass, cupping a hand to her eyes to see better, to see through. Where was the curator?

Tap, tock, tap.

"*Bonjour?*"

Julia assessed her chances. She could just run now, run right past, out the main door; it might take seconds for the murderer to realize what had happened; to turn and see the door swinging, see Julia sprinting away. Would the killer even come running after? Would she take the risk? Attack Julia in bright daylight?

It was the best option. *Do it now.* Before the curator returned and pointed and the woman turned.

Sweat trickled. She was sticky and hot and terrified and immobile but she had to do it. She was about to do it, to run, when she heard a voice, the curator's, heard him sliding back the glass partition.

"*Ah, Mademoiselle, pardon, bonjour.*"

"*Vous êtes occupé?*"

"*Non, j'étais en train de parachuter un Sénégalais!*"

The Asian woman nodded, unsmiling.

"OK, I am going to continue my research. You understand? *Je vais poursuivre mes recherches*. OK?"

"*Oui, oui!*" The curator was grinning, feebly, submissively, like a supplicant; Julia realized with a shiver that even this big and grumpy man was frightened by this small, menacing woman, this thing, this killer, the presence she carried with her was so mesmerising, so unsettling.

The killer turned away. This was it. The danger was passing. Julia was going to survive. To make it through. The curator had said nothing. The killer was unaware of Julia's presence five meters away—

"*Un moment*," said the curator, leaning out through the glass partition. "*Il y avait deux personnes qui vous cherchaient!*"

There were two people looking for you.

The woman swiveled, lithe and tautened, in sneakers and jeans and a dark T-shirt under a fashionably scarred leather jacket.

"When?"

The curator mumbled.

"*Ce matin . . . ?*" The reaction was instant. The rest of the curator's sentence was truncated by a brash clattering of glass. Then a grunting noise. Then a fearsome groan. Julia could not see what exactly was happening. The killer was in the way, muscling and tugging. The grunting was horrible, pursued by a pissing noise, a hissing, and another low groan, then silence.

The killer then turned. And ran. Julia could hear running feet, the killer fleeing, surely. A door slammed open; cold wind blew in from outside, from the parking lot and the drizzle and the concrete Algerian slums.

For five minutes Julia remained crouching, half sobbing, half panting in relief and fear. She texted Alex. *Go home. Now. Please trust me.*

Then she called Rouvier.

The policeman picked up the phone at once and listened to her whispered story in brisk silence. Firmly, steadily, he instructed her: telling her to go to the apartment immediately, where he would send men to interview her. He likewise told her to lock herself in the apartment and answer to no one but him or the Paris police. In the meantime, he was sending cars to the archives of the *Musee de l'Homme.*

Shudders of relief rippled through Julia. Here again, in her soul, was her father, hugging her in the lobby of the ragged old casino in Sarnia.

Tentatively, Julia stood and turned to leave—but she couldn't leave. Because she had seen *what the killer did.* The young "Oriental woman" had punched a hole in the glass partition; then she had evidently pulled the curator's head through the hole, and slammed his neck down, onto the jagged shark teeth of the glass, severing arteries and veins, almost slicing off the entire head. Impaled on the shards of glass, it looked, grotesquely, like a severed pig's head on a butcher's counter.

The man was clearly dead, *absurdly* dead: his blood spooled across the floor, a luxurious shellacking of tacky red varnish. Julia gawked at the blood. She was almost paralyzed by the sight, this astonishing violence.

And then: *a noise.* The distinct squeak of rubber shoes on polished floor, returning. The sickly vertigo of fear made Julia sway, at the cliff edge of death. The killer *hadn't* left the building: the young woman had gone the other way, slamming through doors, making the other doors swing, inhaling cold air; and now she was back in the lobby with her blank, beautiful, slightly distorted face, leering with fierce and logical intent. Julia screamed—she half screamed—and she ran. She ran or else she would die.

Her mind worked at a panicked speed. The parking lot was wrong, the wrong choice. A vast open space: three hundred meters of nothing. The murderer would catch her—the athletic body, the *immense strength*—Julia needed somewhere to hide, somehow, somewhere, until the police reached the museum. She had to buy herself time.

She stayed in the building and ran left, down a corridor, heard the killer running after her. Julia dared not look behind—not out of fear, but at the time it would take: a few seconds delay would mean her death. She sprinted as fast as she had ever run, to the end of the corridor, which darkened and turned and turned again, past doors, and boxes of old leather cloaks, reeking with neglect, then a pile of battered bronze drums, gloomy in the dark. She knocked them over as she hurled herself, the drums falling with enormous ancient thumps, resonant booms like beer kegs. Tumbling into the corridor.

This wouldn't stop her pursuer, she knew. She could hear the loud but easy breathing of this remorseless woman, an athlete's breathing, relaxed, confident, jumping over the Dong Sang drums, vaulting them, almost, like a graceful animal, a predatory feline. Julia threw herself at a door that terminated the corridor; she twisted and yanked it open and slammed it shut behind her. Four seconds. She had maybe four seconds to barricade the door.

With what? She was back in the archives, the vast echoing hangar-like spaces, racked with endless open corridors and a shadowed infinity of shelves.

A totem pole. A British Columbian totem pole, maybe two meters high, carved with eagle heads, vicious beaks of pine and cedar, was tilted against the door, directly to her left. Julia had just enough time to topple it over; it fell as the door was kicked open, blocking the door—but it wasn't enough, she knew that at once. This had gained her another five seconds.

She needed more than that, much more than that—she needed five minutes, ten minutes, before the police got here, or she was going to die. She ran. Hard. Burning up the energy inside her, burning the will to live, running on the fuel of life. Straight into the vast darkened labyrinth of steel shelving and lofty racks of boxes and sarcophagi.

It was a true maze—a labyrinth of ancient anthropology. It was like being lost in a dream, a bad dream of her own teenage studies: anthropology and ethnology and archaeology—the sinister and beautiful cultures of ancient man, now her own death trap. Julia fled past grimy camel palanquins, slowly desiccating in the dryness. A rack of death masks, Senegalese or Cameroonian, smirked in the semidark. One of them fell to the floor as she brushed past, a mask of real human skin, a ghastly wig of real human hair, smiling at the roof.

Then more drums. Running. Perfume bottles of the Maghreb. Running. Moroccan rugs, knotted and ancient. Running. Okuyi helmets from Gabon. *Running.* All the lessons she'd ever had in ethnology were here—condensed into a nightmare. She ran.

A Soto lyre stone, carved in rock, nearly tripped her over. More bronze drums, dinted and somber, knocked at her heels.

And the killer was *still coming,* stalking the passages and open-ended corridors, seeking her, hunting her down. Julia felt like a small fish in coral, hiding, pathetically, from a shark, shirking the effortless and superior species, the top of the food chain.

No. She wouldn't let it happen. She needed to fight back. If she was going to die, she was going to fight back first—but how? A sword. There was nothing here like that. No metal. A club? Yes. A club. A cudgel. Pausing in her heart-straining sprint, she grasped at a human sacrificial club, Tupinamba, Brazilian, a wooden killing club, decorated with scarlet feathers and white jaguar teeth. She could swing that around and maybe—yet even as she practiced she knew it was pointless—one swing and she would *miss* and then the killer would be on her, the long steel knife gutting her open, like the bison at Lascaux. Abject, despairing, she hurled down the club.

What else?

Carpets. Tunisian carpets. A shamanic cloak, musty, made of reindeer, still more drums, then dusty boxes, then another corner to run around and more miles of shelving. At last she began to slow down, her energy was sapping. The sad and angry despair flushed her with fury, but she was running out of life, out of that desire to resist. She grasped at herself—no, she couldn't die like this, not here. Not like this. Not here. But how?

Seconds left. The killer was in the next steel corridor. Those yellow eyes, white in the darkness, glanced through the grille and the cardboard boxing—and narrowed on Julia. *Got you.*

She'd been spotted. Julia was trapped in one of the very last racks of shelves, which ended in a wall, the exterior wall—she was cornered. There was a door, probably an exterior door, beyond the next steel rack, but she was trapped. Entirely trapped. Dragging the last ingenuity from her brain, Julia stopped. This was it. *Think of something.*

If she couldn't fight back, what could she do? If she couldn't run away, how could she escape?

Hide. Protect. *Defend?* She needed to *conceal* herself. Now. Flailing and desperate, she reached for some wooden armor. A breastplate, from Japan, made for a samurai. But this was futile, the killer would tear it away. So what? What could she possibly do? The killer was fifty yards away, rounding the corner. A raptor descending.

There. A coffin, long and black and lacquered with dragons, loomed at the end of the steel corridor. A Chinese coffin, Ming dynasty, from Jiangxi province. She recognized the type: made of *nunma* wood, fire-tempered, incredibly hard. Sprinting to the coffin, she pulled at the heavy lid; even as she stooped, she could hear the rubber squeak of footsteps behind her, running, approaching, attacking. Julia strained to lift the great coffin lid, which rose slowly.

Three seconds. She bent herself double—*two seconds*—and tried to squeeze inside—*one second*—but the killer was here. It was surely too late. The killer was on her. But *Julia was in.* The lid collapsed shut, sealing her inside, with a great booming thud. Now she was encased in this ancient long box. Would it hold?

The knife slammed straight through the crack between the lid and the casket, but it didn't reach her eye. The killer kicked at the coffin, frustrated, then the knife came again, trying to pry the box open. Julia pulled the lid down, tighter, desperately. The crack was widening. The lid was being lifted. Julia kicked, furiously, at the murdering fingers, the hands trying to get at her, to open the wooden sarcophagus.

Again the blade plunged, phallically, through the gap—but the point jarred and halted, and juddered, a centimeter from Julia's pulsing neck. Now the blows were frenzied. The killer was stabbing and hacking, trying to kick the lid off, to expose Julia's face, her body. Another crazy swoop of the blade came lunging through. How long could she resist this assault? More hacking swipes of steel blade slashed at the gap. Julia felt the first cut. A tiny nick of her flesh, and the first blood drawn.

With a rush of terminal horror, she realized that the wood was strong, but the *hinges* were bending and giving way—the lid was going to be shunted hard aside, leaving space for the killer; the next blow through the widening crack would go deeper, the next plunging blade swoop would reach her, stab her deep in the kidneys. She would be a corpse, floating in blood. Julia screamed.

A siren.

Outside, way out there, but quite distinct, Julia heard the caterwaul of police sirens.

The killer seemed to think, and to pause. The kicks and the stabbings stopped.

Julia crouched, fetally, inside her wooden box, tasting the sour and ferric spit of primeval emotion, of instinctive fear and will to live. She listened, tensed and coiled.

Then she heard that distinct, repetitive squeak. The rubber shoes of the killer. Running away? Could it be? The pounding of the shoes faded and was instantly replaced by voices, loud voices, and flash-lights, real lights, proper lights. Doors were flung open. The police were in the building.

The killer had *gone*—she had fled, somewhere else, somewhere not here, leaving Julia encased inside her *nunma* wooden box.

A petite American archaeologist in a 2,500-year-old Ming dynasty coffin allowed herself two sad, angry, urgent tears. Then she turned and strained, threw the lid open, and rose from the casket.

24

Closing the call with Tyrone, Jake resisted the desire to panic. Then he began
to panic. So he got going instead, closed his bag, ran downstairs, and joined
Chemda and Sonisoy in the back of the tuk-tuk. The soft morning air smelled
of fish sauce and garbage and sweet jasmine and two-stroke engines. And
danger.

Chemda looked his way: "You OK?"

"No."

"Me neither," she said, and she squeezed his hand.

Chemda's uncle snapped some Khmer at the driver. The tuk-tuk
swiveled onto the road and they began the journey to the great temples of Angkor, the Bayon, Angkor Thom, Angkor Wat, Banteay
Srei, the East Mebon.

Jake gazed ahead, trying to remember. He had visited Angkor in
his first year in Cambodia. Like any tourist, he'd wandered the miles
of tumbledown sandstone shrines and palaces, the *gopuras* and *lingams*
and terraces of *garudas* slowly being swallowed by the orchids and
lianas and strangler figs of the jungle—he had walked around gawking.

It was, as he recalled, a truly stupendous place. Even Jake's godless
soul had been stirred by the majestic mystery of it all, this city of

monuments, a thousand years old, where once a million people lived and worshipped; a city that was left to the poisonous millipedes and jumping spiders—and the busloads of Japanese tourists queuing for sunset photos beside the *bodhis* of Phnom Bakheng.

This was a very different journey. Fretful, disquieting, dangerous. The air was cool with the promise of heat as the tuk-tuk puttered north on the long straight road to Angkor. Monkeys played by the road between the fallen green husks of coconuts; stall holders cycled their coolers of cold drinks to work; villagers in blue-checkered *kramas* washed naked toddlers under pumps of gushing water.

Chemda said to Sonisoy: "Uncle, could you tell Jake what we discussed last night?"

Sonisoy's nod was terse.

"About a year ago we found a Frenchman, Marcel Barnier, wandering around the temple. Looking specifically in Preah Kahn, where we were researching. We asked him to talk with us."

"Us?"

"Our consortium. Samsara. We have an office in Siem and we are restoring the temples, with EU and Chinese help. Angkor is a World Heritage Centre."

They were passing a vast new concrete hotel, as yet unfinished. A vendor was selling coils of dried snake in the parking lot, and buckets of boiled eggs. The vendor gazed at their tuk-tuk, unsmiling, unfrowning, just blank.

"This man was quite old. Sixty-five, maybe seventy."

"What was he doing there?"

"Apparently, in 1976, a team of scientists and thinkers, all of them left-wing radicals, was invited from Paris to Cambodia. Their mission was to help the Chinese and the Khmer Rouge to create a perfect Communist, a soldier for communism."

"With brain surgery?"

Sonisoy shrugged. his T-shirt was old and clean, with a discreet little picture of a young Elvis Presley on the breast pocket. He glanced along the road ahead, which was almost empty. Jake also scanned ahead: for police, soldiers, danger. Nothing. The road was ominously deserted.

Sonisoy continued: "Barnier did not know that aspect of the story, but after hearing from you and Chemda, I think yes, that must have been one technique used by the Khmer Rouge. Experiments on the brain."

"How did Barnier know nothing about the surgery, if he was part of this same team?"

"Barnier's speciality was hybridization, between species. Men and monkeys. That was another avenue explored by the Communists. It started in the 1920s in Russia. However . . ." Sonisoy looked over Jake's shoulder, at a car that was approaching fast from behind. His face tautened. Jake spun around.

"Relax," said Sonisoy. "Park rangers. We are just approaching the gates. *Relax.*"

But Jake could not relax, not after what Tyrone had said. Indeed, he had an urgent need to express himself, to *explain his fears;* he needed to share and dilute his paranoia. Leaning forward, he informed Chemda and Sonisoy of what he had been told by Tyrone. The manhunt. The tension in Phnom Penh. The price on his head.

When he had finished, Chemda was pale and her expression tremulous. Even Sonisoy's monastic serenity was ruffled.

"OK," Sonisoy said. "This is *not* good. But I know a way to get you to Anlong Veng, it's through Angkor anyway. And we are safe in Angkor behind the fences. For a short while. We must be quick. Here."

He gestured. They were approaching a large wall. The entire fifty square miles of Angkorian remains were surrounded by guards and fences and walls and toll booths, making sure all those tourist dollars and euros and yuan poured into the coffers of Phnom Penh.

Sonisoy alighted from the tuk-tuk, flashed the gatekeepers a badge, and gestured at Chemda and Jake. Jake shrank from the inquisitive stares of the gatekeepers. If these officials had seen a Phnom Penh paper this morning, then he could be spotted, recognized. But maybe it was too early for the news to have made it here?

The tension was an insistent pop song from a tinny radio, repetitive and stressing. The gatekeeper yawned, stared again at Jake—and then shrugged an uncaring smile. Sonisoy climbed back in, the driver gunned the little engine, and the tuk-tuk trundled on, with painful slowness.

"So, let me finish." Sonisoy sighed, curtly. "This Frenchman, Barnier, explained that he had been invited to Phnom Penh but in the end was not closely involved in the process. He wasn't in the loop. Other specialists and scientists, neurologists, anthropologists, psychiatrists, were more favored. Perhaps the Communists decided brain surgery was a better route to their goal. Barnier went home to Lyon virtually as mystified as when he arrived."

"But why did he come to you? Why would he return at all?"

"Guilt."

Sonisoy turned and snapped an order at the driver, giving him directions. He turned back:

"Barnier has a conscience. Since that trip to Cambodia and China so long ago, he has renounced his communism. He sees it as a terrible historical error, and he is ashamed of giving succor to the Khmer Rouge by supporting their regime from the West. A lot of Maoists and leftists in Europe and America tried to justify the Khmer Rouge. Some of them are still serious academics, writers, and politicians. I'm not sure how many have apologized for what they helped to do to *my* country." Sonisoy stared, unblinking, at Jake. The stare of accusation?

Jake twisted in discomfort, physical and mental. The heat was already rising. The tension had topped out hours ago. Days ago.

He thought back to that fateful evening in Vang Vieng. Then he was just a happy, sad, guilt-ridden, cheerful, boozy photojournalist; now he was a hunted man. A prey animal.

Sonisoy was still talking: "Barnier wanted to, I suppose, absolve himself. And he wanted to find out how and why he was used by the Khmer Rouge. So he came to Angkor."

"Why Angkor?"

"What Barnier did discover during his trip was that the KR and the Chinese were also obsessed with history, with some historical foundation to their experiments. And they did many explorations of Angkor. And from what you guys have told me of the Plain of Jars . . . Now I see how it all fits."

"Go on."

"Following Barnier's visit, I began my own excavations based on his scant but tantalizing information. After all, I too am a Khmer, I want to know what happened to my people, why we did what we did. We were the insane country. We had a national psychosis. What happened and why? I want the past uncovered. I want to know." He leaned across the tuk-tuk. "And we have unearthed some materials at Angkor in the past few weeks that may fit these pieces together, especially with this new information from you. And so I am going to show you. And then—" He looked for the first time in a while at Chemda, then back at Jake, "You go north. At once, as fast as possible, across the border at Chong Sa."

Jake nodded.

"We got it, we're not lingering."

Sonisoy was scribbling something on a notebook page. He ripped it out and handed it over, explaining: "Barnier's address and number, in Bangkok. He lives in Bangkok now. When you get there, you could look him up. He may know more than he told us. OK, we go left here."

They all looked ahead. A glimmering sheet of water barred the end of the road, tinted gold by the morning sun. The great serene moat around Angkor Wat temple. Jake remembered that Angkor was built around and on top of and because of water: vast artificial lakes, beautiful and serene *barays*.

Some of them were eight kilometers long. And huge moats, too, reservoirs, aquifers, conduits: all quenching the thirst of the greatest city built before the age of industrialization. Perhaps the greatest city *ever built*. And now the *barays* were glittering gold and bloody yellow in the hot rising sun.

They turned left, puttering around the water barrier. The first tourist buses were already parked under the banyans by the Angkor Wat causeway. From a distance the hundreds of tourists slowly crossing the moat looked, to Jake, like the spirits of the newly dead silently and obediently proceeding unto oblivion, crossing the Styx.

"We're going to the Bayon first."

This temple, Jake knew, was beyond Angkor Wat. It was within the ancient city precincts proper: Angkor Thom.

Ahead of them a wide bridge crossed another moat; the balustrades consisted of two *nagas*, enormous long stone snakes snarling their fangs, forever devouring the warm tropical air, ridden by stone demons, also snarling. And the gate itself was a mouth, a huge yawning stone mouth topped with the serene smiling face of Jayavarman, the king-god.

As they trundled under the gate, driving right under the godhead, kids ran out to sell their trinkets and DVDs and bottles of water—*Mister, mister, you buy, America good, England good, barang, you buy*—while others scampered down from the crumbling great walls, grinning and jeering at Jake, making their eyes round by squashing their faces, laughing.

Children were everywhere, on the balustrades, hanging from trees, running in the road, scampering, laughing—children running and smiling in the street, like his sister. The sadness and grief stabbed at Jake, maliciously; he took out his cheap little camera and grabbed a few shots. He needed to mediate the sadness.

Snap.

The tuk-tuk accelerated under and beyond the gate. For a few minutes they drove in anxious silence, the sunshine flickering in the laurels and bamboo and gigantic kapok trees, as dark, somber birds flapped away. Ahead of them was a palace of enormous stone heads.

The Bayon.

"We get off here first." Sonisoy gestured at the tuk-tuk driver. "He will wait."

The temple of the Bayon was just as Jake recalled it from his cursory touristic visit two years back. A series of large, square, ascending sandstone terraces, delicately inscribed with bas-reliefs of *apsaras* and *garudas,* and serene female deities, *devatas* and *dvarapalas,* and scenes of Khmer life from the twelfth and thirteenth centuries: princesses on palanquins, cockfights and boar fights, scrolling stone tapestries of Hindu myths, the ark of the sacred fire, the churning of the ocean of milk, the god of love murdered by Shiva.

Jake took more photos.

What marked the Bayon was the heads: every significant point in the temple terminated in a pinnacle beautifully carved with megalithic human heads, serene and huge and enigmatic visages of the god-king. Smiling.

They climbed the very narrow stone steps to the innermost enclosure of the temple, the *prasat*. It was hot now. Jake was panting in the impervious sun. It was like they were too close to the sun.

"Jayavarman," said Sonisoy. "The heads of Jayavarman, here in the Bayon, represent the apogee of Angkorian culture, the apotheosis, when the king becomes a living god and society is perfected. Many people find these heads disturbing. I think it is the smiles. The size of the heads, and the eternal smiles."

Jake agreed. He found them awesome but they unsettled him. Maybe it *was* the vast serene smile, slightly different in every sculpted face. He remembered a face, smiling sadly in the dark, a large face, enormous, smiling. Disembodied.

"Now, this is crucial. Look," said Sonisoy. He pointed at the nearest enormous head.

Chemda said, "What?"

"There."

"But I can't see!"

Chemda kicked off her flip-flops and climbed a balustrade to get a better look. Jake gazed at her ankles. She had a delicate tattoo of a scorpion on her slender left ankle. Sonisoy pointed again.

"There. You see the forehead of the god-king. There is a diamond there, a rhombus. No? Carved distinctly in the forehead—like a hole in the head. It represents, of course, the third eye of Hindu mythology: the location of the soul, the place in the mind where God resides. Consider the *bindi* of an Indian woman, the mark between and above her eyes—the same thing. So. Remember this—it's important— because the rest of the story is in Preah Kahn. We must be quick."

Hastily, almost slipping, they made it down the treacherous and mossy steps to ground level. Sonisoy led the way out, past the Terrace of the Elephants, past the Terrace of the Leper King, with its dancing demons and manic *garudas,* skinned Wagnerian sopranos singing mutely through their sandstone beaks at the uncaring forest.

The lane to the west gate of Angkor Thom was unpaved, virtually jungled over. Monkeys swung away as they approached, disappearing into the lianas and the cotton trees. The noise of insects was close to deafening. Jake had heard cicadas rasping before, but this was like a mass screaming, like the whole forest was shrieking in anger, or torment.

Sonisoy led them through another snarling huge gate, topped with another huge head of another god-king, and then they were in even thicker jungle. Cobwebs laced the pathway, invisible but very tangible. Jake spat them from his mouth with disgust. Translucent lynx spiders fled up his arm, until he flicked them off. Chemda fought the red ants that dropped into her hair. Lianas, sticky with some gross exudation, snagged at their arms and legs.

Sonisoy turned, a faint smile of pity on his face.

"Few people make it this far into the jungle—to Preah Kahn, one of the oldest temples of Angkor. Originally a university. Here."

The temple loomed, old and vast and very ruined. More giant *garudas* guarded the walls at every corner. *Nagas* lay waiting on either side of the entrance; headless statues of gods stood as sentinels at the porch.

"Through here, and here . . . left here, just down this way. . . ."

It was a labyrinth of dozing sunlight, ancient darkness, fallen stone pillars, and mutilated stone buddhas. Enclosures, *gopuras,* doorways, columned doorways, and then long, broken corridors where bats nested in the upper corners.

"It's vast," Chemda said.

"Twenty thousand people lived in Preah Kahn at its height," said Sonisoy. "And we don't know what they studied."

He had finally brought them to a kind of open cloister. The far wall backed onto the jungle.

"That place there," said Sonisoy, gesturing, "is unique in Angkor. The only building with round columns. Probably some kind of sacred library. As for what it contained . . ."

It was a roofless pavilion, elegant, empty, desolate. Massive spiderwebs hung like constellations from the empty sandstone windows.

"Books," said Chemda. "It would have contained, ah, books,

parchments, wooden tablets, but they would all have been destroyed by time—"

"Yes." Sonisoy gestured them to the side. "But stone can survive in great detail if it is buried. We have dug around this library in the past year, since our discussions with Monsieur Barnier, and, last week, we found these."

He gestured over a heap of rubble. Beyond it was another pile of rubble, covered in dusty plastic.

Like a magician, Sonisoy swept the large sheet of plastic away. Jake stared. It was still a heap of nothing. They had come all this way to look at some ancient bricks.

"Uncle, I don't—"

"Look harder. Use your eyes."

Amid the rubble stood two larger pieces of stone: pediments, badly worn, with several carved panels; figures etched into the stone. *Apsaras, garudas,* the usual.

"So what?"

Sonisoy sighed in the breathless heat.

"These were special carvings kept in the special library in the intellectual heart of Angkor, the greatest city of its time in the world. They must tell a story—"

"You tell it to us," Chemda said, "and fast. Please!"

"Of course." He turned to his niece. "We all know the prophecy, don't we? Every Khmer learns it: A darkness will settle on the people of Cambodia. There will be houses but no people in them, roads but no travelers."

Chemda finished the prophecy for him: "The land will be ruled by barbarians with no religion; blood will run so deep as to touch the belly of the elephant. Only the deaf and the mute will survive."

"So," said Sonisoy, pointing to the pediment. "Here is the belly of the elephant. Here is the sea of blood."

Jake knelt and squinted. He could barely see what Sonisoy was pointing out. Maybe that was an elephant, that could be an ocean, a ripple of water—or of blood. But now that he was close he could definitely see one thing. One thing was perfectly plain.

"My God, that's a jar! From the Plain of Jars in Laos! This is a carving of whatever happened to those people? In Laos?"

"The Black Khmer. Exactly."

Sonisoy was nodding; his bald head was sweating. He unwrapped his *krama* from his waist and dabbed his scalp, then he returned to the carvings: "When you told me of them last night, I thought of these carvings. Now it all makes sense. Here are people, Black Khmer, being drilled in the head, turning them into warriors. See, there, the drilling." He moved his hand. "And you see the metamorphosis here, and here. From cringing peasant to proud Khmer warrior, when the skull is drilled. These are probably Vietnamese prisoners, decapitated, after the wars, the triumphs of the Khmer."

That was also clear: a row of heads on the ground. The panel was surely showing a great military victory, by Khmers, Black Khmers, on the Plain of Jars. Jake grabbed a couple of photos; poor photos, yet still evidence. Khmers with trepanations . . .

But evidence of *what*?

Sonisoy intoned, "But here, see, in the next panel we see the jars and the weeping women. And the blood and the destruction, the burning of bones, a mass suicide. You see, it is a story, it is *the* story—"

"A story of what?"

"Who knows. But—"

A noise interrupted, a buzz of static. It was a two-way radio attached to Sonisoy's belt. Jake guessed one might just need such a thing, to stay in touch, in such a vast place as Angkor.

Sonisoy unbuckled the radio and talked. His face grew dark, then darker. Angry. He gabbled, and stared at Chemda.

Then he said, "That was the gatekeeper, a friend. Warning me. Someone has spotted you. National police, they are coming for us right now, surrounding the temple—"

Chemda grabbed Jake's hand. She yelled at her uncle: "How do we get out?"

"It's too late, we need to hide—*this way.*"

They were about to be caught. The fear shrilled through Jake's body, a fire siren in the night. Sonisoy guided them swiftly over fallen columns and rubble, through a small empty window that led to a dimly lit, elongated chamber, a virtual tomb of unaired heat.

The room was darkly concealed at the very heart of the temple, the bat-haunted core of Preah Kahn. The three of them pressed flat against the wall. Jake could feel the damp cold sweat of his own shirt. Chemda was next to him, her face a waxen and perspiring mask of unease, the heartbeat visible in her neck, pulsing rapidly.

What next?

They were successfully hidden, for the moment. But they were also trapped inside the cardiac darkness of Preah Kahn. Sooner or later they would be found, in a minute, or five, or ten. Jake was prey, a targeted man. He would go to jail. He probably wouldn't make it as far as jail. They would find a reason to execute him. This was Cambodia. People died with a blink.

Jake stared at the temple wall opposite. The chamber was decorated with a stone frieze. He realized it was a series of smiling, floating, and completely disembodied female heads.

25

The she-demons stared. Jake could hear the police now: young male Khmer voices clacking orders at one another. A far wall was dazzlingly overlit by sun, then a shadow fleetingly shot across it: the shadow of a man. One of their pursuers.

"This way," whispered Sonisoy. He gestured, low, beckoning. They followed. The stone corridors narrowed. A strangler fig tree loomed in the middle of a tiny light well, growing out of the architrave, its enormous roots like muscles and tendons grappling the stonework into submission, arm-wrestling the temple into dust. A spider hung sacred and scarlet, poised on a sunlit web.

They ducked. Another corridor, more voices. The policemen were flooding into the ancient maze of Preah Kahn: it sounded like a dozen, at least, climbing through the *gopuras,* patrolling the *naga* balustrades, pointing flashlights and guns into thousand-year-old alcoves where blind white salamanders feasted on the pristine darkness and scuttled from the hideous light.

Sonisoy's shaved head was brightened by another shaft of sun, slanting through the broken roof. He glanced all around. Thinking— and gesturing.

"Along here—"

It was pointless. Jake felt the utter futility dragging like leg irons as they scrambled over the fallen columns and pediments and the cracked and tumbled bas reliefs. They were going to get caught. Death always caught up.

The young cops were engulfing the place, he could hear them everywhere now, those dark, high, clamorous Khmer vowels, clashing, unpleasant, stern and yet juvenile. They could not escape.

Abruptly, Sonisoy stopped and raised a hand. He was pointing through a stone window, at an open space. Great kapok trees loomed beyond a wall, like watchtowers around a concentration camp.

"See. The lions of the stairway, there—"

His gesture led Jake's eye to a stone lion.

Sonisoy explained: "There's a small path at the right of the lions, the stone lions, you see it?"

"Yes."

"That path leads to the fourth enclosure and then it goes under a wall—we dug a tunnel to extract rubble."

Jake leaned forward, excited: "So we go, we use the tunnel!"

"Wait!" Sonisoy hissed, quiet and urgent. Another clamor of male voices passed right behind them, just a wall away.

"Jake, you go, you're the one they want. Chemda and I can stay here, get captured, nothing will happen to us—"

Chemda's intervention was fierce: "If Jake is going I am going."

"But, Chemda."

"No!" Her eyes burned in the darkness. "I want to find the truth about my father. *And I want to be with Jake.*"

Jake looked her way. Churned.

"Stubborn little Chemtik, always *stubborn.*" Sonisoy sighed and put a hand on Jake's shoulder. "Just *look after my niece.* Please. OK? I'm going to run that way"—he gestured backward—"making a *lot* of noise to distract them, so you two will have a few seconds as they all come after me. Make sure you *use those seconds*—" He clasped Jake's shoulder tighter, and said, "Then, when you get to the outside, just *run,* run through the forest, it goes a long way, right to a baray, Srah Srang, no one goes there, just villagers, locals, no tourists, no police—you can grab a ride to Anlong Veng."

The nearest policeman was coming around the corner: Jake could hear the chink of rubble as black boots slid against the clitter.

Sonisoy gazed up at the half-revealed sky, his eyes worshipful and concerned, misted with sadness. "So, now, we split up, in three seconds, two seconds . . . ready?"

"Ready."

Sonisoy ran noisily, left, out into a courtyard, shouting behind him.

"Chemda! Jake! This way!"

Immediately a chorus of excited voices responded—they'd heard him. Sonisoy kept shouting, leading, decoying.

Jake grabbed Chemda's hand and they ducked into the sun, past the lion, down the terrace, down the steps, and onto the path.

There. The path evolved into a short tunnel, under the wall. They slid down the mud and scrambled through darkness and emerged into peaceful light, shattered by a sound.

A terrible scream.

The awful scream was so loud and eerie it seemed to silence the rasp of the jungle; it was the near-inhuman scream of someone being viciously beaten, or worse. And now the cops were calling, barking orders, continuing the hunt.

"*Sonisoy*—" Chemda's eyes shone with the shock. "*What did they do to Sonisoy?*"

The scream echoed again: a man's bellow of pain.

Jake was paralyzed, momentarily. He saw the repetition in his life: he was leaving someone behind, a broken body covered in blood, barely breathing.

But a fierceness entered Jake's thoughts.

"They'll do the same to us."

He wrenched at her hand—she resisted, for a shred of a moment; then she shuddered, nodded, and they ran fast together deep into the jungle, hard along the path, running straight into this forest of noise and heat. It was a humid maze of green. Birds and monkeys catcalled like derisive hecklers. Insects hissed all around, whirring and angry; huge black wasps hovered and dived at their sweating faces; the sunlight flickered crazily through the green canopy.

They ran until they could barely walk, until Jake keeled to the side, gasping, heaving. Chemda hugged his neck, her warm, panting breath feathery on his skin; the two of them were hanging on each other's shoulders, exhausted.

Then Jake looked up.

Ahead of them, beyond the last of the trees, was a waste of water, another sheet-metal expanse of *baray,* like a vast lido of mercury in the hot afternoon sun.

And maybe a village?

Seizing the opportunity, Chemda walked out onto the docile shores of the reservoir, where wooden shacks and some naked swimming children revealed human life. Jake followed, his heart still hurting from the exertions. Chemda was barefoot. Her ankles were bleeding. She curved and slipped her flip-flops on, and dropped her rucksack to the ground. Jake looked at the little bag; he had a similar bag on his back. All their possessions. Two pitiful rucksacks.

He picked up his and followed her. He felt a bleak sense of affirmation as they approached the village, Chemda ahead of him. They were certainly in this together now. She was his and he was hers. Whatever happened.

The village was so sleepy it was like someone had mortared the place with narcotic gas. Women lay on their sides on wooden platforms, dirty and barefoot, snoozing, yawning, breast-feeding babies, their *kramas* on their shoulders. Men sat with their backs against the banyans in the shadows, sleeping. Only the children and the roosters were alert.

An old man wearing a white loincloth came forward. He scrutinized Jake and Chemda; he asked her several curt questions; she replied. He looked like Mahatma Gandhi. His teeth were haphazard but his eyes were kind, and shrewd. The man watched as Chemda took dollars from her rucksack. Then he spoke.

Chemda translated his words for Jake: "There's a pickup leaving here in forty minutes, taking fruit to Thailand. Through Anlong Veng. We can hide in the back."

They had to wait. Jake was glad to wait. His legs were still aching from the run through the jungle, his mind still roiled by the hideous scream in the temple. What did they do to Sonisoy?

The old man led them to a clearing and a kind of communal table for the village. More chickens and children scampered in the dust. Five boys were playing with a shuttlecock down by the waveless waters of the baray, kicking it in the air.

Taking a metal jug, the man poured water in plastic cups for them both. It was cold and delicious. Jake drank it hungrily.

"Aw kohn."

The old man smiled. His eyes held a spark of charm and friendliness, maybe even empathy for these two scruffed, muddy, sweating young people emerging with frightened faces from the jungle. He stood and retreated to the shade of a shack, then came back with a bowl of boiled eggs. He proffered them. Jake realized he had not eaten anything in almost a day. He gladly took one.

As he cracked open the egg he instantly understood his error: Chemda was staring his way, her eyebrows subtly raised. But it was too late. He'd have to eat it now. The rich and pungent smell emanating from the warm boiled egg told him what he was holding.

Balat. It was boiled duck embryo, an egg that had been fertilized and then left to grow for a fortnight or more: meaning there was a crunchy half-formed duck embryo inside. Jake peeled away the soft delicate shards of white shell, trying not to grimace. Sure enough, there it was, inside—the slimy bolus of egg and duck fetus: little feathers, brains, beak, claws, squidgy and gray, almost ready to be born, almost ready to fly, mixed in with the dark yellow egg pulp.

He couldn't say no. These villagers were saving their lives. He didn't dare risk insulting them. Closing his eyes, Jake put the egg in his mouth bit by bit, bone by bone, sensing the slimy crunch of the bird's rib cage and the jellylike squidge of its half-formed brains between his teeth, like chewing silt. Jake shuddered and felt a kind of guilt, the guilt of a carnivore, and yet he ate. *Because he was hungry.*

"We're ready—"

It was Chemda. Jake swallowed the last of the *balat.* And stood. A Toyota Hilux, unexpectedly clean and new, was backing into the clearing. Villagers were loading it with baskets of fruit: apples, mangosteens, papayas, purplish dragonfruit, and enormous durians, with their excessive green prickles.

Jake and Chemda climbed in. They lay on the bottom of the pickup, between the racks of fruit. The fetid, sweet, bad-sewer smell of durian was quite persistent, but they were concealed between the crates.

The old man threw some kind of tarpaulin over the load, and over Jake and Chemda. He whispered to them as they lay there, cowering in the darkness.

Jake said thank you. Chemda said *aw kohn.*

The pickup started. They were on their way.

The journey was long and hot, and Jake spent it watching Chemda sleeping. She was lying right next to him, and her eyes closed almost as soon as the vehicle accelerated away. He sensed her exhaustion. That's why she could sleep in this fetid, cramped space, in the heat and the reek of the durians, as they rattled over the endless potholes of National Highway 67.

Jake was only half-awake himself. His thoughts wandered. He daydreamed. The smell of the durians was like toilets at a hot summer festival when he was a teenager. Glastonbury. The pickup rattled through the gears. He thought of his sister running into the road as the car banged and juddered. Becky, Rebecca. Why was the guilt so persistent? None of it was his fault. His sister, his mother, and yet he felt guilt. It held him. Fuck the guilt.

Reaching down to his rucksack, he unzipped it and retrieved his wallet. Between two fingers he found the photo of Rebecca, lifted it and looked, close, in the gloom. Her undying smile, the guiltless, happy smile. Five years old, then snuffed out. The grief tugged at him like an undertow, like an immense tide he could not resist. Maybe he did not want to resist. *Just let go. Just let it all go.*

He buttoned the photo in his breast pocket. He wanted it close, close to him, he didn't know why. Then he shut his eyes and tried to sleep, but he couldn't; he drifted into turbulent semiconsciousness.

Voices outside came and went in a second as they slammed through hamlets and jungle, and slowed over rickety wooden bridges. Jake shifted and rubbed his eyes. It was dark in here, under the tarpaulin; just a flapping corner of light at the end of the pickup showed dust and road and paddy fields disappearing as they motored north.

He thought of his mother. Dying and smiling. How had she died? He didn't want to think about it. He thought of the demon heads, the women in the frieze staring down at him as they hid at the dark center of Preah Kahn. He thought of Sonisoy, screaming. Everyone was dying now, it was day zero, year zero, they were clearing the city of his life; people were just falling in the gutter of Sisovath Boulevard. Soon they would blow up the bank.

A rattle turned his daydreams into lucidity. The tarpaulin was flung back. The driver was standing there.

"Anlong Veng."

The driver motioned: *climb out.*

Tentatively, Jake rubbed his muscles as he walked away from the pickup. The sun was less hot now. They were in the main square of some tiny impoverished town where boys played volleyball in the middle of the dusty road.

Chemda was on maneuvers already: paying off the driver, and talking to another, younger man in a faded red Klang Beer T-shirt.

She turned and explained to Jake: "We can rest here." She gestured down a shady lane that led to a kind of promontory. "This man is Rittisak, he will help us."

"But—" Jake stared around. Some guys were drinking palm wine at a wooden shack a few meters away, looking curiously at the muddied Khmer princess and the scruffed-up sweating white man. "Are we safe here?"

"We are safe here. This is Anlong Veng, the Thai border is on top of those hills there, the Dangrek Escarpment, Chong Sa crossing. This is the last place the Khmer Rouge ruled, until 1998."

"OK."

"The locals hated the Khmer Rouge so much they still hate everyone, the police, the customs—if we are outlaws that makes us their friends—we are safe here, well, for a few hours, but then"—she looked at Jake's face—"then we move on. As you said. We have to get to Thailand."

Their new friend, Rittisak, was beckoning, his hand turned down, flapping, requesting them to follow. The path led through a

grove of shady trees, past a burned-out Soviet truck, to a large concrete house.

"In here," said Chemda, following Rittisak through a door and
up some steps.

The house was bizarre, empty and furnitureless and still hot from the
day's sun, and it was decorated with amateurish murals, of Angkor Wat
in an idealized jungle setting; Disney-eyed deer were feeding at overly
crystalline lakes, elephants bathed in the sapphire waters, watched by
monkeys so cheerful they looked as though they were drugged.

But what made the house truly bizarre was the view. On three
sides of the almost wall-less house stretched a plain of water shining
red and yellow in the setting sun, with the faint spicy reek of decay
breezing off the waters. Sticking out of the water, like burned arms
and charred fingers, were thousands of dead tree stumps, sometimes
entire dead trees, all black, stricken and ugly. The watery graveyard
of trees extended many miles, sullen and tragic, to a sudden rise of
hills beyond. It looked like a First World War battlefield, like the
Somme or Ypres or Passchendaele—inexplicably flooded, and set
beneath a decrepit tropical sun.

"What the fuck is that?"

Rittisak bade them sit down. They sat. Jake asked again: about the
view, the peculiar lake.

Chemda explained, quietly, as the sun folded its cards behind the
Dangrek Hills.

"This was Ta Mok's house."

"The Khmer Rouge leader?"

Chemda nodded, rubbing the mud from her hands on her skirt.

"Look at me. Filthy. Yes, Ta Mok, the Butcher—Pol Pot's friend—
the only man crueler than Pol Pot."

"And that . . . fucking graveyard over there, the lake?"

"They call it the Butcher's Lake. Because Ta Mok made it. In the last years of the Khmer Rouge, when they ruled this final corner of Cambodia, Ta Mok had the peasants dam a river and build this lake, an artificial lake, but it went wrong, it just killed the trees, killed everything."

"Why?"

"They say he did it to bury all the corpses. Even to the very end, the Khmer Rouge were slaughtering people, they killed many thousands of peasants around here, and, ah, locals say that the remains are out there, concealed under the waters, poisoning the waters, forever."

Chemda sat back. Her hands behind her, she was talking with Rittisak, and frowning. She explained: "Rittisak says that to get across the border we have to move tonight. In the dark."

"Good idea."

"But there's only one route, only one way to avoid checkpoints." She stared outward, at the watery desolation, and nodded. "Yes. We have to go that way. It's the only way. It's dangerous."

"No."

"Yes. We have to get across the lake."

26

Quelques spéculations sur les origines de culpabilité et de conscience dans les grottes paléolithiques de France et d'Espagne.

Sitting in the darkened apartment, Julia thought, deeply. This was the title to Ghislaine's essay, the essay that was sought by the killer.

"Some Speculations on the Origins of Guilt and Conscience in the Paleolithic Caves of France and Spain."

What did it mean? What did it imply? What was he thinking?

The origins of guilt?

The others talked, quietly. She didn't notice any of this. She didn't notice Rouvier standing pensively at the window, she didn't notice Alex murmur a question then disappear into the kitchen—because she was remembering the sensation she had felt by the stones, the Cham des Bondons.

Guilt. She had felt some kind of guilt. Mournful guilt. And now she had this clue; for all the horrors of her experience in the archives, she possessed a clue. Maybe there *was* a link between the skulls and the murders—*and maybe the cave paintings, too?* And if there was a link, it was something deep and serious, it had to be. She could sense the outlines of something, in a tactile way; she was like a blind person touching an abstract bronze sculpture. Art. Bones. Wounded skulls.

A part of her thrilled at her discovery, even as she shriveled at the memory of the killer. Plunging the knife at her eye.

Officer Rouvier was nodding again. Light, softly filtered by the half-closed blinds of the Carmichaels' Marais apartment, was making subtle stripes across his kindly face. Like a man behind horizontal bars.

Maybe they were all behind metaphorical bars, Julia thought, quite suddenly: they'd been hiding in here for forty-eight hours, barely daring to visit the boulangerie. Policemen had come and gone, interviews had been taken and recorded, but Julia and Alex had been stuck here, in a darkened apartment, together and isolated.

Alex came into the room from the kitchen, clutching his third mug of tea; he sat on the sofa, saying nothing. Rouvier gestured at the sheet of paper with the essay title carefully written thereon. *The essay that had, for some unknown reason, disappeared.*

"Miss Kerrigan. Can you explain it to me, briefly? Recall that I am a humble detective from the farthest provinces. A *péquenaud*." He smiled, charmingly. "I may not understand complicated science. How does your new theory connect with this *missing* article by Quoinelles?" The smile faded. "And all the murders?"

Julia offered a pinched smile of her own. "As I said, I don't have a theory. Just ideas. First you have to know a little bit about the evolution of the human mind."

"Of course."

"*Behavioral modernity* is a term used by some scientists to express the idea that humans made"—Julia glanced at Alex, then back at Rouvier—"a kind of Great Leap Forward in their cognition and cultural development around forty thousand years ago."

Rouvier asked, "Evidenced how?"

"Well, firstly, the birth of art—the cave paintings. But there are other signs at this time of humans suddenly changing their behavior, signs of advanced and abstract cognition. Hunting becomes much more elaborate and efficient—animals are corralled and herded over cliffs, showing significant forethought. Music and game-playing emerge, refined bone tools are manufactured, barter is seen between tribes; and religious rituals become complex, including proper burials. All these behaviorisms sharply differentiate *Homo sapiens* from previous hominid forms, such as *Homo erectus* or *Homo neanderthalis.* Basically, the idea is that we quite suddenly became fully human around forty thousand years ago."

"Why did this change happen?"

"Two main perspectives. One is a sudden genetic mutation in human DNA, another is an actual change to neural structures of the brain, evolution of the brain itself. Maybe in the frontal cortex! No one is sure."

The sounds of the Paris traffic filtered into the quiet apartment.

"And you believe Professeur Ghislaine was investigating this?"

"Perhaps yes. Surely, yes. Just look at his essay title. '*Guilt and Conscience in the Paleolithic Caves of France and Spain.*' We also know he was interested in the trepanned skulls: his very first work, as a student, was done in Lozère, where he probably encountered the theories of Prunières and—and we know Annika was an expert on the cave art of Lascaux and Gargas—"

Rouvier raised a hand. "You are referring to the skulls you found in your caverns, and the same skulls, and damaged bones, found by Pierre-Barthélemy Prunières a hundred years ago, in the same region?

"Sure, but—"

"And because this Prunières mentions Cochin China, you believe that, somehow, this ties it all in to the murders . . . by a Cambodian, a possibly Asian killer. Yes?"

"Yes." Julia felt herself blushing. She was slightly angry at herself: she should be advocating her ideas better than this.

Rouvier sighed. "But. I am still a little unclear. How are they tied together?"

"I don't know—but I know they are! They must be! *I just haven't worked it out yet.*" She stopped, with a stammer. Why was she almost shouting? Why was she so histrionic?

The apartment was quiet. Alex was looking at the slatted windows, a faint trace of embarrassment on his English face.

Julia felt, absurdly, like she had failed Rouvier, the way she had once disappointed her father; but she also felt an injustice. She couldn't piece together the lost essay just like that, she needed time, and clues, and maybe luck. And given enough time, she might prove she was right. Because she was right. She was energized by this idea: *I am right.*

Not only was she right, she was surely just repeating someone else's excellent analysis. Ghislaine's. Indeed, she even felt a slight resentment that Ghislaine had got there so long *before* her: she had thought herself so insightful, that day on the Cham, sensing the guilt in the past, the stones, the bones, yet Ghislaine, it seemed, had been there already—*the origins of guilt and conscience?*—and he had maybe achieved a much smarter, deeper, older explanation. Something that circuitously led to his death?

Maybe. But how could she explain this series of hunches and guesses to a sober and practical policeman? She couldn't.

Rouvier was standing. He walked to the long windows of the eighteenth-century apartment and pulled down a few slats of the modern gray blinds, looking out at the softly rumbling traffic. He spoke to the window: "I do not know. I am not a Tarot reader of ancient times. It is a fascinating idea but I am not sure how it helps us."

Julia subdued the last of her enthusiasm. She felt mortified, almost scorned; Rouvier was just being his normal self: polite, charming, sensitive. Yet it was as if her parents were in the room, pouring kind but skeptical cold water over her teenage dreams of a serious archaeological career. Inside her was the old rage at being patronized.

"However," Rouvier added, "there is one aspect . . . Hmmm . . . I wonder . . ."

"Wonder *what?*"

"The fact that this essay disappeared. This is interesting, and maybe relevant." He turned and faced her directly. "You say that the article is mentioned in, if I have the word, bibliographies—it is referenced and indexed? Correct?"

Quickly, she answered, "Yep. The essay was only ever published in one magazine, an extremely obscure academic journal. There might only have been a couple hundred copies ever printed. But all these copies have gone! Not in the libraries. Taken and not returned, maybe destroyed. Weird . . . is that weird?" She was unsure of herself now.

Rouvier was sitting down again. "No. It *is* unusual. And, as I say, it possibly relates to something else we have discovered."

Alex spoke, for the first time: "What?"

Rouvier smiled. "Exactly how old was Ghislaine Quoinelles when he wrote this?"

"Twenty-two."

"*Oui.* And already he was being published in academic journals, no matter how obscure. We know he was building quite a reputation, a famous radical. And yet, soon after this, his career *dwindled*. He went to Cambodia, he returned to France, and he promptly disappeared into obscurity, back to where he came from, where he did his student work, the caves of Lozère—and there he stayed. Despite the dazzling promise of his early career, it all dwindled away."

"Yep," Alex interrupted. "And he never told me—or Julia—about any of this. The essay, I mean. And Annika never mentioned it. It's like he suppressed it, denied its existence. Denied his past. Rather odd."

Rouvier hunched forward, his flecks of gray hair almost silver in the fading light. "But maybe not that odd? Or at least not unique." He reached into his briefcase and lifted out a piece of paper with a photo. Julia recognized it immediately. The same poignant photo of the mission to China and Kampuchea in 1976. That gallery of smiling young faces, in the hot Phnom Penh sun, with the queerly empty boulevards in the background.

The detective waved an eloquent hand across the photo.

"We have now completed our investigations into these people. They were scattered across the world. Yet they share two things, apart from their membership of this mission."

"Yes?"

"Many of the careers, of these men and women, subsided after this Asian adventure. They were very bright young people, of course Marxists"—he said the word with a definite moue of repugnance—"but nonetheless clever. Future stars of science, if the English phrase is suitable? Yet so many of them appear to have deliberately returned to obscurity after 1976. Strange."

Alex interjected. "You said they shared two things? What was the other?"

Rouvier's sigh was abrupt, yet emotive.

"It took us several days to follow up their careers and life stories, because of that obscurity, and because they had dispersed so globally. But, the truth is, we are too late."

"Sorry?"

"They are nearly all dead. Already."

Julia asked: "You mean . . . they were murdered? Like Trewin and Annika?"

Rouvier's gray eyes met hers.

"Most of them. Possibly. Yes. The older ones died naturally. Many of them appeared to have committed suicide, but now we think—we estimate—that if we look again at these suicides they might turn out to be murders. And some have just been clearly and plainly *butchered*. Over the last three years. Therefore, after much investigation, our foremost guess is that the killer has been slowly slaughtering the rest, working her way through a list, probably a list she extracted from Trewin, by torture. She has been taking revenge, gradually, over the last three years." Another short sigh. "Of course, no one noticed a pattern before, partly because this mission to Cambodia was so secretive that no one knew of the historic links between the victims, and because the murders were subtle, often disguised as self-murder. And anyway, who would associate the suicide of an elderly psychologist in Los Angeles with the tragic death of, say, a sixty-five-year-old archaeologist in Geneva eighteen months later? But now, now we do see the pattern. A vivid pattern."

"Is anyone left alive?"

"We have failed to trace two people. We know, naturally, about Marcel Barnier, the expert in hybridization. He is also apparently in the Far East, or at least he was until recently—we have reports of him in Cambodia itself a few months ago."

Rouvier pointed a manicured fingernail at a second figure in the photo. Julia leaned to see a tall, smiling blond face in the back row of the photo, with a ponytail. A Hawaiian shirt. Arrogantly smiling. "This man, Colin Fishwick, may also still be alive. A neurosurgeon from Princeton, he moved to Hong Kong in the 1980s. We don't know where he is now, but we have no record of his dying."

Rouvier sat back. "So there it is. Just two men left. The killer will evidently seek them out. And kill them, too, if she can find them; then her task will assuredly be complete."

Alex said, "Why did she kill the archivist? And attack Julia?"

"A most sensible question. Probably just a *reaction,* the fear that she had been recognized, a sudden desire to silence a witness. This is a violent killer, very violent: there are elements of extreme cruelty in some of the later killings alongside clever forethought. It is as if the killer is getting angrier as time passes, or maybe she is allowing herself to take more *brutal* revenge, to use more animal savagery, as she nears the completion of her task."

Julia noticed the deliberate phrasing.

"Animal?"

Rouvier nodded and smiled, this time rather bleakly. "Ah yes, Miss Kerrigan. Perhaps you have elucidated this for yourself?"

She shrugged. She knew where this was going, but she didn't want to articulate it. The idea was too insane.

Rouvier was less bashful.

"This may all sound incredible, I know. But given all the other information we now possess, it seems very possible that we are dealing with some experimental form of . . . hybridization. Or maybe some experiments at a higher anatomical level, maybe even neurological? Hence the simultaneous interest in cranial surgery? How *else* do we comprehend the links with Ghislaine's grandfather, the crossbreeding experiments? It all seems too rich to be coincidence." The suavity returned. "Perhaps I am reading too much science fiction, perhaps my theories are becoming as florid as the novels they sell in Carrefour. Who knows?"

Rouvier swept up the photo and slid it back into his briefcase. The traffic noise from the street was more noticeable now: rush hour had arrived.

"*La circulation!* I must go. Before I depart I can relieve you of some minor burdens." He glanced at Alex, then at Julia. The room was dark now: a late November twilight was falling swiftly outside. "We have no more need of you, at least for the moment. You are surely not on the killer's list. You do not need protection. I can also understand if you wish to leave France, after the horrors"—he looked at Julia, piercingly—"all the horrors that you have experienced. If so, the Gendarmerie de France will not resist, though I would like it if you let me know where you go, if you go. We will need you as witnesses at some point. But for now—*au revoir.*"

They shook hands. The room was very dark. When the officer was gone Julia turned on a lamp and poured herself and Alex some glasses of dark scotch whiskey, and they sat alone and silent on the sofa for several hours, drinking slowly, occasionally cuddling or kissing, saying nothing.

But when they went to bed, Julia could not sleep. Instead she lay there, watching the filtered shadows cast by the moving car lights outside, watching them slide quietly across the ceiling. Like the shadows on the wall of a cave, cast by a timid firelight. Fearful shadows, images of animals, frightening shades.

The next morning was wet and dreary, the sky a true Parisian *grisaille.* Julia didn't feel like doing anything or going anywhere. The puzzle wasn't even half solved. And she felt desolate. Emptied. Unsatisfied. She sat down on the sofa and stared at nothing and didn't even eat breakfast. Finally, she retreated to her laptop. Research. She had nothing else to do. She was a scientist. She could *research.*

But there was almost nothing to go on, just her own hunches and guesswork and wildly ambitious intuitions, and she was frankly bored with them. How about hard facts?

The one fact she had was this essay title, and the name of the obscure magazine. The *Journal of French Anthropogenesis.* The magazine was long defunct, and many of its editions had disappeared from this earth—but maybe she could find out more about the magazine itself.

An hour of furious key-tapping gave her an answer. One of the editors of the journal was mentioned in another obscure journal in the footnotes of a French government website. The trail of connections was flimsy, attenuated, and Julia had the peculiar notion she was grasping at a cobweb, a network of ephemerality that could disappear with a single, too-eager touch. But a network of connections, nonetheless.

The name of this editor was intriguing. He was called Sergei Yakulovich; and he was apparently a senior editor of the *Journal of French Anthropogenesis* when Ghislaine submitted his essay.

And who was Sergei Yakulovich? The name was Russian.

The same website gave her a brief but piercingly relevant biography.

Sergei Yakulovich: a Soviet primatologist who for many years studied at Lomonosov State University, specializing in the relationship of human brains to primate brains.

Julia's eyes were alive with excitement.

There was more: *Since 1979 Sergei Yakulovich has been director of the Center for Primate Research in Abkhazia, Georgia; controversially, the center is best known for its experiments into crossbreeding between primates and Homo sapiens.*

The revelation was a physical sensation, a slap across the face. This guy was running a center that *still did research into crossbreeding. Between men and animals.* The editor of the magazine that published Ghislaine's essay was *still alive. Still out there. Still working. Still contactable.* In Abkhazia, in the insurrectionist wilds on the periphery of the broken Soviet Union, by the Black Sea.

Julia's troubled and excited mind flew across the world to this place. She tried to imagine it; she failed. She looked back at the screen. The website even gave an e-mail address for Sergei Yakulovich. In Abkhazia!

She knew she was going to contact him. As soon as possible. Because: Maybe he had a copy of the essay? Maybe he knew all the answers? And his career—human-primate hybridization—fitted the features of the puzzle too well. It *had* to be relevant.

But she also had to be clever. She couldn't just e-mail and ask this Yakulovich guy straight out. Maybe if she did that, he would say nothing, pull down the shutters, thwart her one viable route through the maze. So maybe she could even *go there*. To Abkhazia. Why not? She just about had the money and she certainly had the time—and maybe she now had the ambition, even the confidence—after resisting the killer in the archives. And she had nothing else to do—the idea of now going home to London, retreating to teaching and winter and the quotidian pointlessness of her failing career, seemed ludicrous. Not after all this.

Alex wandered into the room. He was munching a croissant and carrying an unread copy of *Le Monde.*

"Morning, sweetheart?"

"Morning," she said.

"Hey. Are you OK?"

She nodded. "Yes, sure, yes."

As she watched him sit and not really read the paper, she knew her answer: she was probably going to do all this alone. She'd had enough of men patronizing her. Her father. Her boss in London. Even Alex was embarrassed by her wild ideas; even Rouvier was very charmingly unpersuaded. All the men in her life, from Dad to Ghislaine, they had scoffed, or condescended, or both—even when they meant well. Now she would show them all—and prove herself. Earn and demand their respect.

"Shall I make some more coffee?" Alex asked.

"Yep," she said. "Coffee would be good."

27

He didn't dare look down. He didn't want to look across, or behind him, or anywhere. He could feel the silt, or maybe something less acceptable, between his toes. A persistent cold breeze froze into him. Moonlight sheened the waveless water, silhouetting the black dead trees against the deadening silver.

The Butcher's Lake. They were a third of the way across; already it was long past midnight.

"Here."

He reached out a hand for Chemda. She had slipped in the rotting mud.

"Thanks."

Jake hauled her up onto a kind of island, with its one requisite black spar of dead tree. A large white night bird, alarmed by their arrival, flapped away into the depths of sky, toward the silent tropical stars. The whiteness of the beating wings dwindled into dark.

Rittisak glanced back at his charges as they squatted on the mud bank, regaining some energy. His dark face was fathomless in the gloomy moonlight.

"It's taken us two hours already," Jake said to the Khmer, who shrugged. "How much longer?"

"No English, no English."

Jake pointed to his wrist, where a watch might be if he hadn't taken it off. "I said . . ."

But he said nothing: he gave up. He turned to Chemda to translate. She was barefoot and smeared with mud to the knee—but they were all barefoot and smeared with mud, indeed Jake was muddy to the *shoulder*. He had already slipped over once as they tried to ford the expanse of water, nearly collapsing into deeper grayness, splashing noisily, making the night birds clack and disperse in agitation, making Rittisak frown and whisper and put an urgent finger to his elegant Khmer lips: *shhhhh!*

At Jake's request, Chemda translated. Rittisak answered. She translated again.

"Just another three hours, ah, more or less. He says the next bit is the worst . . . then it should get easier, shallower, I think."

They rose and slid down the mud of the islet shore, and Jake girded himself for his near-submersion. The cold cringed into his ankles with a sensation of sickliness, like sudden gangrene. He wasn't sure if he was imagining it, this definite feeling of viscosity to the water, this cold and unpalatable oiliness. Perhaps he was just spooked by those stories of bodies dumped here, drowned here, the Butcher's thousands, cached underwater, like Ta Mok had been some kind of human crocodile, storing food.

The tiredness washed over him as they followed Rittisak's delicate path, picking the shallowest route through the deceptive waters, the chilling wide swamps. He gazed, half-dreaming, at these strange black-and-white night birds, raptors, vulturesque, posed on so many trees. Did they feed off the corpses? Was that why they roosted here?

Chemda slipped again, and he reached out to steady her. He wondered if he loved her.

The trudge continued. It was a hypnotically repetitive process:

wait for Rittisak to seek his path through the quagmire, then follow his footsteps exactly, then lean against a poisoned tree, then turn and make sure Chemda was OK.

Then repeat.

They were halfway across now. When he leaned against the next dead tree, Jake looked behind and squinted in the moon-tarnished darkness; he could see Ta Mok's house, back there, on the dry ground. What must the Butcher have felt? Sitting there in his concrete villa with the stupid paintings, looking at this reservoir of death that he had decreed? Where the ospreys fed on the fish and the flesh, carrying the carrion of his victims to the distant kapoks on the Dangrek Escarpment? A sliver of wind goosefleshed the water around him. Another bird streaked the bleak whiteness of the moon, then disappeared.

It was three or four a.m. But was it really? How long to dawn? Was that the first skein of silvery blue on the far horizon? Maybe it was just some dismal Cambodian town staining the sky with its naked lights hung on stark concrete poles.

Rittisak was talking and pointing. Chemda came up close and held Jake's muddy hand as she listened. She explained:

"Says it's, ah, the last kilometer, we go that way, then we can climb the hills—some of this is deep—we need to be careful. But we are nearly there."

Nearly there, they had *nearly made it.* Jake's spirits surged with hope as they waded the greasy cold water. Soon they would be climbing up the hills, then they could rest in the dry, warm shelter of the forest, then it was an easy slip across the border, and then: safety! After all the terrors came Thailand. And trains and telephones and a talk with Tyrone. Jake yearned to be in Thailand, to be in a country that was not haunted by two million ghosts, a country that wasn't one giant *neak ta,* one giant spirit house, with more specters than citizens.

The waters oiled between his legs, making a silver-and-rainbow coil in the moonshine. Jake stared down, absorbed.

A face was staring up at him.

He lurched, swayed. And reached out a hand for a branch of black wood.

"Are you OK?"

"I'm fine."

He lied. He was sure he'd seen a face, a kind of face, a skull, a skull with flesh on it, bobbing momentarily. Or had he? Jake had no time to sort the nightmares from reality. It was all a nightmare. Now he could hear a fat sudden noise behind him. A splashing angry noise, coming close. The trees were denser here, the moon was partly clouded, the light was so poor: Was it someone pursuing them, or some animal?

He didn't know who panicked first. Chemda maybe, maybe even Rittisak. But they panicked, all three of them. From the obedient procession of the last four hours, suddenly they were all running, or trying to run, wading the waters of a childhood nightmare, unable to progress, yet still running, slipping, gasping.

"I'm stuck!"

He reached behind and grasped her hand and tugged; the ooze clutched at her, lecherously; but then the mud yielded—and she was free, and shuddering, and waving him on. The splashing behind them was louder. They struggled forward. But now, all around them, the water was roiled, like a saucepan coming to the boil.

With a scum floating on the surface.

Jake fought his urge to give up, to go back, to do anything but *this*. Chased by the splashing, they were wading through *bodies,* or at least floating bones. Shin bones. Human arms and femurs. The lake was brimming with dismembered cadavers, floating like sad and small gray logs, brought to the surface by the disturbance.

The victims of Ta Mok.

The smell was an abomination. No wonder the night birds roosted here: the shrikes and the ravens. Ospreys. Fish vultures. Butcher-birds. Despair and denial mixed with Jake's revulsion, and his fear, but they had to keep wading, escaping whatever pursued them.

And now the moon shone down—on a tiny ripple of hope. Jake squinted, and yearned. They were *nearly there:* the hapless attempt at a shoreline where the artificial lake met the artificial beach. Rittisak was *already* up on the shore, reaching out; Jake caught the hand and was assisted onto dry land; behind him, Chemda raced up, spitting and shivering. She squatted on the black soil and she swiveled.

The moon broke the clouds, once more, revealing their pursuer: *just a water buffalo.* Halted angrily in the water, amid the floating bones. A gray image in the lighter grayness.

Rittisak clapped his hands. The buffalo snorted contemptuously, then turned and waded away.

For a moment they sat panting, and trembling, and rubbing the mud from their hands and feet as best they could, using leaves and ferns. They all coughed the filthy water from their mouths. Still no one spoke. Chemda seemed on the verge of tears, but as ever she strangled them at birth. Manfully.

A religious silence ruled. Total silence, *omerta.* Maybe, Jake thought, what they had witnessed was *beyond* conversation, simply too harrowing to discuss. Maybe they would never mention this again. Not to anyone, not to each other, not for as long as they breathed.

"Climb," said Chemda. "We have to climb."

28

"Let's go."

The climb began. It was sharp and prickly, but it was dry, and better than their ghastly course across the Butcher's reservoir. Roots ripped his hands. Chemda held on to Jake's arms. Rittisak was a sherpa of nimbleness, choosing rocks as footholds, helping them up, adeptly pointing at branches they could use to ascend. Jake wondered why Rittisak was so assiduous in his assistance: the villagers here were much friendlier than in so many other places. Maybe they just hated authority, like Chemda had said, and a couple of outlaws, like he and Chemda, appealed to their rebel spirit.

Ten strenuous and sweaty minutes later they were on top of the cliff, near a concrete shack. The moon shone on more dead trees, burned trees; maybe slashed and burned by the swidden farmers. There was a definite sense of dawn in the air, a virginal stirring, as birds timidly chirruped.

Jake said, "We need to rest a few hours, Chemda. Tell Rittisak?"

The two Khmers spoke Khmer. Jake saw Rittisak shrug, uncomfortably, then accede. *OK. Sleep here.* Jake lay down at once—right inside the fetid concrete shack. His rucksack was a pillow. Chemda lay beside him and sleep came at once, like a kidnapper, hooding him brutally. Darkness.

He didn't care. He slept and he dreamed as he knew he would dream: he dreamed of bodies and faces drowned underwater; he dreamed of his mother like a mermaid, his sister, too, the lost women underwater, sighing and singing, sirenic, disinterred, waving their pale limbs, beckoning.

He woke to blazing patches of sun on the ground, shaped by the small concrete windows. Eight a.m., maybe. Jake suppressed his shivers of simultaneous heat and cold. And then the juddering memory of the lake returned, and his anxieties spiraled. He felt feverish. Could this get any worse? What was happening to him? He felt an overwhelming urge to see the picture of his sister one more time. But where was it?

He recalled: buttoned in his breast pocket, where he'd secreted it during the long truck journey from Siem Reap. Fumbling for his pocket, he reached for the photo. But the pocket was unbuttoned. It had come undone. The photo was gone. Slipped away, or washed away, no doubt, when they were wading the lake. Only shreds of moist paper remained. She had dissolved in the water. His family had finally dissolved.

It was difficult to fight the emotions, the keening loss. Yet he tried. But even as he fought the grief, the chilly possibility slit open his thoughts. The possibility he had been ignoring for days—yet not quite avoiding. And this final slice of grief tipped him into speculation. Abject, degraded speculation.

Was he *cursed*? Had he been cursed by the spider witch?

This was, of course, ridiculous. He was a rationalist, a materialist, the most convinced of atheists. He wasn't scared of death, of ghosts, of vampires or God or gravestones or hell. He despised and rejected the absurd and clattering parade of *human religion and superstition*.

And yet, despite his anger, he couldn't wipe away the sensation, the creeping and ridiculous idea. That ghastly witch, the nouveau crone in her sequined turquoise jumper, with the black spider excrement in her chewing black mouth—maybe she really had done it: cursed him, cast a terrible spell. Bad luck, evil luck, was pursuing him like a feral dog. And now he had lost the photo. Lost his sister all over again.

The sun shone brightly through the little window.

Chemda was awake. She was standing and dressed, and listening to Rittisak. He was talking quickly in Khmer—and his utterance made her blanch, visibly.

"Pol Pot's house," she said, and her face was trembling. "My God, we are in Pol Pot's old house. Where he spent his last years. Sometimes tourists come here. Ah. God . . . Of all the places. We have to go."

She was obviously shaken. They needed to leave at once. Jake doused his face with bottled water, slung on his socks and boots, then he and Chemda helped each other with the rucksacks and shared a brief, silent kiss, and they walked into the jungle.

There was still a deathliness to the area. This was not the vibrant, overly fecund jungle of Angkor Wat. Patches of burned or dead vegetation dotted the forest. Birds sang: apologetically, and uncertainly. Or maybe Jake was imagining it. He hoped he was imagining it, just as he wanted to believe he had imagined the skulls and skeletons in the water, the jaunty flotsam of genocide.

Two hours and five kilometers of jungle pathway found them in the outskirts of a village. Rittisak looked more relaxed in the sunlight. His job was close to completion. He pointed one way and talked and then pointed another way.

Chemda turned: "He says the main road is just there, so we must be careful, but the Chong Sa crossing is also very close, we just have to hack through this last field . . . take the path, along a ravine, get across the frontier."

They slipped down the ravine, but the route was confusing, it forked several times. At one point it led them to a clutch of houses, the busy road to Thailand taking them horribly close to danger; but another turning seemed to head for the wilds, toward that unguarded and very wooded border a few kilometers east.

They walked away from the houses, sweating, silent, and scared. Burned trees lined the narrow lane. And then the path widened to a clearing.

Everyone halted.

In the center of the scruffy clearing was a small linear hump of soft mud, surrounded by a wire fence. A low and rusty iron roof protected the mud from the rains and the sun.

Rittisak was pointing.

"Pol Pot grave! Where they burn body. Dump him!"

Jake stared, dumbfounded. This was the grave of the dictator? *Pol Pot's grave?* It was poignantly rudimentary. It could have been the lyrically humble grave of a great poet, a pauper's grave for a neglected genius—and then, Jake thought, maybe it *was* just that: the Mozart of death was buried here, this was the grave of an eerie prodigy, an autistic savant, a grinning mediocrity who somehow killed, murdered, his own country.

Offerings had been placed next to the grave. Some incense sticks were burning, planted in a sand-filled jar of instant *tom yum* noodles. Red apples shriveled beside a pile of silver coins. And next to the grave was a wooden spirit house: someone had actually installed a wooden shrine to honor the dead shade of Pol Pot. Jake moved close and saw: inside the wooden house were two dolls, Mr. and Mrs. Pol Pot. Jake marveled.

Rittisak was speaking. Chemda interpreted:

"He says people come here to pray, to, ah, seek help from the spirit of Pol Pot. The shrine was erected by some Thai guy. He won the lottery after praying to Pol Pot's ghost. Hey. Do you think I am allowed to piss on this grave? Ah, are women allowed to do that, or is it just a guy thing? Anyway, please—let's move."

He had never heard Chemda speak coarsely before; she barely ever swore. Chemda turned away from the grave in disgust.

But Jake lingered. He was impressed by the florid paradox of the scene: the grave of a lunatic and atheist dictator, the man who murdered monks and pulled down temples, the man who didn't just hate God but tried to stamp God into the dust—the grave of this unbeliever had been turned into a shrine, a place of superstitious worship where peasants prayed to a Communist ghost, a Marxist deity; it was the most perfect irony, quite sumptuous. It *had* to be recorded.

Almost reflexively, Jake took out his camera from his rucksack and aimed the lens.

Rittisak was edgy and fidgeting. Chemda was anxiously gesturing: "Come on, Jake, quick, we need to go!"

"Just a couple more shots, wait, just a few more."

He knelt in the dust and grabbed some images, just a couple more. Raising his tiny camera to get a wider shot, he stepped back; then he looked at the digital image and realized he hadn't properly framed the four soldiers who had just walked into the clearing with guns.

The four soldiers with guns, who were now aiming them at Jake and Chemda and Rittisak.

"Chemda," he whispered.

Way too fucking late. How stupid was this? How stupid had he been? So quickly, so easily: they had been captured. The soldiers were smiling, and laughing, waving those guns. One was snapping orders, triumphant. Shouting in Jake's face.

Jake reeled at his own idiocy. His rasping stupidity. It was his fault.

If they hadn't lingered for him to take the photos, the soldiers might not have overheard them, marched off the road, and found them at the stupid little grave.

Rittisak had a gun pointed to his head. Chemda likewise. Jake felt the numbness of defeat. He allowed himself to be handcuffed. Everyone was handcuffed. The soldiers were arguing. Smiling and laughing—yet arguing. The youngest soldier handcuffed them all in brisk and ruthless silence. The apparent captain shouted his order. The youngest soldier shrugged and shook his head.

Again the soldiers argued. The captain pointed, with a metal bar in his hand—he was giving it to the younger soldier and barking his harsh Khmer sentences as he did. A metal bar? In a lonely clearing? Chemda was covering her face with frightened hands.

The revelation came to Jake like the flush of a sudden and terrible sickness. *The soldiers were deciding whether to kill them.*

A bird sang melodiously somewhere. It was done. The soldier saluted. The arguing ended. Jake could hear a car on the road, and a radio, and a cockerel crowing the tropical morning. He could smell cooking, he could smell woodsmoke and forest and sunbaked garbage.

This is how it happens, he thought. Not with choirs or angels or poetry, but with the smell of garbage.

Chemda tried to speak; the soldiers ignored her. They pushed Rittisak to his knees, making him buckle and kowtow. They kicked Jake to his knees, too: a foot brutally stamped the back of his legs so he crumpled into a praying position, supplicant in the sunny dust, praying by Pol Pot's grave.

The smell of garbage.

He twisted to see Chemda. She was being led to the side, like she was special. Jake knew, with a shudder of quiet despair, precisely how his death was going to happen. He'd been to the killing fields of

Cheung Ek. This is how they did it. This is how the Khmer Rouge slaughtered their countless victims, with a primitive and simple efficiency. Make them kneel down, swing the iron bar, crush the skull from behind. Next, please. *Why waste a bullet on death?*

He could hear Chemda crying now, heavily. The soldiers murmured. The decision had been made, so they were just doing their job. Rittisak was staring at the sky. Jake stared at Pol Pot's grave. The incense was still burning. A trail of ants led from the brushwood to the shriveled apples, to an empty bottle of chili sauce.

The soldier approached with a rusty iron bar, a car axle, maybe. He was going to swing the bar and bash out their brains. Jake closed his eyes, waiting to die. Chemda sobbed in the darkness of his mind. He could hear the man giving orders. Yes, that's it, kill them now. The world devolved to a still, silent point in the singularity of his life: here at the end of his life, he thought of his sister, and laughter, and his mother, and sadness, and Chemda, and Mama Brand Instant Rice Noodles gently rotting in the sun.

29

Monkey lab, thought Julia, what's that in Russian? Didn't she write that down somewhere?

Grabbing her notebook, she turned to the middle-aged man with broken, taped-together wire-rimmed spectacles, standing in the desolate, carless parking lot of Sukhumi railway station.

"Obez . . . yanii pitomnik."

The man nodded. *"Da! Obez'yanii pitomnik."* His nylon shirt was greasy, his chin unshaven, his tie stained. His helpful smile was keen.

The man was pointing down the road. Julia followed his gesture with a reflux of dismay: the streets in front of the station were potholed and syphilitic, the sidewalks cracked and weed-sprouted. This town seemed to be like every other town on this polluted eastern shore of the Black Sea, decaying, smelly, depressed, half destroyed by recent wars of irredentism and secession. A post-Communist, ex-Soviet statelet at its worst.

"Da!" The man pointed, once again: his hand firm and vigorous, his fingernails dirty. He seemed to be telling her to go straight, then right, then up a hill. *"Obez'yanii pitomnik!"*

"Spasibo," said Julia, putting away her notebook, quickly walking on.

The weariness was lurking. She was very tired from the flight from Paris to Moscow, the flight from Moscow to Adler, and the train down the gray-drizzled waters of the Black Sea littoral. But Julia was nearing her goal, so a surge of adrenaline was masking that tiredness. She walked quickly into the town.

The subtropical sea port was chilly and dank, and alienating. Julia wished Alex were here. In the end she had decided to tell him what she was doing, and she had been entirely unsurprised when he had declined to join her. He had said, "Sweetheart, you are mad," and had tried to dissuade her, but she wasn't to be dissuaded. And so here she was.

Maybe he was right, she was mad. She was in Abkhazia. Even the destination was mad.

What was she hoping to find? The truth? Yes, the truth no one else would try to uncover, the truth about the skulls, the caves, the bones, the cave art, the truth about Annika's death. Perhaps she would find nothing.

She passed a brace of cafés where women with ugly leggings sat in the grubby windows staring with expressions of grief at their own babies yowling in plastic strollers. A tramp was slumped in the shelter of a broken tram stop plastered with peeling adverts, its glass grimy and cracked. Office blocks that seemed too derelict and window-smashed to be useful nonetheless disgorged workers heading home for the night.

Julia glanced at her watch. Would it still be open? She *so* wanted not to stay here for a night. The place was demonically gloomy and depressing.

No. She had to grasp her fears, defeat them. Remember what the man had said at the station. *Top of the hill.* That's what he said, in Russian. Or had he actually been speaking Georgian? Or Abkhazian? Who knew?

Julia marched on, looking left and right as she did: wary, alone, conspicuous.

The shame of the place, Sukhumi, was that it must once have been pretty: a crude, demotic but nonetheless charming spa resort, a place celebrated in those idealistic Communist summers of fifty years ago, the summers depicted in faded photos of the Khrushchev era, communism under the palm trees, where pasty white Russian workers with their fat, happy wives in big black bathing suits had their four weeks' vacation in the sunny sanatoria of the Black Sea coast, in Yalta and Sochi—and Sukhumi.

Now only the palm trees remained, trees diseased and old, trees dusty and sad, trees shredded by bullets, or trees just dying a slow death in front of a closed Constructivist cinema. Ice-cream stands were shut for the winter. The cold of evening approached.

Her route was taking her straight uphill now, as she collected stares from Slavically pale shoppers and darker Muslim and Georgian faces. She paused on a cracked street corner. A noisome smell was emanating from somewhere. The smell of a badly run zoo?

Her instincts were confirmed. A few yards later she was confronted by a chain-link fence, ripped uselessly in places, and a sign high up on it that said, in several scripts and languages, one of them English: Institute for Experimental Primate Pathology and Therapy.

The gate was open. She went in. Lab workers in dirty white coats passed her as she entered; the staff were leaving the compound, going home for the night, and they gave the better-dressed Western woman a few suspicious glances, and then just apathetic glances.

Julia was alone.

The compound was huge: a large, lush, drizzly, and litter-strewn garden full of dusty cypress trees and rusty metal cages where apes and monkeys sat balding and fidgeting; some of the condemned and neglected creatures had numbers tattooed on their pale shaven chests; little monkeys, with the saddest eyes, stared up at the curious stranger, like neglected children discovered in a terrible orphanage.

Julia remembered the feeling she got when she descended the steel ladder into the Cavern of the Swelling, in the Cham des Bondons. This was similar: a descent, physical, temporal, and moral, into one of the world's darker places. And yet a descent she *wanted* to make. To find out the truth you had to go into the caves.

She passed more cages and enclosures. One contained a pair of forlorn gibbons, another seemed empty—but then she saw, squatting behind a cardboard box, an orangutan, apparently sobbing. A mangy gorilla was hunched in a corner of another cage, next to a pair of wilted chimpanzees, quite inert with unhappiness, smeared with their own filth.

A much smaller cage between these larger enclosures imprisoned a delicate little monkey, a rhesus, maybe. It was screaming and gabbling, running frenziedly from side to side, touching one row of bars then shrieking and running to the other side to touch the bars there, and shrieking again, like it was being electrocuted every time it touched the bars. Half its head had been shaved. It was surrounded by orange peel and scattered grain, and green-yellow pools of urine.

"Jesus," she said to herself, almost brought to tears. "Jesus Jesus Jesus."

This place was disgusting. Why couldn't they just keep the animals clean, or let them go?

For the money? Maybe. She had read in her research that the impoverished Abkhazians made money from it as a zoo in the summer: people came to laugh at the shit-flinging gibbons.

The main door loomed. Julia reminded herself of her persona, constructed for the e-mail exchange with Sergei Yakulovich. She was a top archaeologist, a friend of Ghislaine. She was writing a paper about his career and achievements, following his tragic end. She would be very honored to meet an old colleague of Ghislaine, like the great Yakulovich.

The e-mails had worked to a point, although she had elicited no direct information from the man. But he had eventually, after some persuasion, agreed to a meeting. *If you really wish to know more about my work, come and see me. I am a busy man.*

And so here she was, on the shores of the Black Sea, in a primate lab, in Abkhazia.

A sign seemed to indicate the main entrance. She pressed a big Bakelite bell button and the door opened. A brassy blond secretary with blotchy skin and bad teeth sat in the reception area packing her handbag for the end of the working day; with a friendly shrug at Julia's pitiful attempt at speaking phrasebook Russian, she showed Julia directly into the director's office, a large room with peeling paintwork, a grand wooden desk, two big clumsy telephones, and faded photos and maps on the wall.

The man himself was seated at the desk. Sergei Yakulovich. One-time editor of the *Journal of French Anthropogenesis*. The director of the Institute for Experimental Primate Pathology.

Yakulovich stood as she entered; he smiled shyly and tragically, shook her hand, and swapped pleasantries. His English was good, and he was proud of it. He spoke even better French and German, apparently, as he informed her. He invited her to sit, as he returned to his seat behind his desk. Julia gazed. With his grubby brown suit and wistful face, he looked like a pensionable version of one of his own monkeys.

Julia attempted a question, but she was interrupted by the blond woman with the snaggly teeth—she was carrying a tray with two tulip-shaped glasses of black tea and a saucer of scarlet raspberry jam. The glasses tinkled as they were set down. Sergei Yakulovich tapped his watch and smiled at the receptionist, indicating she could go home at last.

She put on her plastic coat and said goodbye.

They were alone in the primate laboratory. A cold, rainy evening was falling outside.

"So. Shall we begin?" The director was stirring jam into his tea as he spoke. "I am honored by the presence of an esteemed scientist from America. The reason I would not reply to your e-mails in more detail is that we get many mischievous requests. Journalists and so forth. I am not a suspicious man but our science here has been caricatured once too often. But you have the manners to come and visit us. So I shall respond." A tiny, telling pause. "As you can perhaps surmise . . ." His sad old eyes looked briefly at the peeling paint of the room, then through a window, at the Abkhazian dusk. "We are not the place we were. We are not blessed with so many serious scientific visitors these days. Just sightseers, and those who willfully misrepresent our work. Work we are very proud of." He smiled, suddenly, a pip of raspberry jam lodged between his yellow front teeth. "Now. You are writing a paper on my friend Ghislaine Quoinelles? That is correct? Poor Ghislaine. A good colleague. Killed by some . . . madman, I understand? I try to follow the news here, but it is difficult, we have so much to do . . . in our remote little fortress of science!"

"Yes . . ." said Julia, and she paused at the memory of her friends. "So, you see . . . I'm writing about Ghislaine. As I mentioned in the e-mails, I am interested in many aspects of his life. How his research intersected with your work, what made you colleagues. Maybe you could tell us what you have been doing here."

Another monologue ensued. The director had a kind of spiel.

"This was the very first primate testing center in the world. We were once the envy of the West. A thousand scientists worked here at our peak. As you can attest, our behavioral and medical experiments put us at the very forefront of the most groundbreaking medical discoveries. We even trained monkeys for space travel. Look."

The bald director pointed at one black-and-white photo pinned to the wall behind him. The picture showed a pair of fragile, gawky, long-limbed, nervous monkeys strapped into two airline seats, with big grim metal bars to keep them in place. The monkeys wore white headbands giving their names in Cyrillic.

"Yerosha and Dryoma. Early pioneers of Soviet space flight. Yuri Gagarin's direct predecessors!"

His laughter was sad.

"These were the glory days. But then we had . . . *perestroika,* and then the Georgian-Abkhazian war. The soldiers stole primates as mascots, some were killed in crossfire. They nearly destroyed us." He exhaled wistfully. "Most of our scientists fled to set up a new center in Adler, in Russia. Many monkeys were killed. But I prefer to think of happier times."

The director waffled on about the palmy days of the institute, when Ho Chi Minh and Brezhnev and Marshal Zhukov and Madame Mao were regular guests, when the scientists would fly to Texas—in America!—to give lectures to the backward Westerners. Julia found her senses wandering. The smell of monkey shit was detectable even inside the office. The sound of screaming, of that mad little monkey in the farthest cage, was mercifully muffled.

She nudged the dialogue along. "Tell me about the crossbreeding experiments?"

Sergei paused for a moment and stared straight into her eyes, quite disconcertingly; then he continued his apparently well-worn speech.

"*Da.* In the 1920s there was a plan to create a man-ape hybrid. Supposedly this would become a Soviet superman. The news said this . . . in their sensational way—but the truth is Stalin and the politburo just wanted a very reliable worker, with great strength and a less inquiring and distracting intellect, perhaps also a soldier who would be, as it were, devoid of conscience, therefore a better and harder soldier, therefore able to replace real men on the battlefield. Thus we could have saved human lives! The idea was humane."

"I see."

"It was a long time ago, Julia Kerrigan. The tests were conducted, originally, by Ilya Ivanov. You may know of him, eminent Russian biologist. Around 1900 he had perfected the technique of artificially inseminating mares; soon after this he produced crossbreeds between several different species. This is a picture of him here."

Julia stared at the wall: at another black-and-white photo. An old man with a white beard and a white mustache—like Sigmund Freud in his later years—smiled softly back. He had a wise and paternal face.

"Professor Ivanov commenced these experiments in Africa, then in association with Albert Quoinelles, Ghislaine's grandfather, at the Pasteur Institute in Paris. . . . Then the experiments were moved here to Sukhumi."

"How successful were they?"

Yakulovich shrugged and sipped the last of his tea. "He took semen from human males, siphoned or collected from masturbation, and then he injected it into female chimpanzees, although nothing came of that."

Julia repressed a shudder.

"And what then?"

Yakulovich shook his head. A wary expression crossed his face. "This is a very detailed analysis of my work? I thought we were here to discuss Ghislaine?"

"Er, yes, of course." Julia was flustered. "I was coming to that."

The director gazed at her and said, "It is rather curious, yes? Just a year ago another friend of Ghislaine came to visit me."

"Who?"

"Marcel Barnier." His eyes had a certain sly brightness. "Yes, yes, another great French expert on crossbreeding, and a good friend of Ghislaine Quoinelles! Look, I have Barnier's card here, he came to visit us just a year ago, to talk. I knew of him through Ghislaine's work in China and Cambodia."

The director was proudly flourishing Barnier's card. Julia took the card from his hand. She examined it. Her soul was sickening but she was determined to remain calm.

"Do you mind if I write these details down, Mr. Yakulovich? Barnier would be an interesting person for me to talk to. About Ghislaine."

"By all means. Barnier is . . . a very clever man, a very clever man, a veteran like me, determined that the best of Communist science should not be discarded by history along with the less good aspects."

"OK." Julia felt the time had come. "About Ghislaine. There's one particular question I thought you might be able to help with. I mentioned it in the e-mails, but as you say, you needed to meet me to talk."

"And here we are. Please ask."

"The *Journal of French Anthropogenesis*. Do you remember it?"

The director frowned, and shrugged, and said, "Not so much. A little. It was . . . just a . . . small journal, in the late 1960s, sympathetic to our Marxist-Leninist principles."

"But you were the editor!"

"Was I indeed? Aha." Yakulovich's smile was still slightly stained with jam. "Yes, I believe I was the token Soviet! *Da!* I did no real work for them, it was an honorary position. I may have read some of the contributions."

She felt her hopes revive. Tentatively.

"So you might recall a particular essay—something you might have selected, got peer reviewed—by Ghislaine Quoinelles, when he was very young. In the early 1970s. An essay on guilt and conscience?"

A pause. A heartbeat of a pause.

"Well now." Yakulovich sighed. "I don't know. We would have welcomed an essay from Ghislaine Quoinelles, of course, simply because of his name. His patronym? His surname, I mean."

"His grandfather?"

"Yes, yes! Ghislaine was the grandson of Albert Quoinelles, who was a true comrade in arms! A Communist, and also a great scientist, a specialist in our field. So yes, if Ghislaine Quoinelles sent us an essay, maybe we would have read it with interest. This is true." He hesitated, delicately. "But this magazine published many essays, I believe. And . . . I am trying hard, but I am afraid I cannot recall this *particular* essay."

"But—"

"Please! Do not chastise me! I can barely remember my wedding anniversary, as my wife will confirm, let alone an essay written forty years ago. Hah. My friendship with Ghislaine developed later, in the later 1970s." The smile was now entirely mirthless. "So is that it? Is that all you came to ask? It is perhaps a long journey for so few questions."

Julia sensed she was failing. And yet she also sensed, paradoxically, that she was clueing into something. Ghislaine's essay was, for now, a cul de sac. But what was this about Barnier? Marcel Barnier was the man in the photo. Why had he been here?

It seemed the pieces of the puzzle were scattered, but they *were* somewhere here, or hereabouts.

"Mr. Yakulovich, why did Barnier want to talk with you?"

"He wanted to know how far our work had proceeded by the 1970s. We discussed what the Chinese wanted from us, and so forth."

"How far had it gone, your work?"

Yakulovich hesitated, visibly, and the quietness was prolonged. Julia could hear the monkeys, clacking their teeth in their cages outside. The old man glanced at the darkening window and back at his guest. His mouth was shut and his lips were thin. His wisps of remaining gray hair hung lankly to the side, uncombed. But then he shrugged, in a beyond-caring manner.

"Journalists always like to ask about this. Usually I never reply, ever, it is so very controversial. But you are a scientist, a fellow scientist, Julia Kerrigan, I can trust you. You have made the effort of visiting us. I can be much more open, as we are on the same team! *Nyet?* The same side, yes?"

"Yes. Of course."

"And we are also alone now! The laboratory has closed for the day. So let us be frank and open and transparent, as scientist to scientist!" He sipped his tea and grinned. "This is how science proceeds, is it not? The scientific method, the open exchange of data. And I am proud of what we achieved here."

Julia was desperate for him to get on with it. She wanted the truth, she could *feel* the truth near at hand yet obscured, like a shadow passing behind baffled glass.

Picking up and toying with his teaspoon, he continued.

"We had a little more luck with impregnating human females. Eventually."

"Luck?"

"At first there was no success at all, with the artificial insemination of primate sperm into humans. We faced complete failure. So we asked ourselves: Why the failures? We decided that artificial insemination *itself* was part of the problem, that we needed actual coitus to produce viable embryos."

Julia ignored the revulsion inside her; she smiled falsely and asked: "Coitus, you mean actual . . . *sex*?"

"Yes! Intercourse! It is well known that artificial insemination between humans has less chance of producing viable offspring than actual intercourse. We do not know the precise reasons for this, but intercourse acts as an ovarian stimulant, vaginal peristalsis is greater, all sorts of complex chemical and anatomical processes take place in sexual congress that surely aid the successful fertilization of eggs and the creation of viable embryos, so it was speculated that we should try coitus across the primate-human barrier."

She asked, as dryly as possible: "How?"

He set the teaspoon down.

"The idea that we enslaved women from Guinea or some other old French colony is absurd. No. We had volunteers."

"Women *volunteered* for this?"

"Why not?" Sergei laughed a high, wheezing, old man's laugh. "The women were not expecting to . . . bring up their half-breed babies, just go to full term, parturition. I have letters here in my desk"—he slapped the wood—"from women happily and bravely offering themselves. They were good young Communists in the good old days. They were happy to lend their wombs to Stalin. Or Khrushchev. Or even Brezhnev."

"What happened?"

"We realized it was a question of accustoming the primate rather than the human. The woman can, of course, rationalize her situation, and lubrication can be artificial, but the primate has to be aroused. We experimented on denying apes sexual outlet; that is to say, denying them mating or masturbation, then giving them olfactory stimulation with human pheromones, then allowing them to copulate with a fitting receptacle, a human-female-shaped doll. This was promising. So then we moved on to primate-human couplings, to coition with the live subjects, the human volunteers." He smiled wistfully in the semi-darkness. "We also learned from the Romans. Yes, it is true! They used to have a spectacle at their great circuses where they would herd virgin Christian girls, girls condemned to die, into the Colosseum. The girls' genitals were drenched with the urine of chimps and mandrills, then the Romans would unleash a troop of sex-starved apes into the arena, and the beasts would rape the girls to death. Of course, the depravity is distasteful. But also very useful! Why should we not learn from this?"

His face was pale with sincerity. "So we realized we could maybe drench the vagina of a female human volunteer with some chimp or orangutan urine and that could work. And we came close, we were coming close, we achieved fertilizations, which were swiftly followed by abortions. Who knows what we might have achieved if we had been given just a few more years." He sighed. "But there it is. We ran out of money and time, after that came Gorbachev and the war, and here we are, helpless, feeble, impoverished. No one wants our science. That is why it is good to meet you. A real scientist with proper perspective, not this modern, sentimental hysteria."

Sergei Yakulovich paused. Like a man semiproud of something very secret. Dying to tell, yet still wary.

"Would you like to see the last of the donors, the ape who came closest? Then we can conclude our discussion of Ghislaine Quoinelles. Poor Ghislaine."

Julia said, "Why not?" Even as the puzzle dragged her further in, her mind yearned to escape. This ghastly place. *She wanted to burn it down.*

The director pushed back his chair and led them through the

offices. He stopped at a cupboard, opened a door. It contained guns, or maybe stun guns, and cattle prods, and rope, and neck irons. Yakulovich selected an electric prod.

"Don't worry, we won't need it, he is too old, but we have rules on safety."

It was dark outside, but harsh lights illuminated the laboratory compound. Yakulovich was bumbling along in his brown suit, humming a tune. He paused at the cage of the sobbing orangutan.

"Boris!" he crooned through the cage bars. "Boris! *Boris u nas posetitelyei!*"

The old man found a key in his pocket and opened the cage door.

"You don't have to do this," said Julia.

"No, no, it is no problem. I want to show you that we are still treating our primates well, they are not unhappy, they are friendly. And the friendliness is key, they need to be accustomed to humans, to like us, and trust us—the reason we managed to mate Boris with human females is that he trusts humans: from birth he was trained to like us, therefore the coitus could take place." Sergei found a mandarin in his pocket and waved the fruit at the squatting creature. *"Boris, moi drug, ya prinesti plody!"*

The ancient orangutan unhunched the long arms from his hairy face. His streaked eyes gazed from the dark depths of his prison. Then the ape shambled with painful slowness across the cage to the open door, into the brightness of the compound lights. Its eyes expressed a sadness deeper than anything Julia had witnessed. A black, black sadness, unfathomable, like coal mines of sadness. Sergei Yakulovich was stroking the ape's forehead.

"See, perfectly tame. Of course, very old now. No longer interested in the girls!" The director laughed. "But before, when he was subadult, he was our most promising ape. He fertilized three human wombs. We came closest with him. But that was before everything was shut down. Such a tragedy."

The orangutan looked at Yakulovich. He was sniffing. The ape was sniffing the air. It turned its wide sad face and sniffed at Julia. Sniffing in the direction of her face, her stomach. She inched away.

The ape inched forward.

"Do not worry," said Yakulovich, brightly. "Boris is not a threat."

Julia was gazing in disgust at the ape's groin. A small erection was visible.

The director gazed quizzically at Julia.

"Miss Kerrigan, you have strong pheromones? Perhaps you are premenstrual? This is an unusual reaction. He is reacting to you."

She shook her head.

"Please. This is disgusting."

He bridled. "But why? What is so disgusting?" His expression was an uncomprehending sneer. *"This is just science!"* He seemed affronted. "If you are offended by this then you should talk to the Chinese!"

"What the hell does that mean?"

Yakulovich shrugged. "Exactly what I say? The Soviet Union sold all its data to the Chinese in the 1980s, when we were too poor to defend ourselves. Indeed, I asked Barnier what had happened to our research, how it had progressed in the East. He could not be explicit, he refused. But this is what Barnier told me." The director sighed, expressively. "Barnier said simply this: *'The Chinese took it much further.'* Who knows what they did, Miss Kerrigan, who knows? The Chinese! They are entirely without scruple, they are the new Roman Empire, who will govern us all!"

Sergei Yakulovich turned back to his favorite prisoner and stroked the orangutan's forehead. Crooning in mumbled Russian. Julia stared at the bleakness. The drizzle was falling again, the stench of shit was pervasive, the orangutan was stroking his scarlet penis, and the little rhesus monkey was still shrieking, running to one side of the cage, and screaming, and running to the other side, and screaming. Julia gazed at the sad eyes of the orangutan. Sad and crying, yet guiltless. There was no conscience there: just suffering.

Suffering. And libido. And rage.

In a single second Julia was unsure what she saw. Yakulovich sailing backward; the great long arm of the orangutan extending past him; and suddenly a dark and heavy flash as the ape leaped toward her. Julia seemed to pivot away, on instinct, and run. But the ape had her, it grabbed at her neck and pulled her brutally to the floor. She tried to struggle free, writhing on the damp ground, skidding her heels against the rain and urine and concrete, but the animal was enormous: huge and pungent.

Now she could feel the large, inhuman hands between her legs. Ripping her panties away. Julia gasped.

And the little monkey was still screaming, running across the cage, and screaming.

30

The blow didn't come. He waited. Still nothing. Khmer voices rose to a clamor, more voices, shouts even. Jake opened his eyes, looked left: beside him the soldier was still wielding the rusty iron bar, ready to execute him and Rittisak. But the iron bludgeon was hanging, unused, and the soldier himself was gazing offstage, with a distinctly nervous expression.

Why?

Villagers, *at least a hundred of them,* coming down the path from the main road, shouting and yelling and clutching ugly long knives and hatchets and machetes and old Russian rifles. Even pitchforks.

He glanced Chemda's way, the tiny fledgling of hope in his heart. Chemda had shrugged off the uncertain grasp of her captors, and she was marching to greet the mob. Despite her ragged flip-flops and her muddy skirt and her dirty hair, she still looked like a Khmer princess, bold, proud, self-possessed: she was talking with the villagers, they were smiling at her, waving their fists in triumph and anger, gesturing furiously at the soldiers: the captors.

They were being rescued. The would-be executioner dropped his cudgel to the ground and backed away. Raucous shouts apparently demanded that Jake and Rittisak be unhandcuffed.

The youngest soldier nodded, and humbly shuffled up, and turned a key behind Jake's back.

He was uncuffed. Rubbing his raw wrists, he stood in the hot sun and stared at Chemda. The incense from the offerings to Pol Pot perfumed the smiles they exchanged, frightened smiles. Rittisak was also released. Jake crossed to Chemda's side, walking around the low grave.

"Why . . ." He was almost muted by the reversal.

Chemda told him, "Your friend. He did this."

"Tyrone?"

"Yes. Ah. So they say, these people. He has contacts here and he called them last night and asked them to help us, to watch out for us, and he said they *should* help us *because of what I do*." She gestured at the triumphant crowd of Khmer peasants in their vests and *kramas* and dirty sandals.

"They know I am trying to get the Khmer Rouge imprisoned, and they want me to go on with my work. They want me to bring the tyrants to *justice*." Her dark eyes looked up at his. A shine in the dark tropical depths of her eyes told of her emotion. "I thought they were going to kill you. Jake, I thought they were going to *kill you*."

"Trust me," said Jake, "so did I."

So he had Tyrone to thank for his life. Of all people: laconic, selfish, hard-assed Tyrone McKenna. Jake felt a surge of love for his cynical friend, and he smiled at his own sentimentality.

But he was also swallowing the vinegary aftertaste of his intense fear. He breathed deep and long. His leg muscles were still weakened from the terror, and he felt like he might just crumple to his knees, right here and now, by Pol Pot's graveside. He had been oddly calm, the moment that Death had approached, Death the dull functionary,

Death who casually took his sister and his mother, Death the offhand commander of the killing fields.

But now he had survived, Jake was suffering the emotional aftershocks. Palpitations. The sweats. He tried to assert control over his own reflexes. Breathing deep.

A few meters away, the Khmer villagers were yelling at the soldiers, who were now silent and cowed. One of the locals walked up to the apparent leader of the squad and simply took the submachine gun from the soldier's weakening hands.

The large eyes of the young Khmer soldier blinked rapidly, in anger or terror, or cowardly relief. But he did not move. He was rigid. Jake realized the soldiers were now, probably, in fear for *their* lives: outnumbered a hundred to one, caught by an entire village in the act of brutal, Khmer Rouge–style execution, in a region riven with loathing for the Khmer Rouge. The troopers knew they could die, any minute.

"We mustn't let them kill them," said Jake to Chemda. "The locals, they can't kill the soldiers."

Her face was contorted with disgust, but she nodded. "You're right. Ah. They don't deserve to live, but you are absolutely right. We need to be . . . inconspicuous."

"And we're still *stuck,* Chem. There's no way we can just sneak down the ravine, not now, there are other policemen around—"

She shrugged impatiently. "So we'll have to cross the border, at the official frontier."

"No way. Come on. They'll stop us and send us to Phnom Penh."

Her frown was fierce. Jake gazed around at their rescuers. A possibility evolved in his mind.

"I have an idea. We could ask these people . . . to help? To come with us? With all of them we have a chance."

Chemda didn't even reply: she turned and she talked with the villagers. The villagers nodded and yelled, urgent and keen. And Chemda was smiling a half smile.

"They're going to help."

The crowd moved as one. Jake realized it was working. *They were being escorted to the frontier.* The soldiers were left behind, guarded and disarmed. The huge crowd of locals was now walking boldly up the burning sunlit road to the frontier, just a few hundred meters away.

As the mob approached the border, Jake saw the look of astonished alarm on the faces of the Khmer customs officers in their little glass kiosk. The officers had obviously been briefed to watch for escapees matching Chemda's and Jake's description; they had surely been told to stop them and arrest them at once, to prevent their crossing. But they obviously hadn't expected Jake and Chemda to be accompanied by half of Anlong Veng.

What could five border policemen do against maybe a hundred angry people with knives, guns, and rusty machetes?

The crowd fell into an oddly solicitous silence as it met the white wooden boom that marked the Cambodian frontier. Jake saw the blue-and-red stripes of the Thai flag fluttering languidly from a flag-pole, a hundred meters farther on; he saw Thai faces leaning to the window in the glass-and-steel office, observing the strange scene unfolding on the Khmer side of the border. Behind the Thai officers, he could just make out the kindly portrait of a bespectacled King Bumibhol of Siam, hanging on the wall.

Jake wiped the sweat from his eyes and assessed the situation. He knew they would have little trouble getting *into* Thailand. Their pass-ports were in order: British and American citizens could enter Thai-land freely and get a visa anytime.

But Jake and Chemda still had to cross the Khmer border first. Would his plan work?

The Cambodian officers inside their kiosk were making frantic phone calls. Two of the officers had guns drawn—the revolvers were laid significantly and blatantly on the counter before them. But the crowd, still ominously silent, moved closer, gathering around the kiosk. The sheer weight of numbers threatened to topple the little building; the sad little office, with its sad men inside, rattled and vibrated.

Victory came quick. The guards surrendered: behind their grimy panes of glass they did deep submissive bows, with their praying hands high above their heads: they were doing the *high wai,* the deep inferior *samphae* of total submission.

The fattest Cambodian border guard urgently beckoned Chemda and Jake to his little hatch, past the white barrier. His hands were shaking and sweat was dripping in long rivulets down his chubby, frightened face.

Wordless, he took their passports. He glanced at the crowd behind the barrier.

He stamped Chemda's passport, he stamped Jake's passport. With the same weak, unspeaking demeanor he waved them on. His face said, *Just go, please. Go. Now.*

But Jake lingered for a second, savoring the moment, this tiny refreshing moment of his victory, in all the recent tragedy of flight and defeat; Chemda walked over to Rittisak, who was smiling, at the front of the crowd. She hugged him.

Then she ran back and took Jake's hand, and they walked the hundred meters of no-man's-tarmac, to the bigger, glassier office on the Thai frontier.

"Sawadee kap!" said the Thai border guard. He glanced down at

their passports. His smile was brief, but subtly meaningful. "Thirty-day visas?"

"Yes," said Jake, "thirty-day visas." He clutched Chemda's hand. *"Kappunkap."*

Jake found them a cab to Surin, a badly abused Toyota Corolla with a fat Isaan driver and maybe thirteen monastic amulets hanging from the rearview mirror. He gazed ahead of them as they motored past the cane fields, and so did Chemda. Their mutual good mood, their sense of wide-eyed astonishment, at their own gruesomely belated good fortune, had already dwindled; it was entirely gone by the time they reached the train station, whence they had decided to catch the night train to Bangkok. To Bangkok and Marcel Barnier.

At the station, Jake took out his little camera. He still had this precious new camera with the precious photos. He had lost his sister's photo, but now he had new photos. The slight sense of resurgent possibility elevated his mood once again. Get the story. Pin down the past. Defeat the world, just for once. Be a real photographer. Yes, he could still do *that*.

At a newsstand in the station Jake picked up a copy of the *Bangkok Post;* he was surrounded by Thai workers reading manga. Half interested, half anxious, he flicked the pages as Chemda bought the tickets.

But he soon stopped flicking pages.

The *Post* had an article about him and Chemda. UN worker missing from Phnom Penh . . . granddaughter of Sovirom Sen, noted Chinese-Cambodian businessman . . . photojournalist linked to the disappearance. . . .

The article was very small, and tucked away, and neutral in tone: it didn't accuse Jake of anything, but it did mention the reward for Chemda's return, and the mere fact that the article was printed in the most important Thai English-language newspaper brought the rest of Jake's unease surging back. Who might try and claim that reward? And how?

The afternoon hours ticked by until the night train's departure. Jake drank bottled water and cans of cold Japanese coffee and sat nervously on a station bench, next to Chemda, both of them trying to be inconspicuous. He telephoned Tyrone.

Tyrone told him to shut the fuck up and stop being so "minty" when Jake tried to say *thank you, you saved my life*. Tyrone listened to the epic story of their escape from Siem Reap, and swore and even chuckled, and his good humor helped dispel the darkness, just a little.

Tyrone asked: "So you're going to Bangkok?"

"Yes."

"To find Barnier. You don't give up, do you?"

"Not after all this, Ty, no, I don't. You said I had a good story and I'm on it. I want it. And Chemda wants the truth. What happened to her family. But we need somewhere to stay, incredibly discreet. Near this guy's apartment, in Nana. You know Bangkok. Any ideas?"

"Yes . . . The Sukhumvit Crown, Soi 8, you can only find it if you go the wrong way down Soi 6."

"Anything else? Any other advice?"

"Stop walking across lakes filled with corpses."

"Ty. Please God. Ty!"

"You should buy new sim cards for you and Chemda, now you are in Thailand . . . use True, no, DTAC, just give a few people the numbers. Use the phones sparingly."

"Thanks."

"*Mai pen rai*. Stay in touch. And remember, you are still in serious shit. People will come after you in Bangkok. They won't do it openly, but they will try. Be very, very, very, very fucking careful."

As instructed, Jake went straight to the nearest convenience store, at the front of the station, and bought new sim cards for himself and Chemda; they swapped numbers, he texted the number to Tyrone. He sat down on the bench again. Waiting. Passengers came and went, eating fishball noodles at the fishball noodle stalls. Amputee beggars lifted their stumpy arms, pincering plastic cups of loose change. Commuters yawned. Policemen patrolled. Their train was ready. They climbed on the carriage.

They had bought first-class berths mainly because first-class berths had a tiny shower. The shower was risibly small but Jake didn't care: as the train rumbled out of town he stepped straight in and rinsed away all the mud of the Butcher's Lake, and all the grease from Pol Pot's house, and all the dust from Preah Kahn, where Sonisoy was taken. He only wished he could sluice away the terrifying memory of kneeling there, in the dirt, by a shrine to the ghost of an atheist dictator, waiting for a man to casually smash his brain through his mouth with a rusty iron bar.

Crack.

Chemda was already fast asleep in the bottom bunk. She had held his hand as she fell asleep, but now the hand was limp and unconscious, and he folded it onto her breast, and he climbed the bunk-bed steps to slide between his own crisp, clean white cotton sheets. The sensation was unfathomably blissful.

The train was rattling through the dark Isaan countryside. The comforting rattle of a train, ta-chakkating over the points, soon lullabyed Jake into sleep.

Most of his sleep was undisturbed. He woke just once, when they pulled into a hick little station with moonlit palm trees, at about five a.m. Hushed voices muttered outside in the tropical stillness. Jake sweated in the airlocked compartment. Who was that? Outside? Someone quietly passed down the train corridor, seeking a berth, whispering. He waited, tensed with fear. But nothing happened. Chemda's unconscious breathing was regular and low.

The train pulled out. At length he fell asleep again and this time he dreamed—he dreamed of someone hitting his head and his head being smashed off his body, and then somehow he was looking down at his own head fallen to the ground and the head rolled over, and it was his mother's head, smeared with violet lipstick. *The eyes opened.*

Jake woke with a jolt. Their compartment was bright with morning sun, and skyscrapers and motorways paraded past the uncurtained window. Chemda was awake and dressed.

"We're here. Bangkok."

She leaned over and kissed him.

His returning kisses were slurred, reluctant. The dream had been so vivid; why did he keep seeing this image, the disembodied head?

"Chemda." He wanted to confess, to share, to divide his anguish. He'd had enough of lonely wondering. And he had been through so much with this girl, why not tell her?

He felt he was falling in love with her. He had no idea what falling in love meant or felt like, but if it was something like this, then he was happy to call it love, so yes, he was falling in love with Chemda Tek. But love meant he had to be truthful. He wanted to be truthful.

"Chem, I keep having these dreams. Sometimes daydreams. Nightmares, just idiotic nightmares, but they are persistent, this image I see."

He told her. About the head, the floating heads, his mother's face.

As his story unfolded he watched her expression turn from curiosity to concern—to piercing anxiety.

"The *krasue*," she said. "What you are seeing is, as far as I can tell, the *krasue*."

She explained further, quietly.

"A *krasue* is a malign spirit, cannibalistic, ah, bloodsucking. It appears mainly at night. It manifests itself as a woman, usually young and beautiful, with . . ." Chemda winced. "With her internal organs hanging down from the neck. Because she has no body. So she floats, with her spine and her organs trailing behind."

"OK." Jake swallowed hard. "And what does she do? This demon?"

"The *krasue* preys on pregnant women. It uses . . ." She sighed. "She uses an extended tongue to catch the fetus, by, ah, probing inside, up the vulva and inside the womb to devour the fetus. This causes diseases during pregnancy. Or so many Southeast Asians believe."

"Sorry?"

"Jake." She held his hand tight. "I know you don't believe this stuff, and it sounds like a cartoon, but this really is an *iconic* demon, all across my part of the world. The legend comes from ancient Hindu India but it is deeply rooted in Cambodia, and Cambodian voodoo. The Filipinos have their own version, the Manananngal; the Balinese have the Leyak. Some call her the *arp.*"

"What about Angkor? I saw something like this in Angkor. A sculpture on the wall."

"In Angkor they are called *kinarees*. Female spirits. But it is basically another *krasue*. They are everywhere. This icon is everywhere. There are legends and prayers about *krasue,* spells and stories. Even horror films."

He stared at her. She looked at him. The train stopped, they had arrived. They had to disembark.

Chemda said, "The thing I don't understand is . . . this is my culture. Not yours. This is not your culture. So why are *you* dreaming of an *Asian* demon?"

31

"Boris vyĭti!"

Yakulovich was stabbing at the orangutan with the cattle prod, poking like some effete and feeble swordsman. But the shocks were strong: Julia—in her desperation—could feel them herself, faintly conducted into her body through the writhing muscles of the ape, frazzles of pain and pungent fear. She struggled under the gross, surging weight, pushing at the leathery skin.

"Teper', Boris v vashu kletku!"

The orangutan began to cringe and shirk the blows; another shock from the prod dislodged the ape completely and sent him loping into the cage, which Yakulovich shut, and locked, with fumbling hands.

For a moment Julia lay numbed and flat on the slimy concrete; but then she seized herself and sat up. She was bruised but unharmed, terrified but unviolated—the orangutan had got no further than her arms and thighs. But the ape had ravished her sense of herself: she could never forget this. The electric prickle of the cattle prod.

She stood. Swaying a little. But she stood. Brushing dirt from her long skirt and her top. Brushing and brushing. Yearning to shower. To wash the hot musky smell of the primate's fur from herself—and from her clothes. No, she would burn the clothes. The way she burned her clothes after Sarnia.

The director was actually weeping as he gazed her way—weeping like a child, sobbing like a doll designed to cry.

"What can I say—I am so sorry, Miss Kerrigan." His sense of disgrace was obvious, he even lost conrol of his previously immaculate English: *"Miss, sorry, mne ochen' zhal, etogo nikogda ne sluchalos ran'she! I sorry. Vy dolzhny byt gormonal'nye. Opyat' ya proshu proshcheniya—"*

"Whatever," said Julia. "You stupid man. You . . ."

These curses dwindled to nothing. What was the point? Julia had seen and done enough. The orangutan was hunched at the far end of his cage, his long arms curved over his face. The eyes were big and sad and thoughtless.

She had to get out, now. Julia had everything she required from the Sukhumi Institute for Primate Pathology. All the information it could ever provide; maybe even some vital clues.

But now she urgently needed to bathe.

Walking to the gate, and then to the top of the hill, she scanned the bleak Sukhumi streets. She was searching for a hopeful sign between the drooping palm trees. Looking for something saying *Hotel*.

For once, she lucked out. *Hotel Ritsa*. Its light was flickering in the drizzle half a kilometer down the hill, beside the arthritic tramlines, toward the coast.

Julia ran down, dragging her reluctant bag, and checked straight in. The reception area was dusty and careworn. The elevator was probably dangerous. The sheets in the bedroom were nylon. The showerhead belched spurts of lukewarm water. It felt mildly paradisiacal.

She showered, long and hard, and then crept into bed, and drank her bottle of duty-free Georgian wine—using the bathroom tooth-brush mug—and then she slept, in the nirvana of scratchy nylon, for many hours. And then she woke, and went down to a hotel breakfast of processed pink ham slices with pickled eggs.

When she came back to her room, she showered once more: one final cleansing. But this time, when she stepped onto the bathroom tiles, to dry her hair, she lingered at the mirror, and she gazed: appalled—and intrigued.

Her pale arms and thighs were liberally covered in bruises, purple handprints made by the orangutan. The bruises showed where the beast had grasped her, and groped her, fiercely clutching at her flesh. The bruises were dark and livid.

A tingle unsettled her as she stared at these contusions. The tingle of an idea. The fingers were all there: the fingers of the animal's hands, guiltless, brutal, different, undaunted. Guiltless as the boys who attacked her in Sarnia.

Then she thought of the Hands of Gargas: their poignancy, their sense of remorse. Human hands, so very old. And full of a strange regret.

Julia smiled at herself.

Yes? Yes maybe. Perhaps she *had* it. The key. The code. The glimpse of a glorious solution.

She had it.

Refreshed, revived, and filled with excitement, she sat down at her laptop. And she worked, hard, putting these pieces together. The cave art. The trepanations. Guilt and conscience. The guiltless ani-mality of the orangutan. The guiltless savagery of men reduced to animals in the back of a VW van.

Yes! The idea positively thrilled her. She was *using the past*. She was turning the past into something purposeful, something directed. She was also aware, somehow, that she was masking—denying and subverting—all the accumulated horrors, with *thinking*. But she didn't care. *Because she was getting ever closer to the truth.*

It took her many hours; it took her several days. To break the monotony and refresh her mind, during these days, she took breaks to make phone calls on her cell phone, which miraculously worked; and to send e-mail from a small, dingy café that served Abkhazian tea with saucers of gooseberry jam.

Most of her calls were to Michigan, or to Alex, and full of lies. *I'm fine, don't worry about me.* She knew they would only tell her to come home; of course there was no way she was going home, not when she was this close to the Truth.

Nearly all of her e-mails were to Marcel Barnier. He, apparently, was the link. The next link. He was maybe the only man who could tell her if she was actually correct.

He didn't reply. Not once.

Julia wasn't surprised. She sat and sipped her gooseberry-flavored tea, and she surmised that Barnier was avoiding the world. All these Western scientists and intellectuals, these Marxists who once visited Cambodia, must surely by now have realized what was happening to them: that they were all dying. Even the most isolated and friendless would have seen at least one or two news reports, especially of the spectacular later killings in France.

So if Julia wanted someone to confirm her theory, Marcel Barnier was the only one, because he was the only one left—yet he wasn't replying. Perhaps, therefore, she should just go there? And see him? It had worked before. Yes, perhaps she would go there, when she had broken open the intellectual puzzle.

And on the third day she did it, she cracked it: *she had her theory.* Standing back from her laptop, which she was using in the hotel lobby, as the cleaners made their daily yet farcically halfhearted attempts to clean her room of forty years of Soviet grime, Julia almost gloated. It was just three pages of thoughts. *But it was the truth. Or at least her version of the truth, a truth that had been entombed in the past for decades and, in some senses, centuries.*

It was the Gospel of the Ice Age. It was the Spiritual Confession of Mankind, written on cave walls thirty thousand years ago.

Julia had, for the first time in her life, completed something: finished a journey, made that amazing discovery; she had restored an extraordinary thesis to the world. The fifteen-year-old girl still inside her, the girl who almost wept at the terrible Hands of Gargas, was exultant, and gloating, and almost happy, despite it all, because of it all. She smiled quietly to herself.

"*Spasibo.*" Julia accepted the bill from the lobby waiter for her canned, sweetened orange juice. Then she got up, walked across the tram-clanging boulevard to the Internet café, and booked the next flight from Adler to Moscow, and then from Moscow to Bangkok. She had just enough cash left in her savings for a few more flights and cheap hotels. She was going to use this money, the last penny if necessary, to see Barnier, whether he wanted to see her or not. This was her life, her moment. After this nothing seemed to matter; if she ran out of cash, who cared? Not her, not anymore.

A Valium let her sleep on the plane to Moscow, a Xanax let her sleep on the plane from Moscow to Bangkok. She needed energy for this confrontation: she was spiraling into the black hole of the truth, where destruction and oblivion lurked, where the killer herself might be headed—but the risk felt almost good, she was unmoored now, floating on the tidal bore, surfing her success to the mouth of the river. Gloriously free.

Maybe the gravity in all this was her own pride, dragging her to danger. But she *was proud.* As the Thai Airways plane landed at Bangkok she woke from a dream of herself receiving a prize for a great discovery. The man giving her the prize was her father. Then

Rouvier. Then Alex. Her mother was apparently locked out of the
Nordic hall. The walls of the hall were covered with paintings of
huge cats.

"*Sawadeekap!* Thai Airways would like to thank you . . ."

She stirred herself: stashing her new clothes in the holdall, grabbing her laptop, filing out of the plane and exiting customs. The heat
outside the airport was welcome, a wet cocoon of humidity. After the
chilly, stale dankness of Sukhumi, this rich tropical Siamese closeness
was better.

A cab? She got a taxi from Suvarnabhumi Airport, into the city.

Julia stared across the elevated highway at the myriad skyscrapers
as they sped into town: Bangkok, it seemed, was another lusty and
furious Asian megalopolis, with wild high-rises and huge elevated
freeways and vast adverts for Japanese cars and English-language
schools and South Korean TVs.

And Bangkok also had the answer to everything. Perhaps.

"You say Soi Sick?" The cabbie was talking. "Soi Sick, Sukhumvit? Near Sukhumvit?"

"Yes. I think so. Soi, er yes, Soi Six."

She mumbled to a stop. What if the address on the card *wasn't*
correct?

She had no choice.

"Sorry, sorry, lady, I pay money."

The cabdriver was handing over cash at a tollbooth, but when the
gate opened they merely inched ahead: they'd hit the real urban traffic, the cholesterol of Asian prosperity. The cab stopped again and
started again, slowed and stopped. The endless traffic massed, and
moved, and slowed, like an organic process, peristalsis.

She gazed across the city. Again. Flashes of distant lightning
zagged silently between the skyscrapers and the imperious Hitachi
adverts: a storm over the Gulf of Thailand.

Then at last the traffic parted and the taxi swooped left and over a disused railway track, and now they were in the florid and gristly urbanity of central Bangkok, with the street-side kebab stalls, the upmarket European shops, the amputees lying outside British pubs, sushi bars, Bookazine outlets, French restaurants, and enormous marble megahotels squeezed between Bangladeshi tailors and Chinese jewelry shops.

"Soi Sick! No Soi Eight? You sure? Sure-sure?"

The cabdriver's smiling Thai face was a wry question.

She repeated her answer: "Yes, Soi Six."

The taxi swerved right, down Soi Nana, the commercial sex district. Middle-aged Western and Japanese men sat with unfeasibly teenage girls outside bars pounding the Rolling Stones and AC/DC into the twilit street. Female flesh exhibited itself everywhere, languid, brown, sheened and exposed. Painted toenails. Vivid lipstick. Girls from Isaan ate fried cockroaches and fried beetles and sweetened coconut rice with chunks of fresh mango.

It was dark now, and the streets were bright. Julia saw Coyote Bars. Man4man Massage. Lolita Sauna. Bangcockney Pub.

Pachara Suites. Right in the middle of the red-light district.

"Here," said Julia, the tension accelerating with her pulse. She alighted and tipped the taxi driver.

Pachara Suites was a gleaming, thirty-story condominium, with elegant slate fountains and a wall-eyed man begging outside using a Yum Yum noodle jar as a cup. The man's blind eye looked like a mung bean.

Julia found the glossy lobby deserted—she heard, too audibly, the squelching of her sneaker soles as she walked to the faraway elevator. Eighteen floors above, and down another long, bright, empty hallway, she located the door. She knocked.

Silence. An eyehole opened for a second, then occluded. Was

someone behind the door? Checking her out? Or was this someone else? Was this the most absurd chase of a very wild goose?

Julia knocked again.

The eyehole shut. A latch was turned.

Finally the door opened, just an inch: the door was secured with three chains. An oldish, intelligent face peered out. Julia recognized an aged version of the young smile in the Phnom Penh photo.

It was Marcel Barnier.

His wild liverish eyes looked at Julia. He was holding a long knife in his hand. But as he absorbed what he was seeing, he seemed to relax. The faint trace of a pout glistened on his wet lips. A gourmet's air kiss. Desirous.

"Fuck. Ah. You are Julia Kerrigan! The *glamorous* archaeologist? I Googled you. Saw your . . . *photo*. Yes. Yes, yes. I got your e-mails. Forgive me for not replying, but . . . Why the hell did the doorman let you through?"

"Uh."

"Why? I told him not to. Was he not there?"

"No."

"Fuck." The face concealed behind the door swore twice, and sighed. "Fucking noodle head, Supashok. They shoulda kept the last doorman. Ai. Maybe he went for a pipi. OK . . ."

Dropping the knife on a table to his side, he unlatched one chain, then the second, then the third. He opened the door and gazed at her creased jeans and jet-lagged face.

"You understand that I am being very fucking careful. Come in."

"Thank you."

Nervous, hopeful, quite terrified, she stepped inside.

The apartment was in chaos. Cardboard boxes sat on the floor, full of books and paintings. Furniture was partly dismantled and stacked against the wall. Half-empty bottles of Johnnie Walker and completely empty bottles of Jacobs Creek Grenache Shiraz stood on tables and in corners next to copiously overfilled ashtrays.

"I am moving. Yes. And yes, I am an alcoholic. For reasons I am sure you understand. To escape, to save my life. I used to escape through fucking liquor, now I have to escape for real."

He looked in Julia's eyes.

She nodded and said, "I think I know why."

"That's good. That's good-good. Save a lot of horseshit talking."

His French accent had been entirely erased and replaced by a kind of coarse, slangy, slightly bizarre Anglo-American-Oriental English; his breath smelled of whiskey and cigarettes and garlic. Presumably, decades of living out here, speaking the only Western language anyone understood, English, had beaten the Frenchness out of him.

"You look stressed. Very charming, but stressed. Ah-ah. We can have a fucking drink, no? The fridge will be the last thing I empty." He laughed, angrily. "But so what—I like a drink, it keeps me cheerful. What is it they say about the French, a Frenchman is an Italian in a bad mood? Hah. *Ein bier, meine freunde?* I will have wine!"

Julia said yes. Barnier laughed again and slipped into his kitchen and returned with a beer and a glass. He looked at her inquisitively as she sipped the Tiger beer.

"You want to know everything I know. Yeah?"

"Well. As I also said, um, I have some ideas of my own. I wanted to see if I was . . ." The beer was refreshingly cold. She drank. "See if I was right."

"The great mystery? Maybe we can inform each other, *ma bichette.* Trouble is, I do not know everything. You may know more than me." Wariness and mischief and anxiety mixed in his gaze. "But maybe not. Maybe I know quite enough already. And someone ought to hear my story, before I escape." He gestured at the boxes. He took a glass of red wine from somewhere and swallowed a huge gulp. He lit a cigarette and said, "So, ask me your questions."

"But. It needs time. And you seem, sorry, I mean—you must be very on edge. When are you going to go?"

Barnier paused, and exhaled smoke, before he answered. He slurped once more at the wine and ogled Julia's blond hair. His own hair was thin and brownish gray; his clothes were relaxed and youthful, though not in the embarrassing way of Ghislaine: just jeans and a gray T-shirt, stained with drops of red wine. Loafers. No socks. A suntan. A man keeping himself reasonably in shape apart from the alcohol. But the face was frightened and the lips were stained red with tannin.

Then he said: "I'm going. Somewhere, very soon, where that witch of a killer, that *krasue,* won't find me. I have read all the newspaper reports. I have read the shitty police e-mails, but not replied. I do not trust anyone. Fuck. 'Course I am on edge. She's coming for me—here."

Julia said, "Do you know who she is? The killer?"

"No. Not exactly."

"Do you know why she is killing all these people?"

"Revenge!" Barnier tapped ash, and stared at her with a sudden expression of deep and existential fear. He was scared. He was really and visibly *scared.* But then the bravado returned. "Yes, it is revenge—it is surely revenge—for the poor Khmer millions we helped to destroy. And I cannot blame them, you know? That is the poignancy. I cannot blame them. The fucking things we did, the Marxists, us, me, Danny the Red and the rest of us, all the reds now in socialist governments across Europe, we gave the Khmer Rouge succor, we told the world their lies, we were their useful idiots, maybe we fucking *deserve* to die. But if I am gonna die then I am gonna die happy.

Do not go gentle into that good night, but rage, rage, and order some hookers and blow." His eyes flicked around the room. "Come. You are right. If we want to talk, let us do it in a good place, somewhere safe, somewhere there are pretty girls. *More* pretty girls. And these are naked. We can have lady drink short time. You know you are not the first person to come and see me today. I am suddenly an attraction, a destination, a tourist honeypot."

"How?"

"A girl from Cambodia. Chemda Tek. And her boyfriend, Jake . . . Jake something. A photographer. A Brit." He belched smoke. Profanely. "They found me this morning. They, too, are frightened. They are also pursuing these mysteries. I told them to go away for a while 'cause I must pack, and I told 'em I would meet them in a bar this evening, a nice busy bar with lots of witnesses. It's at Soi Cowboy." He dropped his cigarette butt in his glass of wine. The cigarette whispered and died. "I have a feeling no woman would ever just walk into this bar alone, so we should be safe. C'mon, 's go. Because staying here feels like sitting, waiting to die, a target."

"Who are they? These people, what do they want?"

"I am not totally fucking sure. I was drunk when they told me. Hey, it was eleven a.m. Let them explain, *non*? Come, if we are to talk we might as well all do it together. Somewhere safe. This way, *moumoune*."

They took the long elevator ride to the ground floor, then a short walk around the corner, then ten minutes down thrumming Sukhumvit Boulevard, with Barnier gazing down each junction as if he expected to be run over—or attacked—at every junction; and then they crossed the Asok walkways, whereupon they were immersed in another sex-district strip of the most garish neon, with go-go bars and massage parlors and love hotels and small baby elephants carrying drunken Western boys on a stag weekend who threw hopeful leers at the harlots enticing them into Sheba's and Suzie Wong.

The bar they apparently wanted was called Baccara. It was luridly advertised in scarlet light, and inside it was dark and noisy and big and full of Japanese men staring at a central stage where maybe thirty or forty nubile girls were dancing in gauzy bras and equally transparent miniskirts.

But then Julia realized the Japanese men in their sofas and armchairs were not staring at these girls but staring *up*. She followed the communal gaze. Above them was a glass ceiling, and on top of it about twenty more young girls danced languidly to Chinese pop music, naked apart from tartan schoolgirl skirts, wearing no underclothes at all.

"Biggest no-panty bar in the world!" Barnier's laughter was like a vulgar heckle. "The Japs love it here, and the girls love them back. You know why? You wanna know what the girls call Japanese men? Mr. Four. They call Jap johns Mr. Four—"

"I'm sorry—"

"'Cause they pay four thousand baht for a fuck, they last just four minutes, and they are four centimeters long! Hah. Look, there's our good friends. Let's get some Tanquerays and tonic and talk. Corner left, nine o'clock."

Julia followed Barnier's gesture and noticed a particular female figure sitting discreetly in the darkest corner, with her back to them. Her body language was stiff and uncomfortable; she seemed Asian, judging by the petiteness, the dark bare arms, dark long hair. Julia empathized with any discomfort the woman might be feeling: they were virtually the only two women in the bar who weren't half-naked, or dancing, or serving drinks.

The woman's companion was a young white guy, tall, presumably Jake. Julia glanced back at the woman. Her profile, seen obliquely, was familiar in other ways.

The shock of recognition was liquefying. This was no ordinary Asian woman. This was no coincidence.

Julia swayed as the cliff edge of fear dropped around her.

Barnier was gesturing to a smiling bar girl.

"*Nong?* Hello? *Sawadee?* We go talk-talk with friend over there? Gin tonic. Bring three. *Kapkap.*" He pointed at the table, then turned to Julia. "Let's go over."

"No. Stop."

Barnier didn't hear her. Julia whispered again, urgently: "Stop!"

She reached out a hand and pulled at the Frenchman. He was bemused.

"Eh? What is it?"

A pause. Julia hesitated. Maybe she was wrong? She wasn't wrong. That long dark hair, the curve of the back, the profile.

She was right. As she stood, immobile and silent with shock, Barnier shoved on and walked to the table and said, "Chemda, Jake! Look! I have brought yet another exciting new friend. I am such a fucking *wanted* man."

Jake rose and offered a hand and said hello to Julia. But Julia's focus was still fixed on the face of the woman: Chemda Tek.

Then Chemda Tek spoke.

"Hello?"

This was it. The final proof.

She even had an American accent.

Chemda Tek was the killer.

32

Jake watched this woman's reaction with astonishment: the American woman, Julia, was refusing to sit down. She was muttering, half-shouting, she was frightened and gabbling and staring at Chemda.

Finally she managed to say: "It's her. It's her."

Barnier turned to Julia.

"What?"

Julia pointed directly at Chemda.

"Her. That's *her*. That . . . *thing*. It's *her*."

"That's who? She's who? What are you saying?"

Jake listened, confounded.

The American stammered: "That is . . . the same goddamn person I saw in Paris. The woman who killed the archivist. The curator. Who tried to kill me. That's *her*, the killer—"

Jake stood. "You fucking *what*?"

Barnier was leaping away from the table, as if the bar stools had just been electrified. Chemda suddenly reached for Jake's hand, her own hand damp and trembling. Trembling violently. Jake was standing and shouting.

"How can you say this?"

The Frenchman turned, shouting at the staff, demanding that they chuck Chemda out of the building and instantly fetch the police. Bar girls were gathering. Staring. And in the middle of the flashing lights and the thumping music Julia stood, still, her face awash; transfixed, appalled, terrified; Chemda gave the appearance, in the melee, of a little girl lost and bewildered.

Jake gazed, motionless. What the fuck was happening?

Even the pantyless schoolgirls were agitated, peering inquisitively down through the glass ceiling, trying to work out the reason for the hubbub. Several Japanese men were pointing, alarmed.

Now Barnier ripped it all up, yelling at everyone.

"Get that bitch out of here, *nong*! *Papasan*? *Mamasan*? Now! Get her out of here before she fucking knifes someone——"

Chemda found her voice. It was uncharacteristically weak.

"But. . . . but *it's not me*! How *can* it be me? I have been in Cambodia. Jake, tell them!"

But Jake was staring at Julia's face, the pale, soft face of the young archaeologist, and it spoke a kind of truth. The woman really believed what she was saying; she really believed this outrageous accusation.

Jake swallowed his next words. Momentarily, he was dumbfounded. Chemda flung his hand away.

"You believe them, Jake?"

"No, of *course* not!"

"But you do. You do! I see it in your face!"

"I don't. Sorry. A moment. Only . . . *Chemda*——"

But it was true, she was right, even though a few seconds' consideration told him that the accusation was absurd, he had let the shadow of a doubt pass across his face: thinking of her odder behavior; inviting him to the Sovirom compound——

His Khmer girlfriend was staring his way, with tears jeweling on her eyelashes. She was finally breaking, after all of this—she was falling, losing, unhinging.

"Don't ever speak to me—ever again—"

Chemda pushed aside his protesting arms; she stepped down from the table and strode through the parting crowds, through the g-stringed dancers and the Taiwanese tourists and the trio of fat and chortling white businessmen just coming through the doorway curtains.

The curtains rustled and closed. Chemda was gone. The bar returned to life. Lady drinks were fetched. Someone ordered short time. Once again, the clientele stared up at the glass ceiling, where the girls in plaid miniskirts and no underwear resumed their bored and languid shuffle.

Jake was momentarily paralyzed by anger and guilt. Run after Chemda? Phone her? Give her space? Why had he let the doubt even enter his mind? The idea that she was the killer was beyond absurd, it was physically impossible—how could Chemda have been flying to and from Europe to kill people? Just surreally ridiculous. And then there was the moral impossibility: Chemda. Of all people. No. Not Chemda.

But then why did Julia appear so genuinely shocked and convinced?

The American woman was tentatively approaching. She put a hand on Jake's shoulder.

He shrugged it off. Snapped in her face.

"You are *wrong*. She's been with me in Asia for the last few weeks. Every minute of every day. What you said was *grotesque*."

Her answering expression was pained.

"Mr. Thurby. Jake . . . I'm sorry, but I thought it was true—"

Barnier was behind her.

"So you think, Julia, it might *not* be true? Then why did you fucking *say* it?"

"Because it *was* the same woman, only with darker skin! I'm not joking. I wouldn't joke. Not about this! Chemda is the same, only with much darker skin. But the same age, same eyes, same face, same stance, same everything else." Julia frowned. "Jake, does she have any siblings? Close in age?"

Jake shook his head. "No."

"Then I don't . . . understand. An identical killer? Maybe they are cousins . . . or what?"

"Who cares. Let me through."

He shoved between Barnier and Julia, pushing himself into the sordid bustle of Soi Cowboy.

The street life of Soi Cowboy was blithely ignorant of the turmoil in Baccara. Freelance whores were eating sausages on sticks outside Rawhide, fake monks were begging sorrowfully at the corner by the Dollhouse.

Where was Chemda?

Jake tried the phone three times. Nothing. Voice mail. He went back, walking up to the doorman of Baccara.

"Did you see a girl? A Khmer girl, running out of here?"

"Nnn?"

"A dark girl? Please, which way did she go?"

The doorman grunted, and shrugged—and pointed at another bar.

Jake demanded: "Lucky Star? She went in there?"

A shrug—then another curt but directed nod.

"Girl."

Pushing urgently through the Cowboy crowds, Jake entered the indicated bar.

Lucky Star. It was dark. He squinted, saw two naked girls on a stage, one wearing a pelvic harness and a strap-on dildo, penetrating the other, time and again. The girls writhed and moaned, robotically. The music was Debussy: "*Claire de Lune.*" Men in the shadows were silently throwing fifty-baht notes onto the stage.

Jake ran right out. Despairing, depressed, desperate. Evidently the doorman had thought Jake had just wanted girls. Girls on girls.

It was all disgusting. Soi Cowboy disgusted him. Meeting here had been some kind of joke by Barnier, a repulsive joke by a sick and frightened man.

He was never going to find her. Maybe they would kill her. Whoever they were. His anxiety surged. Raged. A monster from the swamp. At the corner of Soi Cowboy by the Dutch pub, he anxiously phoned his hotel on the off chance, as a last chance—but the receptionist had not seen her either, and that was that.

His hopes had gone.

Jake looked up and down the glittering lights of Asoke Boulevard in terminal dismay. A bleeping from his phone; a text message.

Kdnapd. Car. Plz help. Dont know where. lease help Jake help.

33

Twenty-four hours later and Jake still hadn't heard anything. Her phone was, of course, switched off. He'd waited for hours in the hotel just hoping, but it was hopeless.

In desperation, feeling his sense of himself begin to dissolve, he had even tried calling Chemda's mother and grandfather, risking everything—but all he got was the Sovirom maids, who answered his questions with impenetrable Khmer. He was lost; he was unmanned and enfeebled; he understood no one; and now he was sitting in a street-side bar in central Bangkok with Julia and Barnier.

Marcel Barnier's breath smelled of whiskey. He always smelled of whiskey. He had apparently been drinking on the sois of Sukhumvit, nonstop, since the incident in Baccara, as he was too damn "motherfucking scared" to go home to the flat in case "the witch" came to kill him.

It was accepted by all that the witch, the killer, was not Chemda. Julia had been tearful and profound enough in her apologies on that score. But that didn't answer any of the other questions. The questions that *burned* through Jake. Where was Chemda? Who'd taken her? The Laotians? Her family? The Khmer Rouge loyalists? Would they come for Jake? And if they did find Jake, would they bother with a kidnapping? Maybe they would just *kill him,* as they had so nearly done in Anlong Veng.

He remembered the smells and the senses of that moment: involuntarily praying in the dust by Pol Pot's grave; staring at the incense sticks planted in the old noodle jar; smelling the rotting trash. Waiting to die, like a tethered goat. He knew that could happen again at any moment—but he couldn't flee for his life.

Because of Chemda. He couldn't leave Chemda to her fate. Not now, not ever. He had lost two women in his life. This third he would find again. He had to, or his life was smoke and ashes.

Jake turned and looked at his drinking companions. Julia— miserable and guilt-ridden and earnest. And Barnier, drunk and frightened and smirking. But at least they seemed relatively *calm.* Jake was far from calm. He was nervy. Jumpy. Twitching. He wanted to do something. *Anything.*

"Tell us? Why have you asked us here, Marcel?"

The Frenchman languorously swallowed another shot of Mekong whiskey.

"I want to know what you have discovered, I want to compare notes. Apparently Julia has a theory."

"A theory?"

"What happened in Cambodia thirty years ago. Julia says she has worked out why. The theoretical *basis.*"

Jake switched his anxious gaze to the pale American woman.

"Yes," she said, very quietly, as if speaking to herself. "Well . . . I believe I might have pieced together the intellectual idea that underpinned what happened in Cambodia in 1976."

"So! Now is the time to tell!" Barnier grinned, quite vulgarly, maybe a little desperately. "Ideas, theories, discoveries, whatever. Confess! It might help us, and it might even help Chemda. No? *Allez, les braves!*"

Barnier lit a cigarette and inhaled the smoke through his nose. Jake stared, in nervous depression, at the ecstatic neon glow of the nearest sushi bar, and then he shrugged at his own bleakness. He looked at his cell phone. Nothing. Nothing at all. Nothing piled on nothing.

They had nothing better to do, nothing else they *could* do. Why not discuss, why not do this?

He motioned at Julia.

"Go on?"

In five very dense minutes, she outlined her theory: but she did it in precise and deeply confusing scientific language. The words were long and slippery; Jake found them hard to follow. His thoughts persistently drifted to Chemda. Barnier had no such problems, he kept saying, "Yes, yes," grinning self-consciously and exhaling cigarette smoke in clouds of triumphant approbation, like he was winning a game of poker. By bluffing.

"It's a stunning thesis," said Barnier when Julia had concluded. "It is surely right! This is surely what Ghislaine's essay must also have affirmed. *C'est magnifique!* You are a true scientist, and a sleuth!"

Julia looked half anguished, half pleased. Jake was entirely confused.

"Can you guys explain it a bit slower, in more simple terms. Remember, I'm just a bloody photographer. A snapper."

Julia offered a sympathetic smile. "Of course. Sorry. First you have to know a little bit about the evolution of the human mind."

"OK."

Patiently, and more slowly, she explained *behavioral modernity:* the accepted idea that men and women made a Great Leap Forward in their cognition and cultural development around forty thousand years ago. Jake nodded.

"So, cave art, music, religion and stuff, proper burials, and tool making, they all . . . this is the first time we see them?"

"Correct," said Barnier. "Abstract mentation! Teamwork in hunt-ing. Even humor is born. We see many, many signs that the human mind, the human spirit, quite suddenly changed during the Ice Ages."

"Why did it change?"

Barnier puffed smoke at a passing tuk-tuk and answered: "Genetic mutation. Or change in the neural structures. Or both! No one is sure."

"So . . . In which case. Go over it again? The *entire* thesis?"

Julia nodded, shyly, and answered: "It's actually quite simple but, like I say, very relevant. In essence I believe that the birth of the art evidenced in the cave paintings shows the birth of guilt, and this guilt is the key to the modern human condition."

"And . . . ?"

"Around 40,000 B.C. it also seems that we, as a species, became truly aware of . . . of death. Hence the complex ritualization of burials. And a corollary of this is that we humans must surely have become aware that we were killing our fellow creatures, condemning them to death—and so we began to feel guilty over this slaughter. Guilt for . . . who we are."

Jake looked again at his cell phone. Nothing. He glanced at the rumbling Bangkok traffic. The pink-and-yellow Toyotas reflected the streetlights, casting a subtle glow on Julia's animated face.

"The intriguing nature of this theory," she continued, "a theory that, as I say, I am sure Ghislaine Quoinelles first brought to birth, is that it neatly explains many puzzling aspects to the great Paleolithic cave art of France and Spain, and this art is, in itself, the strongest evidence we have for the Great Leap Forward."

"Puzzling aspects?"

Julia answered:

"*The obsession with animals.* All the great caves are just *filled* with drawings and engravings and even sculptures of animals, galloping animals, herding animals, animals charging, animals copulating. Animals being speared to death. Various people have tried to explain these obsessive animal paintings as part of some ritual, to aid the hunt, to magically enable better hunting, but then why show so many animals—like horses or lions—that were rarely if ever hunted? Alternatively, why not *just* show hunts? Others have claimed the artworks are mere doodles, but then why are these paintings often so beautiful, so inaccessible, so treasured, so carefully hidden at the very ends of caves?"

Barnier interrupted: "This theory might appeal to an artist like yourself, Jake. Julia believes that the cave artists were, in a sense, returning to the scene of the crime! They were working through their own sudden guilt at seeing these animals suffer. A psychological reaction to trauma."

Jake's nodding smile was faint. The word *trauma* reminded him of Chemda. He glanced at his useless phone, then forced himself to focus on the argument:

"Sure. Er. That's interesting. Sure. But this theory seems a bit *fragile*?"

"There is more," Julia continued. "My theory—Ghislaine's theory—*this theory* also explains why we see animals that were never hunted, why we see animals presented so reverently, and the reason is *envy*. The newly modern humans wanted to return to the Edenic state they once enjoyed, the guiltless freedom still enjoyed by the animals they killed. So they painted these animals as a form of worship, envious worship. This also explains several puzzling images of men with animal masks, like the *Sorcier* of the *Trois Frères,* which show men wanting to be animals *once again*. Men were now feeling exiled from their fellow creatures—and they looked back with regret."

Jake frowned.

"OK."

"Another puzzling aspect of the cave art is why there are so few representations of *humans*. I remember my friend Annika mentioning this. That was one of my first clues. I have now worked out the relevance." Julia sighed. "All we have in the caves, in terms of human representation, are a few crude sketches. Most of them seem to be obscene caricatures, insulting, like the heavy-breasted women of Pech Merle, or the grinning imbecile of La Pasiega, or the ludicrous faces of Rouffignac. Why are these paintings so few, and so crude?" Julia barely paused; her question was rhetorical. "Mankind is not known for his lack of vanity and self-interest. For thousands of years we have painted and drawn and sketched ourselves and each other, yet back in 30,000 or 10,000 B.C., when there were *truly* great and skillful artists working, artists who could conjure an auroch or a lion with a few lines, like a Stone Age Matisse or Raphael, these artists refused to depict the beauty of men and women. They either ignored their own kind or obscenely insulted them, as if they despised themselves, despised mankind."

Barnier, intent, and no longer smoking, interrupted once again: "There's lots of other evidence, in addition. I am correct?"

"Yes." Julia nodded, firmly. "For instance, when the few images of men don't show cartoons or abusive doodles, they show men being tortured and speared: in the caves of Cougnac, there are the so-called *hommes blessés,* the wounded men, men being speared to death. Or the tortured boys of Addaura. What despair made them record all this? Why all the horrible and existential self-loathing?"

"So," said Jake. "Why?"

She gazed his way. "Now we come to Gargas. The famous Hands of Gargas. These hands have been a total mystery for a century. Some say they show frostbite in the Ice Age. But why would you go to the trouble of stenciling nasty wounds? Others say the hands must have belonged to a tribe with some kind of genetic malformation, but there is no skeletal evidence for this, and again, why stencil such embarrassing disfigurements? The latest theory is that the fingers are not mutilated or severed, they were bent over before being stenciled, and the hands show a hunting code—one finger closed means *antelope,* two for *auroch*—similar codes are utilized by some tribes today."

Barnier came back, like they were working as a tag team:

"A particularly ludicrous theory. You only have to go to Gargas to see that. The hands are profoundly affecting. Intense. Hands of men and women and children. It's not a few men making signals."

"So, what—" Jake stared at Barnier, and then at Julia. "What do *you* think about Gargas?"

Julia answered: "The strange mute stencils of the hands express *guilt* and they seek *redemption*. The stencils say these human hands have sinned. These hands have killed. Forgive us. We can speculate that the fingers were, at first, mutilated *deliberately* as a kind of atonement, in a shamanic ritual. There is good evidence for this: some tribes did the same in very recent times, like the Tui-Tonga, or the Tahitians—they cut off knuckles and digits—as a form of human self-sacrifice, when the tribe needed to atone for sin, to propitiate some deity, or to mourn a noble death."

A pause. Jake listened intently.

Julia added: "But after these initial amputations, in Gargas, probably the fingers were just bent over for ritual stenciling and the severed fingers became symbolic. But still the cavemen came into the cave to ritually stencil the hands, the hands that killed the noble animals. To express contrition, to seek redemption. To mourn the deaths they caused."

Jake drank some of his Singha beer.

"All right. I'm beginning to understand . . . I think. But the skulls, the skulls and the bones, how do they fit in?"

Hunching forward, Barnier interruped: "Think about it, Jake, think. Here we have, in Julia's magnificent thesis, the unique tragedy of *la condition humaine*. Encapsulated. Uniquely, it seems, we as a species have a sense of shame and guilt for *just being human,* for the sin of simply being ourselves. And all of this . . ." He smiled. "And yet all of this can be prevented with a few slices of the knife."

34

Jake said, "What?"

With surprising deftness Barnier extracted, lit, inhaled, and exhaled another cigarette.

"I will explain the rest. But we need all the information. First, tell me your story. Tell me what you have found."

Jake still wasn't quite there. But he'd had enough of being quiet, so he told Julia and Barnier his side of things, to distract himself. He gave them the whole story of his meeting with Chemda and their flight from Bangkok and the rabid janitor and Pol Pot's grave and even the *krasue*. As he did, he fidgeted and sweated, looking at his phone, looking anxiously up and down the soi at the durian seller and the mango woman and the cackling and pouting ladyboys, the *kathoeys,* the transsexual hookers, with their cheekbones and lipstick and weird tallness and their supertweaked hair: they were like pirated copies of women, like the fake Chanel handbags of women. Brilliant imitations, yet not quite right.

Barnier mouthed a smoke ring as Jake concluded his narrative. Then he spoke up:

"There we have it, that makes it all fit together. Finally! You see,

I too have been doing my own thinking, my own investigation, so, with what you have told me—and of course Julia's decisive conception—I believe we have the total answer."

"Which is?"

"Let's, once more, go back in history. *Oui?* We know that eighty years ago or whenever, Stalin and the Soviets began a long, long campaign to try and create man-animal hybrids, powerful but biddable, strong, guilt-free killers, or robotically servile but very capable workers." He drank half a shot of whiskey in one gulp, and continued. "These experiments were a bunch of crap. They failed, dismally. And no surprise because, as a zoologist, I know the species barrier is just too big. In the end the Russians gave up their project. However, not everyone was so . . . gay, as you British say." Barnier smiled in his bogus way. "The Chinese had been intrigued by the experiments from the start. Madame Mao visited that lab in Abkhazia, the Chinese even bought the data from the lab when it was nearly shut down in the eighties. So we know the Chinese liked the underlying concept—*a fucking lot.* They just didn't like the blundering, clumsy Soviet method. Humanzees. Comedy science."

"How do you know that?"

"Because of the mission. The mission to China and Cambodia. In '76."

Julia quietly said, "Please go on."

"As you know, in 1976 the Chinese government discreetly invited some selected Western academics, historians, scientists—including me—to go to Beijing and Kampuchea for a series of 'conferences.'" Barnier did two drunken quotation marks in the humid evening air, with his nicotine-stained fingers. "But the Chinese conferences were a farce, at least for the zoologists like me. They showed us the Great Wall, they fed us plenty of abalone and *pak choi,* but they weren't really interested in zoology, at least not after the first few days. There was, in short, an . . . undeclared hierarchy. *In the group.* Some were more important than others. Pretty soon, I realized that many other people—the neurologists, the archaeologists, the guys like Ghislaine Quoinelles—they were doing . . . the more *significant* work, behind *closed doors.* The many, many, many closed doors of China."

"So that's the answer," said Jake. "The zoology failed, and consequently they tried a second route."

"Yes, exactly." Barnier belched smoke. "The Chinese plan was this: they still wanted to create a man without conscience, without guilt, without our species shame, but they realized the zoological method was a pitiful dead end. The man-ape stuff, that was nonsense. That's why, in time, they ignored people like me."

"And they went for something more refined, something neurosurgical."

Barnier's eyes shone, a hint of mischief amid the liquor and the terror.

"Ah! Well . . . but wait. To perfectly fit the puzzle together, we must use *all* the pieces you two have provided. Let's go back to France. We know from Prunières, Ghislaine's favorite obscure scientist, that there was a coincidence of trepanation and tribal violence in Lozère, *non?* How did this happen? Very likely the first trepanations began as a rudimentary Stone Age cure for epilepsy. That theory has been around for a while. Call it letting the demons out, if you like, as that's maybe what cavemen called it. But anyway, the reason these primitive surgeries endured is 'cause they actually freaking *worked.* One of the most common forms of epilepsy is frontal-lobe seizures, so-called because they occur in the frontal cortex. So a crude trepanation can, remarkably, be effective after a fashion, if you hit the right spot. But here's the genius bit!"

Barnier eradicated another cigarette as he continued. "The Chinese invited Ghislaine, the grandson of a great *gauchiste* scientist in

Paris, once an expert on crossbreeding himself, to their conference. However, they invited Ghislaine not just because of his political pedigree, but because of his theories. Ghislaine was the young and coming man, the radical, the *soixante-huitard,* the scholar who knew all about Prunières, about trepanations and Stone Age violence, *and* he was the one who had developed these related theories—of human guilt and neural evolution. And listening to all this, to Ghislaine's ideas, the Chinese must have made the final deduction: that these primitive societies in France had achieved some unexpected results from their archaic brain surgery, and therefore these ancient tribes had begun drilling into healthy brains. Deliberately."

Jake shook his head.

"What do you mean?"

"Like this. Imagine you trepan some caveman, because he has fits—epileptiform seizures—and you want to get rid of the demons. But when you do the surgery, it turns out, not only do you get rid of the demons, you turn him into a superior fighter, a warrior, a logical brute. Why? Because, quite by accident, you have chopped out some of the higher evolved structures of the frontal cortex, the neural networks *responsible for guilt and conscience,* the part of the brain that evolved in the Paleolithic, the Great Leap Forward, as Julia so brilliantly confirms."

The traffic surged, a beggar stared, a ladyboy wiggled her tongue at Jake.

"Ah. Jesus."

"Exactly. Fucking *exactly.* So you discover that by drilling brains you can make real nasty, ruthless, *guilt-free* killers. Like feral gorillas but clever, *oui?* An *inestimable* evolutionary advantage." He vigorously extinguished his eighth cigarette and looked across the table. "So that's why we see so many trepanations. All over the world. These Stone Age primitives began to do it on purpose, to make themselves more warlike—but maybe these societies then *collapsed* because they killed too *well*. They collapsed into tribal violence, ritualized torture, executions, mass suicides, even. And this is what we see in Lozère, and the legends of the Black Khmer on the Plain of Jars. Violence and trepanation and tragedy. Hand in hand in hand."

Julia interrupted.

"But of course the crucial point is that the Chinese decided to repeat the Stone Age trepanations. To alter the neocortex."

Barnier accepted his next whiskey, slugged it, and lit yet another Krung Thep cigarette; then he said, "Yes. Using Ghislaine's ideas and knowledge as a theoretical base—the same ideas you have unearthed, Julia—the Chinese must have established a way of chopping the possibility of conscience and guilt out of the neocortex. And then, when they finally felt ready, they must have started their grisly *experiments* on the brain, in Phnom Penh, on live subjects."

Jake said, "But these experiments went wrong. Didn't they? They turned people into zombies. Like Chemda's grandmother."

"Indeed," said Barnier, "it seems so. Looking back, I can see why. If a guilt module exists it must be delicately interwoven with the frontal cortex *and* the limbic system, and the hippocampus. You might get lucky and remove most of it, or you might just leave a drooling lobotomy victim. It's not a question of just neatly spooning a few cubic cc's of conscience from the top of your head. And their surgery was, I am guessing, desperately crude. This was Cambodia in the seventies. So they lobotomized these poor bastards and turned them into alcoholics, rapists, psychotics. Not that the Commies especially cared: they were feeling their way, these were early experiments. Broken eggs for the omelette, eh?" He smiled, and frowned, and gazed at a Muslim woman in a black shroud with a metal nose mask over her face, like a Norman warrior. The Muslim quarter of Bangkok apparently began just north of the brothels and ladyboys.

Now Barnier continued: "My guess is that they must have cut into the wider inhibitory systems by mistake, dopamine reward systems, who knows. But they ended up creating retards or helpless monsters. Like that guy who tried to ravish Chemda, what was his name again?"

"Ponlok. His name was Ponlok."

"So this explains it." Julia shook her head. "This also explains why people *volunteered* for the experiments."

"Uh-huh. Yes, it does, does it not? The real committed Marxists volunteered. They wanted to be perfected, like Cathars, they wanted to be stain-free Communists, to have their guilty bourgeois minds cleaned and purified." He spat smoke. "A quite magnificent dramatic irony, worthy of Flaubert. Given that it happened in maybe the most revolting regime in the world—because if anyone *should* feel guilt it is *the Khmer Rouge.*"

Jake ignored his beer and asked, "So how did *you* end up *here*? What happened to *you* in the seventies?"

Barnier sucked on his cigarette. "Like I told you. First they took us to China, and that was bad, dark, unsettling. And then we went to Kampuchea and that was just . . . Aii, that was just motherfucking *horrible*. As soon as we landed in Phnom Penh I could *smell* it! You could smell the desolation and fear. And there was the silence. Like a dead city, like Venice in a very bad dream. No cars. No laughter. No one talking. Just whispers. Whispers and heat and decay. And those eerie, eerie streets. My God, those empty streets." Barnier downed another drink, and ordered yet another.

Jake said, "But what actually happened? What did you do there, in Cambodia?"

"Same as China. Zero. I was ignored, because by then they knew they really wanted guys like Ghislaine, neurologists and historians and shrinks and the like. These important guys would be whisked away in jeeps, while I would stay in my creepy hotel, staring at the

Tonle Sap, thinking about death. And one day I lost it, I just decided: *enough.* So I sneaked out of the hotel and I slipped my KR handler and I found a bicycle in one of those empty streets and I picked it up and rode out into the countryside." He shook his head. "And I saw for myself. Out there, in the countryside. Oh my God. I saw the truth, Jake. I saw with my own eyes the fucking reality of their perfect Marxist revolution. Everyone was wearing black, black pajamas, building these stupid irrigation canals, in the sun, carrying mud in baskets, barefoot. Sliding around in the mud. Skeletal. *I saw people pulling plows.* People. Not animals, *people.*" He gazed, furious, at nothing. He continued. "They weren't even robots, they were beasts, beasts of burden. Silent serfs. No one spoke. I cycled around and stared and listened and I heard nothing. Just people working in the mud. And it was then I realized: this place was a prison, just one big prison. An entire country turned into a concentration camp, a whole nation doing forced labor." He coughed angry smoke. "That did it for me. I rode back, I was trembling all the way. Almost sick in the street. Pretty soon I started asking questions and I got one or two people to talk, and they told me about the killings, the many killings. People were being killed for anything, for wearing glasses, for planting their own potatoes, for speaking a foreign language, for loving their children too much, for writing, for talking, for dancing, for laughing—you really could get killed for laughing in Cambodia under the KR, you could get your head smashed against a tree for being happy, *because laughter and happiness were capitalist,* and soon after I just *quit.* They let me go, all they did was tell me not to talk about the conferences, and I didn't. Other people got more stringent restrictions: they were told to lie low for their whole careers, afterward. So no one would guess what the Communists were doing. Everyone had to conceal their discoveries and sacrifice themselves, to the greater project—revolutionary Marxism."

Julia said, "And that's why Ghislaine went back to Lozère. That's why he reacted so weirdly when I found the skulls."

Barnier agreed, vehemently: "In his later years, he must've been fucking conflicted, like your friend Annika said. There he was, once a brilliant young scientist, with a brilliant new theory, based on the skulls and the bones of Lozère, the cave paintings, and Prunières; and yet he was told to trash it, to forget it, to destroy his essays, to kill his own career. And then along you come and you find some more skulls, and he is reminded of all this, the waste of his life and his theories."

"He was told to do this, to stay silent," Jake asked, "because it's what the Cambodians wanted?"

"Ah no." Barnier shook his head. "No no no. Not the Cambodians. The Chinese, of course. *The Chinese were in charge of the whole thing.* That's what I always understood, this experiment was always a Chinese operation, they had the money and ambition and the idea, but they used the little Cambodians, their lunatic Maoist acolytes, the craziest regime in the world, as useful lieutenants. The Chinks were farming it out to the Khmer, outsourcing, franchising."

"Why?" Jake asked.

"This was '76. China was in turmoil. Mao was dying. The extreme Maoists needed somewhere to work *undisturbed,* and Cambodia was their death laboratory, a fucking socialist *playpen.*"

A beggar with no legs dragged himself past Tony Roma's pizza outlet.

Jake asked, "And what happened to you *then*? Why are you here? Why were you in Abkhazia? Why have you been traveling around the world, trying to work out the past?"

Barnier exhaled smoke, his face sallow and his brow darkened. It seemed that he'd grown sick of himself.

"Because I have my own searing guilt at being involved in any of this. I *remember* '79, when the Khmer Rouge fell, I *remember* watching my TV in Lyon and seeing it: all my worst suspicions confirmed, the whole damn country had devoured itself, inside out, two million dead. A quarter of the nation. The nation that cut off its own legs, gouged out its own eyes. And that's when I renounced it, that's when I was born again—a capitalist. A simple capitalist and proud of it." He was glaring at Jake defiantly. "I moved to Hong Kong, then LA, and then Singapore, and I used my guilty brain and became a day trader, a money broker. I wanted to be as un-Communist as possible, and it did the trick. I made my money and I fucked myself a lot of poontang, and, you know what, if I have to die now then to hell with it, kill me, kill me, for I have sinned. But at least I'm not a cunting Communist, not anymore."

Barnier drank the residue of his whiskey in one toss. "And in the last couple of years I have used my money to try to find out what really happened in China, and Cambodia. I went to Angkor, 'cause I knew the KR were interested in Angkor. I went to Sukhumi. But none of it really made sense, until now. Until lovely Miss Kerrigan told me this theory, and you told me your story. I suppose I should be thankful to you both. Explaining just how evil my life has been." He laughed. Bitterly.

A tuk-tuk driver swerved past, swigging from a Leo beer can. Jake looked at his phone, ritualistically. But Chemda was not going to call. She was gone. Maybe for good. The phone was silent.

Jake leaned and poured himself a glass of the Mekong whiskey. It was harsh and sour and necessary. He drank it fast, poured himself another. The mosquitoes were biting, the women in burqas waddled past the whores in their hot pants.

Julia was talking.

"I have one final query, Marcel."

"Eh?"

"You said to that guy in the lab, in Abkhazia, 'The Chinese took it much further.'"

The Frenchman was gazing nervously down the crowded street in a reverie of half-hidden fear. He alerted himself, and turned.

"Aii. Yes. Yes. That's right. I did."

The American woman leaned forward, serious. "How do you know this? How do you know they carried on?"

Barnier had maybe his sixtieth cigarette of the evening poised, unlit, between his fingers. He cracked open a Zippo lighter and flamed the tobacco. Then he plumed a blue maribou feather of smoke and said: "About a year ago I got an e-mail, out of nowhere, from my old colleague Colin Fishwick. My old comrade in arms from Democratic Kampuchea. Fishwick!"

"The neurologist!" Julia said. "The other survivor, from the photo."

"The only one alive, apart from me. We e-mailed about the killings. The way we were all being . . . knocked off? One by one. He wanted to know what I reckoned, how dangerous it was. I said I was damn terrified and I was looking into the mystery and I was going to flee if it all got too close. Fishwick said the killer was probably coming for *him,* too, but he was so hidden away he felt safe. For the moment."

"OK."

"The e-mail exchange ended soon after that," Barnier added. "But Fishwick let one thing slip. I asked what he was doing. And then he confessed. He said he had been recruited *again* by the Chinese. He'd been enticed back—big money—to develop things. He hinted it was the same stuff he had done thirty years ago. Whatever that was—I hadn't guessed at the time. Now we know. Anyway, he said he was *still* working at a lab in Yunnan, in a very obscure, very remote place. Balagezong, quite near Zhongdian. It's in the lower Himalayas. Hard by Tibet."

Jake stared across the dirty table.

"You say he is . . . *still* working?"

"*Yep.*" Barnier nostriled smoke. "Right now, in this remote corner of China, Balagezong—it seems they're still wielding the scalpel, they are still chopping out guilt and conscience. *They are still doing the operation.* The only difference is . . ." He paused and gazed warily around, then added: "This time, apparently, according to Fishwick, this time they've got it *right*. And that—"

He stopped abruptly. His face was a cold-sweated mask.

35

The Frenchman was standing.

"*I just saw Chemda!* Over there. By the *kathoey* bar." He hesitated. "*Unless—!*"

Jake was already running down bustling Sukhumvit, barging past the white men and their miniature girlfriends; but he felt a surprisingly strong hand pull him back.

Barnier's whiskey breath was hot in his face.

"Think—this cannot be your girlfriend—think—it must be the killer—why would Chemda be skulking around. *Jake?*"

The good sense was chilling. But Jake didn't care: he had to take the risk. It might be her. He wrestled himself free of Barnier.

"I'm going to look. Where was she, *exactly*?"

Barnier puffed his exasperation.

"*Idiot.* There. There. Fucking madness. She was there. I am going back to my apartment, lock myself in—get my bags—and then I am fucking *gone.*"

He turned and paced away, joining the crowds, another older white guy among the younger Asian girls and the he-shes. Jake found Julia at his side.

"Let me help."

She helped, but it was swiftly obvious the search was fruitless. They searched up and down Soi 2, and Soi 4, they ran past Beer Garden and Foodland Supermarket, they pushed past the freelance hookers and the Saudi wives and the blind karaoke singers warbling their terrible songs.

Nothing.

"Maybe," Julia suggested, "maybe Barnier imagined it. Probably. He is drunk."

"He is delusional." Jake spat his disappointment. "Fucking drunken lunatic. Ah, fuck . . . *Fuck it*." He rubbed the tiredness and despair into his face with weary hands. "Come on. I don't believe he saw anything. Let's go to my hotel. See if Chemda left a message."

This was, of course, pathetically hopeful, as he knew: but he had no hopes left.

The American woman was silent as they paced down hot, busy, nocturnal Soi Nana.

"Jake, I'm sorry. For what happened in that bar. Chemda."

"It's OK. I believe you. And I also know the killer just *can't be Chemda*."

They were at the corner of Soi 6. A whore in a microskirt was bowing to a small shrine, a spirit house, erected in front of the Shakerz Coyote Tavern.

"So who is it?"

"A clone?" Jake sighed. "Who knows. If they can cut your conscience out of your head, what *can't* they do? Clone you? Multiply you? Your guess is better than mine."

Julia put a hand on his tensed, muscled, angry shoulder.

"We'll find her."

"Yeah. Of course we will. Somewhere in Asia. Where shall we start looking? India?"

They walked quickly down Soi 6, past the Sukhumvit Grand with its saluting guards, where a snicket of a side road led under papaya trees. It was a cloistered spot in the kineticism of the city: two Thai kids were sitting on stools playing guitar, softly, like troubadours in the moonlight. Another spirit house lurked in the very darkest corner.

Julia said, "What about her family?"

"Speak to them? Sure. That's the obvious solution, isn't it? I even tried. But I don't think they *trust* me, they already think I kidnapped her, whisked her away into danger. Can I blame them—"

"But she was already in trouble when you met her, in Laos, right?"

"Yes, but . . ." Jake sighed. "Since I met her she's got into a lot *more* trouble. And I wonder. Maybe it *is* my fault? Blundering into situations I don't understand? That's the thing with Cambodia, Thailand, all these countries—you think you have grasped a situation, then it turns out it was entirely the opposite, it all meant something different." He gazed at the lobby of his hotel, the Sukhumvit Crown. Desolate. "Jesus, what are we gonna do?"

As if it was an answer, he felt a buzzing in his pocket.

His phone, blinking an American cell number. Tyrone. *Tyrone.*

He eagerly clicked ACCEPT.

"Ty?"

"Hey. You OK? Any news of Chemda?"

"So you heard. You got my message?"

"Yes, but—"

"We don't know where she is, Ty. Just gone. I've been trying to ring you. Do you know anything? Just . . . desperate."

"I'm trying to tell you. Look . . ." Tyrone's drawl hinted at something. A revelation.

"What, Ty? What?"

The silence was sharp. Then Tyrone answered: "I have good and bad news. I think I know where Chemda is."

"Where? Jesus! Is she OK?"

"She's OK, probably, at the moment. Probably."

The signal from Phnom Penh faded out. Jake sprinted up the steps to get better reception, waving at Julia as he did: *wait here, this is important, sorry.*

Tyrone was back on the line: "I did some investigating for you."

"Like how?"

"I had a brainstorm when I got your message. Figured her dynasty must know something. I just went to the Sovirom house, the compound, and I did it—I confronted her mother. And she fessed up. She fessed up and broke down. They've had a kidnap note."

"Who is it? The Lao?"

Jake stared at the dingy hotel parking lot. Julia was sitting on the steps, staring at the darkness. The boys had stopped guitaring songs. A rat was nosing between garbage bags, a fat and brazen tropical rat.

"Chemda is in China." Tyrone sighed. "Yunnan. Right up by the Tibetan border, a place called—"

"Balagezong!"

An intake of breath.

"Yep. Jesus, Jake. *Balagezong.* How do you know that?"

Jake hastily explained—the conversation with Barnier, the terrible brain surgeries. Somewhere in Phnom Penh, Tyrone swore his surprise.

"Wow. OK. That makes sense. Total madness, but a lot of goddamn sense. So that's what they are doing. And that explains why Madame Tek was so freaked—"

"What do you mean?"

Tyrone paused. "Prepare yourself. Really. *Prepare yourself.* I'm sorry. But through her crying jags I pretty much got the impression, from Madame Tek, that some physical threat had been made against Chemda, that they were threatening to do something awful to her, unless Sovirom Sen gave them what they wanted."

"Which is? What do they want?"

Tyrone did a verbal shrug: "No idea. Maybe just money. But apparently he has flown to Yunnan, to meet them, to try and get his daughter back before they—"

"Cut open her brain. Section her brain."

The rat squealed as it fought another rat for a piece of rotting carp head.

"Yeah. Yes. Sorry, Jake. I'm sorry. God. But yes, that must be the threat. Chemda's mother was just a *mess,* crying a river, crying like the fucking *Hudson.*"

"I'm going there. Balagezong. I have to go there."

Tyrone protested: "Jake Jake *Jake.* C'mon, calm down. I figured you'd say that—but c'mon—think about it, this is very very dangerous now—"

"Ty, they already tried to kill me. In Anlong. Can it get any worse? Now they are going to cut open Chemda? Turn her into some fucking zombie? I'm going, tonight."

A very short silence. Then a long sigh. Then: "OK, mad Englishman. I'll do my best from here. Try and get more information. I know you are Mr. Guilt Trip, but this isn't your fault, Jake, you didn't do this—"

"But I love her and she saved my life in Laos and I love her. I'll call you from China."

He broke off the call and stepped over to Julia. With as few words as possible he explained the situation. Her face trembled at the corners of her lips. Guilt spoke without words.

"So I'm going to leave tonight, now, sooner," said Jake. "First I better go and tell Barnier, then arrange flights, to Kunming—"

Wordless and quick, they made the corner of Soi 6 and Soi 4 to Pachara Suites. It was just a three-minute walk, past the Seven Seas restaurant with the girls in old Singapore Airlines dresses, past the squid sellers with their racks of rubbery ganglions ready to char-grill.

At the last junction, they heard the ambulance sirens.

Sprinting around the corner, they saw it all: the flashing red lights, the police cars askew on the sidewalk, and a man drenched in red paint being escorted from the lobby.

Jake watched, quite stunned.

It wasn't a man in red paint. It was a Thai man in blood.

He was covered in gore, splashed energetically with human blood, and he was handcuffed and being manhandled by two policemen.

Crowds were gathered, people were hanging off balconies, staring down at the emergency, at the sirens and the unholstered guns and the swiveling red lights. At the man covered in blood being tugged toward a police car. Jake recognized him. The doorman from Pachara Suites.

He pushed through the onlookers, and two cops with white gloves, but another policeman stopped him from going any farther. Jake shouted across the yards that separated them.

"Hey! Supashok? You remember me? Supashok! Jake Thurby."

The face turned.

"Supashok? Remember? I was with Chemda? The Khmer girl. This morning—you let us see Mr. Barnier? It's me, Jake—"

The terrified man regarded Jake, and then he yelled. He screamed and he pointed:

"You! It was her—your girlfrien'! She kill him! I let her in then I hear scream!"

Jake backed away. A Thai policeman was pressing down on the doorman's head, forcing him into the car. Supashok was still shouting at Jake, in English.

"She kill him. Your girlfrien'. Kill him!"

The cops weren't listening to his screaming words; probably they couldn't understand English. They didn't know the doorman was accusing Chemda of killing Barnier. But soon the doorman *would* speak Thai. And explain. And soon the cops would get it.

Shrinking even further into the crowds, Jake grabbed Julia's hand and they paced away, discreetly, and then less discreetly they jogged—and then they fled. Running from the blood, running from the scene, running down Soi 6, running past the Heidelberg German pub, where the hookers and the midgets sat outside on their bar stools cackling and laughing and eating rice noodles and saying, *Meester, meester. Welcome, welcome.*

36

"Guilt."

"Why do you feel so guilty?" Jake gazed at her and shook his head. "Don't think like that. You didn't know."

"If I hadn't accused Chemda, she wouldn't have run out of the bar—she wouldn't have been snatched." Julia rubbed her face with both hands. "I have two thousand dollars left, nothing to go home to, I have screwed it all up. Let me do this, let me come with you and try . . . and save her."

Jake sighed. "But maybe you should at least have rung that guy. The policeman in France?"

"Rouvier."

"Yes, him."

"How could I?" Her eyes were bright and sad—and honest. "I'd have had to tell him everything. He'd have got straight in touch with the Thai police. Who would detain you, because you were implicated by the doorman, at the murder scene. Then you'd be stuck in Bangkok."

It made sense. Jake knew it. He swiveled and squinted through the scratchy plastic of the window.

Julia added: "I'll call Rouvier when we are safely in China. At some point."

"*Safely?*" Jake almost laughed. He didn't laugh. The Thai Airways jet was banking toward Kunming. The City of Eternal Spring. The capital of Yunnan. Monotonous blocks of housing stretched along a lake; factory chimneys trailed pennants of smoke. Polluting the future.

"She must be a relative, or something." Julia's voice was pensive, musing. "I don't understand how they can be so similar yet different, sometimes a man, sometimes a woman. An identical twin would be a girl."

"Chemda," said Jake. That's all he could think about. His lover. *Chemda.*

And the irony.

All his life he had wanted danger and risk, well, now he had it, but in the most unexpected way: he had the risk and danger of love. You fall in love with someone—you endanger your soul and your happiness. He saw that now. He was a war reporter of the heart. Taking those risks, capturing that . . . what? That thing. That moment.

Jake turned and regarded Julia. He watched her as she gently placed her hands on her stomach. A protective gesture, like a beautiful quattrocento Madonna in a painting. Shy, yet subtly determined. Destined, yet gracious. He made one more attempt.

"Julia, you know the killer will *also* be going to Balagezong. To find Fishwick."

"Yes."

"So go home?"

"No."

The plane trundled to a stop at Kunming Airport. Red-and-yellow Chinese flags hung limply from a large arrivals building, in mild sunlight. Chinese script jangled everywhere, with no English translations.

"We'd better run, we need to *run,* we connect in a few minutes—"

They made it, with six minutes to spare, sweating their way aboard. The next flight was even bumpier. A Dragonair prop, a fragile domestic plane. Half the passengers were red-cheeked, eyes slitted against upland wind, laughing and drunk; half wore furry hats: these were Tibetans, mountain people, businessmen trading timber and yak meat and caterpillar fungus from the Himalayas.

Their destination was Zhongdian, way up in the wilds. Jake stared out at scenery of remorseless ruggedness, vast gorges, abrupt Manhattans of mountains, and then deep, wide, pristine cold lakes, chips of blue crystal embedded in rumpled green baize.

Julia was asleep; a talkative Chinese man in a cheap suit and nylon shoes on Jake's right was keen to practice his English.

"Only build airport last year!" said the man. "Before build airport take many, many day to go Zhongdian. Five day by truck. Now one hour plane good! It is good, yes. New China!"

The man did a thumbs-up at Jake. Then he added: "You American?"

"No. English."

The Chinese man frowned cheerfully.

"English bad. You sell us many opium. But now we are friends, make money, yes!" He laughed. His laughter was tanged with some rancid alcohol, but it was slightly cheering, amid the unalterable terrors.

Jake had already noted the cheeriness of the Chinese, on the planes, in Kunming Airport, chattering and smiling and smoking and spitting, like nouveau riche Italians with tuberculosis: a whole nation making money, a whole nation winning the lottery of capitalism. There was no sense of cynicism, just wide-eyed amazement at their own good luck.

This was not the menacing Chineseness evinced by the stories of Balagezong and the *experiments.* And yet this cheerful, friendly, nakedly capitalist China *was also* the China of the concentration camps, and Tiananmen Square, and Tibet, and the tens of thousands in slave labor, and the live harvesting of organs from prisoners. And what else? What weird surgeries? What weird surgeries right now being done to Chemda, her face sliced open from the nose up, to get at her conscience, to slice out her personality?

Swallowing his overpowering fears, Jake took the chance to show the strange address to the Chinese man. He frowned.

"Ba . . . la . . . ge . . . zong? Hnh." The man spelled out the syllables audibly and slowly. "Yes. Bala . . . ge . . . zong! Shangri-La gorge, Sichuan border, I think. Very, very difficult reach, beautiful but much difficult and danger."

"Why?"

"Big mountains. Road bad. Many . . . Gra . . . Gra . . ."

The man was trying to find or pronounce a word.

"I know how say . . . not. River ice. Not move."

"Glacier?"

"Yes! Many. Like Deqen. Deep, deep valley, people no speak any language you know. Danger, danger. See there!"

The Chinese man pointed a gold-ringed finger at the looming landscape as they descended. The greenery of southern Yunnan had given way to higher altitudes, to brown vistas, brown plateaux and gray-bluish lakes and glittering peaks of frosted ice. Jake could see wooden houses and emptiness and strange wooden structures draped with drying fodder and barley sheaves, dotting the cold, sunlit, hardened tawny fields.

"This place Zhongdian—no law, no government till 1960! Not even Tibetan law. No army. *Unexplored.* And this place"—he stabbed the same beringed finger at the slip of paper—"Balagezong. Even worse! You must be careful . . . get guide take you. One road only. So danger."

Zhongdian Airport was an incongruous outpost of angular

modernity in the empty Tibetan-Yunnanese plateau: pyramids of glass and steel surrounded by shivering lakes and shallow dun valleys. As soon as the door of the plane opened and the air breezed in, Jake was hit by it: the heart-pumping altitude. They were at 10,000 feet, abutting the true Himalayan plateau. From here it was a level but fifteen-day crow's flight to Lhasa. The altitude was an insistent pain, he could already feel it in his skull, the headache. His body screaming to adjust, like a car engine burning the wrong fuel.

"Christ," said Julia.

"We're at ten thousand feet. Are you OK?"

She smiled, but in a fragile way.

"I spent a summer in the Rockies, as a student. You get used to it. Kinda."

Jake carried Julia's bags as well as his own, and he felt like he would collapse with the effort. But they had to endure, they had to find Chemda: right now she could be under the knife, being mentally amputated, truncated, *severed*.

It might already be too late.

Sharply bright air greeted them at the exit. The parking lot was full of Tibetan families with wide fur hats and cherry-rose cheeks and slope-eyed smiles, squinting in the dazzle of the cold, harsh sun. Jake was reminded of the upland brightness of the Plain of Jars, the contrast of high altitudes and subtropical latitudes. This was even more severe. The sky was a soaring, virginal, Saint Lucy blue.

He saw his mother staring at a stained-glass window. The image was too painful.

A Chinese man with gold teeth and bright red sneakers approached them in the sun-stark parking lot.

"Taxi?"

"We need a hotel?"

"You go hotel, hui!"

"Then we need to go to this place." Jake gave up on conversation and showed the man the slip of paper, with *Balagezong* written in Mandarin and in English.

The man frowned.

"But very difficult. Guide. Taxi take Zhongdian. Hotel. Guide maybe help. Difficult."

The highway from the airport to Zhongdian was empty, apart from a few taxis and farmers' jeeps and a yak in the middle lane and some very sleek black Mercedes with tinted-black windows, traveling in speedy convoy, all swerving carefully around the yak.

"Government," said the driver, then he rolled down his window and spat. Ahead of them was the grubby high-altitude city Zhong-dian. The Baimang Snow Mountains loomed beyond, absurdly clear in the clear, cold air, a row of somber patriarchs in white churchlike hoods. An inquisition.

The drive was fast.

They entered the concrete laterals of New Zhongdian, a grid of Chinese banks and dusty government offices and PLA troop trucks and running raw rivers that passed under broken concrete bridges. The place had a frontier feel, wild, lawless, full of men in gangsterly dark glasses and Tibetan women in red-and-purple headscarves, step-ping over potholes, heading for the Many Wonder supermarket. Can-tonese pop music warbled from loudspeakers, deafening entire street corners. Yak shit and noodle packets littered the pavements.

They checked as swiftly as possible into the biggest hotel, seeking anonymity. The hotel boasted a fake lake in an atrium with fake cement storks sitting on fake islands.

No one knew anything about Balagezong. It was as if the place didn't quite exist, not like real places. Julia packed two small bags for them to take along, as Jake inquired about their destination. But it was useless. No one spoke English, some of the staff didn't even speak

Chinese, just dialects of Tibetan. But then, as they hoisted their bags to step outside, a brisk and small Chinese man arrived at their side with a noiseless smile, and he glanced at the now very creased piece of paper and said in his unexpectedly good English:

"I am the manager of the hotel, it is our pleasant to meet you. I hear you wish to see Balagezong."

"Yes. As soon as possible."

"But this is a very, very difficult place to reach. Why don't you visit Bitahai Lake instead? Jade Dragon Mountains? We have the black-necked cranes here, it is the season."

"We want to go to Balagezong."

"But, but it is too difficult." His smile was bright and determined. "You must need a guide, and such tremendous luck with the weather. I do not know if you can be doing this. It is so far, it is past the heaven villages. Instead you visit the rhododendrons, or day trip to Dali! See Tibetan dancing."

"We want to go to Balagezong."

The manager sighed. He shook his head and a faint hint of a scowl crossed his face. Then he tutted.

"So. I will help." He snapped fingers at a bellboy. "You go to the Lijiang Teahouse—take taxi from here past old town square. Ask for a young man, Tashi. *Xie Xie.* My boy will help you." His smile faded and then it was gone. The manager disappeared.

The sun was harsh on the street, so bright it was a painful process to open an eye; simply seeing was painful. Jake put on his sunglasses. Julia did the same. But everything was painful, not just the sun. Walking was painful. The blood in Jake's veins was pumping; he wheezed. He thought Julia looked unwell. Should he allow her to take these risks? Did he have the right to stop her?

"Come on," she said as the bellboy waved down a taxi. "Every minute—remember? *Every minute matters.*"

Jake wasn't sure he could get used to this: the altitude was like some slow but insidious constriction around his brain, heart, and muscles, as if he were being medievally tortured from the inside, with thumbscrews and gyves. But then he thought of Chemda being dissected and altered on a slab, and he hurried to the cab.

The old town of Zhongdian was a mazy parade of decrepit houses and Yi tribal shops and squawking scarlet parrots outside Tang dynasty pavilions abutting rackety flagstoned plazas, where Naxi women grilled yak-meat kebabs on open braziers; the sun was so bright it made the very darkest shadows even darker—and there in the shadows, by the Lijiang Teahouse, they found Tashi. He was a young Tibetan in jeans, with a rough leather jacket and a plausible manner and dazzling white teeth.

"It will be great difficult, rough, two days, maybe, but I have car. Very, very danger, two hundred dollars. We go now?"

Jake and Julia swapped a glance. Jake took out some more bills. Four hundred dollars.

"Keep us alive. Get us there. *Fast*."

Tashi smiled widely.

"We go now."

An urgent walk down a cobbled road took them past the headquarters of the Chinese Communist Party. The big red flag fluttered halfheartedly. Jake stared. Swastikas were inscribed on an ancient Buddhist doorway. Sun symbols. The car was muddy and robust: an old Japanese pickup. They climbed in and rattled out of the last straggles of Zhongdian.

"How long to Balagezong?" said Jake.

"Ten hours. Maybe more. We sleep in house. On way."

The vastness of the Tibetan plateau engulfed the speeding car. They passed herds of cudding yak and indolent dzo, yak-and-cow crossbreeds. They saw newly built Naxi farmhouses of unseasoned wood, and gatherings of villagers in purple-and-red headscarves sitting in yards under the Chinese Communist flag. Black-necked cranes shimmered off the alpine lakes, flocks of wistful and fragile beauty wintering from the colds of Siberia.

Tashi was laughing as he drove, telling them what he felt about the Chinese.

"Sometimes, before, I get angry about the Chinese, what they do to Tibetans. So now I say fuck the Chinese. And that is what I do. I fuck the Chinese, I fuck Chinese girls in the discos." He laughed. Then he said, "Why you wan' go to Balagezong? You are in trouble? No one ever want to go there, not tourist, not Chinese, not Tibetan."

Jake stayed dumb.

Tashi shrugged and laughed and said, "I do not care. No p'oblem. I used to sleep on a snooker table. I help you. Police arrest me many time, drink, fight!"

Children ran out to stare at the car as they passed through a ramshackle village: children in sheepskins and leather skirts. Then the houses dwindled and some higher brown slopes showed cataracts of snowmelt. The confusion of seasons was unnerving. Spring and winter and summer in one place at one time. The road skirted a blue mineral lake surrounded by an eerie forest draped with green moss.

Then, at last, as the sun died behind the summits, Tashi pulled off the rubbly road into the forecourt of a huge, old wooden Tibetan house, in an entirely electricity-less village, where an old snaggletoothed crone smiled at the door. This is where they would sleep. They climbed steps above a barn of stored barley and steaming livestock, into the house itself.

A pungent fire of fresh-chopped wood burned beneath a cauldron in the center of the shadowy darkness. Pieces of flattened pig face and racks of yak trotter hung drying from the eaves. Jake saw a portrait of Mao on a poster on one wall. On the opposite wall was a large photo of the Dalai Lama. *Thangkas*—Buddhist paintings—hung behind protective screens of rippling silk curtains.

Mao stared at him. The Dalai Lama stared at him. The cured flat pig faces hanging from the eaves stared curiously at him with their squashed brown cheeks and lashy little eyes, like the face of someone run over in a cartoon. Jake struggled not to think, obscenely, and upsettingly, of his sister. Why were these thoughts bombarding him? It was surely the witch, the *krasue,* unnerving him. From afar. But if he was bewitched, he was going to fight it. He had to fight, for Chemda.

Even as he sat here, she could be on the slab, her brain vivisected.

Tashi said, "You are hungry?"

"Yes."

"The old woman, she is friend of my aunt. She will feed us."

The request was passed to the woman, who nodded and called in turn to some ponytailed granddaughters, who emerged like petite and nubile genies from the intense darkness. Food was served. The house was filling with Tibetans. The whole family was eating walnuts and boiled broad beans and yak chops and oily cubes of rancid pork fat in sesame.

Tashi wiped his greasy hands on his leather jacket, then said, "OK, I ask about this place. Balagezong."

He spoke with the woman. She nodded. Then she looked at Jake and Julia and shook her head. An angry sadness lurked in her dark expression.

Tashi explained: "She says it is very bad place? She says do not go. Men with scars live there, dead men live there, I not know what this mean."

"What?"

"She says death is there. Much death there. Scarred men, ghost there. They live in heaven village. She say do not go." He repeated her words. *"Do not go to heaven villages. Because you will not come back."*

37

The heaven villages: unnerving images floated into Jake's head. He resisted them; sourcing his resolve. Focusing on Chemda. He wanted information.

"How far is it? Balagezong?"

Tashi sighed. "A few more hours only. But a dangerous road. Now we sleep. Maybe tomorrow you feel different and go home. I hope so."

"I will not. I will not feel different. We have to leave early."

The Tibetan man shrugged and smiled a lopsided smile.

"You are in trouble. I can see. I will help. As we agreed."

Tashi stepped into the shadows and sat down on a bench—talking in Tibetan to one of the girls. Flirting. Her soft little giggles filled the silence of the house under the Snow Mountains.

Night fell, quite abruptly. Jake wondered if that suddenness had something to do with the heart-straining altitude, but he couldn't work out the science. He got up and stood at the glassless window, watching the stars over the snowy summits, and he reached into his pocket for his cell phone.

But there was, of course, no signal. And who could he call, any-way? Who could really help? Tyrone? The police? He was *hunted* by police.

They were on their own.

Dogs barked in the bitter cold outside. Jake pocketed his phone and retreated from the window. He lay down on some straw bedding next to Julia and whispered some reassurance to her, and somehow they slept.

He woke at dawn, or just before dawn: the sky had an aurora of pinkish green at the very edges of the endless darkened blue. A noise had disturbed him. Everyone else was asleep, but the noise was Julia being sick; she was being sick at the bottom of the wooden steps. He rose and went to help, but she waved him away.

"I am OK. Go back to sleep."

He obeyed; and for once he did not dream.

Morning came harsh and stark and blue and cold, and it was like waking up asthmatic, the air was so thin. He drank some black tea, his hands nursing the hot metal cup, and he looked at Julia's pale face. The altitude was exhausting him; he wondered what it was doing to her.

"Julia," he said, "you really have gotta stay here. Let me reconnoiter. You stay here, please?"

For the first time the American woman seemed to succumb to some inner weakness. She nodded.

"I don't feel so good. At all. Maybe . . . OK, maybe I will rest just for today, then you will come and get me?"

"Yes," said Jake. "I will check it out. Then come and get you."

There was no mention of what Jake was going to do. He had no *idea* what he was going to do. He just had to keep moving and he hoped it would sort itself out. He could see Chemda, lying on the table, her hair shaved, her scalp peeled back, an arc of skull removed.

They walked down the steps to the car. The view beyond the farmhouse yard, up the valley, was stupendous.

"Now," said Tashi. "We go now. If we must go."

Jake turned and hugged Julia. She was still pale and she was shivering. He said, "You should go back to Zhongdian. We can get you a lift."

"No. I'll wait. *Find Chemda.*"

Then she kissed him on the cheek. He got in the car with Tashi and waved goodbye, and then they drove on down the winding high mountain road in silence. The plateaux and ranges stretched ahead of them. Jake took photos. He saw a bleached yak skull sitting in a brown meadow by a brown and frothing creek. The teardrop sky ached in its blueness. He felt like he was driving finally to heaven. The heaven of another god, another time.

"OK," said Tashi, "this the dirt road the lady tell me about. This is where it get very dangerous. First down, then up, into the holy mountains. She say we take secret route, to this mountain, is mountain of the snow goddess. Heaven villages there, with the men. We go behind the mountain."

He pointed at one vertiginous and beautiful peak: a slender pyramid of gray and ice against blue, immense and intractable, maybe 20,000 feet, streaked with white snow.

And yet they were heading *down* an awesome gorge. The drop was precipitous. It grew humid as they dropped, richer with oxygen, the jungle encroached, replete with mighty ferns and palm trees. A monkey hooted. Parrots alarmed the air with crimson feathers. The chasm was gut-numbingly deep, three kilometers or more.

Then they bottomed out and they were ascending again, switchbacking right and left and right, and for an hour they made a dizzying ascent, back up to a plateau. They passed three humble villages, implausibly remote. Tibetan women in bare feet and embroidered turbans were sitting in a field digging turnips, the holy mountains rising behind them.

"These the heaven villages," said Tashi.

"Why are they called that?"

"Is the fog. Thick fog, so thick it go into houses. You wake up you are on a cloud, in heaven. And because when you reach this far, you never come back. Like you have died and you are in heaven."

They left the heaven villages behind. Ahead of them the road forked. Tashi stopped for a moment and climbed from the car and surveyed the mountains, sniffing the air; he got back in and they took the smaller and humbler road. This lesser road was barely passable: it had once been paved, but the winds and rain had reduced it to a glorified goat path.

Yet they drove. The car protested and rumbled. A stubborn pair of yaks barred the road, and they shooed them away with hoots and curses. The car spun on, taking the switchbacks in tight sweeps. The track disappeared under a cataract; it seemed they were lost; but then Tashi pointed. Beyond the water, and a grove of trees, the road recommenced.

They drove, left and right, left and right. Climbing even higher into the sacred cirque of mountains, scraping gravel. Nearly spinning off the road. The anxiety rose with their ascent.

They were close now.

"We have come around the mountain, from the back," said Tashi. He was not smiling. His face was twitching with nerves. He pressed the throttle. The final turn brought them out onto a flat yard of gravel space and a couple of dirty concrete shacks. Like very big urinals.

Tashi braked, the car stopped. What now? Jake peered through the dirty windshield. The lunacy of everything he was doing began to hit home; as soon as he stopped moving, the stupidity kicked in. He wasn't armed. He didn't even have a weapon. What did he expect to do? Walk into this place and rescue Chemda, like some superhero? Maybe he should have waited for Tyrone. Or something.

Maybe he should have cooked up a plan. He squinted again through the dust.

What?

A group of men had emerged from one of the shacks. Faces pointing toward Jake. They were moving hesitantly. Staring. Shuffling. Uncertain. Bizarre.

And then they started running—toward the car.

Jake saw the scars on their foreheads.

"Go!" said Jake, unnecessarily. *"Go!"*

Tashi was already squealing the tires, hurriedly backing away, an emergency turn. But the scarred men were at the car, and one of them was yanking at Jake's door, pulling it open; Jake had the absurd sensation that they were being attacked by apes, by a troop of primates; he felt himself tugged out of the seat by several hands. He shouted to Tashi, who was still swinging the wheel.

Jake was pulled clean away, and he watched the wildly swinging car door clash against rock and snap from its hinges—the car swerved; the men were shouting; Jake was trapped by the hands, the men were holding him, but Tashi was thrashing a second reverse and then roaring down the road.

A cloud of descending dust.

Tashi had escaped, but Jake was captive. The men with the scars looked at Jake and they nodded, and one of them said something in Chinese.

The others agreed.

"Hui!"

Jake was briskly dragged into a shack. He writhed in the clutches of the men, he fought and he bit and he struggled as they entered the darkness, the shadows of the building; but then he saw one taller man step over, contemptuously tutting, barging between the others. The man carried a large metal wrench. He raised it over Jake's head. The crack of pain was intense; Jake ceased his struggling, barely conscious now.

He watched, head throbbing, with a kind of detachment, as they carried him into a further room and chained him to a rusty iron bedstead with a small machine sitting next to it. A small machine? It was a grimy machine, like a food processor, with tubes emanating from it. The clear plastic tubes were smeared red on the inside.

Smeared with blood?

The uncertain implications of this made him struggle, fitfully, just one last time: he rattled at his straps and yelled for help—but again the taller man came across and lifted the metal wrench. Yet again he clattered Jake, brutally. And this time he did it so hard that Jake blacked out at once.

He awoke—moments later, maybe minutes later—to a strange sensation. A sharp prickle. In his arm. He looked down. There. They were sliding a steel needle into the crook of his arm. A second jab of pain, on the other arm, followed the first. It was another long needle, sliding in.

Tubes were now attached to the inserted needles. Numb with horror, Jake watched the men intubating him. He felt the coarseness of the leather restraints, saw the spray of old blood on the ceiling. It was all from his dreams, from the nightmares: the tongue of the *krasue,* the many tongues of the *krasue,* probing inside—seeking his innards.

The machine was switched on with a casual flick. It was now buzzing and humming. It was, of course, a pump. An electric pump. The men looked at one another and shrugged. Job done.

The machine suctioned and pumped, rocking very slightly from side to side, a small but effective electric pump just doing its humble task.

Jake twisted against his straps and gazed down at his feet, tethered to the iron bed frame. Now he could see bulky glass canisters beyond the end of the bed. The vessels were slowly and imperceptibly filling up with bright scarlet blood, dripping down the inside of the glass vessels. Making fat carafes of blood. Flagons of rich crimson blood.

Jake's blood.

The electric pump ticked over.

Jake began to gasp, to croak, to stridulate. He was dryly croaking as the machine vacuumed and sucked the lifeforce from his flesh. As the pump ticked over.

He rasped, in his agony, like a dying insect.

38

Julia waited wearily and headachingly·in the house on the road to Balagezong. For two days she stood cold and frightened at the window, like a fisherman's wife. She watched the herdsmen patrolling the mountain paths, she saw a man carrying a huge creamy red-and-yellow yak skeleton on his back.

She counted the stones on the roofs of the houses, she watched the black-necked cranes glide against a blank white sky.

Guilt and determination held her at the window, waiting for Jake. Then, as her fever worsened, she retreated to her bed of straw: she was half convulsed with cramps, listening semiconsciously to the creaks and moans and smells of the Tibetan farmhouse. Her cold limbs shivered. The woman with the teeth came across and medicated her with cups of warm barley wine poured from a tin thermos.

She lost track of time. The only indications of daytime were the spears of light through holes in the timbered ceiling, shining on the flattened pig faces—plus the noise of occasional laughter and singing outside. And then even these dim sounds melted into a white noise of pain and fever.

The smell of yak dung rose from the livestock below. The fever climbed inside her bones. The cups of yak-butter tea tasted like her own bile. She lay back in pain. The loneliness was intense. No one spoke English, she had no one to talk to. The old woman and her granddaughters came and went in her dreams, her half-dreams, her daydreams.

Men came and went. A Frenchman. An American. An Englishman. But through her perspiration she realized she was hallucinating—it was the Tibetan men, stomping into the house in the evening to eat their chicken feet and spit the bones into the fire, brutal daggers tucked under their jerkins. Some of them gazed in curiosity at the white woman with the bright hair, the woman dying in their house; they stared at her stomach.

Amid her dreams she wondered if they could see through her—see the faint skeleton of the child she never quite had, inside her red uterus, like a fossilized bird with its Jurassic feathers preserved in soft red sandstone. Like a ghost baby, a smoke baby. The grandchild she never gave her parents, the baby she aborted after Sarnia.

The ghost of her guilt, still stalking her across the world after these many years.

Her dreams melded. Dreams of Alex, making love to her by a lake, with frightening flocks of storks and cranes. She was trembling all the time now. Once she woke in a swinish perspiration and saw the old woman eating blue plums. The plum juice drooled down the woman's face. Where was Jake? Where was Tashi? They had gone, gone forever, everyone was gone, smoked, ghosted. The kippered pig face stared across the room.

Was she going to die from this thing, finally?

She almost didn't care—until she cared. At some unheralded moment—five or six days in, maybe seven, she summited, she topped the mist-shrouded mountain of her illness without even realizing.

The fever abated.

After that Julia slept properly, undreamingly, and when she woke she felt a firmness in her bones, an energy returning. She sat up. She stood—for a second. Then she slumped into the wooden seat by the fire, where she rubbed her stiff legs and eased her aching neck, before sorting through her bag.

There. Julia examined her phone. And sighed. The battery had died long ago. Even if she could somehow, miraculously, find a signal, the phone was dead.

What was she going to do? Wrapped in an embroidered blanket, she shuffled to the window.

Her hopes had finally gone, likewise the rains. Jake was not coming back. Maybe he was dead. Surely he was dead. But she *had* to help him, just in case. She wasn't going to stop now. She'd come this far, the idea of turning back seemed perverse. She had to help him, and help Chemda. It was her duty.

Julia gazed out.

The corn was laid on the top of the houses to dry in the new winter sunshine. Two Tibetan men were singing a song as they worked in the yard, sawing logs. An eerie dancing song. She followed the tune with her mind, gazing along the valley, sensing an idea. What she needed was electricity, therefore what she needed was a big building, somewhere that might have a generator, and an electrical outlet, so she could recharge her cell phone.

The biggest building in the valley was large and tiered and far away and painted white. A monastery? It looked, from this great distance, like a monastery from a picture of Tibet. The palace in Lhasa.

She crossed the room and asked the old woman, who was busy shelling walnuts. What was the place at the end of the valley? The woman shrugged and smiled, toothlessly, blankly. Of course she did not understand. Julia signaled, and pointed and gestured: *Big building. Up there?*

Miraculously, the woman nodded and smiled properly and said,

"Songzanlin!" And then the old lady did a praying motion with her head, like a Buddhist monk, chanting.

It was a monastery, a lamasery. Julia hurried downstairs and out into the dry, dry sun, her head still faintly swimming with the altitude, and she hitched a ride from a youth on a motorbike, riding pillion along the dun-hard valley. She barely knew what she was doing, or why: maybe a nonexistent God the Father would speak to her at the lamasery. Guide her movements. Certainly she needed an outlet for her phone, and the only likely place in the entire valley was the most significant building of all.

The drive took a frustrating twenty minutes. Past a trail of Tibetan tribeswomen carrying enormous wicker baskets of grasses on their backs. Bent over by the burden.

Songzanlin was tucked hard against a mountainside, tiered and bleached and dazzling in the sun, like a terrace of snow mountains, like the very mountains that it faced across the sloping brown fields. The ancient steps up to the white monastic buildings were steep and knackered. A few stray pilgrims were climbing the steep archaic steps on their knees. A yellow-robed monk was playing a trumpet made from a human thighbone, heralding the heavens.

Julia ascended to the temple yards, where some old men spun the prayer wheels, the fat brass cylinders that shone in the sun as they revolved, squeaking on their ancient axles. Prayer flags of red and faded yellow and a washed-out blue fluttered and rippled in the stiff cool breeze, by the ancient white stupa.

She entered one of the chambers: the temple halls of Songzanlin. It was wooden, old and enormous. She felt stupid and angry now. There was no electricity here. The lamasery was as ancient and isolated and powerless as the village down the vale. Monks were kneeling on rugs and praying with palmed joss sticks, chanting their nodded incantations, whispering in sacred Pali beneath the lotused statues of the Buddha, beside the gilded frescoes. Smoking butter lamps scented the darkness; men in maroon robes came and went, wearing tall yellow hats.

Julia coughed the smoke and stepped outside, desperate and defeated. She had been defeated. Jake was maybe dead. Chemda cut open. It was all her fault. The guilt was a pain in her mind, an actual headache in her frontal cortex, in the center of her chest, her stomach.

What now?

An intricately carved red-and-yellow wooden platform was standing in front of the largest hall, and it was filled with sand—and the sand had been planted with a hundred vermilion shoots of incense. The perfumed smoke trailed in wisps into the blue and sunny haze.

She turned.

A face.

A recognized face.

It was the killer. Coming toward her. The young Asian woman. It was her. At last. Confronting her as she had done in Paris. And this time there was no hiding, and no escape.

In the bright mountain light Julia could see the woman so much better. It was Chemda and yet it wasn't. The white face had gone. Yet it *was* Chemda, almost.

"But . . ." said Julia. "But . . ."

Was this it, then? Was this where she was going to die? Here in Songzanlin monastery?

"Julia Kerrigan?"

Yes, the voice was American. It was definitely *her.* Chemda and not Chemda. So nearly identical. Long hair, deep eyes; only a strangeness in the bones spoke of a difference. The killer was a few yards away, approaching across the terrace of the monastery. How did she know Julia's name?

Julia swiveled—and she ran. She ran to give Jake and Chemda a final slender chance; but as she ran she tripped on the steps at the top of the great processional stairway of Songzanlin and she fell. A monk shouted, she was falling, the sun was bright, she kicked and smashed against the steps, she cracked her head with a blinding pain, and the agonies shot through her back.

Get up. She had to *get up*. But she couldn't move. Something was wrong, something had snapped. The killer was running down the many steps toward her, but all Julia could see was the astonishing liters of blood.

Running and pooling between her legs.

39

Death was near. Jake could sense his presence in the grimy room, Death the Bureaucrat with his infinite checklist, ticking the boxes, auditing names, eyes unsmiling behind his rimless spectacles as he went down his list. Baby smashed. Tick. Sister killed. Tick. Mother dead. Tick.

He could hear the gurgling noises of his own blood, the last of his blood, filling the glass bottles.

Yet even as he heard this he was *staring* at his mother. His dead sister and his dead mother floating under the Butcher's Lake. Their white arms waving, beckoning him down, and down. He yearned to join them, at last, in the nothingness; to commingle his ashes with their ashes, to meld his nonexistence with theirs, to sing the song, to be standing in church as a small boy once again, still loved, still mothered, still holding his mother's hand as she stared at the stained-glass window, gazing up in adoration: at the robes of blue, Saint Lucy blue, the blue of the Virgin.

The beloved mother. The forgiving mother. Who left him, who left him alone in this life. Until the only thing he could do was run away, so he had fled to the very ends of the earth—and yet here he had found her again, the mother he hated, he loved, he hated, and his sister, frail and floating, two floating female heads, disembodied, *kinarees* with wings on the sandstone of Angkor.

The blood siphoned and guttered, the last fluid ounces were draining into the bottles: like pilfered gasoline on the streets of Phnom Penh, on the road to Skuon, where the spider witch had cursed him.

The *krasue* sucked. She was inside him. The demon. Sucking out his blood. Like Chemda sucking him in bed with her seven black tongues.

He rasped. Choked. Shuddered. The last blood was nearly taken. He was inside. He was outside. He was blind now. He couldn't see. His sight had gone. But he could hear voices. Was he hallucinating? One of the voices was Tyrone.

Tyrone? He realized he was purely dreaming now.

He blacked out.

40

She watched the blood run between her legs. A viscous and violet-red pool of sadness. Then she felt strong arms behind her, helping her to her feet. It was the killer, the Chemda lookalike, helping her.

Helping her?

Two monks ran over and assisted Julia down the last steep and broken steps of the lamasery, to the broken street. Julia felt everything blur at the edges, as if she were staring through a smeared lens at the world. A car was waiting, an incongruously new car; Julia was gently lifted into the backseat. *The killer drove.*

The car raced over the potholed road. Julia was trying not to cry in pain, trying not to cry in despair. Someone had given her a large white rag of cloth, and she clutched it between her thighs, sopping the blood. The pain surged; she gazed urgently out the window, where Tibetan Yunnan was immortally unconcerned by her situation.

The barley dried in the sun, stretched across the tilted wooden frames. Tibetan women marched along carrying their wicker baskets of wood, singing and laughing as they worked. And Julia was bleeding from her loins in the rear of a car being driven by a murderer.

Back at the house. She was back at the house with the snaggletoothed old woman and the pretty granddaughters and the piles of dung drying in the byre under the bedrooms.

Smiling and frowning, the women attended to her: cleaning and rinsing and bathing her, using hot water from the tin thermos, hot water from battered saucepans heated over the brazier. The pig faces stared down, their eyes batting little lashes of surprise. The women were well-meaning and ill-equipped and they tried to tell her, via sign language, what she already knew: she had miscarried. She had been pregnant. All these years after the abortion she had thought she was infertile, that something had been damaged, internally, by the termination. So she never took precautions. Because she didn't have to. And yet she was still fertile.

And yet again the baby had died. It all made bitter sense now. The sickness, the throwing up: even the way the ape reacted in Abkhazia— to her "unusual pheromones."

Pregnant. Pregnant by Alex. But not pregnant anymore, and probably not pregnant ever again. She had almost fulfilled her parents' dearest desire; but she had failed them, again. Ghost children, smoke children. All she did was produce smoke children.

"*Dzo*—"

The women were talking in Tibetan. Julia was cleaned and finally dressed and then they carefully sat her, like a large fragile doll, on the long wooden bench, so she could stare out the window. But Julia was looking the other way: staring across the room. At the killer. All the time the killer had lurked there, in the shadows, between the *thangkas* and the picture of the Dalai Lama.

Julia didn't care about anything anymore. The killer wouldn't have helped Julia if she meant Julia harm. Julia wanted to *talk* to this strange, silent young woman. This brutal murderer.

"Who are you?"

A soft breeze rippled the silken thangkas.

"Soriya." The killer spoke, and walked closer. Her accent was quite clearly American. "You know you had a miscarriage? It's not life-threatening, the pregnancy was not advanced."

"Why did you help me? You tried to kill me before."

"I know pain. I understand pain."

Piercing curiosity filled Julia's thoughts. Maybe the killer—Soriya—would explain. And Julia yearned for an explanation, for the truth, for something to fill the emptiness that now grew inside her, the horrible void; the tears came rising to the surface, but she fought them.

"OK." Julia sat farther along the bench. Inviting this woman—this woman?—Soriya to sit beside her.

Soriya sat down. She was svelte. Young, athletic, wiry. She had Chemda's beauty—but differently. Dark, angry eyes.

The sun was slipping behind the sawtoothed horizon. A cold Siberian wind was coming down from the Snow Mountains, reminding the black-necked cranes of the winter they had escaped.

Gazing directly at Julia, the Khmer woman took off her wig of long dark hair.

Underneath she was completely bald. She had a very faint scar on her forehead.

Julia gasped. "They cut you."

"Yes." Soriya paused, and continued: "Or so I have now calculated. Finally. Someone abandoned me. Chemda's mother, Madame Tek. Chemda's mother is my mother—"

"You are her sister."

"Almost. . . . *Almost.*"

The Khmer woman's smile was shaded with an intensity of pain.

"Growing up in America as a child, I was wild, unhappy, suicidal. I was moved from foster home to foster home. Unwanted. Because I was disturbed, and violent. Not comfortable in my skin. I tried to find out who my real parents were, but the records had been destroyed. I was just another orphan from Cambodia, another product of the chaos, after the Khmer Rouge fell. But my sense of dislocation was worse than that. And why was I scarred? What was wrong with my mind?"

"How . . . ?"

"I am Chemda's twin sister. And yet I am not. I cannot explain now. I don't want to. I was strong, and clever and athletic. I was recruited. Special forces. Then I left the army. But I still wanted to kill. I couldn't control myself. Barely, I controlled myself."

The light in the house was fading fast. Soriya's speech was dark and unhurried and compelling, and Julia forgot about her miscarriage as she listened to Soriya.

"I went to Cambodia. Researching my past. Desperate. I found a guy named Ponlok. Begging, near Tuol Sleng."

"*Ponlok.* I have heard of him—"

"I saw the scar on his head. We shared the very same scar. He told me what he knew, that he had heard a rumor. That the Khmer Rouge tried the surgical experiments on babies, on one baby in particular. He told me I looked like Chemda Tek. He told me it happened in Anlong Veng. I went to Anlong Veng. I found the doctor who did the trick. Madame Tek had *twins*. The doctors did a switch on the mother, told her the second girl was stillborn, a miscarriage. I was whisked away." Soriya's eyes softened, for a second, in the twilight. "I am sorry for what happened to you today."

Julia did not know what to say. She struggled toward a reply.

"It does not compare to . . . what happened to you."

Soriya shrugged.

"No. It does not. The doctor told me, in Anlong Veng, that I was carried off. Like a prize. The prize was me. They took me away and tried the experiment on me, they wanted to see how I would fare compared with my twin. She was the control. It was science. But it went wrong. I was a disturbed baby, feral, epileptic. A failure. They gave me away. Someone adopted me from America. That's how I ended up there, age two, just thrown away like a spoiled chicken steak. In America I got worse. The fighting. Disturbances. Fits and seizures." Soriya paused. "When the doctor in Anlong Veng told me all of this I was . . . even angrier. I threatened him. I was brutal. He told me that one man could explain more, about the experiments, the theory that had mutilated me. Hector Trewin. So I went to England and I tortured some of the truth out of him. And he gave me the list of names and told me about the Western mission. The Marxists. He didn't tell me why they did what they did, but he told me that they helped, helped the Communists do their experiments. And so I resolved to kill everyone. If I had to kill, I was going to kill all the people that did this to me." She gestured at the scar on her head. "*They made me this way.* So I have been slowly killing them. One by one. I have many passports. One of them says Chemda Tek."

"You travel as Chemda?"

"It is easy. When I am dressed like her I am identical—unless you look very close."

Julia could see this was true. Only close up, sitting two feet away, could she properly see a difference in Soriya's face. A faint haze of facial hair, maybe. A stronger jaw, perhaps. The mind affecting the brain? But how?

And yet the face was beautiful, just like Chemda's. Beautiful and dark, and murderous, and scarred.

"What about . . . what happened in Paris?"

"I do not like killing anyone I do not have to kill. The archivist, at the museum? That was wrong. I am ashamed of that. And I am sorry for what I did. To you, too. My temper still surges, I still have . . . many cognitive problems. Violent urges. I can't help it. But

I am sorry I had to do that, and sorry I frightened you. I have been shadowing you and the English guy, for a while. And Chemda. Of course. Following you. Watching you. I followed Barnier to his apartment block."

A puzzle presented itself to Julia. She ignored the pain in her belly and asked: "How did you find me here? *Why* did you find me here?"

"Two Westerners in Zhongdian? Not hard. A few days ago I tracked down a young Tibetan. Tashi. Rumors said he had taken two *gwailos,* two white people, to Balagezong. Neither came back. He told me Jake was taken by men in the mountains. He said you were here in this house. He was very, very frightened. I decided to come and find you."

"Why?"

An evening breeze kicked at Soriya's fake black hair.

"I know who you are. An archaeologist. You have the truth."

"What?"

"All along, all through this, I have been trying to find out *why* they did this to me—what was the point in cutting me open. Trewin refused to say, even at the expense of his life. No one would tell me. I tried to find out more. At the museum, in Paris, I was desperate. That's why I went *back into* the museum, after I did it. After I killed the guy at the door. I wanted that box. Prunières de Marvejols. But you must have moved it. So I was still seeking the truth. And Barnier, when it happened, he tried to bargain for his life, and he told me you and he had worked it all out. But the doorman disturbed me. I had to act quickly. I killed him. Had to. But that meant he couldn't explain. That leaves you. Only you can tell me what happened. Tell me, please. Why did they do this to me?"

Julia hesitated for a long time. Then she explained. Softly, firmly, lucidly, she elaborated the theory. Outside in the cold evening air the yaks walked along the valley in quiet processional.

At the conclusion, Soriya nodded.

And then she said nothing, gazing out at the brooding turquoise sky. Julia broke the silence:

"Soriya, what are you doing *here?*"

"It's the only road to Balagezong."

"But how do you know all of this? You've been here, to these places, before?"

"Yes." The killer's voice was quite calm, but her eyes burned, staring at the very first stars. "I have been preparing for several years. I got an army pension. Battlefield wounds. Bought me the time, to do this."

"Preparing how? How did you *prepare?*"

No answer.

"Preparing how?" Julia repeated. *"Learning to kill?"*

Her question was brutal; Soriya shrugged and said, "I didn't have to learn that. The army taught me that. No. I tried to learn some languages. And then, as I said, I traced and tracked the different . . . Communists. I also honed my skills over time. Faked suicides. Learned to sedate: by disabling, then injecting. Methohexital. Carefully. Intravenously. You can't just inject it in the buttocks."

"And here?"

"I have been here several times before. I came to Zhongdian, and then to Balagezong. Disguised. Preparing for today. OK. Today. You need to decide."

"Decide what?"

"Tomorrow I am going to Balagezong. The last chapter of the story."

Julia tried to speak; Soriya raised a small, strong, dark-skinned hand.

"I am leaving tomorrow morning at dawn and it is unlikely I'll be coming back this way. So I'll be gone and no one will see me again.

But I can't just let you go back to Zhongdian. And call the police. So my friends here will make sure you stay put."

"Imprison me?"

"Yes. You won't be harmed. But you won't be able to leave. Not for a week. By which point my task will be done. Finished. Either way."

"So . . ."

"The alternative. There is an alternative. If you want, you can come with me. And you can maybe find a way to save your friends."

Julia protested: "But how? *How* can I save them?"

"I have no idea. But I give you the choice because you gave me the truth. You don't have to trust me, I am a madwoman and a murderer, after all."

The wind carried scents of pine and ice through the glassless window. The darkness was fanged with frost.

41

"Dude."

The swamp mist cleared from the Butcher's Lake of his mind. He was still alive.

"You had us worried. Big time."

Jake sat up; he was in a bed. A clean white bed in a clean white room without windows. Tyrone was standing at the end of the bed, laconically leaning, skinny in his blue jeans.

"But . . ." Jake sought his watch. His watch was gone. "Where am I? How long have I been out?"

"Six fucking days! You nearly died. The doctors had to put you in a coma. Induced. To save you. But you should be fine now. We put all your blood back. Those idiots, the morons, on the back road, they thought you were someone else. We didn't think you would take the back road."

"Ty." He was beyond confused. He wondered if he was still hallucinating. "Where am I?"

Tyrone pulled up a chair and sat down.

"Balagezong. In the clinic. Top of the mountain. Bala village. Great views. Shame you haven't got any windows."

The electric realization shot through him.

"Chemda!"

Jake leaped from the bed—but he didn't leap from the bed. A metal clanking noise, and a sharp pain in his ankle, told him why. He was chained: ankle-cuffed to the steel frame of the bed.

Uncomprehending, Jake stared at the irons clamped around his leg. He was a prisoner? Then why was he rescued?

Tyrone tutted.

"Relax. Chemda is *fine*. And here, take this, *madman*." Tyrone threw a plastic bag onto the bed. "Sorry about the leg irons, necessary precaution. We thought if you woke up in the dark and panicked and bolted, you might wander off a cliff. Or get angry or something. Lot of cliffs around here." He grinned. "Hey. You must be hungry, eat the food and I'll come back in a moment. We can talk more. *Lots* to talk about."

Tyrone walked out of the room. Jake stared at the blank white concrete wall. Chemda was OK? What was going on? How had Tyrone made it here so quickly? Had he really been unconscious for six days?

It was too much. He was very hungry.

The plastic bag contained bottles of mineral water and a couple of sandwiches wrapped in foil. Jake drank the water and ate the food. Then he lay back, still hungry, staring at the bruises in the crook of each arm. Where they had tried to drain all his blood.

So he hadn't imagined that.

There were so many questions, it was tiring: physically wearying. He found himself drifting into unconsciousness once again. His sleep was disturbed by the creak of the door.

Tyrone. The American gave him another sardonic smile.

"That's better. Bit of color in your cheeks. For a Brit."

This time Tyrone pulled up a chair, swiveling it so he was sitting reversewise, arms laid on the top of the chair back. Jake gazed, the bewilderment fighting the tiredness in his mind.

"OK," said Tyrone. "Give me your questions."

"All I care about," said Jake, "is Chemda. Where is she?"

"Patience. Jesus, you really do love her, don't ya? She is fine. Unharmed. What next?"

"Sovirom Sen. Did he make it here?"

Tyrone pulled the chair nearer.

"Yes. He's here." Tyrone sighed. "OK. Yes. It's confusing: let me explain. First thing you gotta know. Prepare yourself."

"What?"

"*Sovirom Sen is Khmer Rouge.* And not just that. In the 1970s he was a member of the elite, just beneath Ieng Sary and the Butcher. A cadre. A leader."

Jake fought his utter confusion. "Sen? But Ty, he is a known anti-Communist, famous for it."

"Dude, he lied. He is a liar. He lies. He was the most committed Communist of all. But the Khmer Rouge fell. And of course he is not stupid, he is a very clever and far-sighted man. Sharp as fuck, like all the KR. He realized that to survive and prosper in the postregime era he had to pretend that he hated communism, hated the Pol Pot regime."

"How could you get away with *that*?"

Tyrone's smile was pert.

"You think he is the only one? How many former Khmer Rouge officials are now at the top of the Cambodian government? Some of the more foolish are open about it—many more conceal it, the more subtle operators, perhaps. And the transition is easy. We see it across the world, right? Regimes change, yet the *personnel* stay the same. And in Cambodia everyone assists in the deception. Because the country's tragedy is too large to endure, the grief too immense, two million too big. Only the deaf and the mute survive. And the only exit *is* survival. So they have this conspiracy of denial, of silence, of accepting the common lies." Ty sighed. "Poor old Cambodia. Still, they shouldn't have gone bat-shit crazy, should they? Gooks."

Jake attempted a question: "But what does this mean? Now?

"I have pieced together the narrative, with a bit of help. Apparently the trouble began when Chemda, your beautiful, smart, and determined little Khmer princess girlfriend . . ." Tyrone's eyes were bright. "The trouble started when she took a more detailed interest in the recent history of Cambodia. Working with the United Nations, the 'reconciliation' tribunals. Talking about the babies they smashed against trees. The monks they burned alive. The people they threw into the sea."

"Sen tried to dissuade her."

"Yup. He was worried, but then he reluctantly decided she should have her way. He reckoned she would soon tire of her idealism and meet a young man, and she would then want a family like any good Khmer daughter, and she'd give up the lawyering. But she persisted. And then she began investigating the Plain of Jars. Coming close to her grandfather's history, to his concealed past."

Jake gazed across the room.

"The professors in Laos?"

"They were pressured, and how. By Sen. Khmer Rouge people in Phnom Penh. The Lao. All of them together. And when Samnang topped himself, Sen thought that would be it, that Chemda would quit, yet he could tell from her phone calls that she was determined to continue."

"So her mother got the witch to arrange the *kun krak*. To scare her off. I know that."

Tyrone nodded empathetically.

"Yeah, that bit we know *all* about, right? Madame Tek was aware that Chemda shared her irrational superstitions. The mother hired the spider queen. To do the embryo juju."

"And it worked—"

"But when she got back Chemda was the same girl! Mmm? Right? Still convinced of the need to confront the past. She just didn't realize that confronting the past meant . . . unmasking her own grandfather. And you know how Chemda thinks. She reveres Papa Sen. Father Number One. Sen was like her real dad and Chemda was Daddy's little girl."

Tyrone abruptly stood. He walked to the other side of the room and gazed at a wall chart. A picture of the human brain.

"She loved and revered her grandfather. It would rip her open to know that Grandfather Sen was a friend of the Butcher. Of Ieng Sary. Pol Pot. And Sen in turn, apparently, rather likes his granddaughter's love and respect, so he did not want Chemda's hatred. He needed her out of the country, away from these mysteries. And they had another reason for her to leave."

On the horizon, the truth was rising, like a sickening moon.

Jake asked, "Which was? This reason?"

"People were being killed. Scientists across the West. People who had helped in the experiments they did in Phnom Penh, the experiments that have continued here. Sen knew that danger approached. In desperation he thought maybe you would take her to England or America. She loves you, Jake. She would follow you, if no one else, right? You were their best hope. As a final inducement, Sen arranged for your apartment to be fired—"

"Sen? It was *him*? How the hell was that meant to persuade me?"

"Seems you left the Sovirom compound too soon that morning. You weren't meant to see the actual fire bombs, you were meant to agree to the marriage and then go home and see the already gutted apartment and realize your life was in real danger. You would marry

Chemda nice and easy—and take her far away out of harm's reach, away from the terrible truth. And then *papa-san* would deal with the threat as best he could. But it went wrong. You escaped—eloped, even—and then Sen got angry and decided to take more drastic action. In Anlong Veng. Kill you, seize Chemda. He felt you already knew too much. I saved your ass."

"But what are you doing now, Ty? You saved me then? But what are you doing now? We have to save Chem, get her out of here, away from Sen—"

Tyrone sighed.

"I'm coming to that. You are my friend, Jake, really. I really did save you in Anlong Veng. I was rooting for you, dude, but then a couple of weeks ago . . ."

He paused.

"Tell you what. Maybe you need some visuals." Tyrone walked to the door, pulled it open, and signaled to someone beyond.

Sovirom Sen stepped through; his smile at Jake was halfway between delicate pity and pure condescension. His smile at Tyrone was entirely civilized.

42

Tyrone nodded at Sen and turned to Jake.

"Two weeks ago Sen came to me in Phnom Penh and told me all of this, and he persuaded me that there was a solution to everyone's *problems.*"

Jake was floundering and frightened. He gazed at Sen's untroubled smile; he stammered.

"No—this—no—"

Tyrone tutted. "Hey. Shape up. You are missing one key piece of information. I'm surprised you haven't asked the crucial question. The crucial part of the story is . . . Have a guess. Go on, just try."

"What? What is it?" Jake could hear the needy tone in his own voice. He didn't care. He was desperate. "Tyrone, just fucking *tell* me."

"OK." The American smiled. He was leaning sideways against the blank white wall, arms folded.

"The experiments were all Sen's idea, it was *his* project. He conceived and directed the project. He and a couple of others, back in the seventies."

The grandfather spoke. His bespoke shoes were truly incongruous in the utilitarian concrete room.

"Of course it was me. However, Jacob, it goes rhapsodically further than you have guessed. And here is why I have invited Tyrone into our . . . conspiration. It is a truly astonishing story, and Tyrone is a teller of stories. This is how I persuaded Mr. McKenna, by giving him the story—what we are really doing up here, in the wilds."

"It's crazy, Jake, a total mind-fuck, if you will forgive the expression."

Helpless, Jake asked the only question: "*What* are you doing?"

Sen answered: "Recall, Jacob, how we discussed my loathing of irrationality, of superstition. Khmer legends, Chinese astrology, feng shui, geomancy. You remember our dialogue, Jacob? And remember how I affirmed the lucidity of Japanese Zen Buddhism, the nothingness. The taking away. The beautiful withered garden; the absence of God."

"No," said Jake, struggling with the concept, with the terror in his mind, the sense of something wicked approaching. "I still don't get it."

"So I will illuminate." Sen came forward and tapped the end of Jake's bed, almost paternally. "You deduced that we were trying to neurosection guilt and conscience, and that we failed. Well, in the years since then, the science has moved on."

"How?"

"The original theory, Ghislaine Quoinelle's elegant theory, was that the specifically human sense of guilt and remorse was the price we paid for our sudden leap forward in cognition, for the biological evolution in our neurology, changes that probably happened in the frontal cortex, the most advanced, recently evolved area of the brain. But during our conferences in Cambodia we deduced that the birth of guilt also meant the birth of religious faith, the birth of *God*. Because, when there is guilt, then God is not far behind. Only a god can punish or forgive—and therefore heal the guilt. Heal the species shame of *Homo sapiens*."

His smile was polite, diplomatic.

"Since the 1980s your bold Western scientists have, not uncoincidentally, theorized that there may actually be a God module, a God spot, in the brain. A part of the brain responsible, as it were, for religious belief. People like Persinger in Canada, and Ramachandran, and Zohar, have specified areas of the cerebral cortex that are activated when we have religious experiences, epiphanies, conversions. Do you see the connections now? The brain, they say, is hard-wired for belief."

He paused for effect.

"Of course I—and my friends in the Chinese elite, the Chinese military—we regarded the genesis of these theories with great interest. Because the speculations tie in so neatly with Ghislaine Quoinelles's grand thesis, his ideas about the evolution of the human mind in the Paleolithic, the evolution of guilt and conscience in the cortex, in those . . ." Sen tapped the top of his forehead with a finger ". . . those younger neural pathways."

Jake felt as if he were watching some speeded-up film of a terrible organic process, a beautiful and terrible process. Narcosis, or decomposition.

"You're saying—"

Tyrone intervened: "Jake, he's saying that this is what they are actually *doing*. They have succeeded. *They are doing it.* They aren't just spooning out guilt and conscience to make killers. They are going further: they are cutting out *God,* they are slicing the possibility of God out of the human mind."

"Jesus. Jesus. A . . ."

"A Jesusectomy? A soulectomy. A stupidectomy!" Tyrone's laugh was sharp. "Call it what you fucking will. But yes, that is what they are doing. And why not? How good is that? Get rid of it all, all the stupid fears of ghosts and demons and the bogeyman, all that praying and moaning and tambourine-bashing. Just cut it all out. That's what they do."

Sen stepped nearer to the bed once again.

"But we don't just excise, Jake, we make people new, we manufacture them afresh, we make them perfect, and pure—and anatomically Marxist. Brains that are biologically incapable of belief. Minds that are immune to superstition."

The room was silent for a second, until Tyrone snapped: "And guess what, dude?"

Jake shook his head.

Tyrone leaned near and put a hand on the ankle chain that locked Jake to the bed frame.

"You are going to see the results. We can prove it to you. It really works. It's not the brutal intrusion you think, it *works*. It's a miracle. It makes people better, smarter, happier. I've *seen* how it works, I've already met some of their successes, which is how Sen won me over."

Jake gazed with pure and instantaneous hatred at Tyrone, and at Sen, and their chortling complicity. Of course. *That's* why he was chained to the bed. In case he got murderously angry.

"You did it to Chemda. You always despised her superstitiousness. You hated that in her. You said it yourself—" He yearned to throttle the smiling patriarch. "So you cut it out? You fucking did it to *Chemda! Your own granddaughter?*"

Tyrone turned to Sen, who raised a consoling hand:

"So we have done the operation already. Why not? This is someone you love, someone very special. This means you will be able to . . . see for yourself the . . . *transformation*."

43

"Please. Wear this, over your clothes. It is time for you to meet Chemda. We are going outside, and it's a little cold."

Sen was offering him a coat.

Two men came in, imperviously unsmiling Chinese guards, in some kind of uniform. They unlocked the shackle on Jake's ankle. He swung his legs out of the bed and stood. As he did, he waited for the sense of weakness in his limbs; yet he felt nothing. Nothing? Nothing. He felt quite fine. Completely normal. Yet also anguished.

What had they done to Chemda?

He would have taken on Sen and Tyrone, here and now—but the silent guards were armed.

Neatly piled on a table, he found his clothes: clean boots and clean jeans, a neatly pressed, blue-striped shirt.

Dressed, and wearing the coat, escorted by the guards, Jake followed Tyrone and Sen through the door into a corridor, with a rectangle of silver and dazzling light at the end. A glass door.

Jake pushed the door and stepped onto a sunlit terrace, where he saw one man sitting at a large table laid with food for many. Jake recognized the figure from the photograph Julia had shown him: it was Colin Fishwick, a much older Colin Fishwick. The smile of Phnom Penh had been replaced by the sad, sad face of Balagezong.

Balagezong.

Jake stared across the table on the terrace, at Balagezong.

The laboratory complex was set on a vast butte of rock. Surrounding them, guarding them, even, was a hamlet of Tibetan houses, themselves surrounded by turnip fields and yak paddocks; a lane at one end of the village led to a white stupa where prayer flags rappled on a promontory of rock.

The sky was faintly veiled; blue skies smiled behind the translucent mist, like Buddhist paintings under rippling silk *thangkas*.

A noise. He turned.

Chemda.

She was approaching the table, her expression distant and opaque. He scanned her body and her head for signs of injury, but she seemed intact; yet the eyes were different, untrusting, clear but untrusting. He walked around the table and embraced her, and she kissed him.

The guards had hung back. Tyrone and Sen loitered at the other side of the table. Observing. They knew there was nothing Jake could do. He was imprisoned here, with his fate. He kissed Chemda again. And confirmed the bitter truth.

The kiss was different.

"Chem?"

Detaching herself from his arms, she said, "I'm OK. Thank you for trying to save me. Ah. Ah. What can I say."

Her eyes said *I love you* but her words were worryingly staccato.

What had they done to her? She was different.

She pressed a hand flat on his chest and shook her head, and a tremble in her mouth told him she was near to tears. She shook her head again—as if she were trying to say goodbye but couldn't quite bring herself to do it.

All she said was: "I'm OK. They kept me here. Wouldn't let me see you until they had done that thing. Their surgery."

"So you know it all? The whole story?"

Her dark eyes avoided his gaze, her voice was low and murmuring.

"My grandfather, S-37, my family, his role, I know it all. Sonisoy? Anlong Veng? All of it. Ah. What can we do now, what choice do I have? It is too late anyway."

"Chem?"

Her eyes lifted. They found his regard and she said: "How do you feel? How do you feel about me now, Jake? Now they have done this?"

He gazed at her and gazed around, and he surveyed the meaningless circle of summits, above the plunging and pitiless gorges. And he knew that what he really wanted was to have sex, maybe with Chemda, with her firm, eager breasts. Or maybe with one of those cute Tibetan girls in the village, with their rose-apple smiles.

But he didn't love her. He wanted to fuck her. But he didn't love her. *He didn't love Chemda anymore.*

It was true. Why deny it? He just didn't love her, not in that special, ludicrous way. No. She was beautiful and sexy and he liked fucking her. Of course. She was a fine woman, intelligent, moral, and he respected her, he could imagine her as his wife, but love? That was all absurd.

He didn't love her. Love was a neurochemical reaction, a disorder of the hormones, a ruse designed by nature to make men procreate and then hang around with some yowling brat for at least eighteen months until the trick of love expired like free software with a time limit, so no, he didn't love her, but he still admired her and he desired her. And they were friends.

Jake happily smiled and kissed Chemda on the cheek, and she looked at him fearfully and said:

"What have they done to you? Jake? Tell me? How do you feel?"

Her soft hand went to his head and she touched the top of it, and, as if he had been injected, he felt a stab of sharp pain.

His hand reflexively went to his head, to the scar. A scar? He had a scar on his head.

He was freshly scarred. The top of the forehead.

44

The guards were at his side. They forced him to sit.

Tyrone sat beside him, and talked: "Don't think of it as someone cutting out your soul, think of it as cosmetic surgery. Or laser tooth whitening! Don't be a fucking pussy all your life."

Jake stared at his friend. His old friend. His mortal and immortal enemy. The world spun on an axis of inversion.

"You did it already?"

"We did it already. You were in a coma, so we took the opportunity."

"But what—what was the point? I'm . . . already an atheist."

"Ah, but *are* you? Or were you?" Tyrone smiled, and the mountain air was as cold and bright as his smile. "Always struck me that you're one of those people that *hates* God rather than actually not believing in Him. Take a long look at all that load of guilt, the guilt you carry, what is all that but the same guilty God module working away in your head?" Tyrone pointed at his own head, and twisted a finger.

"But Ty, you—"

"All that shit about your dead mom. And your sister. Don't you ever want to draw a line, move beyond the guilt and grief? Dude, your dead mother has been sucking the life out of you for too long. *Get rid.* You are like someone born attached to a dead twin, and you're still dragging the corpse. So we decided it was time to cut the cord. *Snip!*"

"You fucker. You bastard."

"Me?" Tyrone laughed. "Ungrateful. I arranged all this for you. Don't you get it?"

"How?"

"Because I saw the story. Let Sen explain."

Sen sat on the other side of Jake. Chemda was across the wide white table, her face covered with her hands. He wondered if she was crying. He didn't care. He felt a certain unburdening—in that he didn't care.

He didn't care.

Sovirom Sen narrated, gesturing languidly at the low-slung concrete buildings:

"This is, I like to believe, the most amazing laboratory in the world, doing the most amazing work. But the Chinese have lost faith in us. You see? We used to be funded by the Chinese military. We were rewarded with proper guards and equipment and resources, precisely because we could manufacture those perfected soldiers for the PLA. But these days, it's all change, always change."

Tyrone stepped in: "All that organ-harvesting, brain-changing shit, it's bad PR for the new superpower. And the Chinese ardor for communism has abated now they've all got BMWs. So they got a bit dubious."

Jake swiveled in his seat, Tyrone put a restraining hand on his shoulder.

"You aren't going anywhere, Thurby. So you may as well listen. You want to know what's going on, right? So. As we were saying,

Sovirom Sen is not so popular anymore, so he has been forced to employ his *mistakes*. Those guys with the scars at the back gate, who tried to pump out all your blood. They need a lot of blood for these surgeries—these guys have been told to take blood off unwanted guests, if they get the chance, but not just anyone. But they won't listen. They're a symptom. This place has problems."

"Still don't—Just don't get it. Why do it to me?"

"*This* is why you should have stuck to the camerawork. You're just a photographer, a monkey, a snapper. You're not a writer, not a real journalist. You never really saw what a great story you had here, did you? But I did, I sensed it, from the start. So I get to do it."

"You're doing all this . . . *for the story?*"

"Yes! And what a fucking story!" Tyrone closed his eyes, and his voice stiffened: "Hard by the Himalayas, in the high green forests of wild north Yunnan, expert Chinese scientists have perfected the most astonishing neurosurgical procedure in history, the removal of religious belief, excised from living brains."

He chuckled. "That's not a bad opener, isn't it? That's my Pulitzer, right there. So yeah, when Sovirom Sen came to me, asking for my help, explaining everything, yeah, I saw how we could work together. I saw the synergistic possibilities."

"You did it for the job. Fuck."

"Sure. Because Sen needs money and backers for his experiments to continue his work. Not least, he will need a new location, new backers, very soon—when Beijing closes him down. And to get these new funds he needs publicity, he needs the story *out there. He needs the world to know his success.* And that's where I come in. I am going to write it up, me, me, the real writer." A sly smile. "But *before* he gave me the whole story he said I needed to prove my credentials, prove my commitment, give him something he wanted—so, yes, I told him where you two were staying in Bangkok, so he could grab Chem, get her away, take her to China. I persuaded him not to touch you, because I am your friend! Your savior! But I also knew this was only a stopgap."

Tyrone stared Jake in the eyes. Unblinking. Then he continued:

"Put it this way: I knew that no matter how many times I rescued your ass—you were *still* in love and you would come a-running after Chemda, and Sen would, eventually, try to *kill* you *again* for being an irritating bastard. And he would, eventually, succeed. But what could I do about this?" Tyrone turned, for a moment, his profile framed by the blue Bala sky. "And then, a day later, as I thought about the story, *the way the story could work*—well, then I had *another* worry, Jake: I realized that if I was gonna make the whole thing sing, give the story real emotional impact, I needed to convince people of the good work. The final and eventual success."

He smiled with an almost believable sincerity. "Because, let's face it, this is a hard sell. So many have been scarred or lobotomized. Mutilated. Turned into monsters. So I knew I needed a truly positive payoff, something for everyone to invest in, some powerful narrative to distract from the failures, some dazzling human interest, a personal case of a man whose life was transformed—for the better, Jake, so much for the better—by this incredible new surgical technique." A tiny, theatrical hesitation. "And then I had my epiphany. Of course! I suddenly thought of *you,* pal, old guilt-ridden, superstitious *Jake Thurby.* I saw that I could kill several birds with one prizewinning stone—if I made *you* the end of my story! I could finally save you from Sen and yourself—and at the same time I had my brilliant ending. *You* would be my human interest, the man rescued from his guilt and neuroses by this neurosurgery. My denouement. *You.* So I told you where Chemda was being hidden, just *knowing* you would go straight to her. No need for any dangerous stuff on the streets of Bangkok, you would come to us. And so you did! And that's where we are, despite a few hiccups. So you see? You get it?" Ty actually winked. "Now here we are, you are a new man, a very different man, sitting in the sweet Himalayan sunshine—feeling cleansed and new. *And that's my perfect payoff* that brings the story to life! You are my *ending*. My Pulitzer. I thank you."

He did a small, sarcastic, vaudevillean bow to his audience. Jake bridled. The guard was standing close, hand on the butt of a pistol.

Sen gestured to the guard to step back. And he turned to Jake.

"Consider things, Jake. The wise man must always consider things. Isn't it rather desirable to be rid of all that lumber, that trash, that compost at the bottom of the mind?"

"Fuck you."

"Perhaps so. But we didn't do this very difficult procedure because we hoped you would become a drooling cretin, a palsied fool like Ponlok. We did this because we really *have* perfected the operation. Thanks to Colin Fishwick here, such a brilliant neurosurgeon, we have succeeded. And you are our latest success, the greatest success. Finally you are rid of religion, the ridiculous guilt and shame and self-deception. Don't you want to be rid of it? We all need to be rid of it."

"Fuck off."

"But I am correct, am I not? It is time we moved on as a species. At present we are still at the Klamath level. Have you ever heard of them? The Klamath are a Pacific tribe, in North America. They are my exquisitely ludicrous favorites, Jacob, my favorite example of the noxious and warbling stupidity of religion. The Klamath worship a flatulent dwarf goddess who wears a buckskin skirt and a wickerwork hat, and whenever the mosquitoes are especially malign on Pelican Bay, the Klamath ask their midget goddess to blow away the mosquitoes by farting out the wild west wind. They also believe the world was initially created out of a minuscule purple berry."

Jake felt the cold wind on his scalp, the shaven patch where his hair had been, where his soul had been.

"Are we any better than the Klamath, Jacob? Are we? When we take Holy Communion or pray to Mecca or commune with the smirking Buddha we are, in essence, still requesting the sixty-centimeter-high dwarf goddess to fart away the mosquitoes, no?"

Jake inhaled; the world was drifting. He tried to fight the sensation. He knew it was pointless. What was done was, incredibly, *done*.

He walked away from the table and gazed across the silent chasms to the silent peaks. The strangeness of it all was this: Tyrone was right, he felt clearer. Calmer.

Happier.

45

"That is Balagezong. We chose it for its remoteness."

Sovirom Sen was standing beside Jake.

Jake said nothing. He gazed at the wildness of the view.

Sen spoke again: "The village of Balagezong is so remote the locals speak their own language. Their own version of Tibetan, barely comprehensible to anyone else. Until we built the dirt roads for the lab, you had to walk five days to reach the gorges. Then another five days to reach the next village. It was perfect for our purposes." He sighed. "Until recently. At the moment we live and work in pristine isolation—but now they want to put a national park here. They will demolish the labs, turn them into stores. And then there will be tour buses, guides, bringing people to the most beautiful place in the world. The last frontier of China. Someone in Beijing wants to make money from the landscape. These days they *all* want to make money." Sen grimaced and gestured to the left. "The mountain next to it is sacred. White Buddha Mountain. Piquant."

Jake gazed at this imperious summit: the slender yet mighty gray pyramid of stone was delicately striated with snow.

"Twenty-two thousand feet. The Holy Mountain of Balagezong. Of course, you will no longer *feel* the holiness. Correct?"

Jake sought inside himself for his reactions, his new and true reactions: and with another jolt of surprise, a reflex inflected with more delight, he sensed that he *did* feel differently. That cringing awe was gone, the shrivel of feeble smallness, the reverential humiliation of man confronted with the ineffable hugeness of the universe. *Gone.* Instead Jake surged with species pride. I am me. Alive. I am conscious. Man, noble man, the most noble work of evolution.

"I feel . . . different, cleaner. Lighter."

Sen laughed. "Of course you do. You have had a parasite removed, a prion of stupidity. The most poisonous of mental viruses."

"I feel, somehow, more free? Maybe *blithe* is the word."

"Absolutely so, Jacob. And you will get used to it. Very quickly. We find that our subjects need only a few hours to adjust. Indeed, the swiftness of the transformation is remarkable, given the complexity of the neurosurgery. Mr. Fishwick is truly a genius, which is why we pay him the salary of a European soccer star. This is, of course, not very Marxist, but we do what we do! The end *justifies*."

A Tibetan villager passed close to the terrace, carrying a basket of juniper wood. Jake smiled at the villager, who glanced his way and nodded, with a feudal humility, touching a forefinger to the fold of his purple headscarf, then he walked on along the mountain path, to the lower fields.

Sen continued, "Our early operations, our first surgical errors, these were, I accept they were . . . tragic errors. I am candid enough to confess this. My wife volunteered and I could not stop her, likewise my son-in-law. It was perhaps foolish to try such ambitious surgery with the primitive facilities and incomplete knowledge we had at the time. But we were true Communists, as we remain today.

Keen and zealous, Jacob—and ardent for perfection. And you cannot make an omelette for the emperor without breaking thousand-year-old eggs. I did my utmost to help those we maimed. I employed Ponlok. Many of our guards are wretched victims of our earlier, botched operations. But the tragedies of my wife and Chemda's father only fueled my desire to get it right. I knew the ultimate goal was worth any suffering. And so we learned over the decades by trial and error, and now we have succeeded."

Jake stepped forward. Hesitantly. Something else was echoing in his mind, a lost voice, an absent voice, telling him . . . something.

Leaving Sen behind, he walked down the steps of the terrace onto the path. He followed the route of the peasant for a few seconds, then paused in the hard, high mountain sun.

The spectacular view stretched away beneath him. A precipice fell to the tiered and tile-roofed houses of the heaven villages, maybe a kilometer down; then small enclosures of jasmine and apricot trees; and then the mighty gorges beyond, infinitely deep. Black, subtropical, three kilometers down, a different world. They were surrounded by cliffs and gorges and mighty summits. Maybe the most beautiful place Jake had ever seen.

And yet his reaction to the splendor was calm, less impassioned. He no longer wanted to take photos. He didn't need to mediate the beauty or the terror, the world was what it was. Not so frightening. Mountains and sun, cliffs and turnip fields. Barefoot women with headscarves crouching in the mud, tugging roots. Jake didn't care too much. He didn't care at all.

He didn't care.

That was the difference, that was the substance of the change. His mind was entirely lucid now, deliciously clear, clear as the air of Balagezong: he could stare across an unclouded landscape at last, to the blue remembered hills.

He saw himself as a small boy. Running down the road with his sister. This memory was new, this memory was old, this memory had lain locked away inside him for so long—but now all the doors of perception had been slammed open, the fire doors, the barriers he had erected to the truth: they had all been blown away. And he remembered.

Jake was seven and his sister was five, and they were running down a street from school and then Becky *tore herself* from *his* hand and ran laughing stupidly into the road, and Jake saw again his sister hit by the car, thrown like a gruesome doll, batted casually to the side and broken, blood everywhere, dead. Her body smashed. Blood framed her blond head and her white eyes rolled and stared.

The heaven villages stared up at Jake; he stared down. He was standing above heaven, superior to heaven. *I don't need you anymore.*

All this time he had been thinking it was his fault: all this time, somewhere inside him, he had felt the gnawing guilt, without quite knowing why, because he had repressed the memory. But the memory was now presented to him, and he was glad amid the tragedy.

His sister, his poor sister, she had run into the road and there was nothing he could have done. It all happened in a second. *Not his fault.*

Energized and heartened, Jake paced back along the yak path to the stupa at the other end of the village. A Tibetan man in *chuba* and cotton trousers was spinning the glittering brass prayer wheel. He acknowledged the white man with a vacant, smiling shrug; Jake smiled back and sat on the steps of the stupa and gazed at the elegant triangle of the Holy Mountain. White Buddha Mountain. The forests were hanging from the steep gray slopes, catching the mist in their dark green branches.

And here came the second memory, delivered to his feet, small and sad and insignificant. A rabbit returned by a dog. A shot bird, feathers scattering forlornly.

His mother. Jake could remember the chain of events, with new and superb clarity. He had woken in the night, age nine or ten, and seen a face looming above him: his mother, crying, her long hair wet, whispering in the dark and saying goodbye, saying, *Jake, I love you, I will always love you,* and kissing him. And then she was gone.

A white face, in the night, the white face of his mother, with the dark tang of wine on her breath—hovering and then gone. The next morning they realized she had left them—abandoned them all. Broken and drunk and unable to bear the grief of Rebecca's death, she had fled.

Eyes locked on the warm blue skies, Jake seized upon this simple truth. *That* was why he had dreamed those dreams. Women with white faces and disembodied heads: it was no witchcraft, it was just a hidden echo, a concealed trigger.

It had just been a tragedy. It was not his fault. It was just a meaningless tragedy that happened to a piteously small boy—himself.

The guilt was gone, the darkness was dispelled. He was just a man confronted by meaningless suffering, in a pitiless world.

Meaningless.

Jake stared at the meaningless mountains and the ridiculous stupa and the pointless Tibetan villager. The futility was quite extraordinary. That all of this, all that was visible everywhere—forests and sky and high cirrus clouds and villagers and Chemda on the terrace, and Zhongdian and the cement storks, and Bangkok and England and people everywhere, and all the death and suffering—it was all bitterly and blissfully pointless.

Nothing, nothing, nothing. The Zen and withered garden of nothingness. There was no meaning to anything—and in that absence of meaning there was a logical beauty. Of sorts.

Now Jake felt a swaying sensation. And a pain in his head, under the scar, a stinging itch. And he was *hungry.*

His body needed nutrition, so he marched back to the terrace, where they were still waiting for him. Ty and Sen and Chemda and Fishwick were sitting at the wide tables, now laid with Tibetan food.

Chemda's expression was shocked and sad. Tyrone's expression was wry and intrigued.

"So how do you feel, trooper?"

Jake pulled up a chair.

"I feel OK. Better."

"Better?"

"Better than I have felt . . . in a long time."

Tyrone applauded. "There, told ya."

Sovirom Sen nodded with satisfaction. Even the melancholic Fishwick managed a wistful smile.

Only Chemda was unhappy. She reached out a hand and touched Jake's hand; her sadness was obvious. He gazed at her fingers, with the bitten fingernails.

"And what do you feel about me?" she asked.

"Yeah, better," Jake said. "C'mon, of course, better about you and everything! Hey. Can we have some food? I am starving."

Tyrone laughed again. "Guess you're truly mended."

Chemda took her hand away from Jake's. He didn't care, his stomach was protesting its emptiness. He filled a plate with apples and barley bread and a fat dollop of red goat stew and tomatoes in oil and mustardseed. And he ate, lustily and hungrily, chasing his food with slugs of barley beer and salted tea from big mugs.

The food was bizarre and it was delicious: he had never had a finer meal. He was free. Jake was a free man.

Jake returned to his celery in sesame, the hard yak cheeses and momo barley dumplings, even as he ignored the shouting. Then he couldn't ignore it: cars were pulling up; shouts and gunfire echoed across the mighty valley.

Shouting? Gunfire?

Jake gazed down from the terrace.

Men were streaming through the village, into the lab, running past the lab. Men with scars.

They were firing their guns in the air, shouting at everyone, blind fury showing on dark faces.

Lucidly frightened, and calmly alarmed, Jake stayed immobile. More shouts from behind the lab told Jake that they were surrounded and trapped.

Sen was on his feet, yelling. But the men with the scars ignored him, crudely laughing, jeering, even.

Jake stared.

In the middle of the gang, at the foot of the steps leading to the terrace, was *Julia*. And next to the American woman was . . . Chemda. Except Chemda was also sitting next to him at the table.

The other Chemda strode up the steps. She had a gun, and she was aiming it at Sen. Her face was calm, determined, and entirely merciless.

46

"I am Soriya. Chemda is my sister. And you—" *The gun was pointed at Sen, standing defiantly on the top step.* *"You, of course, are my grandfather. The man who did this to me."*

The young Khmer woman took off a wig, and Jake saw the scar on her bald scalp.

"When I was six months old."

The scar was faded, almost white.

Soriya Tek turned to the Chinese men, the other men with scars, with their rifles hoisted or pointing. They were the same mutinous guards from the back gate, the men who had tried to bleed Jake out. She spoke to the men.

"Here. Just as I promised you. Revenge. Now." A step forward; a blunt gesture. "Kill them *all,* except for her"—Soriya pointed at Chemda—"and him." She was pointing at Jake.

"He is one of us. See, the scar. Spare him. Kill the rest."

An uncertainty prevailed. Some of the men moved toward the terrace, others lingered; Soriya said, more loudly: *"Tā shì wǒmen měi yīgè rén. Bèijiàn tāshā sǐ, qíyú!"*

The men moved, properly commanded. In moments the terrace was crowded with the guards. Jake could smell the sweat on them. Beer and yak butter and dirt. Sen was led down the steps, then Fishwick and Tyrone.

Only Tyrone was struggling, shouting. Only Tyrone was fighting.

"Jake, for fuck's sake, tell them. Tell them, dude! Fucking tell them! I've got nothing to do with this—"

The mob of guards was dragging Tyrone to the nearest cliff, just a few meters away; the cliff plunged, gruesomely, right down to the heaven villages. Maybe half a mile or more.

"Jake, please, fucking please, Jake. Tell them!"

Jake observed Tyrone's struggling. He considered, clearly and logically, the fact that Tyrone had betrayed him: no matter that the surgery was a success, Tyrone had risked Jake's life for his own purposes. Did he deserve to live? Maybe not. And there was another factor to be considered: if Tyrone was dead then Jake had no rival, he could tell his own story. Make all the money. Jake stepped down the terrace, Chemda following him. He approached his friend. His ex-friend. He gazed into Tyrone's terrified eyes.

"Mate," said Jake. "I'm sorry."

He stepped away.

The men dragged Tyrone the last meter to the edge of the cliff. Chemda was gazing at Jake, appalled; Jake didn't care.

Let Tyrone die.

Now the American was crying. The hard-assed Tyrone McKenna was sobbing like a child, pleading for his life.

"Please, no, Jake, *pleeeeeease.*"

Soriya gestured.

Tyrone was thrown over the cliff. Jake peered over. His friend actually twirled in the air, the drop was so huge. The spectacle was *fascinating.* Jake watched his friend smash against an outcrop of rock;

an interesting pink blur of blood showed the body exploding with the impact. The corpse bounced and disappeared into the gorge.

Julia was sobbing.

Soriya turned to Fishwick.

"Him next. *Tā de xià yīgè.*"

Fishwick was dragged to the side of the cliff by the sweating guards. The sun shone down on them all, harsh and uncaring. The neurosurgeon was not even struggling; his expression was resigned. His gray ponytail hung limply in the sun.

But Chemda intervened.

"No, please no—*don't kill him!*"

Soriya turned. "Why not?"

"I am your sister, am I not? Your twin sister? Do this for me. *Spare him.*"

Soriya paused. A brief flash of emotion crossed the killer's dark, impassive face. Illegible emotion: Sadness? Grief? Something profound and repressed. Jake watched, deeply intrigued. Julia was staring his way.

"For my sister?" Soriya gestured to the guards. "Ach. What does it matter. Let him go. I don't care. But I will kill my grandfather. Bring me the axle."

Fishwick was released; Sen was pushed to the edge of the precipice. The pine trees whispered in a mountain breeze; the gorges yawned, dark and hungry.

"Kneel," said Soriya.

The grandfather knelt. Sen looked up and said, very quietly: "How did you get past the main guards? The *inner* barrier?"

Soriya shrugged. "They thought I was Chemda. They were confused." She waved a hand at the sweating, scarred men, the excised men. "These other guards, your *mistakes,* they have decided to help me. I discussed this with them many months ago. I came here in secret. We agreed to all of this. They agreed. You invoke no loyalty,

Sen. You mutilated so many. And without faith or fear or love, they care for nothing. There is no one to help you. Everyone in the laboratory has scattered. They know the PLA is coming."

Sen smiled. "But you think this upsets me, daughter? Please. I am not grieved. I am not ashamed, *I am proud of you*. I wanted to create the perfect Communist child. And behold: I succeeded. Because here you are, guilt-free, devoid of mercy, and purely logical. My beloved granddaughter. Biologically atheist."

"You gave me away. How beloved is that?"

"We thought you were a failure! You were taken in the anarchies, the dilapidations, when the Khmer Rouge finally collapsed in Anlong Veng. I never knew what happened to you, do you understand, my child? I didn't dare hope that you had lived—the baby with the seizures, the fits—and yet, when I began to hear of these pitiless slayings, these cruel and clever murders, I knew. I aspired, Soriya, I hoped that you lived, that you thrived. I sensed you were coming, and I wanted to see you. So I could compare you with your superstitious sister, the control experiment. See if you had evolved. And I regard you now with true delight. My wonderful and beautiful experiment. My perfected, liberated, and entirely godless granddaughter."

Soriya had taken a rusty iron bar from one of the guards. A car axle.

"I am not a granddaughter, I am not even a woman. I am not a man either. I am nothing. You made me into a *nothing*. Barely human. You severed me from everything. A freak with no breasts. See."

She tugged open her shirt. Jake winced at the pale scar tissue she briefly exposed. A double mastectomy: two more wounds.

"By the time I was eighteen, I was desperate. Why was I so sick in the head? What was wrong with me? Why did I feel that something was wrong, something was missing? So I began to think maybe I was the wrong sex. And I went to Bangkok. And I had sex reassignment surgery." Soriya sighed tersely and rebuttoned her shirt with one hand. She went on: "The surgeons cut off my breasts, took out my womb—and gave me hormone injections. Testosterone. And they told me to walk like a boy. This was meant, or so I hoped, to make me better. Turning me into a kind of *kathoey*. A she-he." She snarled at her grandfather, and clutched the iron bar tighter. "*Yet it didn't work.* Of course. I was just angrier than ever. I had mutilated myself for no reason. I went back to America. Went back to being a girl. With no breasts. Mutilated. A man with no penis. Then I joined the army. At that, I was good, a surprisingly strong young woman. All those testosterone injections, all the steroids. So all this has been useful. It has helped me get here, where I can kill you."

Sen's smile was gone; for the first time Jake saw confusion on the old man's face.

He mouthed a word but Soriya cut him off.

"Turn that way. *Turn that way.* Cheung Ek. Tuol Sleng. Highway Five. This is for everyone who died. For all the people killed by communism. For the country you beheaded. Turn that way."

The first shudder of fear trembled at Sen's mouth.

"You really think that I should die—"

The iron bar swung into the back of Sen's head: the sound of the skull splitting was pulpy, organic, a plashing crack. The brains squirted into the dust, the broken head gaped open, pornographically. Soriya sneered at the sight, then she kicked the twitching body off the edge of the cliff.

"Now, you, give me a gun."

One of the guards handed a revolver to Soriya.

"Throw me off the cliff when I'm finished. At least I can kill myself without guilt. The one thing they gave me."

She turned and walked a few meters down the cliff and put the gun to her head, and, like she was slaughtering a hog with a bolt, she fired. Another shower of blood, another splatter of bone.

The weeping sound was Chemda—she had turned away from the scene, crying. Jake watched, absorbed. He watched as the scarred men did their duty: Soriya's twitching body was hurled off the cliff. Vultures circled down the gorge, seeking the carrion.

Patches of blood and splinters of bone were glistening in the sun. A yak stared placidly at the men, who had already begun to disperse. The guards were drifting away, some now running.

Within moments, Fishwick, Julia, Chemda, and Jake were standing on the edge of Balagezong village. Quite alone. The wind murmured in the Yunnanese forests, soft breezes fluting their grief.

Or was it grief? Where was the grief?

Jake touched the scar on his head. It was stinging. He could feel the pain in his mind at war with the clarity. Guilt *was* still there, in his mind, yet he could not connect with it; it was a cherished poem he had forgotten, a beautiful song he could not quite recall. Just like his love for Chemda.

He felt suddenly blinded. He was blind to something. He had lost a sense. How could he have done that to Tyrone? Why didn't he feel remorse?

As he touched his own face, he realized he had wetness on his fingers. Astonishingly, he seemed to be crying. But he didn't know why.

"Chemda," he said, "what have they done to me?"

She reached for his hand. Jake could feel the moistness, like tears, on his face, but he didn't know what it was for. He wasn't crying. He was just leaking. He was just fucking *leaking*. He was a machine, a dead battery, he was Soriya, he was pitiless. A soft machine leaking oil.

Jake hunched down. He wanted to make himself small, to hide from the world. This was bitter and disastrous, everything was futile.

Chemda stooped and kissed him and she whispered: "There is something we can do."

47

She repeated, "There is something we can do. But there are dangers. Colin told me, a few days ago. That is why I asked Soriya to spare him."

Fishwick knelt beside Jake and spoke. He was hesitant, repressing a stammer or deep emotions.

"The operation we did on you was cryosurgical. Stand . . . please. . . . Let me *explain*."

Jake allowed them to guide him to the terrace. He sat down and gazed out at the village. It was apparently deserted. No doubt the locals were hiding, frightened by the gunshots. The hideous scene enacted on the cliffside. And yet, now everyone had gone, the guards, the lab workers, Sen and Tyrone and Soriya all gone—it was eerily peaceful. A deceptive serenity enveloped Balagezong. The mist drifted in and out of the heaven villages.

How could he have let them do that to Tyrone?

Fishwick explained:

"It took us many years. To . . . perfect the surgery. Eventually we realized that the solution was conceptual: the God module should be treated as a difficult and inaccessible *brain tumor*. You can imagine Sen was pleased with the metaphor. The analogy. Religion and guilt as a malignant cancer, in an otherwise *healthy* organism."

Fishwick shrugged and continued: "But I haven't got time to explain it all, the Chinese authorities will *surely* be here soon, with the army—and if my operation is to succeed I have to work *immediately*."

Jake was bewildered. Julia and Chemda were sitting together in silence. Like sisters. He said, "Operation?"

Fishwick explained:

"The God module isn't just a little blob of tissue in one part of the human brain. . . . Using ultrasound, PET scans, MRIs of Tibetan monks, and *many* other analyses, we finally established that the God module was an extremely complex system centered in the frontal cortex, but linked to the hippocampus, the amygdala, the thalamic nuclei, and elsewhere, like a vicious, octopoidal *tumor.* The . . . the best way of treating these invasive and complex tumors is cryosurgery: the use of extreme cold produced by liquid nitrogen, or argon gas, to destroy abnormal tissue."

"You froze my fucking soul?"

"If you like. The nitrogen is circulated through a hollow instrument called a cryoprobe. A ball of ice crystals forms around the probe, freezing the unwanted cells. So *yes*. . . . We freeze the soul to *death.*"

The snow on the Holy Mountain glittered in the afternoon sun, crystalline and prismatic. Fishwick continued, his mild face aged with remorse:

"But there is a problem. Although we have, *theoretically,* perfected the surgery, that is to say, we have created stable and functioning minds, anatomically incapable of spiritual belief, or religious delusion . . . I have noticed that the outcomes are still . . . *suboptimal.* There is often something missing, which cannot be adequately defined. A flatness of the emotions, or a lack of psychic music. A kind of deafness. I have concluded that many humans are probably meant to believe. They have evolved to believe. Consequently, taking away this possibility, in some patients, is a grave error. . . ." He sighed.

"Perhaps you, too, Jake, were meant to believe. You have merely repressed this belief for many years, because of the traumas of your youth. You are angry at God, but you still believe in Him, deep down. At least you did believe, until we did what we did. The *surgery.*"

Jake blustered. Helpless.

"But what's the relevance. Now. How does this help me?"

Chemda said, "Reversal. It can be done."

"What? You're gonna reverse the surgery? You thaw my brain?"

Fishwick assented. "Somewhat crudely put, but essentially . . . yes. Over the years, as my doubts have developed, even as we got the procedure right, I have been theorizing and experimenting on . . . the possibility of *reversal.* I have never tried it on live human subjects, just animal tissue. But I believe it is quite practicable. Your neurones are frozen; in a few hours they will die. But if I thaw them with the same probe, *right* here and *right now,* it is possible I can undo the procedure. But there is also a chance you could end up . . . cognitively deficient, very badly damaged. You might even . . . not survive. I am sorry. I simply *don't know.* I think it will work, but I cannot be sure." He sighed. "It is a leap of faith."

Silence returned.

No one spoke.

Jake stared at the mountain, wisping snow from the summit. The mountain he had no desire to re-create, to mediate, to photograph. He remembered the blood on the grass. The blood and the shattered bone.

Then he gazed at the black-throated gorge, down which they had hurled Tyrone. His friend. His flawed, greedy, ambitious, cynical, and selfish friend. Who had saved him in Anlong, who had arguably tried to save him here. The friend Jake had casually chucked to his death.

And now he turned to Julia. She had been silent all through this, but she responded to his gaze. Lifting her phone, she said, "I can get us out of here. I've been in touch with Rouvier. When we reached Bala, there was finally a signal. I spoke to him several times. He has been working for us; he's spoken to his superiors, who have spoken to European governments. He thinks the Chinese government probably wants this over, hushed up. They might do a deal. Just expel us." She shook her head. "But the army is coming. So if it's going to happen, it's going to happen soon. You really don't have much time. You need to decide."

Jake's gaze rested, finally, on Chemda. The face he could no longer love.

48

He lay back on the neurosurgeon's table, which was more like a tilted throne. Bright lights shone down on his scalp, while a silent nurse sorted through a cutlery of steel tools. The nurse was the only other staff member who hadn't fled. What pitiable fact had kept her loyal to the end?

"I will have to do the anesthesia myself," said Fishwick, from the far side of the room. He offered Jake a melancholy smile. "Don't worry, I *do* know what I am doing. It's the surgery that is problematic. Potentially."

Jake stiffened with anxiety. He gazed around the empty, white, laboratory-like chamber. Chemda wasn't present; she had told him she couldn't bear to watch. Jake wondered if he could blame her for this.

"How long will I be under?"

"Two hours. We need to work fast."

Two hours, Jake thought. Just *two hours.* And then what? The terrors were gathering at the door of his future. Would he wake, and, if he woke up, would he still have a mind? Did he even want the guilt to return?

The silence in the room, while Fishwick washed his hands at a metal sink, was unbearable.

"Talk to me," Jake said. "Please. Talk to me."

"Of course."

"Just talk. Tell me what are you going to do, after all this?"

Fishwick sighed.

"I would maybe like to make some repayment . . . for what I have done. Perhaps I could work in Chinese hospitals, treating epilepsy with neurosurgery. The procedure is, er, *similar.* Religious visions and spiritual epiphanies closely mirror the neural process of epileptic seizures."

Staring into the bright white light of the surgery lamps, Jake absorbed this thought.

"So you think religion is just *a kind of epilepsy?*"

Fishwick gazed at the paper towel in his hands.

"Well . . . as I implied, before, over many years, I developed doubts about the *whole concept.*"

"Doubts. And?"

"I was once, as you know, a devoted Marxist. But as I investigated the links between Marxism and social structure and religion, it struck me that . . ." Fishwick allowed the nurse to snap some rubber gloves on his wrists. Then he continued: "It struck me that the worst societies are nearly always the atheist societies. Hitler's Germany. Mao's China. Stalin's Russia. And the Khmer Rouge, of course, Pol Pot's Cambodia, the most brutal of all, the most violently atheist. The land of the prophecy, hmm? The land without religion. And so much *blood.*"

"So . . . ?"

"In just a hundred years atheist Communists and atheist Nazis killed hundreds of millions . . . comprehensively more than any religion. And yet they did it for ideological and philosophical reasons, they did it for reasons which were themselves *quasi-religious.*"

"And what does that mean?"

The tools of Fishwick's business twinkled in the overbright lights; the stainless silver scalpels, the exquisite cranial drills.

"This is the real reason that they are going to close down the lab, Jake, why even the hard-core Communist Chinese lost interest in Sen's work. It turned out that the people who had the surgery, the *Godectomy,* here, they ended up with as little interest in communism as they might have had in Islam . . . or Zoroastrianism."

"Why?"

"*Because communism is just another belief system.* Hmm? Another irrational belief system that uses the *same neural structures.* Communism relies on faith and devotion and revelation, it has sacred texts—*Das Kapital,* the Little Red Book—it has saints, prophets, and priests. It believes in a heaven, a Utopia, which is just a heaven on earth in their case. And Marxism is just as illogical as the *craziest* faith: everywhere that communism has been tried it has failed, dismally." The neurosurgeon leaned to check an oval glass dial on one squat and glinting machine. "Yet still the true believers believe, they are sure we shall see heaven on earth. They have, after all, faith."

"Except an even more destructive one," Jake said. "A savage and godless faith. Right?"

"Yes. A religion with no morals, quite lethal and disgusting. Leaving millions killed. If communism is their Koran, if Marx is their Bible—then it is a Bible of the Dead." He paused for a long second. "And many of our *patients* were proof of this equivalence: following the operation, it turned out they were all *deeply* skeptical of communism, just as skeptical of communism as they might be of Mormonism, or horoscopes. And when the Chinese realized that Sen's laboratory was churning out people with no faith in the orthodox stupidities of Marx and Mao, that's when they lost interest."

Jake was sweating now. Hot and sweating.

"Ironic."

Fishwick agreed, with a pensive smile. And stood close.

"We're nearly ready. Jake . . . the temperature levels of the thawing process are vitally important. There's just a few moments to go. . . ." A quiet word was swapped with the nurse.

Jake said, "Keep talking. Before I change my mind. *Please?*"

Fishwick obeyed. "As it happens, Cambodia also provides the most interesting *counterexample,* on which I have often reflected. Indeed, a year or two ago I began to vigorously reexamine all the ancient history. For instance, I went back to Site Nine in Laos—they preserved just one site intact for researchers. And, crucially, I also visited Angkor." He was staring into his own surgical lights. "Ah, *Angkor Wat.* Perhaps the greatest and most beautiful preindustrial society we know: *exquisitely* advanced, enchanted, a kingdom where government was truly united with the image of the divine, of the godhead—"

"The faces of the Bayon."

"Yes." The American tilted one of the vast surgical lights a fraction of a centimeter. "You know, the builders of Angkor even left a sign to show that they knew the importance of proper faith to civilization."

"The diamond in the forehead of the great Bayon faces."

The light was shining on Jake's forehead. Fishwick answered:

"Yes. Perhaps instinctively, the builders of Angkor knew the *preciousness* of true religion. They even guessed where it might lie, the God module, in the head. They certainly remembered the terrors of the Black Khmer, trepanned, lobotomized, and godless . . . on the Plain of Jars." There was another murmured conversation with the nurse. The surgeon swiveled, and explained: "Jake, this is it. In approximately ninety seconds, the cryoprobe will be at the correct temperature. So if you want to turn back, you need to speak up *now.*"

Jake's heartbeat was chaotic: skipping with fear. He quelled his terror with another question.

"No. I want to know why you carried on with the surgeries, if you had these doubts."

Fishwick nodded, his face a shadow behind the lights.

"Because I kept *convincing* myself . . . against the growing evidence. After all, there are *so many* good, solid, Darwinian explanations for why religious faith has evolved. And yet I also had evidence of the necessity of faith. People who have faith are healthier, happier, they live longer, they even have stronger immune systems. This is scientific fact. So I became . . . very confused." The nurse was calling Fishwick to scrutinize a larger machine, which resembled an ECG monitor. The surgeon softly spoke to the nurse and returned to his theme. "Then, one day, quite recently, I discovered another very curious fact during my research. It's Parkinson's disease. People who have Parkinson's, even the mildest form . . . are less likely to be believers."

The nurse was standing with the rubber mask, ready to hand it over.

"And that means?" Jake grasped at the last shreds of this reality. "What does that mean?"

"It is therefore at least arguable that *atheism is a form of dementia.* Imagine that! *Atheism is a kind of psychosis, a mental illness.* The healthy mind is, very, very truly, a mind that believes." An electronic chime rang across the room. "OK, Jake, that's the signal. The temperature is critical, we need to do this . . . *right now.* We can't wait any longer."

"Wait, I want to know." Even as the rubber mask of anesthesia was clamped over his mouth, Jake felt the cry of a question in his godless mind. "I still don't know *why. Why does it make us happier? Why are we meant to believe?*"

But his question was met by the black silence of unconsciousness.

49

"How do you feel?"

"The same. Different. *I don't know.*"

Jake was awake. Sipping a hot drink. He had been conscious for an hour, in the dark, but now the lights were on, and Fishwick was gazing at him with a quizzical expression.

"Perhaps you need to see . . . to go outside. To assess your reactions."

Jake knew what this meant: go and look at the world, go and see Chemda. Find out whether his guilty soul had been retrieved from erasure.

He stood. Again he felt an odd composure, a sweet stability; not the quailing weakness he expected following serious surgery. Did this mean the surgery had worked? Or simply done nothing?

At least he could talk. He wasn't a drooling fool.

A loose jacket slung over his shirtsleeves, he stepped out of the room. At the end was that dazzling silver oblong: the glass door that gave onto the terrace, the door that opened to the truth.

He walked and pressed the glass and he breathed the thin light air of Balagezong. Julia and Chemda were seated at the tables and staring his way. In a crushing second he realized: he felt the same, he felt nothing. He felt nothing for Chemda.

The truth was so anguished, he couldn't bear to describe it. His face must have spoken eloquently enough: Chemda turned away. She put a hand to her eyes, disguising her emotions. Jake didn't know if she was crying or not. He didn't especially care. The sun shone down. No one said anything. There was nothing to be said; nothing was ever going to be said, ever again. Faint cirrus clouds striped the sky beyond White Buddha Mountain.

Within hours of the surgery's completion Jake was able to confirm this cold realization—the operation had totally failed: the sense of detachment remained just as before, the feeling that he existed in a world where all music had been subtly removed.

But at least he hadn't died, or been calamitously lobotomized. And the guilt about his mother and his sister, that was still gone.

The first days of his recovery he spent lying in bed or sitting quietly on the terrace with Chemda, feeling awkward. Sometimes Chemda tried to smile, to touch him, to kiss him. But his inert reactions eventually dissuaded her. And in time she simply retreated to her room.

And left him alone.

Next day, the soldiers came. The army, and then the police. This was less alarming than they had feared. As Julia had promised, Rouvier had done a politic and convincing job, through the French, U.S., and U.K. governments, in ensuring that they were saved from custody; and in neutralizing the complexities.

Rouvier was apparently aided by the attitude of Beijing. The Chinese surely wanted to cut a deal; they were evidently embarrassed by the whole business. Jake even suspected they had actively held off from taking over the lab complex so as to let events play out; so that

Beijing was ultimately untainted by the whole scandal. With that outcome, the authorities could plead a plausible ignorance—and flush the whole unsightly business down the latrine of history.

Jake saw this desire in the way the officials behaved. The police were brisk and efficient yet eerily detached, uninterested. They questioned them several times, and questioned Fishwick, they took photos of the "crime scene," and they took away equipment for tests, but it was all rather cursory. Jake was sure that the photos and interviews would be simply trashed, at a convenient moment.

And then the specialists and the soldiers departed and it was just the ordinary police. One of them was particularly friendly.

Jake was sitting alone on the terrace, sipping his fine *pu-erh* tea. The young, smiling, English-speaking Chinese policeman came over and looked at Jake's scar and said that Jake was allowed to stay a few more days in Balagezong, for "rehabilitation and recuperation"—two words the man found very difficult to pronounce. But then, the policeman implied, it was *definitely* expected that Chemda and Jake and Julia would make themselves strangers. Go back to Bangkok. Go home. Go anywhere. Just go a long way from China.

Then the policeman made the first and only reference, albeit oblique, to the unspoken deal. He gestured across the mountainscape and smiled and said, "You are a photographer, no? Maybe you should do some photographs of the beautiful gorges here. Publish them. This is the only reason to come here. This is all people need to know, yes?"

Jake had a blanket over his knees, like an invalid at the beach. He nodded. He knew what this remark meant. *Their silence was indeed being bought.* The Chinese wanted the troublesome foreigners gone, but they would let them go only in return for silence. The policeman smiled again.

"People do not want to know about the old China. They need to know about the *new* China! No? And the National Park of Shangri-La Gorge is coming! That is what you must tell people."

"Shangri-La?"

"Yes. Xianggelila." He laughed. "Shangri-La. The name is taken from the book by a British man, I believe? The secret Himalayan paradise. It is good idea—good brand. It will change the lives of these peasants."

"They'll build a proper road?"

"Yes, yes! And many toilets, and cafés. Shops! And why not? This is most beautiful place in the world, so there must be toilets and cafés and buses and shops. It will be wonderful. This is progress!"

He grinned. "And now I say goodbye. There is last village truck leaving for Zhongdian in four days. *You must take that.* We need to begin the . . . destruction of this . . ." He winced with distaste. "This laboratory. The army will return to do this job. So we can build the park."

"Yes," Jake said, sensing the resignation in his own voice. "We'll go on the last truck. Thank you."

The man turned and briefly saluted and the hollowness returned.

But another person was hovering. Fishwick.

He pulled up a seat beside Jake. He poured himself a glass of pu-erh tea.

"I'm also leaving this afternoon. With the authorities."

"What are you going to do?"

"As I hoped, they have agreed to let me work . . . with epileptics."

Fishwick stirred his long spoon in his tea.

"Jake. I just wanted to say something. Do you recall . . . the last question you asked me, just before the surgery?"

"Yes. I do. *Why are we meant to believe?*" Jake squinted at the American.

The older man hesitated, then pointed with his long steel spoon and said, "Look at that mountain. The beauty of it. It is eloquent, is it not?"

"Sorry?"

Fishwick momentarily closed his eyes. And he spoke quietly:

"The answer to your question only came to me a few weeks ago. I was standing by the stupa, Bala stupa, under the Holy Mountain, and somehow it dawned. I saw. I *realized* that perhaps the God module evolved for the most profound and obvious reason of *all*."

"Which is?"

"It's not a byproduct, it's not a spandrel or a parasite or a trick, it's not even something to keep us chatty and cheerful and healthy . . . it's . . ."

"It's what?"

Fishwick gazed at Jake. "We evolved eyes to see the sunlight. We evolved ears to hear the wind. And our minds are wired for faith . . . *because?*"

"You mean we are meant to believe because there really is a God? *You have become a believer?*"

The surgeon shrugged, and gestured, once again, at the sublimity of the landscape around them.

"You know, the villagers here, they were once so isolated, just sixty years ago, they thought they were the only people in the universe. *Imagine that?*"

But Jake didn't want to imagine that, he didn't want to imagine *anything*. He didn't want to think of his own cold, withered future, gray as the sands in Sovirom Sen's Japanese garden. So he stared at the gorges and at White Buddha Mountain. He stared at the nothingness.

Fishwick was sighing. "I really do *have* to go. I am so sorry the surgery proved irreversible. All I can say is—have a little hope. Sometimes neurones can heal spontaneously, we don't know why. The mind retains its many mysteries. Goodbye, Jake."

Jake watched him descend the steps and disappear down a path that led to the rear of the laboratories.

The wind from the forests was mild. But his tea was cold. And the hollowness inside him was profound. Like a silenced bell.

50

The days passed, the nullity abided. Jake dreamed of nothing. He stared at the sky. The day of their departure approached.

On the seventh day following the failed operation, Jake woke early and looked across the bed.

It was empty.

There was a note on Chemda's pillow, in an envelope.

He took out the notepaper and read.

> *I know you don't love me anymore; and I know you can't help it. This is too painful for me: because I still love you.*
>
> *Goodbye.*
> *C*

He put the note back in the envelope; he dressed. Trying not to think. The very last truck was due to leave Bala this afternoon. He wanted to run outside and race down the valley. He didn't know what to do.

Julia was sitting on the terrace.

"Chemda has gone," he said.

She stared at him, and her gaze was searching. "I know. She told me last night. A villager was taking his fruit to Zhongdian market at dawn. She went with him in the pickup. I'm sorry, Jake."

He sat down. Staring at his own hands, then at Julia.

"What are *you* going to do? When we finally get . . . away?"

The American woman sighed. Her expression was strained.

"I don't know. I really don't know. Not anymore."

Jake said nothing. But the silence seemed to embarrass Julia, so he stood, straightened his chair, and continued his walk past the terrace tables.

The day was bright and clear, sharp and mountainous. The villagers were tilling their steep brown fields. One old woman gave him a broken smile as he walked the path to the stupa.

Positioned on a large, high promontory of rock, the stupa overlooked one of the most spectacular stretches of the canyon. Down there were the heaven villages; much farther down was the cascading river, a juvenile tributary of the Mekong.

The Mekong. The very concept threw up a kaleidoscopic series of recent memories. It seemed to Jake as though he had been following the great Mekong all these weeks, from Vang Vieng to Luang Prabang to Phnom Penh to Yunnan. The mighty Mekong. And now he was near the source, where the crystal waters tumbled, violent and tragic.

He climbed the last steps and placed a hand on the stupa. Silence enveloped him.

The only noise came from the wind horses—the prayer flags fluttering in a stiff sunlit breeze. Each flag, of red and blue and faded yellow, was written with the wishes of the villagers, praying to the holy mountains.

Remorse fell like a silent snow. What had he done? He had lost everyone. His sister, his mother, his friend, now Chemda.

Everyone.

In a few hours the last truck would leave Bala village and take the long road to Zhongdian. And he would be on it. Running after Chemda. He was going to find her. He knew he would spend the rest of his life trying to find her, if that's what it took. He could feel the wind carrying him.

A chillier gust kicked up. The little prayer flags fluttered in the silent breeze, petitioning the universe, filling the quietness. Arms of snow embraced the rocky summit of White Buddha Mountain: like a mother, folding a son in her love, and never letting go.

51

"What you did was very brave. Audacious!"

Officer Rouvier steered the car around a corner. Ahead of them, through the drizzle, Julia could see the distant stones of the Cham des Bondons, dark and elegiac. It was as if they had been waiting for her to return; as if they *knew* she was coming back.

"I don't know about bravery," she said. "I just did what I did. What I had to do. Thank you for collecting me from the airport."

The Frenchman smiled, slightly, and squinted at the pattering rain.

"You have already thanked me twice, Miss Kerrigan. But I am still confused. What are you going to do now? You really want to spend the winter out *here*?"

He gestured at the bleak and rainy moors; the wind-lashed causse.

"My college in London has given me another few weeks' paid leave. Because of . . . well . . ."

He didn't reply to this. They drove past a farm's broken gate, where a brace of horses looked dismal and forlorn in the wet. Another lonely standing stone loomed through the mist.

Julia recalled her own ideas. Of Easter Island. The monuments to a violent and dying culture.

Rouvier spoke: "So you will go back to London in the spring?"

"Maybe. Maybe not. I like to think that I have choices."

Rouvier agreed. Then he said, "You also have a very good brain, Miss Kerrigan. Your theory, about the caves and skulls, it was right!"

"Ghislaine's theory."

"No." He spoke firmly. "*Yours*. You do not know what he wrote, and you either discovered it again, or you made a better one. I am *sure* you made a better theory. So it is yours."

The rain was the only sound, discreetly chattering on the car's roof.

They were very near Annika's old cottage now. With that realization she felt a reflux of fear and grief, which she strove to quell. *This is just a place. Just an old cottage. That's all. Just an old house.*

She spoke, quickly: "I've rented a small farmhouse for about two months, it's in the next village from Vayssière. Les Combettes. It's very cheap in the winter."

Rouvier nodded. "I'm not surprised. Most people escape in the winter. This is not Juan les Pins in August. They should be paying you for *staying*." He softly smiled her way. "It will be lonely out here?"

"I don't mind loneliness."

"But . . . Mr. Carmichael?"

She shrugged. "Things change."

"*Bien sûr.*" He nodded, slowing the car as they took the last turn for Vayssière. "I know this all too well. I am now divorced myself. Ah . . . this rain. *Il pleure. . . .*"

"*Dans mon coeur, comme il pleut sur la ville?*"

Their shared laughter was gentle. He stopped the car a few meters from Annika's front door. Julia glanced across. Yes, her car was still there. Where she'd left it, all those weeks ago, when they had quit the place to go and see Ghislaine's body. She'd never got around to picking it up again. And now here she was. Picking it up again.

Like a chauffeur, Rouvier came around to her side of the car and helped her out. Then he assisted in carrying her bags to her car and stowing them on the backseat. Neither of them looked at Annika's cottage window as they worked. The small window that gave onto the sitting room.

When her stuff was in the car, Rouvier stooped and kissed her hand in an unselfconscious way. As he looked up, he said, "If you get really lonely, you must call me. We can drink a pastis in the excitement of Mende."

"Thank you. It might be nice to do that. In the big city."

There was another exchange of smiles, tinged with sadness. Rouvier opened his door, started his engine, and was gone.

For a moment Julia stood, tense, in the faint drizzle; sensing the presence of the past. Then she climbed in her car and briskly drove to the next village down the road. Les Combettes.

It took her just two hours to install all her stuff in her rented cottage. The kitchen of the little house had a good view of the stones. So did the window above her desk. Julia ignored the view: instead she sat down, took out her laptop, and put it on the desk, alongside a small bottle of water.

Her fingers were poised. She opened a new page, and typed:

Some Speculations on the Origins of Guilt and of Conscience in the Paleolithic Caves of France and Spain

For a second or two she stared at the words on her screen. Then she erased the sentence and gazed at the blankness, at the drizzle on the windows, at the lawns and moors. A shaft of bleak sunlight had pierced the clouds; it shone down on the fields, making the sodden feather grass sparkle, momentarily: a sudden harvest of jewels. She tried again:

The Sad Hands of Gargas: On the Origins of Human Guilt and Religion in the European Ice Age

Nodding to herself, she took a sip of water, and then she added three more words:

By Julia Kerrigan.

Turn the page for a sneak peek

at Tom Knox's upcoming novel

978-0-670-02664-7

Coming from Viking 5/2/2013.

Viking
A member of Penguin Group (USA) Inc.
www.penguin.com

VIKING

1

Trujillo, Peru

It was a very strange place to build a museum. Under a Texaco gas station, where the dismal suburbs of Trujillo met the cold and foggy deserts of north Peru, in a wasteland of concrete warehouses and sleazy cantinas. But somehow this sense of being hidden away, this strange, sequestered location, made the Museo Casinelli feel even more intriguing: as if it really was a *secret* museum.

Jessica liked coming here, whenever she drove down to Trujillo from Zana. And today she had remembered to bring a camera, to gather crucial evidence.

She opened the door at the rear of the garage and smiled at the old curator, who stood, and bowed, as courteous as ever. 'Ah, Señorita Silverton! You are here again? You must like the, eh, naughty pottery?' Her shrug was a little bashful; his smile was gently teasing. 'But I fear the keys are in the other desk . . . *Un minuto*?'

'Of course.'

Pablo disappeared into a room at the back. As she waited, Jessica checked her cellphone, for the fifth time today: she was expecting an important call, from Steve Venturi, the best forensic anthropologist she knew.

A week ago, she had arrived in Trujillo – taking a break from her studies amongst the pyramids of Zana; she'd brought with her a box full of fifteen-hundred-year-old Moche bones. This package had in turn been despatched to California, to her old tutor in UCLA: Venturi.

Any day now she would get Steve's answer. Was she right about the neckbones? Was her audacious insight *correct?* The anxiety of waiting for the verdict was increasingly unbearable. Jess felt like a teenager awaiting exam results.

She looked up from the silent phone. Pablo had returned from his vestibule flourishing two keys, one big, one small. As he offered them, he winked. *'La sala privada?'*

Jessica's Spanish was still pretty mediocre, and for that reason she and the kindly curator normally conversed in English – but she understood *that* phrase well enough. The private room.

'Si!'

She took both keys from Pablo and saw how he noticed her slightly trembling hand. 'It's OK. Just need a coca.'

Pablo frowned. *'La diabetes?'*

'I'm OK. Really.'

The frown softened to a smile. 'See you later.'

Jess descended the steps to the basement museum. Fumbling in the darkness, she found the larger key, and opened the door.

When she switched on the light it flooded the room with a reassuring glow, revealing an eccentric and exquisite treasure trove of ancient Peruvian ceramics, pottery, textiles and other artefacts – gleaned from the mysterious cultures of pre-Colombian Peru: the Moche, the Chan Chan, the Huari, the Chimu.

The light also shone on a dried monkey foetus, grimacing in a bell jar.

She tried not to look at it. This thing always creeped her out. Maybe it wasn't even a monkey, maybe it was a dried sloth, or some human mutation preserved as a gruesome curio by Jose Casinelli, forever offering the world its sad little face.

Briskly she walked past the bell jar, and bent to the glass cabinets, the vitrines of pottery and treasures. Here were the stone pestles of the Chavin, and here the exquisite burial cloths of the Nazca in faded violet and purple; to the left was a brief, poignant line of Quingnam writing, the lost language of the Chimu. She took out her new camera and adjusted the tiny dial to compensate for the poor-quality light.

As she worked, Jessica recalled the first time she had come here, six months ago, when she had begun her sabbatical: researching the anthropology of the pre-Columbian Stone Age in north Peru, making a comparative study of religious cultures across ancient America. Back then she had been almost a total ingénue, unprepared for the shock she was about to encounter: the high weirdness of pre-Inca Peru, most especially the Moche. And their infamous 'naughty pottery'.

It was time to visit the *sala privada*.

Taking out the smaller key, she opened the creaking side-door. A further, darker, tinier room lay beyond.

Few people came to the tiny Museo Casinelli, fewer still entered *la sala privada*. Even today a distinct aura of embarrassment surrounded the principal contents: the Moche sex pottery, the *ceramicas eroticas*. They were certainly too shocking and explicit to be shown to children, and conservative Peruvian Catholics would regard them as obscene works of the devil and be happy to see them smashed. Which was why they were kept in this dark and private antechamber, deep inside the secret museum.

Jess knelt, and squinted, preparing to be shocked all over again.

The first row of pots was asexual, merely distressing: on the left was a finely-crafted pot of a man with no nose and no lips, fired in exquisite black and gold. In the centre was a delicate ceramic representation of human sacrifice, with dismembered bodies at the foot of a mountain. And over here was a man tied to a tree, having his eyes pecked out by a vulture. Carefully, she took a photo of the last example.

Disturbing as these ceramics might be, they were just normal mad Moche pottery. The next shelves held the real deal: the *ceramicas eroticas*.

Working her way along them, Jess fired off dozens of photos. Why did the Moche go to the trouble of crafting erotic pottery like this? Sex with animals. Sex with the dead. Sex between skeletons. Perhaps it was just a metaphor, maybe even a joke; more likely it was a dream-time, a mythology. It was certainly repellent, yet also fascinating.

Jessica took some final photos, using the camera flash this time, which reflected off the dusty glass of the vitrines. As she concluded her task, her thoughts whirled. The Museo Casinelli had done its job, as it always did; and the feeling was very satisfying. It really *had* been a good choice of hers, last year, to come out to north Peru, one of the final frontiers of history, maybe the last great *terra incognita* of archaeology and anthropology, full of unknown cultures and untouched sites.

Jessica shut off the lights and retreated. Upstairs, Pablo was trying to text something into his phone. He abandoned the effort, and smiled at her. 'You are finished?'

'Si! Gracias, Pablo.'

'Then you must go and have some *glucosa*. You are my friend and I must look after you. Because you are the only scholar who comes here!'

'That's not true.'

'Well. It is nearly true! I had some visitors last week, they were quite uncouth! Philistines seeking out . . . thrills. And they were unpleasant. Asking stupid questions. Everyone always asks the same stupid questions. Apart from you, Señorita, apart from you!'

Jess smiled, returned the keys, and stepped out into the polluted grey air of Truijllo.

The city greeted her with all its noise and grime. Guard dogs howled behind fences of corrugated iron; a man was pushing a glass trolley full of quails' eggs past a dingy tyre shop; a blind beggar sat with a guitar on his lap – it had no strings. And above it all hung that endless grey depressing sky.

It should really all be lovely, Jessica thought, here at the equator. It should be tropical and sunny and full of palm trees, but the strange climate of north Peru dictated otherwise: this was a place of clouds and chilly sea-fog.

Her cellphone rang; immediately she reached into her bag. She'd expected it to be Steve Venturi but the screen said it was her boss at the dig at Zana, Daniel Kossoy, who was also the overall leader of TUMP, the Toronto University Moche Project. And, as of last month, also her lover.

'Jess, hi. How's Trujillo?'

'All good, Dan. All fine!'

'Where are you now, then?'

'Museo Casinelli. Just left—'

'Ah, the sex pots!'

'The sex pots. Yes.' She paused, wondering why Danny was ringing. He knew she could handle herself in the big bad city. Her silence invoked his real purpose.

'Jess, have you heard anything from Venturi? I mean, we're all on tenterhooks up here. Were you right? About the vertebrae? It's like being in a cop show – the tension and excitement!'

'Nothing yet. He did say a week at least, and it's only been eight days.'

'OK. Well. OK.' A brief sigh. 'OK. Keep us informed? And . . .'

'What?'

'Well . . .' The pause implied unspoken feelings. Was he about to say something intimate, something personally revealing? Something like *I miss you?* She hoped not; it was way too soon in their miniature romance for any such declaration.

Briskly, Jessica interrupted, 'OK, Dan, I gotta go. I'll see you in Zana. Bye!'

Pocketing her phone, she walked to a corner to hail a taxi. The traffic was intense: fuming trucks loaded with charcoal growled at the lights; mopeds weaved between dinged Chevrolet taxis and crowded buses. Amongst the urgent chaos, Jessica noticed one particular truck, speeding down the other side of the road.

Going way too fast.

Jess shook her head. Peruvian driving wasn't the best. It was normal to see trucks and buses tearing down highways as if they were the only vehicles in the world, taunting death. But this was something different.

She stared: perplexed. The truck was *speeding up,* accelerating, leaping over a kerb, horribly dangerous. Somewhere a woman screamed. It was heading straight for – straight for what, *what was it doing?* Where was it going? It was surely going to plough into the grimy houses, the tyre shop, the tired glass kiosk of the quails eggs seller—

The Texaco garage.

The truck was heading straight for the garage. Jessica gazed – rapt and paralysed. The driver leapt from his cabin; at the last possible moment someone grabbed hold of Jessica and pulled her to the ground, behind a low wall.

The crash of glass and exploding gasoline was enormous. Greasy fireballs of smoke billowed into the air. Jess heard dire screams, then frightening silence.

'Pablo,' Jessica said to herself, lying, shaking, on the cracked Trujillo sidewalk. 'Pablo . . .?'

2

Rosslyn Chapel, Midlothian

Everything you could read about in the guide books was here, in Rosslyn chapel, the great and famous fifteenth-century chapel of the Sinclairs, ten miles south of Edinburgh. The bizarre stone cubes in the Lady Chapel, the eerie carvings of exotic vegetation, the Dance of Death in the arches, the inverted Lucifer bound in ropes, the Norse serpents twined around the Prentice Pillar. And all of it was lavished with alluring detail, teasing symbolism and occult hieroglyphs, creating a splendid whirl of conspiratorial intrigue in weathered old stone. Right next to a gift shop, which sold special Sinclair tartan tins of Templar shortcake, baked with special Holy Grail motifs.

Adam Blackwood sighed. His last assignment as a full-time feature writer for the *Guardian*, and it was on the mighty commerce of nonsense that was Rosslyn Chapel.

'You OK?'

It was his friend, and long-time colleague, Jason the Photographer. With the usual sarcastic tilt in his south London accent.

Adam sighed.

'No, I'm not OK. I just lost my job.'

'Tchuh. We all lose our jobs.' Jason glanced at his camera, adjusting a lens. 'And you're not dead, are you? You're just thirty-four. Come on, let's go back inside the chapel, this shop is full of nutters.'

'The whole *town* is full of nutters. *Especially* the chapel.' Adam pointed through the glass door at the medieval church. 'Everyone in there is walking around clutching *The Da Vinci Code*, looking for the Holy Grail under the font.'

'Then let's hurry up! Maybe we'll find it first.'

Adam dawdled. Jason sighed. 'Go on then, Blackwood. Cough it up. I know you want to *share*.'

'It's just . . . Well I thought that at least this time, *my very last assignment*, I might get something serious again, just for the hell of it, a serious news story, as a parting gift.'

'Because they like you so much? Adam – you got *sacked*. What did you expect? You punched the fucking features editor at the *Guardian* Christmas party.'

'He was hassling that girl. She was *crying*.'

'Sure.' Jason shook his head. 'The guy's a wanker of the first water. I agree. So you're a great Aussie hero, and I'm glad you decked him, but is it really so surprising they snapped? It's not the first time you've lost it.'

'But—'

'Stop whingeing! You did a few decent news stories, amongst the dross. And they're sacking journos all over the world. You're not unique.'

This was a fair point. 'Guess not.'

'And you got a bloody pay-off. Now you can bog off to Afghanistan, get yourself killed. Come on. We still got work to do.'

They walked out of the shop into the forecourt. And stared once more at the squat stone jewel-box that was Rosslyn Chapel. A faint, mean-spirited drizzle was falling out of the cold Midlothian sky. They stepped aside to let a middle-aged lady tourist enter the ancient building. She was carrying a dog-eared copy of *The Da Vinci Code*.

'It's under the font!' said Adam, loudly. Jason chuckled.

The two men followed the woman into the chapel. The Prentice Pillar loomed exotically at the end. A young couple with short blonde hair – German? – were peering at the pillar as if they expected the

Holy Grail to materialize from within its luxuriously carved stone, like a kind of hologram.

Jason got to work. Tutting at his light meter, taking some shots. Adam interviewed a Belgian tourist in his forties, standing by the grave of the Earl of Caithness, asking what had brought him here. The Belgian mentioned the Holy Grail, *The Da Vinci Code* and the Knights Templar, in that order.

Adam got an initial glimpse of how he might write the piece. A light but sardonic tone, gently mocking all this lucrative naivety, this cottage industry of credulity that had grown up around Rosslyn Chapel. A feature that would explore how the entire town of Roslin, Midlothian, was living off the need of people in a secular age to believe, paradoxically, in deep religious conspiracies. No matter how absurd and embarrassing they might be.

He could start it with that GK Chesterton quote: 'when people stop believing in God, they don't believe in nothing – *they believe in anything*'.

Adam turned as a baritone voice resonated down the nave: one of the more pompous guides, holding a fake plastic sword, was pointing at the ceiling, and reciting some history. Adam listened in to the guide's well-practised spiel.

'So who exactly were the Knights Templar? Their origins are simple enough.' The guide levelled his plastic sword at a small stone carving, apparently of two men on a horse. 'Sometime around 1119, two French knights, Hugues de Payens and Godfrey de Saint-Omer, veterans of the First Crusade, got together to discuss over a beaker of wine the safety of the many Christian pilgrims flocking to Jerusalem, since its brutal reconquest by the Crusaders of Pope Urban II.' The guide's sword wobbled as he continued. 'The French knights proposed a new monastic order, a sect of chaste but muscular warrior monks, who would defend the pilgrims with their very lives against the depredations of bandits, and robbers, and hostile Muslims. This audacious idea was instantly popular: the new King Baldwin II of Jerusalem agreed to the knights' request, and gifted them a headquarters on the

Temple Mount, in the recently captured Al-Aqsa Mosque. Hence the full name of the Order: the Poor Fellow-Soldiers of Christ and of the Temple of Solomon, or, in Latin, *Pauperes Commilitones Christi Templique Solomonici.* Ever since then, the question has been asked: was there also an *esoteric* reason for this significant choice of headquarters?' He hesitated, with the air of a well-trained actor. 'Naturally, we can never know. But the Temple Mount very *definitely* had a mystique: as it was located above what was believed to be the ruins of the first Temple of Solomon. Which,' the guide smiled at his attentive audience, 'is thought, in turn, to be a model for the church in which you stand today!'

He let the notion hang in the air like the fading vibrations of a tolling bell, then trotted through the rest of the story: the Templars' rise and supremacy; the twenty thousand knightly members at the very peak of the Order's strength; the great, Europe-wide power and wealth of the 'world's first multinational'. And then, of course, the dramatic downfall, after two proud centuries, when the French king, coveting the Templars' money, and envying their lands and status, crushed them with a wave of violent arrests and ferocious torture, beginning on one fateful night.

The guide flashed a florid smile: 'What was the date of that medieval Götterdämmerung, that Kristallnacht of kingly revenge? Friday the 13th, 1307. Yes, *Friday the 13th!*'

Adam repressed a laugh. The guide was a walking store of clichés. But entertaining, nonetheless. If he'd been here for the fun of it, he'd have been happy to sit here and listen some more. But he had just seen something pretty interesting.

'Jason . . .' He nudged his friend, who was trying to get a decent shot of the Prentice Pillar.

'What?'

'Isn't that Archibald McLintock?'

'What?'

'The old guy, sitting in the pew by the Master Pillar. It's Archibald McLintock.'

'And he is?'

'Maybe the most famous writer on the Knights Templar alive. Wrote a good book about Rosslyn too. Proper sceptic. You never heard of him?'

'Dude, you do the research, you're the hack. I have to worry about lenses.'

'Very true. You lazy bastard. OK, I suggest we go and interview him. He might give me some good quotes, we could get a picture too.'

Advancing on the older man, Adam extended a hand. 'Adam Blackwood. The *Guardian*? We've actually met before.'

Archibald McLintock had sandy-grey hair and a demeanour of quiet, satisfied knowledge. Remaining seated, he accepted Adam's handshake with a vague, distracted grasp.

An odd silence intervened. Adam wondered how to begin; but at last the Scotsman said, 'Afraid I don't recall our meeting. So sorry.' His expression melted into a distant smile. 'Ah. Wait. Yes, yes. You interviewed me, about the Crusades? The Spear of Destiny?'

'Yes. That's right, a few years back. It was just a light-hearted article.'

'Good good. And now you are writing about the Chapel of Rosslyn?'

'Well, yes,' Adam shrugged, mildly embarrassed. 'We're kind of doing another fun piece about all the . . . y'know . . . all the Dan Brown and Freemasons stuff. Templars hiding in the crypt. How Rosslyn has become so famous for its myths.'

'And you want another quote from me?'

'Do you mind?' Adam flushed, painfully aware he was disturbing a serious academic with all this fatuous, astrological absurdity. 'It's just that you famously debunked all this rubbish. Didn't you? What was that thing you said? "The Chapel of Rosslyn bears no more resemblance to the Temple of Solomon than my local farmer's cow-shed is modelled on the stately pleasure dome of Xanadu."'

Another long silence. The tourists whispered and bustled. Adam waited for McLintock to answer. But he just smiled. And then he said, very quietly. 'Did I write that?'

'Yes.'

'Hm! A little piquant. But why not? Yes, I'll give you a quote.' Abruptly, Archibald McLintock stood up and Adam recalled with a start that the old man might be ageing but he was notably tall. Fully an inch taller than Adam, who was six foot two.

'Here's your quote, young man. *I was wrong.*'

'Sorry?' Adam was distracted: making sure his digicorder was switched on. 'Wrong about . . . what?'

The historian smiled. 'Remember what Umberto Eco said about the Templars?'

Adam struggled to recall. 'Ah yes! "When a man talks about the Templars you know he is going mad," You mean that one?'

'No. Mr Blackwood. The *other* quote. "The Templars are connected to everything."'

A pause. 'You're saying . . . you mean . . .?'

'I was wrong. Wrong about the whole thing. There really *is* a connection. The pentagrams. The pillars. The Templar initiations. It's all here, Mr Blackwood, it's all true, it's more strange than you could ever realize. Rosslyn Chapel *really is the key.*' McLintock was laughing so loudly now that some tourists were nervously looking over. 'Can you believe it? The stature of this irony? The key to everything was here all along!'

Adam was perplexed. Was McLintock drunk? 'But you debunked all this – you said it was crap, you're famous for it!'

McLintock waved a dismissive hand and began to make his way down the medieval aisle. 'Just look around and you will see what I didn't see. Goodbye.'

Adam watched as the historian walked to the door and disappeared into the drizzly light beyond. The journalist gazed for a full minute as the door shut, and the tourists thronged the nave and the aisles. And then he looked up, to the ancient roof of the Collegiate Chapel of St Michael in Roslin, where a hundred Green Men stared back at him, their faces carved by medieval stonemasons, into perpetual and sarcastic grins.

3

Rosslyn Chapel,
Midlothian, Scotland

'OK, I'm done. Got it all.' Jason stood and stretched. 'The upside-down angel thingy, Mary Magdalene by the fire extinguisher. And a cute Swedish girl bending over the tomb of the Earl of Orkney. Short skirt. Plaid. You all right?'

'Yes . . .'

Jason theatrically slapped his own head. 'Sorry. Ah. I didn't get a shot of your old guy – what was his name?'

'Archie McLintock. Professor McLintock.'

'So,' Jason capped his lens. 'He give you any good quotes?'

Adam said nothing. He was wrapped in confusion.

The silence between the two men was a stark contrast to the hub-bub of tourists coming into the building: yet another tour guide was escorting a dozen Japanese sightseers into the nave and pointing out the Templar sword on the grave of William Sinclair, 'identical, they say, to the Templar swords inscribed on Templar tombs in the great Templar citadel of Tomar!'

'Hey?' said Jason, waving a hand in front of Adam as if testing his friend's blindness. 'What is it?'

'Like I said. Just something . . . a remark of his.'

'Okayyy. Tell me in monosyllables?'

Adam stared hard at the carving of the Norse serpents at the foot of the Prentice Pillar, and there, on the architrave joining the pillar the famous inscribed sentence. *Forte est vinum fortior est rex fortiores sunt mulieres super omnia vincit veritas*: 'Wine is strong, a king is stronger, women are stronger still, but truth conquers all.'

Truth conquers all.

It was all true?

'Well . . .' Adam exhaled. 'He admitted, or rather confessed, that he had been wrong all along. That it was all true. The Templar connections. Rosslyn really is the key, the key to everything. The key to history. That's what he said.'

Zipping up his light meter in one of the many pockets of his jacket, Jason gazed laconically at Adam. 'Finally gone gaga then. Doollally tap. Too much tainted porridge.'

'You'd think so, wouldn't you? Yet he sounded sane I . . . I just don't know.'

'Mate. Let's get a beer. What's that shit they drink up here? Heavy. A pint of heavy.'

'Just a half for me.'

Jason smiled. 'Naturally.'

They walked with a mutual sense of relief out of the overcrowded, overwarmed confines of Rosslyn Chapel into the honestly dreary Scottish weather. For one last second Adam turned and looked at the church, landed in its green lawn, a greystone time machine. The gargoyles and the pinnacles disturbingly leered at him. A chime, an echoic buzz, a painful memory resonating.

Alicia. Of course. *Alicia Hagen.* His girlfriend. Buried in a Sydney suburb with the kookaburras in the trees and the sun burning down on the fake English Gothic church.

Anxiety pierced him. Now he had lost his job, would he go back to brooding? He needed to work, to take his mind off the past; he had emigrated from Australia to put distance between himself and the tragedy, and that had succeeded – to an extent – but he also needed to *occupy* himself. Or he would recall the girl he had truly loved, who died so pointlessly, so casually. And then he would feel the sadness, like a g-force, as if he was in a plummeting plane.

Adam paced quickly into the car park. The local pub was just there, on the corner, looking welcoming in the mizzle and cold.

'Maybe I'll have an entire pint. And a few chasers.'

'Good man,' said Jason. 'We could—'

'Watch out!'

Adam grabbed at Jason, and pulled him back. Jason spun, alarmed.

'Whuh – Jesus!'

A car shot past, inches from them, doing seventy or eighty miles an hour: an insane speed on this suburban road, skidding left and right, but the driver's intention was disturbingly obvious.

'Christ—'

They ran after the vehicle, now heading straight for a high brick wall flanking the curve of the road.

'*Fuck*—'

'*Jesus*—'

'*No!*'

The impact was enormous. The car smashed straight into the wall with a rending sound of sheared metal and shattered glass. Even at this distance Adam could tell that the driver must be dead. A head-on crash with a wall, at eighty miles an hour? It was suicidal.

They slowed as they approached the car. The crash was enveloped by an eerie silence. Shocked onlookers stood, seemingly paralysed, hands to their mouths. As he dialled his phone urgently for an ambulance, Adam leaned to see: the windscreen was entirely smashed on the driver side, the glass bent outwards like a massive and obscene exit wound: the driver had indeed gone straight through.

Chunky nuggets of glass lay scattered bloodily on the pavement. Shards of metal littered the kerbstones. The driver was clearly dead, his blooded body half-in, half-out of the car.

Jason already had his camera out.

Adam didn't need a camera to record his memories; he would not forget what he had seen. The driver had been *smiling* as he raced past them: smiling as he drove straight into the wall.

And the dead driver was Archibald McLintock.

Also by Tom Knox

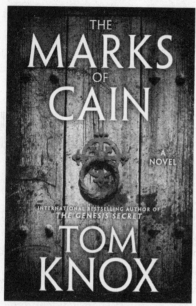

978-0-452-29716-6

978-0-452-29633-6

Available wherever books are sold.

Plume
A member of Penguin Group (USA) Inc.
www.penguin.com